Never Again, No More 5:

Game Over

Never Again, No More 5:

Game Over

Untamed

www.urbanbooks.net

Urban Books, LLC
300 Farmingdale Road, NY-Route 109
Farmingdale, NY 11735

Never Again, No More 5: Game Over

ISBN 13: 978-1-64556-297-9
ISBN 10: 1-64556-297-2

First Trade Paperback Printing January 2022
Printed in the United States of America

10 9 8 7 6 5 4 3 2 1

Distributed by Kensington Publishing Corp.
Submit Orders to:
Customer Service
400 Hahn Road
Westminster, MD 21157-4627
Phone: 1-800-733-3000
Fax: 1-800-659-2436

To Our Realities

Acknowledgments

To the first author of all of our lives, thank you, God.

To my husband, Chris, my blessing in this life as my partner, spouse, best friend, and baby daddy lol, I love you forever.

To my heartbeats, thank you for sharing your mommy with the world so that your mommy can give you the world.

To my dynamic duo of ladies, Diane and N'Tyse, no words could ever express how grateful I am for you both.

To Urban Books/Kensington, I'm forever grateful for the platform and the opportunity.

To anyone and everyone who has supported my untamable journey, thank you.

You've seen the breakup game, the makeup game, the lying game, the cheating game, and now you see the secrets of the game unfold. 'Cause one thing about games—there's no turning back when it's over.

Chapter 1

Trinity

"Oh, my God!" Panic had set in, and I had no clue what I should do. "Think, Trinity, think!" Terrence lay before me, lifeless. "Please, God," I cried. "Please, God." I couldn't lose my Dreads.

Was God punishing me? But why? For leaving a womanizing, abusive, drug-dealin' man to make a better life for myself and my kids? To be a wife instead of a baby mama? To have a career instead of a pipe dream? Was I that bad? What did I do to deserve this? Overspend? I wasn't a bad person. I was a good wife, a great mother, a fair businesswoman, wasn't I?

Was Terrence that bad? Had his d-boy activity come back to haunt him? He wasn't a killer, a thief, or a rapist. He made some bad choices, but so did we all. Wasn't his time spent in prison enough of a consequence? He was stripped of his life once already. Now his existence, too? He wasn't a bad man. He was faithful to me. A great father to his children and another man's. He had a big heart. He was the epitome of what a son and brother should be to the women in his life. He was a real black man. The most sought-after and least appreciated commodity a black community, a black woman, could have. And he was mine. Mine! How dare God take him from me? How dare He?

I wiped my tears with my shirt before running my blood-drenched hands through my hair. "God, I'll do anything. Anything. Just give him back to me. Please." My pleas flowed out through sobs as I held his head and stroked his cheek. "Don't you leave me, Dreads. Do you hear me? I said don't you leave me, goddamn it!"

Suddenly, I felt a cold hand on me. "Ahhh." My head jerked to see what had touched me.

"Ah yo, Trin," I heard Pooch say as he coughed, holding his bloody side. "You gotta help me," he begged as he tried unsuccessfully to move closer to me.

Grabbing Terrence's gun, I pointed it at him. "You killed my Dreads. I'ma send your fuckin' rotten-ass soul straight to fuckin' hell."

"Nah, mama. Wait. Please. You got it all wrong," he begged, still clutching his side. "Fuck! This shit hurts. It's fucking burning." He winced. "I didn't shoot at Terrence, mama."

I pulled back the hammer.

"No! Wait, I promise you . . ." He coughed, and blood flew out of his mouth. "Get . . . get Cal's phone. He's the police. They can track that shit," he struggled to get out. "I promise you I aimed at Cal. I didn't trust the fat fuck."

"How do I know that?" I kept the gun aimed steadily at his head, waiting for him to answer my question.

"Trinity! We don't have fuckin' time for this bullshit." His labored words came out hoarsely. "We all need the fuckin' paramedics."

As much as I hated to agree with him, he was right. Having a pissing contest with him made me lose precious time for my Dreads, if there was even a glimmer of hope that he'd survive. That was enough to kick me into gear and do as Pooch had requested. I kept the gun trained on Pooch and eased Terrence's head to the floor, then ran over to Big Cal, who also lay lifeless on the floor. Wasting no time, I grabbed his cell.

"911, what's your emergency?"

"My name is Trinity Kincaid. I don't know where I am. I was kidnapped. There was a shootout. I'm calling from Detective Aaron Marsh's cell phone. He may be dead, and my husband too. Please hurry."

"Okay, ma'am. I'm linking the number to the police now. Do you have any idea where you may be?"

"An abandoned building? I don't know."

"A stor . . . storage," Pooch sputtered. "2245 Quality Warehouse Storage," he struggled to get out.

"Umm, Quality Warehouse Storage, number 2245," I repeated.

"Are you still being held captive?" the operator asked.

"No. Detective Marsh kidnapped me. He's been shot. So have two other men."

"Is anyone else moving or breathing? And how many people are there?"

"Including me, four. One man, Vernon Smalls, is alive. He's been shot in the side, and he's losing a lot of blood."

"How about the others, ma'am?"

"I don't know." My answer came out shakily as tears flooded my eyes. "There's so much blood everywhere."

"It's okay, ma'am. Just remain calm. My name is Josefina, okay, Trinity?"

"Okay. Josefina." I found myself repeating her name out of nervous energy.

"That's right. So one of the men is your husband?"

"Yes."

"What's his name?" she asked.

Between sniffles, I said, "Terrence. Terrence Kincaid. I call him Dreads."

"And what does he call you?" she asked sweetly.

A nervous chuckle escaped thinking back to the first time we met officially. "Li'l mama."

"Okay, li'l mama. Can you see if he's got a pulse? Take your index and middle finger, hold them together as if you're gonna make a peace sign, but do not separate them. Place them against the base of his neck. If you can't feel it there, try his wrist. Can you do that for me?"

"Yes." I hurriedly walked over to Terrence and felt his neck and wrist. "I don't feel one." At that revelation, I was on the verge of losing it.

"Okay. It's okay, Trinity. We're going to pull them through this. Now can you do the same for Detective Marsh?"

"Yes." I ran back to Big Cal. "I think I feel one for him. It's really faint."

"Is Vernon able to give CPR?" she asked.

"No, he's on his back in pain." I looked over at Pooch. "Pooch!"

"I'm still up. I just gotta rest," he said faintly as his eyes fluttered back and forth.

I got up, walked over to him, and slapped the shit outta him. "Rest, my ass. You are all I have. You will not die on me too. Keep your ass awake!"

He let out a gut-wrenching and obviously painful laugh. "Bitch," he said faintly. "I love . . . love you, Trin," he said and coughed.

"Are you still there, Trinity?" Josefina asked.

"Yes."

"Do you know how to give CPR?"

"Yes. I remember. I'm doing CPR now." I bent down and held Terrence's nose and blew air into his mouth.

"Keep doing that. The police and paramedics are on their way. I'm going to stay on the line with you until they get there."

"Okay." I continued to give my husband CPR. *Fuck Big Cal.* His fucking ass could die for all I cared. I had to try to save my Dreads.

Suddenly, I heard the door slide open. "Aaron! T! Trinity!" The voice sounded familiar.

"Thomas?" I questioned as he ran back to where we were.

Pooch looked up. "Tot?"

Thomas looked at him and pointed his gun. "You muthafucka!"

"Don't," I yelled at Thomas. "The police and paramedics are on the way."

He put his gun away and looked back at us. "Oh, shit," he bit out, tears instantly falling. "My fuckin' truck wouldn't crank. Oh God, Aaron! T!"

"Give Aaron CPR." The command was blunt as I continued to blow air in Terrence's mouth. "Wake up, goddamn it," I fussed at Terrence. "Come on. Come on, Dreads."

"Trinity, did the police arrive?" Josefina asked.

"No, that's Detective Marsh's brother, Thomas. He's giving his brother CPR."

"Okay. He's not a danger to you, is he?"

I really didn't know how to answer that because I didn't know whose side Thomas was on: Aaron's or Terrence's. "Not now," was all I managed to say.

"Come on, bro," Thomas said as he blew air into Aaron's mouth.

"Bro?" Pooch said faintly. "Damn."

A few minutes later the police and paramedics swarmed the building. I explained everything that I knew from beginning to end. Surprisingly, Thomas filled in the missing details. I felt like I was having an out-of-body experience as Thomas and I got into the back of the ambulance with Terrence. I could see everything happening, but I couldn't believe it. And I couldn't stop it or fix it.

Chapter 2

Charice

Refreshed. Revived. Rejuvenated. Relaxed. Reconnected. Those were all the feelings I was experiencing after my weekend getaway with Lincoln.

Ryan had vowed to spend more quality time with the kids and me before training camp began this year, and before he could do that, I needed to be tightened up by my man. So I explained to Ryan that I just needed a few days away from it all before our family vacation and honeymoon so that I could get rewired.

Add that to the list. Lincoln reclaimed (that one too) his rightful throne as the man! There is good. There is great. There is awesome. And then there is—in the words of Tony the Tiger—"Grrreat!" Lincoln was Tony the muthafuckin' Tiger. This trip was better than our trip to Paradise Island back when Lincoln and I were officially together and he'd proposed. Yeah, it was like that.

I smiled to myself as I sat on the plane, smoothing out my flowy white sundress and crossing my legs. Placing my shades over my eyes and leaning back, I wished Lincoln could be there next to me, but he'd left on a later flight so that our affair could remain inconspicuous. I wanted to replay the entire weekend in my mind before I landed. As I dozed off, I thought about the romantic time I'd had with Lincoln.

"I wish I could come home to this all the time," Lincoln whispered in my ear.

"Lincoln! You scared me." I looked down to see him kissing my belly button. I'd fallen asleep on the bed in my negligee as I waited for him to arrive.

"I'm sorry, ma. Let me make it up to you." He continued his sensual kisses, and I moaned. "I take that as a yes."

Rather than speak, I nodded and licked my lips. Lincoln pulled out his massage oils and sensually relaxed every part of my body. He didn't miss an inch of it. From my neck to my toes, he slowly and gently set my skin ablaze with his hands. Then he intensified that with his mouth. From neck to toe and coming back to the creamy middle, he reminded me that he had the thickest, softest, and wettest tongue in the land. And, my God, did he know how to use it. After I'd climaxed more times than I could remember from his tongue action alone, I undressed him, and we headed to the shower.

"I was going to order some food when you landed. I thought you'd be hungry." With a shared giggle, we stepped into the shower together.

A guttural moan escaped his lips. "I was. I ate, and I'm full and satisfied now."

As I turned around and kissed him, our passion grew again. The next thing I knew I was facing forward, pressed against the shower wall, as he stroked me up and down for a back-door entry.

"Now you can call my name out to me," he moaned.

"As loud as I want?" I breathed heavily.

"As loud as you want. You know I'm the only one who can do this body right," he said as he interlocked his fingers on top of mine after gliding his way inside of me. I gasped. He stopped. "Don't tense up," he whispered.

"It's just . . ."

He lovingly stroked me. "I know. I'm bigger," he said, completing my unfinished thought. There was no need to confirm it. We both knew that. "Just trust me like you did before." He reached down and teased my throbbing bud.

Soon my body relaxed as he slowly ground until he reached my comfort zone. Oooh. It was like being reunited with a long-lost friend. Only Lincoln could make me feel like this. I swore a business administration degree wasn't the only degree he got from LSU. If I were a sharing female, I would bottle his ass up and put him on the open market. Hell, I'd make enough money to clone his ass ten times over.

"I've missed this shit so much," he huffed.

"Oh Gawd! Lincoln!" Leaning in close, I could feel his breath tickling my earlobe.

"Feels good, doesn't it? Saying the name that's always on your mind freely, completely. Say it louder. What's my name?" he asked me breathlessly.

Shit. *He was taking me all the way there. I wanted to shout it from the top of the fucking building that he was making me feel so good.* Damn. What have I been missing out on? I swear it didn't feel this good when we were first together. I don't see how it could've. I would've been too foolish over it to let it go. Damn. I was. He let me go. Because of . . . nope. *This was our time. Thoughts of others would fuck it up. Or would they? I smiled to myself mischievously. I allowed myself to think of Ryan, picturing him watching me make love to Lincoln.*

"Shit, ma!" Lincoln yelped. "Damn, you just opened the fuck up," he hissed as I rocked back toward him like a stallion.

"Oooh, Lincolnn!"

"Yeah, that's it, ma. Say that shit," he groaned. "Yeah, baby."

"Lincolnnnnn!" My voice went up to an octave I didn't realize I could hit.

"Gawddamn, Charice. Oooh, Charice!"

"Say it, baby!"

"Chariiice!" he yelled, exploding as I came with him, calling out his name with his body pressed against mine.

"Oooh, baby."

My moans were met with a kiss to my neck. "Damn, ma. What got into you? I loved it, but I'm just saying. You broke me down."

Giggling, I turned my head to the side to view him. "You got into me, baby. All up in me."

He laughed and then paused, getting serious. "I miss this, Charice. I really do."

I leaned back against him as he pressed his back against the shower wall. He held me in his arms, and we stood there letting the water fall against us as we basked in our moment. He held me close as I slowly ran my forefinger up and down his arm, nestling my head back against his chest.

"I love you, ma," he whispered.

"I love you too, pa." And I did. My heart belonged to Lincoln.

The plane's wheels hitting the tarmac woke me from my beautiful reminiscent dream. I looked around for my phone and retrieved it from the floor. I powered it on and checked the text messages.

Tiger: Miss u already.

I typed back.

Yours Only: Me 2. I know I'll have sweet dreams.

Tiger: Your dreams can be your reality.

Yours Only: I know. They are.

Tiger: In a different way, ma.

Yours Only: *sigh* I know that 2, pa.

Tiger: No pressure. I just . . . u know how I feel.

Yours Only: I do b/c I feel the same way.

Tiger: It's hard 2 believe that at times.

Yours Only: Come on, pa. Don't. It was a magical time. Can we just savor that?

Tiger: Yeah.

Yours Only: don't be mad.

Tiger: I'm not. I'm in luv.

Yours Only: Aww, pa. Me 2. Don't ever think I'm not.

Tiger: A'ight. Get some rest, my luv.

Yours Only: what time do u touch down?

Tiger: By 8 tonight. Check on me.

Yours Only: U know I will. I'll hit U up when I get there. Kisses, pa.

Tiger: Luv u, ma.

Yours Only: Back at u.

Lincoln was anxious to have me back, but it wasn't feasible at this time. I loved him. I did. But I had responsibilities to think about. As long as he had my heart, he had me. Hell, I didn't even feel for Ryan like I used to. Lincoln knew the truth. He knew I was keeping up pretenses. In my heart, Lincoln was number one. However, in my household, Ryan was.

Just as I put the phone away, I heard the faint buzz of my other phone alerting me of a new message. *Damn!* I'd just powered it on.

Hubby: Have you landed?

Wifey: Just landed.

Hubby: The boys and I missed u so much.

Wifey: Aww, I miss my fav guys 2. Lexi 2.

Hubby: Had fun on ur me, myself, and I vacation?

Wifey: Plenty. The best.

Hubby: Good. You'll have 2 do it more often then.

Wifey: Sounds like a plan. The best plan you've ever come up with.

Hubby: Anything for my wifey.

Wifey: Thanks, babe.

Hubby: YW, babe. I'll see u in a bit. Love u.

Wifey: All right. Back at u.

"Good Lord, sweetie. You must be really important to have two cell phones," the old lady sitting next to me said.

"Very important."

"How do you make time for your family? Or are you one of those independent women who don't have time for all that jive?" she joked.

Even though she was nosy and being all up in my business, she was amusing, so I figured I'd entertain her questions. "No, ma'am. I'm every woman. Believe that."

"I like that." She pointed her forefinger at me, and then she turned completely toward me. "Pardon my prying, but how do you manage?" she asked. "In my day, my husband was the provider. I stayed at home. Now that he's gone, I'm traveling the world to keep busy. My daughter just recently got married, and when they have a child, I want to have done all I wanted. But it may be a while. I ask because she's a career woman like you, which is so unlike me. Maybe I can give her some of your advice."

Despite her choice to be a stay-at-home mom, she seemed happy. However, it was a shame that she was just now getting to do all the things she wanted. My advice for her daughter wouldn't be much different than what she could've provided to her, but I didn't mind schooling the old or the young. I had been there, done that, and I had the kids and the ring to prove it.

Thinking over my life with Ryan and Lincoln, only one thought came to mind. "Tell her never to sacrifice what she truly loves for anybody else. That's the best advice. As for managing, I'd say I manage very carefully."

She was quiet for a moment as if she was truly soaking in what I was saying. "Thanks, sweetie. I'll tell her. Follow your dreams first. Then keep your business and home life separated but make time for both. Am I right?"

"Exactly, ma'am. Exactly," I said as we stood to exit the plane.

Chapter 3

LaMeka

The pent-up frustration I had been feeling was still lingering. *Ugh!* Why did men have to be so fucking complicated? And I thought women were supposed to be the damn trip. I was so sick of giving more of myself than a man was willing to give to me. Sick and fucking tired. I was one of the realest women in the world. I held my man down willingly. No lie. Hadn't I proved that? I'd been verbally, mentally, and physically abused just trying to hold my family together with Tony, and now here came trouble rearing its ugly head with Gavin. He came into my life with his slick-ass talk and swaggeristic walk, and in one good dick down, I was back on the okey-doke again.

I tried to be careful this time. I remained his friend first, got to know him, and even went so far as to get tested before we had sex. Hell, these days, that needed to be a part of the requirements even for a one-night stand just to make sure a man or woman wasn't being shady and knew their status.

At any rate, I did what I should have done. Even if I hadn't given him the cookie, I'd have been pissed. I'd cursed out one of my best friends and anybody else who gave us their evil complaints because we were an interracial couple. The hilarious part about it was that black men—yes, black men—were the most offended by our relationship. Ain't that a bitch? Like for real? Are you shitting me? The same men who glorify women of other cultures had the audacity to judge me? There was one dude in the grocery store looking at me in disbelief as he saw Gavin walking with his arm around my shoulders. No sooner than we made it to the sugar aisle, there came "Becky" walking up to his cart. Hypocrite. I mean, judging me because I was with the white boy, and he didn't have no brown to go with his sugar his damn self. I wanted to kick the Little Debbies outta his fat ass. Matter of fact, no, I didn't. Becky could have his fat, ugly ass. Our race didn't need no offspring looking like him.

My bad. That was wrong, but I was pissed. Not so much about the hypocrite in the grocery store, but because I would've gladly cussed out him and anybody else from A to fucking Z over Gavin. Gladly. Now Gavin wanted to act a fool on me? Wrong, sista girl. I didn't have to put up with that shit from nobody. Zilch. Nada. It was going through shit like this that made women bitter, remain single, or become lesbians. I was convinced that at least one-third of the lesbian community was made up of women who just got tired of these fucked-up-ass men in the world. I could be wrong, but I couldn't help but feel that way knowing the shit that I'd been through, not to mention my mom, my sister, and my girls. If I didn't love the real "Peter" as much as I did, and it didn't go against my religious beliefs, then hell, I might've considered it myself. I hadn't seen one converted lesbian who had flown back straight yet, so they must know something we don't. But fuck that. I'd rather be single and buy a lifetime supply of AA batteries. That eliminated drama from either sex.

Nobody I knew—including myself—had had an argument or complaint with the Energizer Bunny. As a matter of fact, that would be a great idea. *Somebody call Walmart and tell them I am on the way. Get the stock truck ready, because they are gonna have to restock their entire battery center station when I leave there.*

"Meka," my sister shouted as she touched my arm, scaring me half to death.

"Oh, shit!" I grabbed the rails of my treadmill before I busted my ass, then yanked out my earphones once I regained my balance. "What? I could've busted my ass." My attitude was on go.

"Well, if you kept them damn blaring-ass earphones outta your ear, you could've heard me," she said, throwing her hands on her hips.

Slowing my treadmill down to a creep, I took my towel and wiped my forehead and neck. "I told you I was exercising. You know how I do when I'm getting my workout on."

She peered at the numbers. "Damn, sis. You ran two miles in thirty minutes. Get it, girl."

Ignoring her compliment, I drank a swig of my bottled water. "Misha, what's up?" I wasn't in the mood for all that playful shit today.

She shrugged and pointed behind me. "You've got company."

I stopped my treadmill completely and turned around. Gavin.

His tall frame lingered in the doorway as he gazed at me with sorrowful eyes and a sheepish expression. "I didn't want to disturb you. You were getting it in."

"Well, then don't disturb me, because I still am." I turned away from him. "You can leave."

"Baby, let's talk, please."

Defiantly, I turned to Misha. "See Mr. Randall back to the door, please."

"Who the hell I look like, Geoffrey from *Fresh Prince?* I ain't the fucking hired help around this place." She threw her hands up. "Look, I have to get to the community center. I have a group session. You gotta deal with this one. Keep your head up, Gav," she said as she walked out, leaving me alone with Gavin.

"Be easy, Misha," he said.

Getting off my treadmill, I walked out of the room to make sure my front door was locked and hoping that Gavin would trail behind me, and he did. "You can follow her out as well," I threw out over my shoulder.

"Meka, come on," he pleaded. "What difference does it make how many women I've dated at the hospital? Would you have not dated me if you knew?"

"You lied to me!" I spun on him so fast he jumped back as if I'd startled him. "A couple is not nine. A couple is two. What the fuck am I, lucky number ten?"

Okay, so obviously I couldn't let what Sara and Jeanine told me that day go. That day was like being awakened from a beautiful daydream only to realize you were living a nightmare. How did he figure those gossiping hoes wouldn't spill all his tea about the women he's dated at the hospital and whatever the fuck was going on with his family?

He'd dated nine different broads outside of me at the hospital, and three of those heifers still worked there. He made me look like Boo Boo the fucking Fool in front of my classmates and my coworkers. Here I was prancing around like I was the only one who had unlimited access to the forbidden fruit, and he was passing his shit out on the Sunday morning collection plate. Like Tupac said, I knew men got around, but damn. And then he expected people to take our relationship seriously? No wonder people were looking at me like I was lovesick and stupid. Maybe I was. Hell, at this point, how could I believe I wasn't?

Every woman, every single solitary woman, was exactly the same: milk chocolate complexion, big, beautiful brown eyes, little titties, small waist, and ba-donk-a-donk butts. The only variations besides our job titles were that some women had short hair, medium-length hair, or long hair. At any rate, I never expected to find out that Gavin was getting around like that, and the very least he could've done was prepare me for it. My family was involved, and I had a psycho-ass baby daddy creating mayhem in my life over his ass. This wasn't no fucking game to me. He knew that.

He exhaled, sliding his hands down his face. "I didn't lie. I wasn't specific. Those are two totally different things. I told you I've dated women at the hospital before, and I was clear that it was more than one."

I folded my arms and laughed. "Yeah, more than one and fewer than nine."

"Why the fuck are you creating an issue?"

"Because I got my ass handed to me by coworkers in front of my classmates and there wasn't shit I could do to defend myself or this relationship."

Exasperated, he threw his hands up. "Fuck those broads! This is us. Me and you. Why the hell should you care about some has-been broads?"

"Because I want to know that what we have is for real!" Before I could finish getting all the words out, I had to look away. Tears that I hadn't known I'd hidden sprang forth, and I wiped them hurriedly. After gathering myself, I turned back to face him and clasped my hands together in annoyance. "I want to know that if I'm getting involved in this relationship, I'm not in it alone, and that what we have is special and different. And right now, Gavin, I don't feel so special. I feel like one of the concubines in King Dingaling's royal court. But understand I don't mind being with you. I just want to know that I am

the one and only. No concubines. I am the queen." I finished my rant, allowing all of my pent-up irritation to
flow out before I plopped down on my living room sofa,
putting my head in my hands.

A few moments went by before I felt him ease down beside me. The fragrance from his Armani cologne invaded
my nostrils and threatened to intoxicate me. "Have I ever
made you feel like you're not special?" He paused, but
when no answer came from me, he continued. "Baby, a
few days ago I told you I loved you. I meant that. I admit
there's some shit I should've been a little more upfront
about, but it doesn't change how I feel about you. It
doesn't change the fact that you're my lady, you are special, and you're my queen," he coaxed, rubbing my back.

It was the first time my eyes found his, and that was
when I noticed that he had dark circles underneath his
eyes. It was evidence that he'd been worried for the past
few days that I had refused to talk to him.

"So why didn't you tell me?"

This time he didn't speak, and his head fell forward.

"Gavin, I'm sensitive about this. You know my home
situation. I told you that I loved you that day as well. And
I take my love seriously. The only man I've ever loved
outside of you was Tony. And I loved Tony for nearly
nine years, ever since I was fourteen years old. You know
for yourself the bullshit I went through with him." I took
a deep breath, reflecting momentarily over the hell Tony
put me through. "I just can't take no games. If that's what
this is to you, just walk away now. Just be man enough to
do that for me. That's all I'm asking."

He lifted his face so that we were eye to eye. "Honestly,
I didn't tell you because I didn't want you to trip like you
are now," he confessed.

I sucked my teeth, ready to pop off with an attitude,
but before I could, he cradled my face and shook his head.

"And I ain't saying you don't have a reason not to, but I'm just saying I was tryin'a get my foot in the door with you. I knew there was some shit that was better left unsaid at the time. After we got together, it just never came up. We were having fun, and then the bullshit started with Tony. Then the next thing I knew, you were poppin' off on me during your lunch break. I want you, LaMeka. This ain't no game for me either. I don't know what those chicks at the job told you, but a lot of it is just run-of-the-mill bull. Or they are tryin'a pin on me some crap that happened with a couple of women and claim it as how I am. I'm a man, Meka. I've done some fucked-up shit in my day, too. I've gotten with a few of those chicks just looking for ass. I cheated on one. And hell, I cheated on that one with another chick in the hospital. And I ain't saying this for you to lose faith in me, but I'm saying it so you can know that you can trust me. I can't explain it, but in my gut, deep down inside, I know that you are it for me. You are my queen. And I want to continue being your king."

Gavin sounded so truthful and convincing. His eyes were pleading with me to believe and forgive him. I wanted to. As I bit my lip nervously, I grabbed both of his hands and held them in mine, imploring him once more for confirmation. "How do I know that this is for real?"

"Listen, baby, we didn't have these issues until outside people started clucking in your ear. Understand, I know I added to that, and I accept the role my actions played in hurting you. I apologize for putting you in any situation that embarrassed you or made you doubt me. That was never my intent. So let me ask you, aside from the water-cooler gossip, what does your heart tell you? If you feel in your heart that I ain't real, then let me know you wanna cut me loose. I ain't gonna say I'm going without a fight, but ultimately it's your decision. But if you feel in your heart that this is real, then let's keep on doing what we've been doing and chuck them deuces to them haters, baby."

Maybe I was being too harsh. I wasn't forthcoming with Gavin about all the circumstances in my life at first either, although I was honest before we actually got together. However, looking back, I understood his position. Telling me everything, especially knowing how cautious I was, might have caused me to throw up my barriers and send him on his merry way. In the grand scheme of things, why should I be quick to judge him when he wasn't quick to judge me? He could've easily assumed I had HIV because of Tony, but he gave me the opportunity to explain myself, even after I pushed him away. Shouldn't that count for something? I didn't see many men sticking around after that if all they wanted was a piece of booty to tap. Regardless of how a person was in their past, they could change. I'd changed. Tony had definitely changed. Couldn't Gavin have changed too?

He hadn't given me an actual reason to believe he hadn't. So perhaps, just this once, I could let it go. And so I did. "I was a fool once. I won't be a fool twice. If you lie, tell a half-truth, or manipulate the truth in any specific or nonspecific way to me again, we're done. No questions, no excuses, and no explanations."

He put his hands up in surrender. "Deal. I'm cool with that. Does this mean we're straight?"

"Yeah, we're straight."

He wrapped his arms around me tightly and caressed me. "I love you, baby. I swear I do," he whispered, kissing the top of my head. "And I'm sorry."

When I pulled back to speak, the kiss he laid on me took my breath away. *Damn it.* This damn white boy did something to me. "You know you got me acting crazy over your ass." I giggled.

He pumped his fist in the air as if he were on the TV show *Jersey Shore.* "One time for the Cablanasian!"

"Crazy-ass white boy."

We fell into a fit of laughter before he leaned over and kissed me on my neck and snaked his arms around my waist. "You're making me hot."

"That's the plan," he said low.

I was about to give in when I saw Pooch's name and picture come up on the television screen. "Wait! Baby, hold up." I sat up and turned up the volume with the remote.

"At this time, Vernon 'Pooch' Smalls is at Northwestern Memorial Hospital in Chicago, Illinois, where he is listed in critical yet stable condition. The police are questioning Thomas Marsh and Trinity Kincaid in this gruesome homicide. The details are sketchy at this time. We will keep you posted on this story as more details become available," the news anchor said.

"What the fuck?" I screamed and immediately began trembling as I reached for my phone.

Chapter 4

Lucinda

What the hell did I just touch? I thought when I rolled over and touched an unknown object. I'd been sleeping so hard that it took a minute to focus. All I saw was the color red. Finally, once my eyes adjusted, I saw scattered red rose petals and a dozen thornless long-stemmed red roses on the pillow in front of my face. I smiled and sat up on my elbow, covering my naked body with the sheets.

"Oh, my God," I gasped, picking up the roses and smelling them. "These are so freakin' gorgeous." I covered my heart with my hand. "Aww."

"Not as gorgeous as you," Mike said from the other side of me.

I jumped and turned to face him. "You scared me. I thought you were gone. Well, I mean, not in here."

He sat down next to me, gliding his hand over my thigh. "I left to get those"—he bent his head toward the roses—"and to make you breakfast in bed."

My eyes darted to the nightstand as he lifted a white handkerchief off a tray to reveal bacon, eggs, cheese grits, a bagel, and a glass of orange juice. "Wow. Did you do all this for me?"

"No, I have another girlfriend named Lucinda who is coming over in a little while, and I wanted to cook for her," he joked.

I playfully hit him, and he bent over to give me a kiss. "Shut up." I laughed. "It looks so good, baby. I bet it tastes fantastic."

"You look good, and you taste better." He nuzzled his nose in the nape of my neck.

Basking in the feel of his lips against my neck, I whispered, "You spoil me."

"I'm supposed to." He raised his head and then set the tray beside me. "Open up," he gently commanded, to feed me a spoonful of grits.

That first bite tasted like heaven in my mouth, and I savored it for a moment before I questioned the reason for this beautiful wake-up call. "I love it. But why did you do all this?"

"Just wanted to celebrate our first," he answered.

"Huh?" Confusion was etched on my forehead as I ate a strip of bacon.

"It's the first time you've spent the night at my house as my girlfriend. We've visited each other's spot, but it's the first time we've stayed together, you know, as a real couple."

And it was. It didn't even really dawn on me though. I hate to say this, but after the bullshit I went through with Aldris, I stopped putting stock into much of anything regarding relationships. To me, this "first" was just like any other moment we'd share if we made it together. Don't get me wrong, I enjoyed being with Mike. Over the past week or so, we had gotten closer, and I truly cared for him. However, I was still raw about my relationship with Aldris. Like I said, before Aldris, I had never loved a man so completely. I was a woman scorned, damaged collateral. I hated the fact that Mike was catching the backlash of my failed relationship, but that was the way the cookie crumbled. I spent a lot of time celebrating and acknowledging my little milestones with Aldris and look what happened—nothing. Absolutely nothing. The only milestone that could move me at this point in my life was an actual marriage, and Mike and I were eons away from that.

"That's so sweet of you," I said, breaking the bagel in half. "This is really good." I swallowed hard, trying to avoid that conversation.

He ran his fingers through my hair. "You don't seem, I don't know, enthusiastic about it."

"I am," I lied. "It's just that I am still trying to wake up, baby," I lied again. This was not good. I hated lying to him, but I didn't want him to think I didn't care. I just didn't care as much as he did.

"Okay," he said, accepting that I was telling him the truth, and he kissed me on the cheek. "So what are we going to do today? Go shopping or hit a movie or something?"

I looked at the clock. It was nine thirty in the morning. "Actually, I was going to pick up Nadia in a little bit and have a girl's day out. Take her with me so we can get a manicure and pedicure, do some shopping, eat out, and maybe end it with taking her for some playtime at Jumpin' Jamboree."

"Oh, okay," he said, sounding dejected.

"Baby, what's wrong?"

"It's just that you didn't get here until after midnight because of your job, and the only thing we had time to do was make love and go to sleep. I love the lovemaking now. That's not the issue. It's just that I wanted to spend some quality time with you. Outside of us kickin' it at each other's houses for a couple of hours or so, we really haven't done much together."

"We've barely been together two weeks, Mike. I work, you work, and we both have kids."

Dejection splayed across his face before he put his head down and then looked back at me with pleading eyes. "I understand. I'm just saying I want to do something special with you. I have to work tonight, so I know I won't get a chance to see you until Sunday."

"Well, let me see if my mom will watch Nadia for me on Sunday, and we can catch a movie and do lunch. How's that?" I planted a kiss on his lips.

"You don't have to exclude Nadia. Just include me."

Pump the brakes. I was not bringing him around Nadia for her to know that Mike and I were dating. I'm not crazy, even though what I did might seem to be. It would look strange as hell to my daughter, knowing that Mike and Aldris were friends and I went from about to marry Aldris to dating Mike. Even she was old enough to understand that something wasn't right with that picture. My heart couldn't help who it chose to be with, but at the same time, my mouth couldn't explain it to Nadia either. It was hard enough trying to explain that to my parents and LaMeka. And I wanted to give her a little time to get over not having her daddy, Aldris, around anymore. Then I could ease into this relationship with him to her. Mike had to understand this was an adjustment for the both of us.

I picked up the napkin and wiped my hands, turned my body to face him, and cradled his face in my hands. "Ay, *papi.* You're amazing. I'm thrilled that you wanna jump full-fledged into my life and Nadia's. That touches me like you wouldn't believe. However, you and I need to get to know each other first. We need to continue to build what we have, and once that foundation is there, then you can build a relationship with Nadia, and I can build one with your children."

"Forgive me. I wasn't trying to rush you or anything. I just thought that since Nadia already knew me . . . I'm sorry," he apologized, shaking his head.

"You didn't offend me. I know why you thought it was cool."

He looked me in the eyes and conceded. "You're right. She only knows me as a friend, and I need to give her time to adjust to the change. Like you said, we must get to know each other better as well from the relationship perspective. I get it. I've just never felt this way about anybody, Lucinda. Please forgive me for overstepping my boundaries."

"There's nothing to forgive. Everything is clear and cool." My eyes studied him until I saw his acceptance, and then I kissed him again.

He got up and moved the breakfast tray onto his dresser, then sat back down beside me. "Do we have time for a repeat?" He nuzzled my neck.

I wrapped my arms around his neck in return, pulling him closer. "After everything you've done this morning, I'm more than ready."

He stood up, kicked off his Nike slides, and pulled down his basketball shorts. "Damn. I'm already rockin' up." Not a lie was told there as I watched him rise to the occasion.

Winking at him, I got up and declared, "I have a surprise for you."

"Where are you going?" he asked as he sat down on the bed.

I returned with my heels from the night before and turned on his television to a station that played only R&B music. En Vogue's "Giving Him Something He Can Feel" was on. I slipped the heels on and turned to face him. "You don't mind if I give you a little bit of my alter ego, Ms. Spanish Fly, do you?"

His mouth hung agape as he slowly shook his head as if in a trance. "No," he barely managed.

Slowly, I began to swivel my hips from side to side to the beat of the music, and Mike's eyes grew as wide as saucers. The more I wound and ground, the more labored his breathing became, and he could've used his muscle to chop logs.

"Babyyy. I can barely contain myself."

I waved my finger at him. "No interruptions." My sexy orders came as I bent down and grabbed my right ankle, then carefully extended my leg into the air until it was perfectly aligned with my head.

"Oooh, shit," he moaned.

My smile was laden with seduction as I took that same leg and led it into a full split on the floor. He groaned, rubbing on his muscle. When I got up, he'd already covered his muscle with protection and was ready for action.

"Are you ready to get caught in the Spanish Fly trap?" Immediate thoughts of having asked Aldris the same question numerous times flooded my memories as I struggled to push them back. Maybe it was time to retire Spanish Fly and find a new alter ego.

He groaned and closed his eyes, barely able to nod. I walked to the foot of his king-sized bed and sexily crawled onto it. Then I did a slow frontward flip and peeled out with my ass in his face and my legs in a perfect V-shape position.

"I need you . . . now," he commanded huskily.

Turning so that my back was toward him, I slowly eased down onto his muscle, riding him in reverse cowgirl. As soon as he was completely nestled inside of me, he began to tremble.

"What the fuck?" he asked, bracing himself from succumbing to completion. "I'm so fucking hot, I was about to—"

"Welcome to the Spanish Fly trap."

Introduction complete. The first time Mike and I had sex it was very pure and beautiful. Last night was slow and tender. Right now? Well, right now he needed to get to know the freaky side of me. The side that I'd only felt comfortable showing to Aldris. Today, I needed him to fuck me.

"I love you," he blurted as we began to fuck wildly.

Blocking those words out, I continued enjoying my time with Mike. Mike and I flipped, twisted, and turned as we battled to be top dawg in the bedroom. It was wild, adventurous, fun, and crazy. Our appetite for each other never seemed to run out, and I was matching him pound for pound in our competitive heavyweight bout.

"Oooh, shit, *papi*. I'm about tooo . . ." The words stretched out, and Mike smiled at me as if he'd won this round.

"Lu!" LaMeka's voice came crashing through Mike's answering machine. "I've tried to reach you on your cell, at your house, and at your mom's. I've even called Mike's cell. This is my last resort. If you're there, pick up the damn phone. Something has happened with Trinity. Pooch's ass has been all over the news this morning talking about he's in critical condition at some hospital in Chicago, and Trinity is being held for questioning. They said something about a homicide."

I damn near threw Mike off me and snatched his phone off the hook with trembling hands. "*Ay Dios mío!* Meka! It's me. What the fuck is going on?" Tears streamed from my eyes, and my whole body began to shake as Mike held me in his arms and rocked me.

Chapter 5

Aldris

My body felt like a train had hit it. It was hard to move. I couldn't even open my eyes. I grabbed my head to stop the constant thump pounding against my frontal lobe. This shit hurt so bad my ears felt like they were bleeding. Another drunken episode to ease the pain in my heavy heart.

Every night I had the same recurring dream. I would come home from work, and as I opened the door, Lucinda would greet me. She'd hug me tight and tell me that she was sorry, that she forgave me, and that we could be a family again. We'd kiss, and Nadia would run into the living room, giggling at us. I'd pick up Nadia and tickle her. We would all tickle each other playfully on the sofa, and then Lucinda would cradle my face, kiss me, and tell me she wanted to marry me. I'd slip the ring on her finger and whisper to her the words I'd longed to say, "I do." Then it was as if the devil himself would wake me up from this beautiful and painless dream just so I would realize that that was all it was. Instantly, my world was ugly and painful again. At first, I thought it was the drinking, but whether I was sober or drunk, the dream found me in my sleep. Still, I opted for the drinks. I figured I'd get drunk so I could focus on my hangovers instead when I woke up. Of course, that wasn't working out too good for me.

Two weeks. Two whole weeks. Lucinda had been with
Mike for two whole weeks. I'd psyched myself out to
think this was some type of joke they were playing on
me. Every day I waited for the "aha" moment to happen.
However, the trick was on me. I couldn't have a laugh at
something that was clearly not funny. Two weeks . . . and
counting. Crazy part was I wasn't even mad at Lu. She
was a female scorned. I scorned her. Payback was a bitch
named karma, and I got in bed with that ho every night.
They say what goes around comes around, and I could
say I definitely got what was coming to me. The part that
fucked with me though, you know, the truly fucked-up
part, was my boy. *Ex-boy.* Mike. He hated Lu. Dogged
her every fucking chance he got. Now his bitch ass grew
up a little bit and decided he wanted a piece of my life.
Jealous-ass muthafucka. He couldn't stand that I had it
going on. I had the nice crib, the tailor-made job, and
the finest and baddest lady in the A. Lucinda was smart,
sassy, fine as hell, a great mother, a good woman, and a
freak in the fucking bedroom. And she was all mine. Then
he came and played the "friendship" card to my woman
amid our problems. Friend my ass. The only thing he
wanted to befriend was some of that Spanish Fly.

Ugh! Spanish Fly. Was she giving him my routines?
I wondered if she'd shown him her freaky side yet. I
prayed she hadn't. I couldn't even think about her giving
it to my . . . *Ugh!* The thought forced me to sit straight up
as a tear rolled down my face. I grabbed my bottle of Jim
Beam whiskey, chugged a swig, and hissed the taste away.

"Shit," I cussed, sitting on the edge of my bed and
rubbing my head.

A quick glance at the clock showed that it was a little
after ten in the morning. *Saturday.* At least I restricted
the heavy drinking for the weekends. During the work
week, I usually deadened my pain with a shot of Jose

Cuervo or a glass of Hennessy and Coke. After partaking in Jim Beam, my head was splitting. I closed my eyes and sharply exhaled as I stumbled to a standing position. I had to piss. Bad. I staggered to my bathroom and whipped out Mandingo to relieve myself.

"Ahh," I sighed as I drained some of last night's Jim Beam into the commode, forcing back thoughts of Lucinda. I finished and turned to go back to bed.

"I see you're up," Jennifer said with her arms folded, standing in front of me in a sexy pajama boy-short-and-tank set.

Startled, I jumped and staggered backward. "Damn! What are you doing here? You scared the hell outta me." How the hell did she get in my house?

With an eyeroll, she sucked her teeth. "Jessica and I came over last night, remember? We watched movies, and then you put her to bed. After that, we stayed up talking and watching television while you drank on your Jim Beam . . . and you don't remember any of this, do you?"

I plopped down on my toilet lid. My mind traveled back. *Damn. I did?* I was so fucked up I didn't even remember. "Damn." I shook my head, flashes of last night floating back to me. "Now I remember. Did we—"

"No," she sighed, cutting me off. "You were so tipsy I told you to go to bed. As soon as you hit the sheets you were out like a light. I got up and made us some breakfast this morning, but I couldn't wake you up. Jessica and I ate, and now she's watching television in her room."

I rubbed my eyes. "I can't let her see me like this."

"Then stop drinking," she said plainly. "Aldris, you are floating from one day to the next in a haze. Now you're getting drunk to the point where you don't even remember what happened less than eight hours ago. This is ridiculous, and you need to get it together. I re-

member when you wouldn't even drink more than some
watered-down light beer."

"A lot has changed since then."

"Obviously," she sneered back.

"Why are you here? Why do you care?" I stood up at my
sink and washed my face. I looked like shit.

She walked up to me and hugged me around my waist.
"I care about you, Aldris. I want you to see that, no matter
what, I am here for you."

Laughing in annoyance, I grumbled, "Jennifer, I'm too
messed up for this. I've got to get my head in the right
space. I know you mean well, but I can't do this."

"Why? Because of Lucinda?" she asked with irritation
in her voice.

"Well, yeah."

"Unbelievable!" she spouted, throwing her hands up.
"She fucked your best friend and chose him over you, and
you're still dwelling on that heifer?"

Now I was mad as hell as I spun around on her. "First
off, watch your mouth about her. She's not a heifer.
Secondly, I know what she did, but I did it first, remember?"

"Well, at least I'm not Lucinda's best friend unlike Mike
was to you."

"No, you're just my baby mama and ex-fiancée," I shot
back as I walked out of the bathroom. I got back into my
bed and turned on my television.

A few seconds later she strolled out of the bathroom.
"Here." She handed me some Motrin and a glass of water.
"Take this."

I placed the pills in my mouth and swallowed them
with the water. "Thanks."

She sat beside me. "How long are you going to do this?
Pine away for her? Are you going to drink yourself into
oblivion while she lives her life with Mike? What we did

was wrong, and we must live with it, but maybe it was meant to be. I honestly want what's best for you, Dri, and this," she said, picking up the half-empty bottle of Jim Beam, "this isn't it."

"I know that," I said low, putting my head down.

She stood up in front of me and cradled my face so that I was looking directly at her. "Losing Lucinda is not the end of your world. We need you. Jessica and I need you."

I buried my face between her breasts. "It just hurts so damn bad." My vulnerability was on full display as a couple of tears fell despite my will to hold them back.

"I know." She caressed the back of my head. "I know." She stepped back and kneeled in front of me. "Let me make you feel better, baby," she whispered, and with that, she pulled out Mandingo from my boxers and placed him in her warm mouth.

My head fell back in pleasure. "Wooo shit," I moaned as I grabbed her head and glided it up and down. "Just like that," I groaned. "Damn, Jenn."

"You like?"

"Fuck yeah," I said as she eased back down.

I turned my head to the side, damn near engrossed in the pleasure she was giving me, when I saw the craziest shit in my life: a picture of Trinity, Pooch, Terrence, and two other dudes with the words "Gruesome Homicide" underneath.

"What the fuck?" My eyes bucked at the images again.

"What? Did I do something wrong?" Jennifer asked, stopping abruptly.

"No. Wait. Get up. It's the news." She stood up, and I turned up the volume. The anchor gave brief details of Pooch being in the hospital and the questioning of Trinity and Thomas Marsh in a homicide. "Oh, my fucking God!"

"Do you know these people?" Jennifer asked, confused.

I nodded, jumping up. "Yes. That's Lucinda's best friend." Hurriedly, I ran to my closet to put on some clothes.

"What are you doing?" Jennifer asked.

"I gotta find Lu. I have to make sure she's all right."

"Mike will make sure of it," she fussed.

Glaring at her as I pulled up my jeans, I spewed, "Fuck Mike. Lucinda needs me."

The attitude danced in her body language. "Fine. I'm coming with you."

"No, you're not. Stay here with Jessica."

She threw her hands up. "I can't believe this."

"Well, believe it. I've gotta go." I grabbed my keys and wallet and headed out of the house.

I hated this shit, but I didn't have a choice. Lucinda needed me. I had to be there for her. I went to her house, but she wasn't home. Now, if she knew about Trinity, she could've been at LaMeka's house, but my better judgment told me that she was either at her mom's house or at Mike's. Trusting my first instinct, I went to Mike's. I hated that I was dead on the fucking mark.

Lucinda's car was there, and so was Mike's. Part of me—a small part—wanted to drive off, but I loved Lu too much to give a damn about our situation. This wasn't about getting back with her. It was simply about loving her. And love her I did. I parked my car, shook some Tic Tacs into my mouth, and proceeded to Mike's condo.

"Who is it?" some dude asked.

"Aldris," I answered.

After a few seconds, Mike was standing in the open doorway, and I could see Lucinda, LaMeka, and some white guy sitting in his living room. "Now isn't the time—"

I waved my hands. "I'm not here because of you or for you. I saw the news. I wanted to make sure Lucinda was all right."

"She's fine," he said tensely.

Trying to keep my composure, I asked, "Can I see her?"

He huffed and opened the door. "Come in."

I brushed past him and ran into the living room. Lucinda jumped up from the sofa with a tearstained face. "Lu!"

She sniffled. "Aldris," she said sadly as I grabbed her and held her tight.

"I heard bits and pieces. I had to come to you." I held her as she wept in my arms. "I've got you," I assured her as Meka and the white guy waved at me. I sat down, and Lucinda sat beside me. Mike sat down in his recliner, glaring at us. "What happened?"

LaMeka sighed. "We don't know. We haven't been able to get in contact with Terrence's sister or mom. And none of us has Trinity's number because she was in hiding."

"I found out that she was living in Evanston, Illinois, since they put her name on the television, but all of her numbers are unlisted," the white guy said.

"I'm sorry and you are?"

"My bad. This is Gavin Randall, my boyfriend. Gavin, this is Aldris, Lu's, um, well, Lu's ex-fiancé," LaMeka stumbled.

Gavin and I shook hands. "Nice to meet you," we said at the same time.

"Are you all right?" I asked Lu, wrapping my arm around her shoulder.

She took some Kleenex and wiped her eyes. "I just want to know what happened to her, Dri. Pooch was locked up in a federal prison, so there ain't no way he ended up in Chicago unless he got out. And the last I heard, that crazy ho Sonja or Chocolate Flava, or whatever she wants to call herself, who had been visiting him, was locked up on some drug charges her damn self," she said with exasperation. "I'm so upset, and I can't get

Charice to answer her damn phone. Charice's mom is upset, and the family hasn't talked to Trinity's mom either,
so we are all just lost on what's going on," she cried.

I rubbed her arm as I held her. "Damn."

"I'm sure that Trinity will reach out to you all at some
point. She's probably tied up with the police for questioning," Mike said. "Baby, come here," he said to Lucinda
with an outstretched hand. Lu walked to Mike, and he sat
her on his lap. "Everything is going to be fine. Are there
any other people who may know something?"

Muthafucka.

Lucinda shook her head. "LaMeka and I tried Rome
and Skeet, but they said they haven't talked to Terrence
in months. They are worried too."

An idea hit me. "What about the attorney for Pooch
or the dude Sonja was dealing for? Maybe they know
something. Do you all know their names?"

"Jacob Stein was Pooch's attorney," Lucinda said. "But
it's a Saturday. He's not in his office, and I'm sure his
number is unlisted. He probably wouldn't release any
info to us anyway."

LaMeka hit her head. "Sonja was dealing for that dude,
umm, what's the guy who took over Pooch's cousin's old
spot?"

Lucinda snapped her fingers. "Umm, Skrilla or some
bullshit like that."

"Yeah! Skrilla. That's it. Maybe Skrilla knows what's
up," LaMeka said.

"I know somebody who could probably get us Skrilla's
number," Mike said. We all looked at him curiously.
"Alize," he said, picking up the phone and dialing Rod's
number.

Why couldn't I have thought of that first? I thought as
he called our boy Rod.

"Ay yo, Rod. Is Alize there? Cool. Ask her if she knows a dude named Skrilla. She does. Does she happen to have his number? Or know how we can meet up with him?" Mike grabbed some paper and wrote down some information, thanked Rod, and hung up. "I've got the address for his main spot."

"Let's go," Lucinda and LaMeka said, jumping up together.

I stood up, and Mike walked up to me. "I think we can handle it from here, bruh. We appreciate your concern."

Gavin and LaMeka eyed each other as if some shit were about to jump off.

I looked at Lucinda and then at Mike. "Trinity was my friend too, and if you don't mind, I'd like to tag along to find out what's going on for myself. Is that all right with you, Lu?"

She bit her lip, sighed, and walked up to me. "I appreciate your concern. I really do, but I don't think—given the circumstances—it's a great idea."

Lifting her chin with my thumb and forefinger, I disagreed with her assessment. "It's not about that. It's about Trinity and making sure that you, LaMeka, and Charice are okay."

Our look lingered for a moment before she turned away. She looked at Mike before gently pulling him to the side to talk privately. We saw Mike's face tense up, his nostrils flare, and his face contort as Lucinda talked.

LaMeka looked at me. "You need to be cool, Aldris," she whispered.

I shrugged. "I am. I promise."

Just then Mike nodded, shaking his head in disbelief, and they walked back over to us.

"Let's go," Lucinda said. "You too, Aldris."

We gathered our things, and I was the last one out the door before Mike. He grabbed my arm and pulled me

back. "I've got my eye on you. I promise you if this is a
ploy to try to steal Lucinda back, I'ma—"

"Do what?" I asked, interrupting him. "You screwed
me over, remember? Isn't that enough punishment for
me, friend? Besides, you and Lu are tight now. You have
nothing to worry about. Right?"

"Yeah, right." He nodded and tried to keep up his brave
front, but I already knew his confidence was shaken.
Mike only threatened someone when he felt threatened.
I hadn't been his friend for twenty-plus years and not
learned something.

"Yeah, right." We caught up with the others, and we all
hopped into Mike's SUV. I sat right beside Lucinda and
watched Mike stare at us through his rearview mirror. I
smiled at him and wrapped my arm around her shoulder.
"We need to get there sometime today, Mike," I said. He
grudgingly cranked up his SUV.

"Somebody else needs to invest in a truck so I don't
have to drive all the fucking time," he fussed, and Lucinda
shrugged away from me.

It didn't matter that she did. She'd already allowed
herself to be inside my arms to comfort her and inside
her circle to console her. Thus, my point was proven to
ol' Mikey boy. Lu still cared for me, and what we had
couldn't easily be broken no matter if we were together
or not.

Chapter 6

Lincoln

I arrived home to my big, luxurious, and empty house—
"empty" being the operative word. London was staying
with my mom, and she'd agreed to keep her an extra
night to give me some time to rest from my business trip.
Yep, I said business trip. I knew my parents would never
approve of my relationship with Charice, at least not by
way of an affair. Also, I didn't want London thinking
that was the way that marriages and relationships were
supposed to go. Just because I was having an affair didn't
mean I believed in them. Hell, I knew it was dead-ass
wrong, but like the song said, if loving Charice was wrong,
then I didn't wanna be right.

It all began with my quiet reserve as I fought for the
right to be in my daughter's life. Charice and Ryan contacted me by phone, and we all sat down at my house to
discuss how we would handle the custody with Lexi. As
much as I wanted to beat the shit out of Ryan, I knew that
if I acted a fool, it could risk my relationship with London
and completely stop any attempts at a relationship with
Lexi. Therefore, I did the manly thing and fell back. I
had to put my daughters first. At any rate, through all
Ryan's sarcasm, nasty quips, and snappy comments in
and out of court, I remained the cool, calm, and collected
one along with Charice. "Kill them with kindness" was a
lesson I'd never forget. It helped me land Charice again.

I would never forget the day that Charice admitted how she felt for me. It was like an unsung melody she finally composed, creating music to my ears. It was right before my first visit with Lexi that I contacted Charice to confirm our meeting time for the visit. She'd asked if I could meet her at my parents' old house in Queens again, and I just knew there was gonna be some shit. But I'd agreed. I didn't want to fight Charice in court over Lexi, but I would've done just that had she followed her punk-ass husband in an attempt to keep me from my child. I had planned on telling her just that when I arrived. That time, she beat me there.

"*Hey.*" *I issued the greeting as I climbed out of my F-150.*

"*Hey,*" *she replied, getting out of her McLaren.*

"*I see you remembered your way this time.*" *My sarcasm was at an all-time high as I opened the door to the house and let her inside.*

"*Funny,*" *she sneered.*

"*I'm just saying.*"

She walked into the living room, gliding her fingers down the bookshelf on the way. "*I've always felt so peaceful in this house. Well, except the time before.*"

The sight before me caused me to suck my bottom lip. I wanted to beat myself in the head for watching Charice's ass switch left to right in those sexy-ass low-rise skinny jeans. Why couldn't I get it in my head that she'd chosen her husband and not me? And what right did I have to be jealous about it? She was Ryan's first, even taking his hand in marriage before mine. She did a half turn in her stilettos that showed off the muscle tone in her legs. Being a dancer was in her blood. I could tell by her feet and her posture. Long, slender, sexy legs. She brushed away a strand of hair from her face. Diva. Goddess. Cleopatra reborn. I had to get away from her quickly. Why did I have to get her pregnant? Now I had to be tortured all my life by seeing the only woman I'd ever loved love someone else.

"You okay?" she asked, breaking my trance.

"Huh?"

"You seemed a million miles away. Are you okay?"

Clearing my throat shook me out of my daze. "Yes. I *don't mean to rush you here, but this is an awfully long way to travel just for you to give me the time that I am due to visit my daughter. Can we get on with the point of this meeting?"* Not that I was trying to be mean, but rather, I was trying to contain myself. How could she choose Ryan?

She looked away. "Wow. I didn't realize I was intruding on your time—"

"No, you're not. It's just that I don't see the point of coming all the way out here for something that could've been discussed on the phone."

She walked toward me. Jesus, help me. *She stopped face-to-face with me. "I wanted to talk to you. It's hard to do that with Ryan breathing down our necks. You understand?"*

"True." I nodded, standing with my hands on my waist. "So what's up?"

"Umm, I wanted to thank you for telling me the truth about yourself, our breakup, and Ryan. I truly appreciate that from the bottom of my heart," she said sweetly, staring into my eyes.

"You're welcome."

"And I wanted to thank you for being calm and considerate during this entire process with Lexi. I know Ryan has been a complete ass to you even though you are the one who should be upset. However, you never stooped to his level, and you put Lexi's well-being first. I admire and appreciate that, too." She palmed my cheek with her right hand. "It takes a helluva man to—"

I grabbed her wrist and removed her hand from my face. "What the hell is going on, Charice?" I grew tense from her nearness. "Why are you intentionally fucking with me right now? Hmm? You think this is funny. Are you mocking my feelings?"

She shook her head. "No, Lincoln. I would never—"

"You would never what?" I interrupted, stepping back from her. "Hurt me?"

She stepped back and conceded, "I deserved that."

Rubbing my head, I heaved a sigh. "No, I was out of line. I appreciate you taking the time to acknowledge what I did."

"But?" she probed, eyeing me closely.

"But I still don't get why we had to meet here to discuss this. Is there something that you need to tell me? On the real, if Ryan is trying to renege on his word regarding Lexi, I'm telling you right now to lawyer up."

She put her hands up. "Wait. Whoa. It's nothing like that, Lincoln. Christ. I would never do that . . . again. I thought we were past this."

"I thought so too, but you called me all the way out here to thank me. I'm sorry, but I find that kind of odd. Don't you?"

"No, I don't. But you're right. I did call you all the way out here to thank you. So let me thank you." And with that she walked up to me, wrapped her arms around my neck, and kissed me. "Thank you," she said breathlessly.

I eyed her for a moment, and then I wrapped my arms around her waist and kissed her back. "You're welcome."

We stared at each other and, without another word, went straight at it. "This shit is crazy, Charice. What are we doing?" I asked as we fell on the sofa half undressed.

"Damn. Has it been that long for you? It's called having sex, Lincoln." She eyed me sexily while continuing to unbuckle my jeans.

"Hold the fuck up." I stood up. "The last time we talked, you told me you were staying with your husband. You took your vows. You were honoring them. Now if Ryan has pissed you off today, then take it up with your husband. I'm not gonna be your feel-good sex. You made that decision. Live with it." I put my shirt back on.

She sat up and put her face in her hands. "Okay. Okay. I just thought this would be better, that I could do this if I moved fast."

"Do what?" I asked, irritated.

"Tell you that I fucked up!" she hollered. "God. I love you, Lincoln. I can't stop thinking about you, and I hate myself for it. I thought I could deal with not being with you anymore, but after this shit with Ryan soaked in, I realized just how much I truly loved you, how I never stopped."

Talk about blown away. Everything I wanted to hear and never expected to hear again just rolled out of her mouth in one swoop. To say I was shocked was an understatement.

"Well, say something," she bawled, wiping her tears.

I sat beside her and placed my hand on her knee. "I'm just . . . I don't know what to say to this, Charice. I've wanted to hear those words for so long, and now that you've said them, damn."

She let out a nervous gasp. "You don't feel the same way anymore."

"No. No. Hell no. I do. You're just married. Aren't you?"

"Yes. I am."

"So what happened to honoring your vows?"

"I figured I vowed to be married, not to be faithful. Ryan has screwed me over since I was fifteen, Lincoln. I can't let him take away the one person I have who's real. And that's you. I love my life. It's stable. My boys are happy. But I'm not. So why can't I have my life and you, too? Why can't I be selfish for once?"

"Babe, I get it. But an affair? I mean, why don't you just leave him?"

"Are you not listening to me?" she asked, facing me. "You have my heart. I'll give that to you, but I can't put my kids through more heartache. Ray still calls Charity's name at night in his sleep, and Ryan Jr. looks at her picture every night and cries. They are not ready for another major life-altering shift. They love their dad, and Ryan has finally turned into a great dad. I cannot take that away from them. I want you, but I have a responsibility to my household and my kids. They come first."

"So basically, what you're telling me is that I can have your heart but not your hand in marriage?"

She nodded. "I guess so. Yes."

"What if I say it's all or nothing?" I asked, walking over to the window and peering out.

Suddenly, I felt her arms around my waist. I held them there as she leaned her head against my back. I could feel her warm breasts pressed against me as she still had her shirt off. The feel of her around me felt real and right. It felt like home.

"Then I'd say that you have every right to feel that way. I'd tell you that I wish I could give you my all but that I can't. I would beg you to understand but tell you that it's ultimately your decision. And if you chose to walk away, I couldn't or wouldn't blame you. And although I'd never stop loving you, I'd agree to be your friend, but that would be all that we could ever have. And that on the off chance that you met a woman you'd consider making your wife, I'd buy you a wedding gift and sit idle while she made you happy because I knew that I couldn't."

"But you know I'd always love you."

"Yes, and I would always love you," she confessed.

"So why wouldn't we be together?" I pondered aloud.

"Exactly."

"Is having a little bit better than nothing, though?" The question was more internal, but Charice answered.

"I don't know. I'd rather have a little than nothing at all. But that is me. At least the part that you would have is the very best part of me. However, that decision is yours. You know where I stand and how I feel. This could be the greatest love affair of our lives or the best friendship of our lives. I will live with whatever you decide," she answered.

I knew this was not what either one of us really wanted, but it was a compromise. A compromise so that our two broken hearts could finally mend. How could I turn down an offer of having the woman of my dreams even if I couldn't claim it? Didn't it matter more that we knew where our love stood rather than the world? As long as we knew it, then that's all that counted in my book. More importantly, that's all that counted in hers. Fuck it. I loved her too much to turn down this opportunity. I just had to hope that one day I'd be enough for her.

Turning to cradle her face in my hands, I searched her eyes for any deception, but the only emotion radiating back to me was love. Pure love. The way she used to look at me before Ryan stole away what we had. If her love was with me, then I was going to stake my claim. If I couldn't have her fully, I had to have her to the fullest extent possible.

"You have to promise me one more thing. I swear it is not an unreasonable request."

Her eyes danced with anticipation. *"What?"*

I eased my hand inside of her jeans and rubbed her clit as she moaned. *"That this is also mine. I want your heart and your pussy."* With that, I removed my hand and sucked my finger, never taking my eyes off her.

She smiled devilishly at me, turned, and walked away, stripping. "You have to take it first. Claim it and it's yours." And claim it I did.

Ever since then, we'd been on this whirlwind love affair, and my heart had been full of nothing but love for Charice. But my house was empty. For the first time, I was jealous knowing that just three houses down the woman who should have been my wife was playing house with her husband and my child. How fucked up was that? Extremely. I went to my refrigerator and grabbed a beer. I didn't even have one thing to remind me of the great weekend I'd had with her. No pictures, no souvenirs, nothing but my fucking memories and dreams. I sat on the sofa, turned my television on, and reached inside of my luggage. I retrieved the box that I had taken with me on the trip and opened it.

Her engagement ring. The one I gave her on Paradise Island. I opened and closed the box repeatedly. Then I threw it on my coffee table and took a long-ass swig of my beer. *You have her heart, Lincoln. That's all that matters,* I thought, convincing myself once again that that was enough.

Chapter 7

Charice

Home sweet home. Yeah, right! More like home obligated home. Yes, I was glad to be home. I missed my kids and my students at the dance studio, but this house and this marriage were laughable. I cared for Ryan, and I had love for him, but being his wife wasn't worth the paper the license was printed on. I didn't even let Ryan pick me up from the airport. I had the limo service pick me up just to give me a few extra moments to be free from Ryan.

It was awful that my marriage had been reduced to obligations. Why couldn't I be one of those people who didn't give a fuck about anyone but themselves like my husband? I guess because, despite my transgressions, I had a heart. It pained me to turn my back on my marriage the way that I had, but it was my time now. If there was one thing I learned from my husband, it was that to get what I wanted out of life, I had to take it no matter what. I figured my affair made us just about even. Checkmate.

I walked in the house and sang out, "I'm home." Soon my boys came running full steam ahead, damn near knocking me over as I hugged both of them tightly.

"I've missed you so much, Mom," they said in unison.

"I've missed you guys too." I kissed each of them on the forehead. "I love you guys."

"I love you too," Ryan said, walking in and holding Lexi in his arms.

"Aww, my baby," I cooed, taking a sleeping Lexi out of his arms. "Hey, babe," I greeted Ryan as he leaned over and planted a kiss on my lips.

"Hey, sweetie." He rubbed Lexi's head. "She just fell off to sleep."

I nodded and took her to the nursery to lay her in the crib. She looked like a little angel, a replica of her father. Standing there for a few moments, I reveled at her and then turned on the monitor and shut the door before heading to my bedroom. I walked in my closet and took off my shoes. I was about to change clothes when I felt two arms wrap around me from behind.

"Whoa! You scared me, Ryan."

"I'm sorry. I just wanted to hold you in my arms. Three days without you was harder than I expected. I've missed you like you wouldn't believe. Did I tell you that you look absolutely amazing? And you smell so fucking divine," he said, sniffing my hair.

"No, you didn't, but I can live with the compliment." I giggled and pulled away from him.

As I flipped through my shirts and shorts, he walked up, moved my hair, and began kissing me on my neck. "I've really missed you." I could feel his nature rising quickly.

"I'll bet. I'm going to change and unpack."

He spun me around. "After we make love."

"Ryan, I just got off the plane, and I am very tired. As much as I would love to make love to you right now, my body has given out."

He pouted. "Baby, I'm going fucking loco. Outside of oral sex, you haven't given me the real deal in forever. It's always the business with the studio, errands for the boys, your period is on, Lexi has been a handful, or my personal favorite, you're tired. I've given you an all-expenses-paid 'me, myself, and I' vacation, and now all I'm asking of you is the pleasure of allowing me to pleasure you and to get pleasured by my wife."

"And your wife plans on thanking you for that. I promise." I winked at him. Calling myself his wife was something I said for the same reason he lied about being sorry for his ploy to separate Lincoln and me: it sounded good. "Just let me relax for a little bit. That's all I ask."

Although he still pouted, he conceded. "Okay. You're right. Relax. Just know that I've gone through a whole jar of Vaseline, and I don't plan on replenishing my supply anytime soon."

I kissed him. "Okay, baby." *Plans are made to be broken,* I thought devilishly.

Ryan went back to the living room to watch sports, as usual, as I threw on my shorts and tank top and ran downstairs to grab my luggage. The first thing I did was pull out my camera and flip through the thirty images I'd taken. *No photos of Lincoln. Good.* I'd taken pictures of the island and the hotel, but I was careful that the only ones taken had me and me alone in them or the surroundings. Next, I grabbed my other cell phone and deleted the one message I had from Lincoln. I activated my secret code, locked it, and placed it in the one place that Ryan would never look—my tampon box. Then I unpacked. I'd gotten Lexi an island sundress, T-shirts for the boys and two native toys, and I even sprang for a coffee mug for Ryan. It had a picture of some Jamaican rum and said, "I got wasted in Jamaica." *I sure did—Lincoln wasted. Can't say I'm not confessing it,* I thought, laughing to myself. I took my laundry bag down to the laundry room and put my dirty clothes inside the washing machine and the laundry bag inside the trash compactor. Operation Deep Clean was complete.

When I walked into the living room, Ryan was playing
Madden on the PS4 with the boys. I stared at them for
a moment having the time of their lives with their dad
and Ryan having a blast with them. This was what I
couldn't trade for Lincoln. I'd never had a moment make
me happy and sad at the same time. Don't get me wrong,
there were times when I'd come close to throwing Ryan's
ring and marriage license in his face, but this was the shit
that kept me holding on. I was wise enough to create my
own happiness but loving enough not to disrupt anybody
else's. What Ryan did was truly fucked up, but I couldn't
destroy him like that. I just couldn't. And I damn sure
couldn't do it to my boys.

I walked in. "Who wants presents?" I asked, holding all
the treats I'd gotten from Jamaica.

"We do," the boys sang out as Ryan paused the game.

"One for you and one for you." I gave them each a shirt
and a toy.

"Cool," Ray said. "Thanks, Mom!"

"Did you bring me some of those funky dreadlocks so I
can say, 'Hey, mon,' just like the Jamaicans do?" Ryan Jr.
asked. *Just like his daddy, never satisfied.*

I laughed. "No, but you can put that shirt on and say it.
It's a picture of a Jamaican with dreadlocks."

He laughed. "Cool. Thanks, Mom."

"Just be satisfied that she thought of you," Ryan said to
Junior. "Geez, where do you get that from?" he asked. I
looked at him and laughed. And it was so like him not to
realize.

I showed Ryan the dress I got for Lexi. "This is Lexi's
sundress. Isn't it cute?"

"Yes, that is a gorgeous dress for McKenzie."

I eyed him. *McKenzie?* He never called Lexi by her
middle name. "What's up with McKenzie?"

He shrugged. "Humor me, please."

"Ryan—"

"Her name is McKenzie. You act as if I'm calling her another child's name," he interrupted.

"Why are you calling her McKenzie, though? Everyone calls her Lexi."

"It's bad enough that Lincoln gets the last name. I have to give him the first, too? Just give me that one. You can call her Lexi. I'm calling her McKenzie."

"I like McKenzie. It reminds me of Charity," Ray added.

A hush fell over the house as soon as the name slipped through Ray's lips. Although we'd all made great strides in healing since the death of Charity, our daughter and the missing third of our triplets, instances such as the mere mention of her name could trigger a sore spot in the fabric of my soul. Having Ryan Jr. interject during a heated debate was like adding salt to a reopened wound. However, it wasn't his fault for doing so. It was undoubtedly Ryan's. However, the heat of the moment was felt by all of us.

"Kids, go to your playroom," I instructed them. They eyed each other and hauled tail out of the living room. I crossed my arms. "Why would you do that? That's precisely why I do not call her McKenzie. It stirs up too many emotions with the boys."

"Then you shouldn't have named her McKenzie. You understood that when you named her after Charity," he spewed.

"I just got home and here we go." I sucked my teeth. "You are so extra."

He looked at me as if I were crazy. "I'm not extra. I'm just not going to be reminded in every way that my daughter is Lincoln's child."

"Your daughter isn't. Lincoln's child is Lincoln's child," I fumed with a complete attitude.

He let out a real sinister laugh. "Oh, okay. So you wanna play that game, Charice? Now who's being extra? If I treated McKenzie as anything less than my biological child, you'd fight me, so do not throw that stepchild bullshit in my face when it's convenient for you."

He had a point. However, I was sick of his bitch-ass moods. "And you knew when you married me that I was pregnant with Lincoln's baby. So don't act brand new now. Just because Lincoln is in her life it doesn't change anything. She's got two daddies. Double the love, and her name is Lexi. It was Lexi before Lincoln knew, and it's Lexi now."

He rubbed his head. "I'm not acting new. I just need to be able to cope with this in my own way. Can't you give me that much?"

Cue the role-playing. I was hip to his ass. This wasn't about coping. It was about finding a way to push Lincoln's buttons. It hurt his pride to know he lost this one battle. He'd won the war, so what was one battle? (And he didn't know where Ryan Jr. got his attitude.) I played along. I didn't want him to think I was putting Lincoln before him, which was exactly why he tested me.

"Fine. You can call her McKenzie. I'll call her Lexi."

He smiled. "Thank you, baby."

"You're welcome. You are my husband after all."

"That's right." He gloated, no doubt feeling like a man.

I handed him the coffee mug. "This is your gift."

He looked at it and laughed. "Oh, so you got wasted in Jamaica?"

"So many times I can't even count them." I laughed along with him. *Lincoln wasted all day, baby.*

"Shit. That's why you're tired then. Getting wasted does that to you," he reasoned, sitting me on his lap.

"Yes, it sure does."

"I love you, baby. I'm happy that you had a great time, and I appreciate you working with me on the whole name thing."

"You're welcome. I love you too." And I did. I just wasn't in love with him anymore.

I stood up, and he pulled me into the guest bedroom and locked the door. "I can't wait any longer," he said as he pulled me into his arms and started kissing me wildly.

"Calm down. The boys—"

"Are minding their fucking business, so please mind yours," he blurted, irritated. "I need you to take care of me, Ricey. Damn. You spend all the time in the world tending to everyone else. Tend to me. Your husband."

I felt so bad. I had vowed to Lincoln that I'd only give my pussy to him. But how the fuck was I gonna keep denying Ryan the forbidden fruit? At first I did so because this fool was trying to impregnate me, which he thought I didn't know about. But now I'd made this promise to Lincoln because he was adamant that he wasn't sharing any longer. He'd said that if my pussy was truly his, I shouldn't be giving Ryan any of it. He was right, so I'd promised him. I had to find a way to stick to the oral sex. I dropped to my knees.

"No! If you do that, I'ma blow like a cannon. I want the real deal."

Mentally, I apologized for breaking my promise to Lincoln. I decided that what went on in my household stayed in my household. Lincoln had my heart, and my pussy was his. He was the only one who could truly make her purr and the only man I wanted to pleasure it. I just had to share it. My house was a level playing field, and in here Ryan was the QB. *Sorry, Lincoln.* Part of my wifely duties was performing wifely duties. I just couldn't and wouldn't tell him that.

I stripped down as Ryan did the same, and I eased on the bed. Ryan crawled on the bed with me and began kissing me.

"Shit. It's been so long I don't know if I can last long," he whispered.

"It's okay, baby."

"The second round will be better. I promise," he said as he lifted my legs for his grand entrance. I felt so hurt betraying Lincoln that I wanted to cry.

He pushed but it was rough. *Oh, shit.* I wasn't wet. Ryan wasn't deterred in the slightest. Instead, he attempted more foreplay, and I forced myself to get into the moment. Just as he was about to attempt again, our house phone rang.

"Fuck that phone," he instructed me.

I nodded as he continued to prep me for our lovemaking. Soon the answering machine came on. "Charice," Lucinda's tearful voice came through. "I didn't want to leave this on your house phone, but we can't reach you on your cell. I'm sure you haven't heard the news, but something happened with Trinity. I think Terrence and his cousin may be dead because of Pooch. Please call me."

Ryan jumped up, and I grabbed the phone. "Lucinda!" I yelled as she told me what she knew, and I let out a bloodcurdling scream.

Chapter 8

Pooch

"What do you want to be when you grow up?" my fifth-grade teacher, Ms. Simpkins, asked me.

"Paid," I answered, as the entire class laughed.

Stifling a giggle, she asked, "How do you plan on getting paid, Vernon?"

I thought long and hard. "I want to make my own race cars for NASCAR."

She looked at me with surprise. "That's actually a very good idea. You keep at it, Vernon. I hope one day that you make it, and when you do, please remember me."

I smiled and sat down.

If only that had been the answer I gave to her. It was the answer I started to give, but I remembered what my pops told me.

"Boy, in what lifetime? You think a bunch of politicians and rich white folks gon' let your poor black ass and that little trailer-trash-ass friend of yours into that type of money? Sandy has left your head in the clouds too long. Take a fuckin' look around you, Pooch! This is the fuckin' hood. Ain't no escaping this shit. But you can get money, and that money you will get. You can kill all that nonsense about NASCAR. It's time to build you before you go too soft. You going into the family business. It's *time to step you up. You ain't young no more. It's time to reign, Prince Money. It's time to prepare you to take over the Dope Boy Clique. Me and your uncles, we gonna teach you how to hustle."*

That was the beginning of the fucking end for me. Pops wasn't my real dad but rather my mom's old man, my stepdad. In fact, the only thing I honestly remembered about my real dad, Vernon Smalls Sr., were the last words he told my mom before walking out the door. *"I promise you, I'll be back for you and my son. I love you more than life, babe. Remember that shit."*

After my real dad ran out on my mom when I was 6 years old and he ended up getting killed in a street war, she and Isaac hooked up. Isaac James was my dad's best friend. He was like a brother to all my uncles, and he was the only father I ever had. My pops. Hell, he was the only dad I knew and really loved. He and my mom's oldest brother, Mathias, were best friends. When my uncles took over my dad's operation, they hustled that shit together. Once he married my mom, he became family.

My uncles didn't want my mom selling, so she managed the money and occasionally cooked that shit up. She had to be the one to help raise their kids and me in case something happened to them. Being a no-good-ass hustla was destined for me before I was even born. So you see? I wasn't bad. I'd had real-life dreams that got crushed before I was old enough to know any better for the promise of fast money, power, and respect.

What would've happened if I'd had the foresight to walk away? I could've graduated high school, gone to Georgia Tech, hooked up with some crazy-ass white boy whose folks had plenty of money, and been the king of fuckin' NASCAR today. *Damn.* I could've shown Trinity that side of me that she needed so she would be proud to be my lady. She could've gone to college, been a businesswoman with her art, and we could've been on some ol' black folks high-society shit. I'd be a millionaire with some IRAs— Roth and traditional— CDs, stocks, and bonds, and rubbing elbows with Bill Gates, Steve Jobs, or that rich muthafucka who started Facebook. I would've never had to worry about shit but making sure my money stayed on point and my kid was taken care of. Why couldn't I step up to be my own man? Simple. I thought I was being my own man.

"Pooch," *I heard Trinity's voice say.*

"Yes, baby?"

"Do you love me?"

"Always. I'm so glad you're my wife."

"And I am glad to be your wife." *She smiled at me.*

"Do you see that?"

"See what?" *she asked, looking on curiously.*

"That white light."

"Clear!" someone yelled as my chest lifted.

"It's okay. We got him back. Mr. Smalls, can you hear us? Mr. Smalls?"

"Well, he's stable for now," another person said, but I couldn't make out the image.

Fuck. Where was I? Trinity really wasn't here, and I wasn't married? What the hell was going on? Where was Ms. Simpkins? Where was Pops? Where was I, again? Everything seemed foggy. I heard the constant beep in my ear. *What the fuck is that?* I was trying to move, but I didn't or I couldn't.

"I'm afraid he's not stable enough to talk, Officers. His condition is still critical," a man said firmly.

"Listen, Doc. We are putting round-the-clock police surveillance on him. As soon as he wakes up and can talk, you have them call us. My name is Detective Brandon Michaels, and this is my partner, Detective Bill Nevels. Here is my card," Detective Michaels said.

Detective Michaels. But ain't I in prison?

"Yeah, muthafucka, you are in prison, and I'm gonna kill your muthafuckin' ass!" Wolf yelled.

"Wolf? Where are you?" Panic took over as I searched frantically for the voice.

"Right here!" he shouted, and I saw a pillow coming toward my face.

Struggling for my life, I yelped, "Help! Help!"

"Clear!" I heard the voice through my fog, and my chest lifted again.

"Charging to two hundred. Stand back, everyone. Clear! He's back."

Am I in the hospital? Shit. I gotta get outta here.

I jumped up and snatched off the leads to the various machines monitoring my vitals and pulled out the IV before I threw on my sweatpants and tennis shoes. I ran into the hallway and began walking toward the EXIT sign. The doctors and nurses didn't even notice me as they made their rounds to check on patients. Suddenly, they came rushing by with a guy on a gurney. It was the main runner who'd set up that hit on my spot last year. But I'd killed him. Didn't I?

He sat up and laughed. "The exit's that way, Pooch. It's good to see you."

Crazy muthafucka. Ignoring him, I ran for the big EXIT sign and pushed it open. I stepped out onto lush green grass. It was the greenest grass I'd ever seen in my life. I didn't know where I was, but I just kept walking. As I walked, I began seeing these beautiful angelic stone statues and figures, bringing me a sense of peace and calm. Then I saw a group of people standing around in all black.

"Oh, shit. It's a funeral." After further inspection, I realized that I was in a cemetery.

I tried to run in the other direction, but it was as if my body was jerking me toward the funeral, and I couldn't stop it. What the hell was going on? When I walked to the group of people, I gasped. It was Mom, my uncles, and my cousins. Sitting in the front row in all black and a big hat was Trinity. She was crying and wiping her tears with a Kleenex.

My nerves heightened, and I ran up to her. "Trinity. I'm here, babe. What's wrong?" She never even looked up. "Do you hear me?" I asked, reaching for her. My hand went straight through her arm. "What the hell?" I turned around when I heard a voice speaking.

"My father may not have been the best at being a parent, but he tried his best. He provided for me, and I know that he loved me," a woman said.

The words came from a beautiful young woman. She was the exact replica of Trinity when she was in high school, just a little more filled out. She appeared to be about 16 or 17 years of age. Then it dawned on me. Princess.

"Princess?" I asked, walking up next to her.

"I love you, Daddy. Sleep well. God bless your soul," she said and placed a rose on the mahogany coffin.

"I love you too, baby girl," I cried. "I'm right here. Just look at me, baby."

Trinity walked up to Princess and kissed her. "That was beautiful, Princess. I love you." Trinity pulled her close and hugged her.

"I love you too, Mom."

"Hey! I'm right here. I'm not in this fucking box." I waved my arms wildly in front of their faces. "I'm right here!"

"No, you're not." I heard Pops say behind me.

Spinning around, I asked, "Huh? What are you doing here, Pops? You got killed by Menace when I was in high school. I avenged you though. I killed that muthafucka."

"I know. You did me proud, son, and now it's time to go, Pooch."

"Go? Go where? But that's my daughter. She's grown up to be so beautiful, and Trinity, I love her. I want to make all the shit right with her. Tell her I love her. Apologize. Help her start her business. We can just be friends if she wants. I have to tell Princess I love her," I said, turning to run back to them, but I couldn't. It was as if an invisible blockade prevented me from going back.

"You can't go back, Pooch. Your time has expired. I wish I could go over there to your moms, but we can't. It's time to go," he explained, sticking a Cuban cigar in his mouth.

Tears rolled down my face. It was the first time since I'd lost Trinity that I'd cried. Wait. I'd lost Trinity. She married Terrence. Big Cal. Quality Warehouse Storage. 2245. Shoot-out. Shot. 2245.

Pops smiled at me. "Welcome, young'un. It's time to go, Pooch."

"Wait!" I turned around to look at him, but his back was to me. "Where are we going?"

He turned to look at me, and his face looked as if he were the devil himself. The sight shook me to my core. "I'm taking you home, son. Straight to hell."

Suddenly, I was inside the box. And it was on fire. "Wait! Wait!" I shook the fire off my feet and legs. "I need more time! I need more time! Please!"

Pops was suddenly next to me. "Don't worry. After a while, you can't even feel the heat anymore. All of us wish we had more time, Pooch, but we don't. Lights out. Game over," he said as the fire engulfed me.

"Clear!" I heard the distant but panicked shout. There was movement all around me.

"We almost lost him. He's back, people. He's back."

"Look, he's got a tear," a nurse said. "Can you hear us, Mr. Smalls? Blink if you can hear us. "I guess not yet," she said. The voices began to clear out of the room.

"But I blinked." Although I'd spoken, no one heard me.

"Don't worry, son. I heard you," Pops said, sitting in a chair in the corner of the room as he laughed . . . and laughed . . . and laughed.

Chapter 9

Trinity

I lay in bed staring at the ceiling as tears rolled down the sides of my face. I'd been there all morning and afternoon. I looked over at the clock. 2:00 p.m. *Hmph.* I had no reason to move. No reason to breathe. No reason to live. Couldn't God just take me now? What kind of mother could I be to my kids? I was too messed up. Far too gone. There was just some shit a person couldn't take. I had reached my breaking point. I was done.

Slowly, I dragged myself to the bathroom and opened the cabinet. Sleeping pills. This was it. This was the cure I needed. I needed to rest. I grabbed the bottle and moved in slow motion back to the bed.

"'Take no more than two tablets per day,'" I read the instructions aloud.

I opened the bottle and dropped two tablets in my hand. I closed the lid, and the bottle dropped out of my hands and onto Dreads's side of the bed. I rolled over and picked it up. I rubbed his side of the bed. Empty. It hadn't been slept on. I grabbed his pillow and pressed it against my nose. I could still smell the oil from his dreadlocks. My heart plunged to my toes, and my air supply heaved out of my chest. My emotions went crazy.

"Why?" I cried out to God. "Why? Oh, God!"

At the foot of the bed lay Terrence's cotton pajama pants. I eased out of bed and slipped his pants on. They were far too big for me, but I tied the drawstring and tucked the top in a tight roll before walking to his side of the bed. Sitting on his side, I lay on the bed and buried my face in his pillow, sniffing. His extra key ring, which held keys for the condo, his Chevrolet truck, the house, and my Mercedes, sat on his nightstand along with his Rolex and favorite gum, Doublemint, in their usual spots. The picture of us on our honeymoon along with the last birthday card I'd given him were close by, still intact. Picking up the photo frame, I swiped my hand across the picture and smiled as a lone tear streaked down my face. We were so happy. We'd just gotten married, and he'd taken me to the south of France. The backdrop for the photo was the countryside. It was beyond gorgeous. Standing there holding each other, we looked like the couple of the century. Nothing could spoil our happiness. Nothing. Perhaps we should've applied for visas and moved there, where it was peaceful—safe.

Tears filled my eyes again as I placed the frame back on the nightstand. I picked up the pill bottle and stared at it. I placed the two pills I held in my hand on my tongue and swallowed. Then I opened the bottle.

"I just want to go to sleep." Mumbling those words, I placed the bottle to my lips and dumped another three pills in my mouth.

Turning on my back, I lay there soaking it in. "Sleep. I just wanna sleep," I mumbled as my eyes got heavy. The empty Patrón bottle on my nightstand came into view, and I smiled in a haze. Then I looked at the photo of Terrence and me. "I love you, baby." My eyes closed and I drifted off.

***

"Trinity!" I heard someone yelling. "Come on, baby. Wake up," my mother said, and I felt a slap across my face.

"Umm. Sleep. I wanna."

"No! Wake up!" I heard several voices yell.

Instantly, I felt the urge to vomit. I lurched forward, hitting my head on the toilet lid, and spewed the contents of my stomach into the toilet, heave after heave. I felt cool towels around my neck and face.

"That's it, baby. Get it out," my mom said, brushing my hair back out of my face.

As I leaned back into her arms, I could vaguely see different people. It looked like Lucinda and Charice, but I was so sleepy and so tired. "Umm, Lu?" I mumbled.

"Yes, *mami!* It's me. Please wake up, honey," she cried.

"You have to tell us how many pills were in the bottle, Trinity," my mom said. "Come on, baby. Tell us."

My voice came out in a whisper. "Twelve."

"How many pills did you find on the bed?" my mom asked someone.

"Seven," Charice answered.

"She took approximately five pills," my mom said.

"The bottle says not to take more than two a day," Charice said.

"Don't worry. The paramedics are on their way," my mom said. "Just stay with me, Trinity, okay? I know you want to sleep, but you can't. Okay, honey? You can't."

"Nod if you hear her, honey," Charice said.

As my eyes closed, I nodded slowly. Far in the distance, I heard the sound of sirens.

Sunlight beamed on my face, forcing me to open my eyes. I sat up slowly and stretched. Once my eyes were focused, I tossed my feet to the side of the bed and slipped my flip-flops on. I felt so rejuvenated and alive.

My nightgown flowed long and free as I stood up and walked out onto my terrace. I never missed a sunrise. I wasn't going to start now. As I opened the double doors that led to the terrace, the sun shone so brightly I had to cover my eyes. My feet felt light. I was standing on a cloud.

"Trinity," I heard Terrence say, and I turned around.

He had on an all-white three-piece suit. His dreads swung loosely as he smiled at me, looking fine as hell. Tears came to my eyes. "Baby, I'm so glad to see you. I've come to be with you so that we could be together."

"I know," he said, walking close to me.

I threw my arms around him and kissed him. It was electrifying. I'd never felt such raw and pure emotions before in my life. "We can be together forever. Take me with you."

He smiled at me and cradled my face. "I can't, li'l mama."

"What do you mean you can't?" I asked, getting upset.

"It's not your time."

"But I love you, Dreads. I want to be with you. I'm ready."

Gazing at me sorrowfully, he whispered, "I know, li'l mama. I know. But you can't. It's not your time."

"But—" I cried, and he placed his index finger on my lips.

"I love you, Trinity. No one and nothing ever meant more to me than you and the kids. You are my world, and I will love you forever."

The pain behind his words seared right through me. Crocodile-sized tears fell from my eyes. "But, Dreads, what are you saying?"

"You have to go back and take care of the kids. They need you. Your mom needs you. Your sister and brother and your friends all need you."

"And I need you!" I declared. "I need you to be my husband. I need you to be a father. I need you! It wasn't supposed to be like this. We're married and you promised me forever. You promised me. And I want it. I want my forever." I pounded on his chest. "If you can't stay, take me with you!"

He wrapped his arms around me. "We'll be together one day, baby. I promise. For now, I need you to be there for our family. Raise the kids. Live your best life. Please know that I gave you everything I had inside of me. All of my love and everything I am is with you. It will forever stay with you. Carry that with you. Use it as your strength to go on."

"I can't let you go."

"I don't want you to," he said, staring me in the eyes as he wiped my tears. "Just use that love to go on. I know that you can do it. I believe in you. Promise me that you will do that."

I held him for a long while, and then I nodded slowly. "I promise." Suddenly, I was no longer holding him. He was far away from me. "Where will you be? Will I see you again?"

"Oh, don't worry, li'l mama. I'll be around. I'm never far away. I love you, babe." With his sentiment, he gave me his usual seductive wink.

"I love you, babe," I said softly as he walked off into the bright sunlight.

My eyes fluttered open and scanned across the room as I tried to recognize where I was. My throat felt parched, and I took a deep gulp of air to relieve some of the dryness. That was when I noticed that I was in the hospital. "How long was I out for?"

"Trinity!" I heard multiple voices yell.

There was a flurry of activity around me. I looked around to see my mom, brother, and sister along with

Charice, Lucinda, LaMeka, Ryan, Aldris, and two other dudes standing around my bed. "Who the hell are you two?" I asked the two faces who weren't familiar.

"She's back," Lucinda said. Everyone giggled at that. "This is my boyfriend, Mike."

"And this is my boyfriend, Gavin," LaMeka said.

I looked at Aldris. "So you two . . ." I said, pointing back and forth between Lu and Aldris.

"Umm, we're friends. Right, Aldris?" Lucinda said.

"Yes. I'm here to check on you. I wanted to make sure that you and the ladies were all right."

"It's good to meet you," Mike stepped forward and spoke.

"Wow. It's a pleasure." I looked over at Gavin, and a soft giggle escaped as I reflected on my previous phone call with my girls. "Oh, and you must be the Cablanasian."

My comment released a bit of the tension in the air as everyone chuckled softly. "Fo' sho'. It's nice to finally meet you. I wish the circumstances were better, though," Gavin said.

His words brought me back to my current reality, and I found my mom in the sea of friends in the room. "Any word?"

"You just rest. They pumped your stomach three hours ago. We're lucky that we got there when we did. You'd ingested five of those sleeping pills," she answered.

Her answer was not an answer, or rather not the answer I was looking for, so I sat up to give her clarity about the information I was searching for. "But I need to know—"

"*Mami,* you need to rest," Lucinda ordered, sitting beside me on the bed, interrupting my question to my mother.

"Exactly, cuz. And we're going to make damn sure of that," Charice fussed, sitting on the other side.

"So go ahead and give in, because you can't fight us all," LaMeka added, sitting at the foot of the bed.

"I think you'd better listen to them," my mom said. "And me too. We don't even have to worry about the kids. Consuela volunteered to stay at the house with them for as long as needed. Therefore, your best bet is to listen."

"And us too," my brother and sister said with a firm attitude. I grabbed their hands and mouthed, "I love you," to them, and they did the same.

"Wait. How did you know where to find me?" I asked, looking at my girls as it finally dawned on me that they didn't know where I was living.

"Your mom gave in and called my mom," Charice informed me.

"Not to mention that all of this has made the news all over Illinois and Georgia," LaMeka added.

"Once we found out, I chartered a plane and flew us directly here," Ryan said.

"Ryan! What's up? Still big time, Pretty Boy Floyd?" I joked.

"All day, baby." He gave me dap. I looked at Charice, who was kind of smirking at him. Something was up with that, but I was too tired to ask. I'd pull her to the side later.

Realizing I had no choice but to concede, I sat back in the bed. I didn't have the energy to fight against any of them, and it'd only prove futile in the first place. Rubbing my sore throat, I swallowed again and started coughing. My mom gave me a sip of water and then called the nurse.

I turned to my side, and as my eyes began to close, an image of Dreads sitting in the chair in the corner faded in and out. He winked at me, and then the image was gone. Tears sprang to my eyes as I suppressed my urge to wail out loud. At the same time, a sense of calm came over me, knowing that he was around and that he was never far away. Sleep invaded my lids, and I dozed off.

Chapter 10

Charice

It'd been a long day and a half. Between rushing from New Yitty, to flying to the A, and then flying to Illinois, I was beyond exhausted. I'd shed more tears than the Atlantic Ocean had water, and I was running on zero hours of sleep. We were all shocked and damn near speechless at the twisted turn of events. Then to get to Trinity's house and see her passed out with sleeping pills all around her was enough to make me jump off a cliff my damn self. If only there had been a way, we could've protected her.

I blamed myself. I was family. I should've made her tell me what was going on and forced her to give me some type of contact information, especially being in the position that I was in. Pooch's ass couldn't touch me with a ten-foot pole if he wanted to. Ryan's money was way too long for that foolishness to go down. And Pooch wasn't the mafia, so it ain't like he had connections that tough anyway. I should've done more. I slacked off because I was out of state, out of mind. I fled from my heartache in the A due to the loss of Charity and my failed relationship with Lincoln, and I'd abandoned my girls—my cousin. However, I vowed that if God spared Trinity, I would never do that again. Despite my personal trials, I would always keep my loved ones in perspective.

We'd all left our households so abruptly that I hadn't had time to make sure everyone was in order. Now that Trinity was resting comfortably and was out of the danger zone, I had to check on my children. I sent Ryan to get me a strawberry Fanta, even though I knew damn well there were none in the vending machines. I just needed to be away from him for a while. I sat on the bench outside of the hospital facing the entrance to make my calls. I called home first.

"Mom, I miss you and Dad," Ray said.

"I know, dude, but we'll be home tomorrow. For now, just be good for Ms. Johanna. At least her son is there, and you all can play and drive her crazy."

Ryan Jr. snickered at that and agreed. "Yeah, we are. She's already fussing, talking about, '*Ay caramba*.' You know how Ms. J is."

See what I mean? Just like Ryan Sr. Still, what he'd said was hilarious, because I could just see Johanna's face when she said that. "That's not even funny, and I am mad that I laughed. Junior, you are a mess. I want you to behave, and don't give Johanna any trouble."

"Who, Ryan? Yeah, right," Ray joked.

"I am good. Shut up, Ray!"

"You shut up!" Ray countered.

"Hey! Hey! Didn't I just say to behave? Is arguing behaving?"

"No, ma'am," they said in unison.

"Now chill out and be good. If I get a negative report when I get back, it's going down. Nawimean?"

"Yes, ma'am," they answered.

"Good. I love you guys. I gotta go."

"Love you too, Mom," they sang.

"Dad is going to call you later. Talk to you then."

I hung up and took a deep breath before I dialed Lincoln's cell. After the third ring, he answered. "I'm surprised you called from this line."

"You have Lexi. That's a good reason to call." My focus was trained on the hospital entrance. "Besides, I wouldn't honestly bring that other phone."

"Of course not," he said snidely.

My head snapped to the side, snatching the phone from my ear for a brief second at his tone. "What's with the 'tude?"

"I'd rather be there with you. I should be the one consoling you and seeing you through this situation with Trinity. Not Ryan," he fussed, plain and simple.

Rubbing my forehead, I asked, "Don't you think I'd rather have that too? But—"

"You're married, and my being there would only jeopardize your home life," he finished.

"Exactly," I huffed. I swore this was a fucking merry-go-round discussion with him. He knew the deal when I put it on the damn table. Yet every time he felt threatened by Ryan's position in my life, he got into a defensive mode.

The irritation in his voice was evident as he relented and gave me an update on our daughter. "Lexi is doing fine. She's sleeping now. I just fed her an hour ago." Thank God for the switched subjects.

"That's good. You know if you need any help—"

"Johanna is down the street. I know, Charice," he said plainly, cutting me off again. "Plus, my mom is on her way over here to visit anyway."

"Oh, great! Tell her I said hello."

"I will."

I looked up at the entry to the hospital again. No Ryan yet. *Good.* Now I could move on to the part of the conversation that I'd been itching to have. "I miss you, baby."

"Okay," he replied nonchalantly.

My head fell back in frustration. "What?"

He paused for a moment and then huffed. "Nothing. I signed up to play second fiddle to Ryan, so I can't complain, ma. You handle your business down there with Trinity. Lexi is cool. I'll see you when you're back in the NY," he said abruptly.

"Lincoln—"

"Later, ma." And with that he hung up.

I stared down at my phone in disbelief. Lincoln had lost his mind hanging up on me like that. I wanted to call back and give him a piece of my mind, but I knew better. I couldn't explain why I would be in a heated debate about bringing my husband to Illinois instead of my baby's father without it being obvious that we were having an affair, so I took that one for the team.

Our situationship wasn't ideal, so I knew he was a little aggravated with the arrangement, but like he said, he signed up for this when he agreed to be my sideline lover. I told him that my household and my kids came first. And he had to know that it meant at times Ryan would also come first. Whether I was in love with him or not, he was my husband and a part of my household and daily life. That was a fact that I always had to keep in perspective. The moment I lost sight of that, I'd lose it all. And I couldn't do that. Ryan owed me this life, and I owed happiness to my children. My children's happiness came before my own, so that inadvertently put it before Lincoln's happiness, because having Lincoln was a personal desire for me.

"Everything all right?" Ryan asked.

Shocked out of my reverie, I looked up at him. "You startled me."

"When I walked up you were just staring at the phone. I know you were calling to check on the kids. Is something wrong with them?" he asked. I shook my head no. "Did that muthafucka Lincoln say something to piss you off? I knew we should've let Johanna keep McKenzie—"

I put my hand up. "No, babe, it's nothing like that. I'm just overwhelmed by everything that's going on. Lexi is fine and so are the boys."

He hugged me close. "Okay. I know it's rough, but I'm here for you."

"I know." At that moment, I wasn't referring to just Trinity, though Ryan didn't know that.

"Oh, I'm sorry I couldn't get your strawberry Fanta. I looked all over for that vending machine. I think what you were looking at was the Powerade machine."

I hit my forehead. "Oh, my bad. I'm sorry I had you looking so long," I lied.

He rubbed my shoulders. "It's okay. It's not like you did it on purpose. I know you're stressed."

"Exactly." If only he knew how right he was.

"You ready to go back up to Trinity's room?" he asked.

Standing from the bench and stretching, I nodded. "Yes."

He wrapped his arm around my shoulders, and we walked back in. I slipped my phone in my back pocket and vowed that Lincoln and I would have a long powwow when I returned.

Chapter 11

LaMeka

I fell on the bed in the hotel room, exhausted. All of us were. We'd been at the hospital all day tending to Trinity and trying to console each other. Just being around each other was comforting enough. I was so happy that Gavin and I had gotten past our little rift, because I needed him in the worst way. He'd been my rock this entire time, and I was so grateful for him.

Gavin crawled onto the bed next to me and pulled me close to him. As he held me close, he softly stroked my hair. This was what I loved about him. He knew just what to do when I needed it most. We didn't even speak any words to each other, but he just knew that at that very moment I needed that comfort from him.

"Did you talk to your mother?" Gavin asked.

I nodded. "Mm-hmm. The kids are cool."

"Good," he said.

My cell phone began to buzz. "It's probably my mom again. Can you answer my phone?"

He got up and grabbed it off the dresser. "It doesn't show a name. It's a 404 area code, though."

I fanned it off. "Just answer it. It's probably a wrong number."

"Hello?" Gavin answered. "Were you looking for LaMeka? Oh, then you don't have the wrong number,"

I heard Gavin say. "Since you're questioning me, who is this?" he asked with an attitude, causing me to sit up. "Then you don't worry about who the fuck this is, pah'ner," Gavin shouted.

I jumped up and grabbed the phone out of Gavin's hand. "Hello? Who is this?"

"I was calling your ass trying to be fucking concerned since I heard about Pooch and Trinity, and you got that fucking white boy answering your phone," Tony yelled. "How you take that fucking punk with you to check on Trinity? I'm their friend. We all grew up together!"

"Whoa! Wait a minute, Tony. Who the hell do you think you're coming at like that? I don't owe you a damn thing. We are not together, and how did you know where I was at?"

"As much as you be all up in your girls' asses, I knew you'd hurry up and jump your ass up to Illinois where Trinity is, and besides, I called the house and your mom told me," he answered. "And you took the white boy," he added with an attitude.

"Who was I supposed to take, you?"

"That would've been nice, but you don't even think about me—"

Taking a deep breath, I knew I was going to give his ass the business. "I think about you about as much as you thought about me when we were together. Not at all. Tony, you are no longer a concern for me. You drew your line in the sand with me a long time ago. Don't call my damn phone with this foolishness. As a matter of fact, what you're going to do is stop harassing me and my man. I am with the white boy, and that's where I'm going to stay. If you don't like it, you can kiss my entire ass, 'cause I don't give a good damn. Asshole." Without giving him a chance to respond, I hung up in his face.

"Son of a bitch," I muttered, sliding my phone back on top of the dresser.

Gavin pulled me into his arms. "Don't even sweat that punk."

He was right and I knew it. Too much had transpired to entertain Tony Light. Exhaling, I rubbed my forehead. "I know. He just pisses me off. When he had me, he didn't want me. Going around fucking crackheads and my damn sister of all people! Even if he didn't have the package, why the fuck would I wanna be with his scandalous ass anyway? I must have been on some serious dumb shit to consider being a family with his rotten ass."

As Gavin held me, I heard the deep rumble in his chest. "You are getting gangsta."

"I'm just getting tired. I've reached my breaking point with his loony-tune ass."

Pulling back, he kissed my forehead. "Don't stress. You're amazing and I love you."

God, how I adored this man. "Baby, I love you too. So much."

Just then his phone buzzed. He looked at it and put it back in his pocket. "Who was that?"

He shrugged. "Nobody important."

"You can answer it."

Nonchalantly, he waved off my comment. "I'm here spending time with you and your friends. It's cool. I'll hit them back when we get to the A."

Now as much as I appreciated the attention and the sentiment, the turmoil we'd just experienced speared my gut. There was no way I was letting this slide. I didn't want to start any foolishness, but I wasn't about to be a fool either.

"Why don't you want to answer it?"

"I just told you why."

Naw, something was definitely up. *Fuck that.* "Gavin. Who was that?" I stood back with my hands on my hips.

"Baby, it was nobody," he said with exasperation.

"Well, nobody must be somebody to have your cell phone number, and I want to know who nobody is."

"It's this dude I know. A friend of mine. That's why I said I'll just hit him back later."

I stood with my arms folded, not believing a word he said.

He pulled out his cell phone and showed me the screen as he pulled up the missed call. "See? Look."

"Gary?"

He copped an attitude and put his phone back in his pocket. "Yes, Gary. So now can we drop this damn subject?"

Now I felt horrible. I trusted Gavin, but I just didn't want to make the same mistakes with Gavin as I did with Tony. I had to protect my heart this time. Still, I felt horrible that Gavin was catching the backlash for Tony's actions when he'd shown me that he was nothing like him.

"I'm sorry, baby. That whole mess with the nurses and the women you dated at the hospital is still fresh for me. I apologize. I was wrong."

Gavin calmed down and pulled me to him by my waist. "Woman, how many times I gotta tell you? That is my past. You are my present, and all I see is a bright future ahead for us. As long as I have you and you have me, nothing else matters. This is about me and you."

That garnered a smile from me, and I wrapped my arms around his neck. "How about I make it up to you by hitting the shower with you?" I placed a kiss on his neck as a show of my intent.

His nature rose instantly. "Do you feel that? Ain't no way this is being shared. It loves what it already has, and it won't ever stop loving it," he reassured me. "But you know what? It's been a long couple of days. You can make it up to me later. Right now, I just want you to relax and be stress free, so you go ahead and take your shower. When you get out, I'm going to give you the best back and foot massage. How's that?"

Who was I to turn down a good time? "Sounds like heaven." We kissed again, and I turned to go to the bathroom to shower.

"And hurry before I change my mind," he called out as I switched out of the room giggling.

I had to quit trippin'. Gavin was a great man and an awesome boyfriend. I owed it to him to treat him better. I wasn't going to spend my time believing the watercooler gossip or the haters. I was more than enough for him, and he was more than enough for me. Gavin Randall was my everything.

Chapter 12

Gavin

Once I heard LaMeka step in the shower, I plopped on the bed and exhaled. I had promised myself I wasn't going to date another chick from the hospital precisely because of the situation I was in now. My past was coming around to haunt me. It didn't help that Meka had been scorned so much in her life that she was more used to disappointment than happiness. She was just now beginning to be happy, and I sure as hell didn't want to ruin that for her. She trusted me far too much for that.

Getting involved was a no-go. I knew that from the start, and believe me, I tried my best not to fall for her. The first day I met her, my heart and my loins both began pulsating. Between her brains and her body, I was hooked. Before she cut it, Meka had that short-bob thing going with her hair. It was always shiny and had bounce to it. Her nails were always neatly manicured, her teeth were pearl white, and her skin was flawless. Every day she wore this light and fresh perfume that made her smell like honey. Her scrubs were always fresh and fit her in all the right places. Even outside of the hospital, she was sassy and sexy, never slutty and skankish. Those were all good signs. It meant she kept herself up. So many young women just didn't believe in keeping up their appearance. I understood that not everybody could afford the beauty and nail salons, but damn, buy clothes and shoes that show you care about yourself. All those too-tight clothes made them look like strippers instead of professionals, and the too-baggy clothes made me wonder if they were shopping to impress women. I'm not even gonna get into the shoes. All I'm saying is that if your toes are cutting up the carpet with your shoes on, or your heels got more crust than an apple pie, don't have them joints hanging out of your shoes. Last, but not least, was the bonus round. Tiny waist, B-cup breasts, smooth hips, and an ass so plump you could bounce a dime off of it.

Yes, I said dime. Not a nickel, a quarter, or even a penny, which are slightly bigger, but a dime. You know the ass is potent when you can bounce the smallest object on it and can still watch it jiggle. Every time I saw her, my desire for her heightened.

Then I actually got to know her. It was amazing to find out that she was so young with two children, one of whom had special needs. It showed me her character and her strength. A lesser woman couldn't handle that by herself. Her determination to finish school and her caring nature, charm, and kindness melted me in a way no other woman had. The more we talked, the more I realized she was wise beyond her years, and she gave the best advice. Besides being easy to talk to, she was trustworthy, which was rare for many people. Nothing I ever told her in confidence came back to me. I appreciated that she wasn't a gossiper. The more we talked, the more our friendship grew and the harder I fell for her. Once I realized I had true feelings for Meka, I knew I had to pursue her. It was more than an attraction, because my heart literally ached to be with that woman. When she gave in and gave me a chance, it felt like my soul lifted and went to heaven. I was so elated. She was the total package for me, and I had been on cloud nine ever since. At least, until them talkin'-ass nurses opened their mouths. Now here I was dealing with that bullshit. As if I didn't have enough bullshit facing me.

As I sat on the bed, I eased my phone out of my pocket and pressed REDIAL quickly. I hated to call Gary right now, but if I didn't call him back, he'd definitely call me back.

"Hello?" Gary answered.

"Sup, dude?"

"Nothing much. Just wondering why I haven't heard from you."

"I've been busy. I'm actually busy now." I listened to make sure the shower was still running.

"Then why did you call me back?"

"Because I knew you'd call me back if I didn't." Pinching the bridge of my nose, I asked, "Why are you playing these games? What do you want?"

"I'm hardly the one for games. You know that. When's the last time you talked to Dad?"

I shrugged my shoulders. "It's been a minute. Why?"

"He was right," Gary huffed. "I'll never understand you. Dad has been good to us, and he has afforded your trifling, inconsiderate, uncaring ass more opportunities than you can shake a stick at. Dad says he hasn't talked to you in two months. Why in the world would you not return his calls or call your father for two months, Gavin?"

To restrain my comments, I bit my inner jaw. He knew when I said I was busy that I wouldn't go off on him. *Fucker.* I planned on cussing his ass straight out the next time we talked, because nobody talked to me like that. "You are such a spoiled-ass, daddy's-boy brat. I have a life. I don't live my life through you or Dad."

"You only get this way when—"

"I gotta go," I interrupted him as I heard Meka turning off the shower, and I hung up in his face.

After locking my cell phone, I slipped it back in my

pocket. Then I went inside my suitcase to retrieve the massage oil. Meka walked out with a towel wrapped around her, and as soon as she reached the bedroom, she dropped it.

"I'm ready for my massage." She swayed sexily over to me.

"And I'm ready to give it to you." *Damn.* She was the finest woman I'd ever seen in my life. "Just lie right on the bed, and let me get ready for you."

She did as I requested. Then I walked in the bathroom and removed all my clothing except my boxers. I grabbed my clothes, and as I was getting ready to walk out, I felt my cell phone vibrate. Hurriedly, I pulled it out of my pocket. *Gary.* I hit the IGNORE button and powered it off. At least it didn't buzz while I was in front of Meka. *Thank God for small favors,* I thought as I walked out.

"Took you long enough," Meka joked, lying on her back with her legs crossed sexily.

I licked my lips. "I'm sorry to keep you waiting. I never will again."

I placed my clothes and cell phone on the chair across the room and climbed on the bed with her. This was where I wanted to be. Right here. With my goddess of perfection. Meka meant the world to me, and I vowed I'd never give her up. Never.

Chapter 13

Mike

What a fucking day! I was at the hospital all day watching all the ladies, including my girl, interact with Dri instead of me. I understood I was her new man, but I felt more like the third wheel. Everybody interacted with Gavin just fine. No one treated him like he was a spot or blemish that did not belong. Aldris was the one who didn't belong. He was no longer a part of this clique. Yet here I was the oddball out. Even Ryan interacted with him and Gavin more than me.

I didn't complain to them, but I had every right to do so. Every. Shit was crazy. Here I was in love with a woman who I wasn't sure was even over her ex, who just so happened to be on a trip with us. I knew what her friends were probably thinking—what goes around comes around. Well, fuck that and fuck them if they felt that way. Aldris was the one who fucked up. Not me. I never intended on taking his lady. Six months ago, if anyone had told me that I'd be in this position, I would've laughed and then cussed them out for even thinking some foolishness, but I couldn't help how their relationship ended. I had nothing to do with that. I simply fell in love with the wrong woman who was right for me, and I couldn't help that either.

The person who was pissing me off the most at this point was Jennifer. Yes, Jennifer. Listen, I'm ashamed to admit it, but there had been a plan in place to keep Aldris and Lucinda separated after Aldris had proven he was still the same ol' Dri. For whatever reason, Jennifer wanted Aldris back in a major way. She'd told me that she knew Aldris would confess to Lucinda that he'd cheated, and the only thing I had to do was wait for Lucinda to come around and tell me she wanted to be with me. She begged me to betray Aldris and get with Lucinda if the opportunity ever presented itself so that she could make her move on Aldris. I didn't want to do that shit. I had no intention of following up with Jennifer and her twisted-ass scheme. Actually, it really wasn't a scheme, because she knew Aldris well enough to know how things were gonna go down, and she also knew—from Aldris running his mouth—that I had feelings for Lu. He never should've confided in Jennifer about his insecurities concerning my friendship with Lucinda. Aldris handed her the perfect non-scheme scheme: let everything take its natural course and seize the opportunity when it knocked. I never agreed to it. I wasn't going to do that to Aldris. I truly was not. For one, I never thought it would actually happen. Two, Aldris was my boy. And three, I didn't want to be caught up in no bullshit with Jennifer. But when Lucinda showed up at my house and confessed her feelings, I just couldn't help myself. It wasn't like I forced her to come to me. She did it willingly. And why should I sacrifice my happiness when they weren't going to be together anyway? So yes, I did it. For once in my life, I had found love, and even if it was with the wrong person, I was going to take what I was entitled to have: a real woman and real love.

Well, I'd told Jennifer that Lucinda was mine so that she could make her move. I didn't want or need to know her plan, but I had depended on her to sway Aldris back her way so he'd forget about Lu. In turn, Lu would forget about him. But she wasn't doing what she'd so boldly assumed she could do. Aldris should be halfway back in love with her by now, but instead, he was here up in my girl's face. After Lucinda put that damn Spanish Fly on my ass, I knew Jennifer had to come deep out of her bag of tricks to snatch Aldris. Never in my life had I confessed to being in love during sex, not even great, off-the-wall, "break my back" sex. One round with Spanish Fly had me ready to fucking propose and walk down the aisle in the same day! Yep, it was like that. It may be hard—even damn near impossible—but Jennifer had to find a way to get Dri back because I didn't throw away my friendship with Aldris to lose Lucinda in the process. And I damn sure wasn't giving up on my relationship like some punk bitch.

I'd suffered through lunch and dinner with Aldris, and now I was ready to relax in the hotel with my girl and chill, but the clincher to this evening? They only had three rooms left at the hotel. Guess what that meant. Yep, Dri was shacking up in the room with Lucinda and me. Of course. Ryan and Charice were married, and Gavin and LaMeka damn sure weren't sharing a room with the fifth wheel, so he ended up in our room. Now wasn't this a story for the history books?

"I'm exhausted," Lucinda said as we all walked into the room. She turned to face me and Aldris. "I understand this arrangement is uncomfortable for all of us. However, we have to make it do what it do for tonight. So please, I ask that you two call a truce, and let's be adults about this. There is enough on my plate already, and I don't want to have to referee you guys all night long. Can we agree to deal with this temporary arrangement for one night?" she asked.

Aldris and I looked at each other and grudgingly shook hands. "Deal. Anything for you, Lu," he said as he gripped my hand.

"I feel the same way." I gripped his hand right back.

Lucinda shook her head. "Okay, let me get a blanket and some sheets for you, Aldris. Mike, please help him pull out the coffee table so he can get to the sofa bed." With that, she walked to the bedroom area to get the linen.

I stared at Aldris. He stared at me.

"Let me help you move this so you can get to your bed."

"Any bed will do," he said snidely.

"What's that supposed to mean?"

He shook his head. "Nothing," he replied as we moved the coffee table and pulled out the sofa bed.

"Looks comfy." Yeah, I was being a dick about it.

"Sure does. Good thing I didn't pay for it." He looked at me with an evil smirk. "Ain't that right, Mikey?"

Bastard. Okay, so I paid for the room because I sure as hell didn't want his bitch ass paying for it. It wasn't until just then that it bothered me that I had agreed to foot the bill. At least it gave me leverage.

With a raised eyebrow, I surmised, "The hallway would feel worse though," just so he knew who called the shots.

"All right, fellas," Lucinda said, walking in. "We are playing nice, right?" she asked. We both nodded. "Good. Here you go, Aldris. I gave you an extra blanket to try to cushion the springs on that sofa bed."

"You're so sweet, Lu. Thanks for thinking about me." He took the linen from her hands.

"Did you want to shower first?" Lucinda asked Aldris.

"I can do that." He grabbed his overnight bag and headed to the bathroom. "And I promise not to use up all the hot water." He smiled at her as she giggled.

"I would so kick your ass."

"I know. "Cause lukewarm water is not hot, Aldris,'" he joked, impersonating her.

"You're damn straight it ain't. And I don't wanna hear, 'Well, at least it ain't cold, Lu,'" she mimicked him, and their continued laughter ensued.

Shrugging, I stated plainly, "I don't get the joke."

They both looked at me and quieted down. "You had to be there," they said in unison as they looked at each other.

With the discomfort at an all-time high, Lucinda cleared her throat and gestured toward the bathroom. "I guess you'd better head to the shower," she said to Aldris.

Thankfully, he walked away and into the bathroom with no further conversation or old inside jokes geared toward his failed relationship with Lucinda. *Hatin'-ass nigga.* Once he closed the door, Lucinda waltzed over to the sofa without a word, sat down, and turned on the television. "I guess we can watch the tube until he gets out."

Watch TV? Hell no. Fuck that television. I sat on the ottoman in front of her. "Nah, we need to talk."

She dropped her head into steepled hands. "I know it's uncomfortable. I'm uncomfortable too, but it's just one night."

"It's not that." I picked up the remote and turned off the TV before turning back to face her. I placed my hands on her knees. "I feel like I'm the third wheel with you two."

Leaning forward, she clasped my hands in hers, and sorrow danced on her face. "I'm sorry. I wasn't trying to make you feel that way."

As much as I wanted to let it go because I didn't want to argue around Aldris, fuck that. I needed her to understand my feelings. More importantly, I needed her to respect them because Aldris damn sure wasn't. I couldn't be out here being disrespected by both of them. That shit was a no-go.

"Well, you are. All these strolls down memory fucking lane are downright disrespectful. Do you think he is going to give a damn if you disrespect me?"

She dropped her head at the realization of my words. A beat passed before her eyes met mine again, and she cradled my face. "No, he's not and I am sorry. I didn't realize I was putting you in that kind of position, baby. I really am sorry."

"I shouldn't be coming at you with this right now with all that's going on, but I just couldn't help it. I know that you and Dri have a past—a very recent past—and that bothers me."

"Well, Mike, I can't help that. You know the situation firsthand. I don't wanna disrespect you, but I can't change the fact that three months ago I was engaged to Aldris. That is a fact of life that we both have to live with."

"I get that. What I'm talking about is the closeness."

She groaned uneasily. "Again, three months ago, I was his fiancée. Look, I can't possibly live my life if I don't forgive him for the past. I do. I wish him all the best, but I've moved on with you. You want me to hate him, and I can't."

"No, I just want to know you're not in love with him." The words came out harsher than I intended.

Taken aback, she stood up with her arms folded. I could feel the steam radiating from her body at this point. "That's going to be hard when you think everything that comes out of my mouth is a symbol of my undying love for him. If I ask him if he's okay, if I say hello, if I offer for him to use the shower first, it's all because I must still be in love with Aldris. Damn. He was your friend. You should at least care about him," she mouthed off.

What? I gave away my friendship to Aldris for her, and she wanted to throw my former friendship in my face because of the good bullshit she was on? Hell no. It was my turn to jump up. I was heated now, 'cause fuck that.

"I do care! But I gave that up for you. Now you want me to consider his feelings? You came to me, Lu. To me! You need to make up your mind if it's more important to you to care about me or love him."

With those words, the flame within my hot tamale girlfriend ignited. "So I forced myself on you? Is that what you're saying, Michael?"

"Don't Michael me—"

"I will so Michael you. Answer the question," she seethed.

Being a smart-ass, I nodded angrily. "In a way, yes."

Her nose flared, her eyes narrowed, and she cocked her head to one side, throwing her hands on her hips. *Oh, shit.* This was the storm that Aldris had spoken about. One look at her and I knew without a shadow of a doubt that Hurricane Lucinda was about to blow.

"*Besa mi culo!*" she hollered. She was in my face before I could react. "Ay, *chico,* let me tell you one thing. I never throw myself at any man. You have me fucked up. If you don't want me, step, *papi.* That's all you have to do. 'Cause I will not stand here and take this treatment from you. Not now and not ever," she went off with her Spanish accent thick on every syllable.

Okay. This wasn't going as planned, and what the fuck did she just say to me in Spanish? I hated that, because I didn't even know how to argue back with her. I fought her back with an attempt at her own words. "Well, you can *baja mi ceelo* too."

Over this entire argument, I turned to walk to the bedroom. Great. Why was Aldris standing in the doorway just looking at us argue?

"How long have you been standing there?"

"Long enough." He walked past me. "Are you all right?" he asked Lucinda.

She looked up at Aldris. "I'll be fine. I need a drink."
She plopped down on the chair and dropped her face in
her hands.

"*Quieres que te prepare una copa?*" Aldris asked her.

"Ay no. *Muchos gracías, Aldris. Eso es muy dulce de tu
parte.*"

Another plus. I forgot that bitch learned Spanish. He
was fluent with it and wasted no time showing me that
he could hang with Lucinda in any language. *Note to self:
take Spanish courses.* I was definitely headed to Office
Depot to buy the Rosetta Stone series the moment we
landed in the A. That was for damn sure.

For now, that was enough of that shit. Although I was
still pissed with Lucinda, I would not hand her over to
Aldris on a silver platter, because that was not about
to happen on my watch. Instead of going to the bedroom,
I walked up to Lucinda and took her hand.

"You don't need a drink. Come on. I'm sorry." I pulled
her up and hugged her close. "Let's let Aldris get some
rest. You're good, right, bruh?"

"Yeah, bruh."

"Good night then." With that, I guided Lucinda into the
bedroom with me.

"Good night, Aldris," Lucinda called out as we walked.

"Sweet dreams, Lu," he said.

Once we were inside, I closed the bedroom door and
locked it. I wanted to talk, but when I turned around,
Lucinda was gathering her belongings for the shower, so I
let her be. I knew she was still pissed at me, and I wanted
her to calm down. Hell, I needed her to calm down.
Aldris had already witnessed some of our showdown, and
I didn't want him to see any more. He was probably in
the other room having the laugh of his life, but I would
make sure that I had the last one.

After Lucinda took her shower, I quickly took mine. I didn't want to give them five minutes alone. It had to be the fastest shower in history. Hell, I was out so fast that Lucinda was still moisturizing her arms and legs when I came out.

"O ye of little faith," she said aloud as I pulled out my lotion bottle.

"Why do you say that?"

"Did the water even touch your ass? Do you think that I am so broken over Aldris I'd run to him while you washed your ass?" she sneered, catching on to what I had done.

"I don't trust him. It has nothing to do with you."

"Well, I'm capable of turning down a man. I know you believe that I'm such a whore that I fling myself on the first one available and all, but I don't," she snapped.

I turned to face her. "Baby, I didn't mean that. It's not like that."

"Bite me."

Damn. I was beginning to feel bad for even broaching the subject with the massive clapbacks she was issuing. I'd barely survived Hurricane Lu. Now I had to deal with the riptides, too?

"Do we have to argue? I said my piece. You said yours. Let's be done with it. Honestly, I was wrong and I am sorry," I pleaded while putting on my T-shirt and cotton shorts.

She rolled her eyes before climbing in bed and quipped, "Yeah. Whatever."

She was stuck on our argument, but one look at her fine ass and I'd developed a sudden case of amnesia. 'Cause damn. She looked so hot. Granted, she was only wearing a V-cut tank top and boy shorts, but you just had to know the kind of body Lu was working with to fully appreciate the view. *My God.* Her body was like plow-dow. 36(D)-24-42. You do the math. *Oooh, Jesus.* I knew

Jesus was real because only He could create that much fineness and put it in one human being.

Rather than pounce on her like I wanted, I slowly slid into bed and turned the lights off. After a few minutes, I rolled on my side and slid close to her. "Lu?" She didn't respond and kept her back to me. "Baby?" I wrapped my arm around her waist. "Come on. I'm sorry. Please forgive me. Can you blame me for being cautious and jealous? I'm in love with you, Lucinda."

Those were the words that seemed to resonate with her more. She inhaled deeply and then exhaled. "I hear you."

I moved her hair from her neck and kissed her. "Forgive me."

She giggled. "Stop."

"You know you like it." I laughed and nuzzled my nose in the nape of her neck.

She laughed out loud. "Stop, Mike." The words rolled off her lips sexily, and I kissed her again, showing her I had no intention of stopping. "Okay, okay. I forgive you, *papi*." She laughed. "And I'm sorry for making you uncomfortable again."

Now she turned to face me, and I palmed her cheek. "It's just the rantings of a man who is afraid to lose you. Maybe it was more of me than you. You were just being an adult about the situation. I'm sorry."

She leaned her forehead against mine as she caressed my face in return, signifying her forgiveness. "No, I bear some blame in this too. I'm sorry. I should've done better about your feelings." With that, she kissed my lips, and all was forgotten by me. Suddenly, she laughed. "*Baja mi ceelo*. You are funny."

I chuckled with a hint of embarrassment. "Well, then teach me."

Seductively, she licked her lips. "It's *bay-sah-me-q-low*," she pronounced slowly.

"*Besa mi culo,*" I repeated slowly but perfectly.

"*Sí.* You've got it, *papi.*"

"And what does that mean?"

"It means 'kiss my ass.'" She grinned.

"Oh, yeah?" I asked. She nodded, confirming the meaning. "Gladly." I ducked under the sheets and lightly bit and kissed her ass cheek. "How was that?" I reveled in my inquiry as I came back up to her in a fit of giggles.

"Perfecto, *papi,*" she sang, her Hispanic accent shining through again.

"You're right about that. That GA peach is sweet and ripe." Turning serious, I captured her eyes and professed my affection. "I love you."

Tilting her lips up to mine, she kissed me. What did she do that for? I went in, kissing her deeply and moving to her neck, gliding my tongue to her spot to lightly suck on it.

"Ay, *papi,*" she moaned, commanding me not to stop.

Three loud bangs on the door scared us and caused us to stop abruptly. The next voice we heard was Aldris's. "Can you all keep that shit down? I'm trying to fucking sleep out here," Aldris yelled.

We looked at each other and giggled softly. "I forgot about him," she whispered. I nodded in agreement although I knew I was lying. I wanted him to hear it.

"*Lo siento,* Aldris," she yelled. "It means 'I'm sorry,'" she whispered to me.

"Yeah, my bad, Dri," I shouted. "How do you say 'get some rest' in Spanish?" I whispered to Lucinda.

She shook her head, stifling a giggle. "*Descansar un poco,*" she said slowly.

"*Descansar un poco.* We'll keep our antics down," I added. He groaned heavily and walked off . . . hard.

Checkmate. Game over. Who got the last laugh now? With that, Lucinda and I held each other and kissed again.

Chapter 14

Ryan

"Hey, boys!" I was thrilled to talk to my sons. I missed them so much.

"What's up, Dad?" they shouted excitedly together.

It brought a smile to my face. Their voices were infectious. "Nothing much. I miss you dudes."

"I miss you too," they yelled in unison again.

"What time will you all be home?" Ryan Jr. added.

Mulling it over, I rubbed my head. "Probably around five tomorrow evening, why?"

"He's just mad because Ms. Johanna only allows us to play our gaming systems for two hours. Last night, she caught him playing his PSP when we were supposed to be sleeping, and she took it from him. She said she wasn't giving it back until you and Mom got home," Ray spilled.

"Remind me never to commit a crime with you, Ray. Snitch," Ryan Jr. sulked.

"Ryan." My voice issued the warning. This boy was giving me a headache.

"But, Dad! Come on. Two hours? That's like insane. And she makes us go to bed at nine o'clock. Our bedtime is ten. Like seriously, we only got to watch one hour of *Smackdown*. Then she made Brussel something last night, and I couldn't get up until I ate half of it. That's crazy!" Ryan Jr. fussed.

My kids were becoming the spoiled little rich kids I complained about. I couldn't help but shake my head. Had Charice and I gotten this slack on them? "Your mom and I told you while we were gone that Johanna was in charge. That means if she says your bedtime is at nine, you can only play games for two hours, and you had to eat Brussels sprouts for dinner, then that's what you had to do. She's the adult. You're the child. What I suggest you do—the both of you—is listen to her and be good. And since you have such a problem obeying her rules, it would be fitting to change your bedtime to nine for a month, and I will keep close watch over the PSP for that month as well." Ryan Jr. sucked his teeth. "Did I hear two months?" I asked him.

"No, sir. Not at all. One month is just fine to learn my lesson. In fact, I've already learned. I'm going to help Ms. Johanna with the dishes," Ryan Jr. said. "And Ray can help me."

"But I—"

"That's not a bad idea. Ray, you help him. He washes. You dry, and you both put them away," I cut him off. Now it was his turn to suck his teeth. "Are you aiming for a month-long nine o'clock bedtime too?"

"No, sir." The sulking seeped from his voice.

"Good. You boys be good, and we will see you tomorrow. I love you guys."

"Love you, Dad," rolled out sadly in unison before we hung up.

"Let me guess. Junior got in trouble, and Ray told on him," Charice said, walking into the living area of the hotel room.

Pointing at her, I nodded my agreement. "You know them." I placed my phone on the coffee table. "Charice, I think the boys are becoming spoiled."

Leaning against the doorframe of the bedroom, she crossed her arms. "You just now thought that? I've known that for quite some time."

"Well, why didn't you say something?"

As she eyed me, the smirk on her face was evident. "I do believe I have. You know, every time I said, 'Ryan, they don't need that gaming system,' or, 'Honey, I don't think we should allow them to con us into changing their bedtime schedules.' My personal favorite is, 'Ryan, you are spoiling them.' You always said that your kids had a good foundation and giving them a little leeway wouldn't hurt. Those were Ryan Chad Westmore's exact words."

Oh, yeah. I did say that. Damn. I guess Daddy is a little more spoiled than he realized himself. Well, that was going to change. I wanted my kids to appreciate life's little lessons. I didn't want them to be the dudes no one wanted to be around, and I damn sure wasn't trying to be the parent who was always bailing them out of trouble.

"Well, that changes now. From now on, I'm setting down some ground rules for those boys. Their attitude sucks, and their behavior is getting ridiculous." Standing up, I stretched. "No more perks just for kicks. Now they have to earn them."

"Does that apply to Daddy too?"

"Huh? What does that mean?"

"Part of good parenting is leading by example. Does that mean that you are going to keep your one-year-old Aston Martin instead of trading it in for the new Jaguar just to say you have it?"

Fuck me. She knew she was wrong to ask me that. I'd planned to get that car for the past two months. Okay, so I had a car fetish, but didn't all men? All I had was a Ford F-250, a Range Rover, a Mercedes CLK 500, an Aston Martin, and a pearl black fully restored 1971 Chevy Chevelle. I also had a Harley-Davidson—and a golf cart

with rims, but that last one didn't count. That was only
for golfing at the neighborhood greens. As for the Aston
Martin, I was going to trade that one in for the other. It
wasn't like I was just outright buying the Jaguar. Okay,
so it was actually Charice who told me I'd have to get rid
of one car to get it, but still, I was doing that. Sue me. I
made big money, and I liked to play hard.

"And what about the brand-new Camaro you just ordered? That doesn't count? I mean, since you're trying
to find a way to rationalize your answer in your mind,"
Charice blurted, interrupting my thoughts.

And a new Chevy Camaro—pearl gray with black racing
stripes. *Fine!* Like I said, I had a car fetish. "Well, what if
I get the Jaguar and restrict myself for the next two years
from any more?" My stomach just flopped at the thought
of that.

"How about you don't need it, and you can get a car
when all of the eight that we have now clunk out?" she
asked me. "How about that?"

She had lost her mind. Nah, fuck all that. "Well, I'm
the parent, and they don't have to worry about what I do.
Just do as I say."

She clapped. "Great job, Dad."

"This isn't about me. It's about them." Admittedly, I'd
gotten a little angry at her comment.

"Of course it isn't," she said tersely. "I'm about to get
ready for bed."

"What's that supposed to mean?" I followed her into
the bedroom.

"It means that you love to enforce what you feel is best
on everybody else's life, but you fail to do the same for
yourself. It's never about Ryan because Ryan is okay,
and Ryan has all the answers. Ryan Chad Westmore is
perfect."

What the fuck? Where in the hell was all this hostility coming from? I knew I was a little spoiled, but damn, she just went completely left field on my ass. Didn't I send her ass on a vacation to de-stress? Yes, I did. What the fuck was stuck up her ass?

"What's with the attitude, Ricey? I ain't done shit to you."

"You have this approach to life that the rules apply to everyone but you. And if you don't like the rules, well, you just make some up that fit your standards so you can still do whatever the hell you want to do. That's okay because you're Ryan Chad Westmore, and you and only you are entitled to do that," she said curtly.

She was arguably correct to a certain extent. Men like me are elite. The black Adonises. We are the best of the best. So forgive me for feeling entitled. I was a ruler. Therefore, I made the rules not followed them, but I never hurt anyone. I just made sure that my family and I benefited. Was that too much to ask? And why was the woman I chose to stand beside me in this life treating me like I was anything less? *Oh, that's it.* I knew why.

"This is about the whole name thing with Lexi, isn't it?"

She turned around to finish oiling her skin with baby oil. She smelled so good coming fresh out of the shower, and she was so fine in the silk spaghetti-strap nightgown that stopped mid-thigh. If only she weren't pissing me off right now so I could fully appreciate the view. Women can fuck up a wet dream, I'll tell you.

She paused for a long while before answering. "Yeah, it is. Forget it. I'm over it."

Yeah, now I was damn irritated. "Why is it such a big deal?"

"It's not, which is why I said to drop the subject. It's over, and I'm done with it."

Wiping off her hands, she began massaging her temples, and I realized what the issue truly was. Walking up behind her, I wrapped my arms around her waist. "I know what it really is. You're stressed about Trinity. It's okay. Let me make you feel all better."

"You know what? I am stressed and exhausted from the past couple of days. I just want to get some sleep. Besides, we've both showered already." She patted my arms to release her and pulled back the sheets easing into the bed.

Rejected. I stood there in amazement. "Charice? Go to bed? Really?"

"Are you really gonna stress me with all this drama going on with my family? Can I just have some consideration for once?" she fussed.

Unbelievable. Can she get some consideration? I almost said that when she gave my dick some consideration I would extend her some, but I let it ride. And only because of Trinity. Regardless, I was still pissed. Giving in, I threw my hands up and stalked to my side of the bed and climbed in. "You're right. I don't want to argue. There have been enough senseless arguments tonight. Let's just get some sleep so we both can be refreshed in the morning." With that, I turned the light off, signaling to her my anger and my stance that I was done with the subject.

"Good night," she threw out callously before turning away from me.

Did she just turn her back to me? Muthafucka. So she was dead ass about leaving me with semi-hard wood? I lay there for a few minutes forcing my jimmy to stay at bay. Seriously, a brotha was hurtin'. I rolled over and looked at Charice. Didn't she know how bad I wanted her? How much I loved her? All I wanted was to be with my wife.

I wanted to respect her request, but shit, I needed my wife. Placing my hand on her shoulder, I lightly swayed her. "Are you up, Ricey?"

"Now that you've woken me out of my sleep I am. What, Ryan?"

That attitude pissed me off as much as it turned me on. As horny as I was right now, she could've cussed me out in ten different languages and that shit would be sexy as fuck to me. I decided to tell her the truth. She always seemed to respond better when I was completely honest with her about how I felt. Like I said, Lincoln taught me a lot, but the most important lesson he taught me was how to keep my wife, especially from his ass. That mixed with a few elaborate sentiments of fake sincere apologies should do the trick.

"Listen, baby, I'm sorry. It's just that I can be a little spoiled, and yes, I spoil my kids because I want them to have the best. I want to raise them to always consider themselves as number one. That way they'll always go the extra mile to achieve their dreams. And yes, I was wrong to just call Lexi the name I wanted, but as a man, my selfish pride got in the way. Just like it's doing about the whole sex deal. I just want you so bad. I guess the real reason I want to make love with you so bad, besides the pleasure that you give me, is because I was thinking—hoping even—that maybe we could get pregnant and try for another little girl. Not to disrespect Charity's memory or discount Lexi, just so Lexi could have a sister and bring a little life back to the household."

Hmm, I was getting better. The only lie was the apology about calling Lexi by McKenzie. That was purely for show. Hell, I had to do what I had to do here. I needed to get between my wife's legs in the worst kind of way.

She turned to look at me, and I couldn't read her expression. Finally, she closed her eyes and sucked her bottom lip, releasing a slow and deliberate breath. "Wow. You truly amaze me at times, Ryan. That is the most self-centered thought you could ever have. How do you confess that you want to get me pregnant without first asking me if having another baby is what I want? I have the dance studio in full swing. I have a full life with a baby and two adolescent boys. Not to mention the charity programs that we sponsor as well as the community center that we run. Your schedule in and out of season is bananas, so there is no possible way you could truly help, especially in season, yet you want to add another responsibility to my plate?

"Children aren't baby dolls or toy action figures that you get to play with and put back in the toy chest when you're tired. It takes time, love, care, energy, nurturing, and patience, all of which is stretched thin with me already. I know that you don't get that because the amount of time you spend taking care of the kids pales in comparison to me. I love my children. God knows I do, but having another one at this point in my life is something I neither need nor want. Now that you have thoroughly pissed me off with your inconsiderate ass, I'm going back to sleep before I change my mind and truly blast off on you the way I should have." With that, she turned back around, slapped her pillow hard with her hand, and lay down, muttering expletives the entire time.

Rolling to my back, I couldn't believe what just happened. Charice loved kids. I thought that she wouldn't mind just one more. Was I really being selfish to want to have a child with my wife? Granted, I wanted another child for purely selfish reasons, but it's not like I told her that. What was even more amazing to me was this newfound Charice who was slowly creeping into our marriage. Her personality was changing. Not that I had a problem with strong-willed and strong-minded women, I just wasn't used to that from my wife. It was a good thing that she was developing into a strong black woman, but that strength was starting to fuck with my power in this marriage, and that was the part that I didn't like one bit. I loved Ricey, so due to her current family situation and the fact that she was thoroughly pissed off with me, she'd won this round. Still, the game wasn't over until I said it was over. Whether she agreed to it or not, I was going to plant my seed inside of her so that she could have another one of my babies. That I meant.

However, it obviously wouldn't be tonight. Another sex-free night. My rock was so hard I couldn't even concentrate on sleep, so I stood up, grabbed the baby oil, and headed to the bathroom. Fucking with Charice, I was gonna mess around and get the damn blue balls. I was most definitely releasing these seeds tonight, even if it was only to the toilet.

Chapter 15

Pooch

It felt good to be back at my own house just chillin'. I was so happy to be home I didn't even give a damn that it had been ransacked by the Feds. All I needed was a twelve pack of Bud Light, a couple of Cuban cigars, and the smooth sounds of the Isley Brothers floating through the speakers in my king suite. Yeah, buddy, this was the life.

As I sat down at the desk and made myself comfortable, I heard a knock on my door. Now who can this be? I came home alone, and no one knew I was here. Luckily, the safe that held my gun was still intact. I hurriedly spun the dial to the correct combination and grabbed my 9 mm pistol. I took the safety off and was ready to spill the seeds out of somebody's watermelon.

"Poochie, put that gun away," my grandmother said, walking into my office.

I stood up and looked in disbelief. "Grandma! What are you doing here?"

"What are you doing with a gun?" she asked.

I put the safety back on and put the gun up. "It's for protection. Never mind that. Why are you here?"

"You wouldn't need protection if you hadn't been doing all those evil things you've been doing, Poochie."

"Grandma, it's Pooch."

She laughed, unfazed by my comment. "To me, you'll always be my little Poochie."

I couldn't help but smile. Then I got serious. "Grandma, you died three years ago. Why are you here?"

She sat down and sighed. "I'm disappointed in you, Pooch."

Nothing could bring me down off a high faster than my grandmother's disappointment. I put my head down. "I know I have done some bad things, but—"

"But what?" she cut me off. "Bad things don't begin to describe the things you've done."

Frustrated, I hit the desk before defending myself. "Come on, Grandma! All that ain't even my fault. I was born to be in the business. Every adult in my life besides you taught me to hustle. It's all I know. It's who I am."

She flashed one of her famous smiles at me. You know, one of those smiles that elder people gave you when you knew you were about to be made to feel small. "Poochie, I tried to teach you better. Your mother—God bless her soul—introduced you to everything that was wrong with life, but I tried to give you what was good. I told your mother. She sat back and watched that man turn you inside out. Then they had the nerve to sit up in God's house on Sunday like they were holier than thou. They might've paid for the church mortgage, but they couldn't buy their way into heaven. And neither can you. Don't you remember that you promised me to be your own man and make your own decisions? Don't you remember when I took you to church? Don't you remember your Sunday school lessons? Don't you remember God?"

With a slow nod, I swallowed roughly. "Yeah."

"No, you don't. You've forgotten. You traded in God for drugs, money, sex, and power."

"God ain't got no place for a man like me," I hollered as tears began to form in my eyes. "Not everybody going to heaven, Grandma."

*With sadness in her eyes, she agreed. "You're right.
But that ain't got nothing to do with you. Sure, you were
taught bad things, but you're a grown man now. You
can give that up. Selling that rocked-up death on the
streets, murdering young black men, pimping out loose
women, not taking care of your child, treating your
girlfriend like a piece of merchandise you purchased,
beating her, cussing, drinking, smoking that ignorant
stuff, and carrying on like some kind of wild animal,
that's on you. You ought to be a stone shamed of yourself. Calling yourself a man. You deserve to die and go
straight to hell with Pops," she fussed.*

No matter how hard I tried to stop the tears or how
fast I wiped them, they still kept flowing. *"What do you
want from me?"*

*"Better!" she yelled. "I want you to be better. I want
you to remember what I taught you. Forget what you
know. Forget the life that Isaac introduced to you. Trust
in God. I love you." With that, she drifted away.*

"But, Grandma, I can't do this without you!"

*"Yes, you can, Poochie. Yes, you can," I heard in the
distance.*

I woke up with my eyes blinking. I felt like I was in a fog
and couldn't quite focus on what was going on. Finally,
my eyes made out everything around me. I was in the
hospital. *Oh, God!* I was dead. I jumped up, frantically
tearing out the IVs attached to me. I wasn't going back
in the box. If I had to beg the Lord myself, I promised I
wasn't going back in that box.

"Vernon," Attorney Stein called out.

"Pooch," Adrienne said, worry exuding through her
voice as I continued to scramble.

"Stay away from me. I'm not going down without a fight
this time!"

"Pooch, you're going to tear your stitches. Lie down," Adrienne pleaded.

"That's a ploy to get me back in that box! Why don't you go ahead and show your face, Pops? I'm ready this time."

They looked at each other. "Could he be daydreaming?" Stein asked Adrienne.

"It's possible," she answered, shrugging her shoulders.

"Muthafuckas, I'm right here. Don't talk about me as if I'm not here!"

"Okay, but you have to calm down and get back in bed," Adrienne said calmly.

"Fuck you! This is a hallucination."

Adrienne put her hands up. "I assure you it's not, Pooch. Please."

I swallowed hard. "Well, if it's not a hallucination, then let me slap one of you."

"Pooch!" Adrienne shrieked.

I didn't want to hear it. "Fuck that. After the shit that's been happening to me, either one of y'all is getting slapped, or I'm fucking you up on my way out of this door. Make a decision."

Stein gave in and walked around the corner of the bed. "Go ahead. Hit me."

I pulled back to Africa and slapped the shit outta Stein. He grabbed his face.

"Son of a bitch! You really hit me."

"Oh, damn. This is real."

"Yes, goddamn it! It is real. What the fuck did you think?" Stein yelled. "What the hell is wrong with you?"

"I'm sorry. It's just I kept thinking I died."

Adrienne exhaled. "You did. Technically, you died three times, but they brought you back. You've been out of it now for four days."

"So I'm alive?" They both nodded slowly. I felt my skin and pinched myself. Then I turned to look in the mirror by the sink. It was me. My hair and beard had grown out, but it was me. Alive. Not with Pops. Not in hell. *Oh, shit! You muthafuckas can't stop Pooch Smalls.* "Woo hoo! Yeah, muthafucka, I'm alive!"

Stein and Adrienne looked at each other, confused, but they couldn't help but nervously chuckle at my antics. "We need to call the nurse," Adrienne said.

"Wait." I turned on a dime. "Before you do that, we have to talk about what's going on."

Stein interjected, "Vernon, trust me. We will, but we need to let the nurses know—"

"Fuck that. We need to talk, so sit down."

Irritated, Stein huffed, but they both obeyed my command. Stein filled me in. "Vernon, this is what I know so far. First off, we're in Chicago, so home is a long way away. Secondly, Detective Marsh arranged for your release. This I knew already. Now the only thing left is for you to tell me what happened when you left with him."

"He didn't tell you?"

"No. I can't ask him any questions."

"They must have police surveillance on him like a muthafucka."

The lack of response from either of them told me something was off. Adrienne and Stein looked at each other with regret mixed with confusion this time. Stein patted her hand and motioned for her to speak. "No, Pooch." She reached out and grabbed my hand. "You have to talk to us because we have to know the whole story."

"I will. I just want to go home."

"It's not that easy, Vernon," Stein rebutted.

"Why not?"

Adrienne gently turned my face to hers. "Detective Marsh is dead."

I know I didn't hear her correctly. Did she say what I think she said? "Huh?"

"He died, Vernon. Gunshot wound to the chest from a gun with your fingerprints on it," Stein explained.

Chapter 16

Trinity

The sun shone brightly through the windows. Rolling to my side, I lifted my hand as I blinked the light away. IVs were attached, indicating that I was still in the hospital, but I was so out of it that I didn't have a clue what day it was or how long I'd been there. I felt like I'd slept for years and was refreshed from the sleep yet tired from the ordeal.

Sitting up straight, I looked around. "Hi, everyone."

"Hey, Trinity!" they all shouted.

"We are so glad you woke up. We have to leave in an hour to catch the plane," Charice said, hugging me. "I love you," she added, kissing my forehead. Then Lucinda and LaMeka joined her, tickling me and hugging me as the men and my mom stood around laughing.

"Stop!" I laughed. "I feel like I've been hit by a bus."

"But I hope you feel better," my mom said, walking up and hugging me.

"I do. I have to get up from here. I know I look a mess, and I have to pee."

"She's definitely back." Lucinda waved off my comment. "Your appearance is fine."

I knew she was damn lying. "Give me a mirror." I motioned for someone to oblige. "One of you pretty bitches in here has to have one."

Each of them reached into their purses simultaneously, and I erupted in giggles. "And I'm the Barbie?" They all laughed as Lucinda got to hers first and handed it to me. What stared back nearly scared the hell out of me. "Oh, hell no. You men get out of here. We have got to do something about this immediately!"

After kicking the guys out, my mom called for the nurse, who unhooked my IV line and helped me out of bed and into the bathroom. With my mother's assistance, I hurriedly showered and changed into the T-shirt and sweatpants my mom brought. Charice applied my makeup, and LaMeka hooked up my hair. Thirty minutes later, I looked like I'd never been admitted. Now this was the Trinity I was used to.

"Oh, she's definitely back," Ryan and Aldris joked as the men filed back inside.

"See, they know how we do it," I directed to Gavin and Mike as our laughter ensued.

"So can we get you anything?" my mom asked. "I have to call the nurse. The doctor said if you felt up to it, you could probably be released tomorrow."

"How long have I been in here?"

"Just two days."

"And Terrence?"

"We can deal—"

"Mom! I have to deal with this sooner or later. Where is he?"

She swallowed hard. "Still here."

I stood up. "Take me to him."

"Sweetie, maybe you should—" Lucinda began.

I loved them, and I knew they were trying to protect me from the inevitable, but Terrence was my husband, and I owed him this time. I had to have these last few moments with him for me, but also for him.

"Look, that is my husband. I need to see him. If you all won't take me, I'll go myself. I have to see his face." Not even caring about the fact that I was supposed to be reconnected to the IV, I lifted myself from the bed and made unsure steps toward the door. Not wanting to argue, my mother grabbed my right hand while Lucinda rushed to hold my left.

"Mrs. Kincaid, you're up," the nurse bellowed when she saw me exiting the room.

Looking over at her with determined eyes, I said, "Yep, and I'm going to see my husband."

With the agility of a cheetah, she jumped in front of me. "You need—"

Sneering at her, I planted my feet and tensed at her touch. "Lady, I don't want to hurt you, but if you don't move and let me get to my husband right now, there's gonna be a fuckin' situation."

For a moment, she stood there, her gaze floating between me and my mother. Once she saw that I was serious, she reluctantly moved to the side to allow us all to get on the elevator. My mom held fast to my hand as the elevator made its way to the fifth floor and as we moved down the hall and stood in front of his room. This was it.

The last time I had been in this room was two days ago. He'd died twice in the ambulance—no pulse. They'd revived him. They did surgery to remove the bullet, and we thought that he had an inkling of hope, but more tragedy came. He began hemorrhaging. They'd done emergency surgery on Terrence to stop the internal bleeding, but once they did that, he'd fallen into a coma. The day I took the pills the doctors all told me there was no hope. He wasn't showing signs of improvement and was on full life support. They wanted me to make a decision: maintain the life support or pull the plug. I couldn't do it, so I went home and decided to join my husband. I took the

sleeping pills hoping I'd die and go to heaven with him.
The pain I felt on earth was too much to bear without
him. But Terrence told me it wasn't my time. It was his.
So it was time. Time to let him take his rest. I would be
all right. He'd promised to watch over me, and I believed
him. It was time to let him go.

His eyes were closed, and tears instantly fell onto
my cheeks. My mom walked in behind me as I slowly
approached him. "Baby, I love you," I whispered to his
still body. "I promise you that I will take care of our kids
and that I will always love you. My heart beats so slow
without you, Dreads, but for our kids, I'll make it through
this with the help of my family and friends. You were the
best husband I could have ever hoped for, and I want you
to know that I wouldn't change a thing about our time
together outside of extending it. I love you. Take your
rest now." I bent down and kissed him. Then I turned to
my mom. "Have the kids seen him?"

She nodded. "Yesterday."

I wiped my tears with the back of my hand. I was glad
the kids got to see him one last time. I couldn't put them
through this, though. The funeral would be hard enough.
I decided it would be best if I did this while I had a strong
support system with me, and more importantly, while
my kids were not present.

"Someone call the doctor and the nurse. I'm ready now.
I can take him off the life support." My mom stood there
smiling at me. "What are you smiling for?"

"Damn. I come back from the dead, and you trying to
send me back," I heard Dreads say. As I spun around, he
sat up slowly. "Hey, li'l mama."

"Dreads!" My legs never gave out on me as I found the
strength to damn near sprint to his side again. Once I
made it, I straddled him carefully and started kissing him
all about his face as he held me in his arms. "I love you."

He returned my excited kisses. "I love you too."

"We're gonna just step outside," I heard someone say, but I wasn't paying any attention. I was with my baby— my Dreads—as we continued our emotional reunion.

A short while later, I finally pulled away. "How? They said there was no hope. You died." My words came out as a ramble as a continued stream of tears flowed.

Dreads silenced me with a soft caress to my face. He massaged his now fully bearded face with an unreadable expression on his face. Slipping my hands into his, he gave them a light squeeze before he explained. "It was the weirdest thing. It was like I was outside of my body looking at myself. Then I went into this bright light, and it was so peaceful and serene. Suddenly, I was talking to you and asking you to watch the kids." He lifted my hands, noticing the hospital bracelet. "You were in the hospital?"

The realization of my foolish actions struck me, and my lips began to tremble from the emotion coursing through me. I could've died and never had this again. I could've taken myself away from my husband and my kids. *My poor babies*. It made me feel ill just to think of how selfish I'd been. However, I was distraught with emotion at the time, and I hadn't been thinking clearly. Still, it pained me to have to explain to him what I'd done. But I couldn't lie to him. No more secrets, intentional or unintentional, would be held between us. This time we would do everything right.

"They told me there was no hope for you, so I went home and I . . . swallowed a bunch of sleeping pills."

His face contorted at my words and nearly split me in two. The hurt that oozed from him was so potent it could've leveled anyone in the room. "Aww, baby." He hugged me close, so close it was as if he were attempting to meld us together. "Why would you do that?"

"To be with you. I didn't want to live if it meant living without you."

Pushing me back from him, he gripped my face between both of his powerful hands. His wet eyes held such an intense gaze that I felt my heart would burst from love. "Don't you ever do that again. Ever. If anything had happened to you . . . Just don't ever do that again."

All I could do in response was lower myself into his arms and revel in the sound of his heartbeat with my head on his chest. A long beat passed with his soaking in our newly granted lease on life before Terrence spoke again.

"I wonder if I was dreaming or if I was really talking to you?"

Lifting to meet his face, I confirmed his questions. "Actually, you were. At least our spirits were." His confused look pleaded for me to further explain. "I saw you. You told me it wasn't my time. I thought I'd lost you."

His mouth fell open into the O shape, and his eyes blinked and rose wide. "Wow. I remember I was on my way to the light, and I heard a voice say to me, 'No, you go back too.' And all I remember after that was waking up here with a bunch of nurses and doctors wondering how the hell I woke up. They called your mom, my sister, and Thomas, and they have been taking good care of me. I saw the crew, and they wanted me to surprise you."

"I'm gonna kick every one of their asses," I grumbled playfully. The thought that he'd mentioned Thomas came back to me, and I had to ask about his well-being. "How's Thomas holding up?"

"He's coping. I just don't want him to retaliate against Pooch. There's been enough bloodshed. Even though I can't believe my own cousin shot me and nearly took me out, I'm just glad Pooch made it. I'd hate to be facing murder charges like him," he explained.

"I still have to talk to your attorney and the police—"

He put his finger against my lips to stop me. "We'll worry about that when the time comes. Right now, at this moment, all I'm worried about is my time with you. God gave this to us. Let's just share it."

With that, we held each other through humble tears of joy. Nothing else in the world mattered. Forget the money, the career, the houses, and the cars. All that mattered was family. And God did it. He gave me my Dreads back.

Chapter 17

Charice

The trip to Illinois was an emotional rollercoaster, and I was physically, mentally, and emotionally drained. It was a blessing to know that before we left both Trinity and Terrence were alive and doing well for the most part. Their immediate families were going through a struggle with the tragedy of the events, especially the death of Aaron and Terrence's tumultuous recovery, and I was going to make sure I was right there by Trinity's side as much as she needed and wanted. I knew that Terrence still had a long way to go in his recovery, but as long as we didn't have to put him in a pine box, I was thankful. We all were.

The best part about the whole trip was watching the reunion of Trinity and Dreads. We wanted to surprise Trinity with the fact that Terrence actually made it, but when she hopped up and went to his room, we just watched it unfold. That was hands down the best moment. Trinity refused to leave Terrence's room—hell, his bed even—and Terrence refused to let her go. The doctors finally had to give up and move her into his room. Witnessing true love, soul-mate love, touched me, because in a roundabout way, I knew how Trinity felt. Even though losing Lincoln wasn't as permanent as death, it may as well be due to my marriage. I couldn't freely love the one man I truly loved, and to me, that was a great enough death sentence.

I knew Lincoln didn't feel that I cared, but I did. I'd been back from Illinois for a couple of weeks, and he was still acting dumb. Every time we talked, he was short and smart-mouthed. Outside of him coming to pick up Lexi, I hadn't seen him. Not by my choice but by his. I'd asked him to meet me and he, ever so rudely, told me he was busy. I didn't bother to ask again, and to my surprise, he didn't offer or ask himself. All in all, I needed to know where we stood. Why? The week before Ryan's training camp started, we were supposed to finally take our honeymoon vacation. I'd begged for this trip before I found out about Ryan's deception, and now I wished I could renege. Well, not renege on the vacation. Hell, I wanted to go to the exclusive and secluded resort on the Cayman Islands, just not with Ryan, especially after that fool thought he was going to push getting pregnant on me.

At any rate, I needed to know if I had to get used to being exclusively with my husband, or if I still had a relationship with Lincoln. Fighting off Ryan for five days would be hard, but I already had the perfect plan in place. You know it. Menstrual cycle. But if I no longer had Lincoln, then all bets were off. If I had to learn to live exclusively with Ryan, then I refused to suffer without sex. Damn that. Lincoln may have been better, and I'd rather have Lincoln, but it wasn't like I had complaints about Ryan in that department. This was why I demanded that Lincoln meet me. We had some things to clear up really fast because my next moves depended on his next move.

When I walked into the house in Queens, I found Lincoln sitting at the dining room table. He appeared to be in deep thought. "Sorry I'm late. I had to drop the boys off before I got here, and their friend's mother wanted to talk my ear off."

He shrugged. "I'm used to it."

Irritation displayed across my face. "Used to what, Lincoln? And why are we sitting in here? It's so damn formal. Like we are having a roundtable discussion."

The look on his face showed his bewilderment and disbelief as he let out a deliberate chuckle. "We're sitting in here so I can be separated from you and actually talk. Whenever I'm close to you, I can't make informed decisions. My dick and my heart take over my brain, and then I'm caught up." He pointed to the table. "As for what I'm used to, it's being second to everything in your life, including Ryan."

My teeth clenched together to keep my anger from bubbling over. "Are you still pissed about the trip to Illinois? Come on. That was an isolated incident. I was checking on my family. Don't do that."

"It's not about that. It's about the fact that you were going through an emotional time and I couldn't be there for you to help you through it. Not that I didn't want to or maybe even that you didn't want me to, I just couldn't. And the reason why can be summed up in one phrase— you're married to Ryan."

Inhale. Exhale. Here we go again. "Lincoln, I understand that my being married causes us to not interact with and be there for each other the way that we would otherwise want, but this is an affair. What else can you expect?" It may have sounded harsh, but I was only stating the obvious.

He grimaced, his lips forming a tight line. "I get that. I know what the hell an affair is, Charice. I understand that I signed up for this. At the time, I agreed that having a little bit of you was better than nothing at all, but can't you see that it's fucking with me? Charice, I love you. I want all of you, and I feel like I'm suffocating myself with getting these little morsels of you whenever you feel you want to offer it to me. Outside of that one trip, what have we done? Nothing. Nothing but have sex. I love your sex, but my love for you goes beyond being able to get between your legs."

Unfortunately, he was correct. Even more so, he had a point. Several of them, actually. I swear I didn't realize this shit was going to be this difficult or emotional. Still, I had to plead my case for our arrangement. "Lincoln, you have my heart." I tried to reach for his hand, but he pulled away.

"No, I have your sex. I want your heart."

"You do have it."

"No, I don't. You have my heart. Completely. Everything I have inside and out is yours for the taking. I give it to you freely. Can I say the same for you?"

Tears threatened the corners of my eyes as the realization of his point weighed on my heart. Even still, what he was saying wasn't fair to me. I cleared my throat to clear away the emotion. "Lincoln, you do have my heart. You just don't realize how much."

"Then prove it. Leave Ryan." He opened his arms is if asking me to put my money where my mouth was.

Wait a minute. How did we go from me validating our affair to me going to divorce court? Lincoln had my heart, but I also had a family to protect. I couldn't disrupt my family. I understood Lincoln's point, but he had to understand mine. No matter what, my family came first.

"Lincoln, you know that I want to, but think about my kids. How will this affect my boys?"

"Don't you think Lexi will grow up and wonder why her real father and mother aren't together, too?" he shot back. "I love the boys. I'd gladly raise them with you and Ryan, but you aren't considering Lexi's future feelings either. I understand they've lost their sister. We all lost Charity. Still, it becomes a matter of what you want more out of this life. Do you want to be happy, or do you want to satisfy everyone else? You can't please yourself and everyone else at the same time. As for me, I chose my own happiness. That happiness is with you, but I need the same from you."

Talk about being at a loss for words. Lincoln had really put time into this argument, and though his points were valid and strong, I couldn't be the type of person he wanted me to be. As much as I wanted to be self-centered and leave, I couldn't. Satisfying my boys did mean more to me than anything else. Not that Lexi's future feelings didn't matter, but the boys had gone through difficult times behind the loss of Charity, and I had to keep that first.

"I get it, Lincoln. I do. We're all suffering, but the boys have suffered the most at such young ages. Can't we just have what we have? Don't you like being able to be with me knowing you have my heart and my sex?"

He stood up. "Fine. So how about I only give you a portion of me?" Confusion creased my brow, and without my having to ask, he continued. "You said a little was better than none, right? So how about I take my love back and just give you the sex? Let my heart be free to give to someone else." His anger was evident.

Hurt and shock seared my soul at those words and I jumped up. "No!" The word came out definitively before I could stop it. Had he lost his mind with this reckless solution? There was no way I was agreeing to let him have another woman. That wasn't the deal.

"See?" He pointed at me as if he'd proved a point. "You want all of me, but you're not willing to do the same. That's the selfish part. That's what's fucked up."

Yes, his ultimate point was made, but now I was more concerned with who else he was interested in seeing. What woman had caught his eye, and what was her damn phone number and address? I would solve that issue myself. And yes, I was that damn serious about it.

"So you wanna be with somebody else?"

Disbelief was etched on his face, and he threw his hands up in utter frustration. "No! Are you fucking listening to me? I wanna be with you! Goddamn it!" He began pacing. "I said that because it's fucked up that you expect me to allow you to be selfish over me but you think I should sit back and not be selfish over you. Let's keep it real, Charice. I'm not the one who's married. I'm free to do whatever and whoever the fuck I want. But who I want is you. I wanna hold you at night and wake up to see your face in the morning. I wanna love you completely and know I have that in return. I wanna be there for you through your difficult times and love you through the good. I wanna marry you, raise our kids, and grow old together because I love you. I. Love. You. Period." He poured his heart out, then quickly turned away.

His words held me captive for a long while. I knew that Lincoln loved me and was in love with me, of course, but it was the first time I'd ever seen him get so emotional over me. For the first time since we were officially a couple, I saw the depth of his love for me on full display. It shredded me that we were in the predicament we were in because, ultimately, we wanted the same outcome. We just couldn't have what we both wanted, and I had to get him to understand the difference between what I wanted and what I had to do.

I walked around the table, turned him to face me, and hugged him. "I love you too. I do." Pulling his face to mine, I captured his lips in a succulent kiss. Instantly, he met my passion, holding me close as our tongues explored each other, and then he suddenly tried to pull away. I heard him faintly whimper for me to stop, but I whispered, "No," continuing our fervent kiss.

Soon he gave in, and before long, we were naked and making love on the dining room table. My legs were clasped around his waist as he stroked me long and hard. My back slid up and down against the smooth table slick from the sweat of our lovemaking. He drilled into me with determination. Like he was claiming me, my pussy, my heart, my brain—hell, my soul. Every arch of his back rolled out a deep and determined stroke as he drilled trenches inside of me. He introduced me to the art of missionary, because I'd never been loved down so completely in this position. The way he gave it to me, I doubted any woman had. This man was reinventing sex.

Through my moans, I declared, "Lincoln, I do love you. I love you so much."

"I love you too, baby." He continued his determined strokes, rocking to depths I never knew existed inside of me. "Damn. This feels so right."

"Oooh, Lincoln."

"Ahh, Charice," he roared as he pulled me up in his arms, and we climaxed together.

We sat there unable to move and held each other chest to chest, basking in the afterglow of our high and huffing through labored breaths. Jesus, I loved this man. If only he could feel how much.

Once our breathing had returned to normal, Lincoln asked, "Is this at least still all mine?" referring to the treasure between my legs.

Staring intently in his eyes, I nodded, giving him the answer he desired. "Always."

Pain and worry mixed with love and satisfaction plagued him before he finally whispered in my ear, "I can't let you go. I swear I can't."

I cradled his face, forcing his gaze to meet mine. "Then don't, baby. Don't," I pleaded as we continued to hold each other and bask in our togetherness, even if that moment was only brief.

Chapter 18

Gavin

There comes a point in any man's life when enough is enough. I'd come to that point. I tried to overlook this whole situation brewing between Tony and me, but that muthafucka had tried my patience for the last time. I loved the boys, which was why I never did anything about all the crap their dad had pulled on me. Not even once. But this shit that he just pulled was the last and final straw. It was time for some get back.

He didn't know me. My get back wasn't child's play. It was real. I may not be the one to start trouble, but I definitely knew how to end it. And when I ended it, I ended it. He was about to find out what happened when you let your mouth write a check that your ass couldn't cash.

This fool had the nerve, the fucking nerve, to call children and family services on LaMeka and me, claiming I was beating on his kids. *Me? Oh, how easily he forgets that his cracked-out ass was the one beating and raping his ex-girlfriend.* If it weren't for Meka's fierce protection of her kids, they surely would've been a victim of his drunken and chemically induced episodes.

Sadly, he was playing a game that he didn't realize I held all the cards to, and he failed to realize he was sitting at my table. When you run the table, you have the information. With that information comes power, and with power comes get back, Gavin Randall style.

Luckily, the caseworker who was sent to investigate us was a lady who knew me from several cases I'd assisted with at the hospital. As soon as she saw me, she knew it was a lie. LaMeka and I explained who Tony was and why these random complaints started coming in. I even showed her the police records about when my car and house had been vandalized on two separate occasions. Both reports listed Tony as the possible assailant. Wouldn't you know this dummy had the nerve to call and file the complaint himself? She wasn't supposed to release that information, but information is only confidential these days when you don't know the person who has it. With the information we had to back our story, she made sure the complaint was listed as a false allegation made by Tony and his parents.

He was even dumber, because I had access to something far more vital to him. His status. Aside from harassing me, he'd actually been getting his life together. He'd gotten a job at an auto parts store and enrolled in college. Well, all of that was over. With a little anonymous assistance, a copy of his status was forwarded to his job, from an unknown sender of course.

As for his college education, well, his financial aid was officially stopped. I knew the head of the financial aid department at the college. Tony had lied and said that he was living on his own but didn't make enough money to file income taxes so he could get financial aid. No, sir. He lived at home with his parents, and they were well off, making more than enough to deny his aid. Not only was it denied, but the $3,500 he cleared the previous semester had to be repaid, which meant no higher education until his bill was cleared.

That was the difference between him and me. I had insurance, so replacing my car and the valuables in my house was covered for me. It was a minor inconvenience to pay the deductibles and keep it moving, but having his life shut down wasn't something he could quickly recover from. I didn't want to be that person, but I was done playing games with his ass.

"Gavin," LaMeka called out, bringing my focus back to our dinner table.

"All right, everybody hold hands and bow your head for prayer," I said from the head of the dinner table with LaMeka and the family.

LaMeka cooked one of my favorite meals: smothered pork chops, rice and gravy, black-eyed peas, macaroni and cheese, and cornbread. Damn, I loved soul food. "Most gracious Heavenly Father, we come to you, thanking you for this food that we are about to eat. Bless the hands that prepared it and those who will partake of it. And as always, we thank you for allowing us to come together as a family. Amen."

"Amen," everyone repeated.

"Meka, I promise Gavin is gonna be a preacher," her mom joked.

"A white minister with an all-black congregation." Misha laughed.

Misha was hilarious. I'd heard that a couple times in my childhood, but I couldn't see it. Still, it tickled my soul. Me, a minister? Shit. "Y'all trippin'. Anyway, pass me the black-eyed peas, please."

"Actually, he wouldn't be, because you know he's Cablanasian," LaMeka joked as she finished preparing the boys' plates.

"That's right, baby," I agreed with a finger point.

Suddenly, Misha lightly tapped the table, garnering everyone's attention. "Ooh, I know what I meant to tell you guys! Guess what I heard today down at the center?"

"What's that?" Meka asked after she drank a sip of tea.

"Your babies' daddy's status got leaked to his job, and he ended up getting fired. Well, I was told the company said he shorted the register, but we all know it's because his status got out. They did that on purpose," Misha said, finishing up a forkful of macaroni and cheese.

Meka almost choked. I patted her back. "Thank you, baby. Are you serious?" she asked in shock.

"Yes! No lie. One of Tony's friends from his group session teaches class at the center, and he told me. He was like, 'I sure hope you and your sister didn't have anything to do with that.' I was like, 'No, my sister would never, and I don't have time for that foolishness. Ain't nobody thinking about Tony,'" Misha verified with only the type of sauce she could provide.

Meka pointed to herself. "I know I am not. I would never do something like that. I am not nasty like him. Besides, I just want to live my life in peace."

At that point, even Meka's mother chimed in. "I don't like Tony, but that's wrong to fire him over his illness. People are too judgmental these days. It makes me afraid for you." She patted Misha's hand.

I guess now really wouldn't be a good time to admit that I am the one responsible for all of that. Damn. They are just too nice at times. Forget Tony.

"Well, I just pray it doesn't happen to me. Besides, as dirty as Tony is, he had it coming to him. That's just karma." Misha shrugged.

Meka looked at her and shook her head. "You're young. That's why you say that. Everybody does things they shouldn't. Whether or not Tony learned from the mistakes he's made is neither here nor there. Firing him because he is HIV positive is cruel and inhumane. I just can't agree with that."

"Well, I can," I blurted before I knew it. They all stopped and looked at me.

The frown on Meka's face showed her disapproval. "I can't believe you'd say that. Do you really feel that way?"

I took a long swig of my sweet tea, wiped my hands, and sat back. I'd over spoken myself so there was no need to hide it. "As far as the underlying reason people may feel that they fired him, of course not. It's unethical, unlawful, and dead wrong, but they stated it was because he shorted his register. That's what I'm rolling with. In that case, I stand by what I said. Absolutely. I don't feel sorry for him, and I don't apologize for not feeling that I should feel sorry for him. Why do you ask?"

Meka shook her head in disbelief. "You've never been this heartless. I know Tony has done some messed-up things to you, but I never would have taken you for the type to condone that type of malicious behavior."

Was she serious? *Humph.* "It's not that I'm condoning it or saying that it wasn't wrong. It was very wrong and very malicious. I just don't feel sorry for what he's going through. I look at it like this: you get out of this world what you give to it. If you're sweet and kind, you can expect sweet and kind gestures to follow you, but if you are hateful and nasty, then you can expect hateful and nasty gestures to follow you as well. He is only getting back the same energy he exerts into the world. It's karma, just like Misha said. That is the bottom line."

They all sat there in contemplation for a moment, and as if on cue, they all nodded. "True."

That's right. True. Mission accomplished. "Now let's switch the subject and get back to enjoying our dinner." And that was exactly what we did.

Chapter 19

Lucinda

Dinner and dancing. Yes, I was excited. Mike planned a huge evening for us to get out and have some fun, and we needed it. We'd been so bogged down between work and our kids that we'd basically reduced our quality time to cell-phone conversations and texts. I won't lie though. In a way I liked that. It gave me time to breathe and get used to being alone again. No, not single. Alone.

Although I was in a relationship, I had to get used to being a single parent again. Mike wanted to step up completely and be there for me the same way Aldris was, but I refused. Mike was simply my boyfriend, and Nadia didn't even know that he was that yet. She just assumed that Mike and I were friends as she'd always known we were. Besides that, Aldris had not only been my fiancé, but he had also been a father to Nadia. Having a boyfriend and having a live-in fiancé who was like a father to my child were two completely different situations. I wasn't ready for Mike to step into that role, nor did I want him to. I felt like things took off so fast for Aldris and me, and even faster for Mike and me, that I needed to slow it down a notch. He should appreciate that. Why? It was the only way to tell if what I was feeling for him was really going to last. In my heart I felt I wanted Mike, but I'd never been in love—well, truly in love—before Aldris. I needed the reassurance for myself, and if I'm being brutally honest, he needed the reassurance from me.

Tonight was all about us capitalizing on our feelings and simply enjoying each other. I wanted to be dressy yet sassy, so I opted for my knee-length black cocktail dress with a deep V-cut in the front and back. It accentuated my cleavage and showcased my soft shoulders and back. I loved it. Add to that some four-inch strappy sandal stilettos, and I was fire. With my hair pinned up in a cute up-do and a few sprays of Good Girl, I was ready.

"Wow. You look . . . damn." Mike struggled to speak, shaking his head as he stood in the doorway of my condo. "I'm in awe. You take my breath away, baby." He leaned in and kissed me on the cheek.

"And you don't look bad yourself." I waved him inside so that I could check my house before leaving.

"Where's Nadia?"

"My mom picked her up about two hours ago. Why?" I asked, grabbing my black clutch off the kitchen counter.

"I just thought we'd have to drop her off."

"I've already taken care of that," I reassured him, looping my arm in his to leave.

"So what did Nadia have to say about her hot mama and our date?" he asked, glancing me up and down as we walked out of the door.

"Umm. Nothing." I opted not to reveal that I didn't tell Nadia about our date as I locked the door.

"You didn't tell her you were going out with me, did you?"

His words caused me to pause my stride for a second. *Oh, Lord, here we go.* "No, I didn't. It's none of her business. She's too grown at times as it is." *Please drop the subject.* Those words were said in my mind.

When I turned to look at Mike, he had a scowl on his face. "You know, if I'm going to be in your life, she has to know eventually."

"And eventually she will. Now come on. Let's go and have a good time."

He didn't say anything more as he opened the car door and helped me inside. After he shut my door, I flipped down the visor and powdered my nose to take the shine off. As he walked around to get inside, I prayed he let it go. I was dolled up and overdue for a good time. I had no desire to begin or end our night with an argument over nonsense.

Once we were inside of his SUV, he looked over at me. "I love you, Lucinda, and I want to be a part of your whole life, not just be a portion of it."

Geez Louise. Couldn't we go out and have fun without him being so melodramatic? While I loved that he loved me, him loving me wasn't going to make me tell Nadia any faster, and at this rate, it only slowed the process that much more.

"I understand, but tonight is about having a good time, just me and you. Can we focus on that tonight? I've been waiting all week to unwind and chill out with my man. Let's just relax now and work out the kinks later."

Conceding, he grabbed my hand and nodded. "You're right. This is our time."

Thank God.

Relax and have a good time we did. I expected a nice time but never what he set up. Mike pulled out all the stops. I had no idea where we were going, but when we pulled up at the Hilton Atlanta, I knew. Nikolai's Roof. I'd never been there before, but I'd heard that it was very exquisite and expensive. It's amazing how you can live in a city your entire life and never get to experience the finer things about it, so this was special for me. It was a night out on the town I'd grown up in, experiencing new places with my new man.

I would never say it to Mike, but doing things like this reminded me of how things used to be with Aldris and me during our first six months of dating. We went to all the theatrical plays and dinners and did all the dancing that Atlanta had to offer. Those were the special moments that made me fall head over heels for Aldris. His strong will, intelligence, love for me, and ability to hold me and my child down was what kept me head over heels, though. My oh my, how time changed people. I wondered what happened to that man who hawked me down outside of Club Moet, or who coerced me into going on a date with him at the Varsity, and that man who was able to stand strong on his feelings for me and wouldn't stop until I felt the same way. That was the Aldris I remembered. Did he get too comfortable? Was the pressure behind being a father to Jessica too great? Had we lost our relationship in the midst of trying to straighten it out? Where did we go wrong?

Well, whatever it was that happened to him must have been reincarnated in Mike. For the first time in a long time, I felt young and vibrant again. Mike was putting on a show tonight. I didn't know if he was aiming to please or aiming for a little Spanish Fly. Either way, it was working. I was so excited about dinner that I allowed Mike to order for the both of us.

For my four-course dinner, I had an appetizer of petite kale, a second course of Dutch white asparagus velouté, an entrée of oven-roasted lamb chops, and for dessert, a Macadamia-nut tart. Mike's menu option consisted of the same appetizer as mine, a second course of diver scallops, an entrée of seared beef tenderloin, and his dessert was chocolate soufflé. We washed all of that down with a bottle of merlot.

After dinner, while we waited for our tab, I reached across the table and held Mike's hand and softly rubbed my thumb across it. "Thank you, baby. This was so awesome."

His eyes shone with delight as he returned the gesture. "I'm so glad you're enjoying yourself. This is all I wanted was to spend time with you."

Besides the awesome food, the conversation was great. We took the opportunity to learn more of each other and discuss our family, and he spoke a lot about his children. We'd even done what he called the "top ten things you absolutely have to know about me." Each of us gave ten things that the other had to know about us as a person. The twist was we had to try to guess each other's ten things. Surprisingly, I guessed three of his top ten. Mike had been paying attention to me in a major way. Hence, he was able to guess more than I was, but with more dates like this, I could see myself getting there.

After dinner, we headed to go dancing. Mike's family was originally from Chicago, so he was going to take me steppin' like they do it in the Chi. I was bound to enjoy this because I'd always been intrigued with learning how to step ever since the song "Happy People." This was yet another first for me. Mike was two for two tonight. We were walking hand in hand out of the restaurant, discussing how great the food was, when I heard my name.

"Lucinda?" I heard again. I turned to the side to see who was addressing me and saw Aldris, his boss, Emory, and some other people from National Cross, my old job.

"Hi, Aldris." I nodded my head toward everyone. "Hello, Emory, everyone." Mike wrapped his arm around my waist as we all greeted each other.

"Hey, Dri," Mike said.

"Mikey," Aldris said plainly. "Fancy seeing you two here."

"I was just treating my lady out to a special evening, and you?"

Aldris's eyes lit up with glee, and he gushed, "I got a promotion."

I gasped. "OMG! So you went for it?"

He met my gaze, smiling happily and matching my excitement. "Yeah, I did."

"You know he was a shoo-in," Emory added. "Aldris is a great asset to the company, and we know he'll deliver exceptional work."

"That's great! Absolutely amazing." Aldris stood up and hugged me. "I'm so proud of you. I knew you could do it," I said as we embraced tightly.

"And I thank you for that encouragement." He pulled back and stared directly into my eyes. "I thank you for everything you've ever done for me."

I looked away, and Mike gently pulled me back toward him. "Well, congratulations. We'd better get going."

"Oh, where are you headed?" Aldris asked.

"Nowhere," Mike replied quickly.

To show my pride in my man, I grabbed Mike's hand and smiled. "We're going dancing."

Aldris turned to face him and chuckled. "Wow. That's original of you, Mike. Still taking the ladies for dinner at Nikolai's and steppin' to impress them for the first date, huh?"

"Well, I should always try to impress my lady, don't you think?" Mike countered.

Aldris nodded. "Of course. I just never would've thought you'd take Lu to the same places you took your jump-offs. Lucinda is a helluva lot more special than that. I know I never did." He drank a long swig of champagne and then raised his glass to us. "But to each his own. *Salud,*" he said and turned back to his table.

Although I was damn near speechless, I somehow mustered up enough of a voice to say, "Good night," before we turned to leave.

"Oh, and Lu?" Aldris called out. We stopped, and I turned back to face him. "You look absolutely stunning tonight."

I'd never hightailed it out of a restaurant so quickly in my life. I was pissed beyond belief, but for the sake of argument, I was going to give Mike a chance to explain himself. As soon as we stepped foot in his SUV, we both turned to each other.

"How could you?" we said at the same time.

"Me? No, you!" we shouted at the same time again.

"What? I know you're not blaming me for anything."

Mike put his hands to his heart. "'Oh, Aldris, I'm so proud of you. I knew you could do it,'" he mimicked in my voice. "Hell, that's more affection than you've shown me all damn night!"

"Well, at least the affection I showed you was genuine, unlike your idea of dinner at Nikolai's and steppin'! Is he for real?"

Mike gripped the steering wheel. "Yes, I did it to impress other women, but honestly, for you, it was to show you a nice time. I wanted you to know about me and the things I like."

"So you just had to take me exactly where you took your jump-offs, huh? I can't believe you. Do you know how embarrassing that was?"

"Yeah, about as embarrassing as it was to see you fawning all over Aldris as if you're the best of friends, or better yet, still a fucking couple."

"Oh, go to hell! I was just saying I was proud of him."

"It's the way you said it, Lu."

"It's the way you took it," I spewed back. "You know what? You're making my head hurt. Take me home."

"What?"

"Take me home! I don't wanna step. Call a jump-off. They know how to do it already anyway."

"Fine. Okay." He spun wheels headed toward my condo. Every time we took two steps forward, we'd take two steps back. I hated to think this, but perhaps my decision to be with Mike was a little premature. I was beginning to feel like we couldn't get out of square one in this relationship. I was also beginning to feel like Mike was in love with the idea of being in love with me, because I knew I wasn't anywhere near being in love with him, and after tonight, that chance just got slimmer.

Chapter 20

Pooch

No sooner had I finally woken up from my coma than I was already in federal lockup. *Ain't this a bitch?* I had officially been charged with the murder of Detective Aaron Marsh, and since I was an ex-felon, I wasn't allowed to have guns, so I was also charged with weapons possession. The fucked-up part was that I couldn't even post bond. It was denied, claiming I was a high risk to society. *What the fuck?* I wasn't a high risk to muthafuckin' society, just to any muthafucka who wanted it with me.

I can't believe that fucker died on my ass. He was the muthafucka who had a better chance to live than all of us. As many times as I had seen the piper in my coma, and especially given Terrence's condition at the scene, I couldn't believe he was the one who kicked the bucket. Hell, Terrence's muthafuckin' ass wasn't even breathing when the ambulance first got there. I guess the same things kept us alive: our love for our kids and our love for Trinity. You knew she was a bad bitch when she could bring two muthafuckas back from the dead.

The main question on everyone's mind was, why had I shot Big Cal? Simple. There were two things you couldn't fuck wit' me about—my money and my girl. Big Cal's undercover ass had fucked my operation and fucked my girl in my house. That outweighed anything Terrence ever did to me by a ton. Besides, I did steal that nigga's girl from him by getting him locked up on trumped-up charges and setting him up for a raid, so I charged any foul shit he did back to me to the game. Turnabout is fair play, and karma is most definitely a bitch.

For as much shit as I talked about Trinity and as hurt as I was, I couldn't kill that bitch. For the first time, I understood what it truly meant to love someone. I had a clear shot for her, too. I just couldn't do it. She was the only woman I'd ever loved and the mother of my child. Even though it was fucked up about little man, I still couldn't do it. Big Cal's guns were aimed at me and Terrence. I knew that grimy bastard was gonna try to take us both out, especially after I found out he was in love with Trinity. That was why I shot his ass. He was a cop. I knew if he got one off before me, I'd be a dead muthafucka. Those punks were trained to shoot to kill.

I also knew Terrence would shoot me over Big Cal, being that they were cousins and I posed the biggest threat to his marriage. It made sense. Shit. From a gangsta's perspective, I wasn't even mad at him. If I were him, I woulda shot me too. But I couldn't believe that fuckin' grimy-ass Big Cal shot his own cousin. That muthafucka had to be mental. Over a female who was never his? Even drunken pussy from Trinity had niggas stupid. Her coochie needed to be illegal. When I thought about it, it was kinda funny. All of us were in there shootin' off on each other over the pussy, and at the end of the day, the only muthafucka who could truly lay claim to it was still alive and still with her. Big Cal was maggot food, and I was all shot up and locked up over nothing. Shit was still the same. Terrence was still with Trinity, and she for damn sure was still with her Dreads.

As of now, Stein was working on both my case and Flava's. I still felt horrible that Flava had been caught up in my bullshit, helping me move weight, and gotten popped. Her case was a little more hopeful than mine. I could try to claim self-defense, but that was like trying to sell crack to Jesus. It ain't working. So my best bet was to pray like hell that Terrence and Trinity weren't mad at me so I could get them to testify on my behalf.

Let me back up to Tot, my old connect, for a second. Ain't that another bitch? He was Big Cal's brother, my former right-hand man turned undercover pig. Those niggas had me on some ol' triple-whammy bullshit. Instead of getting Terrence locked up, I shoulda put this nigga on my team for real. This nigga infiltrated me like a muthafucka. I'd finally met somebody who outsmarted me in this street-game shit. It may have been fucked up, but I honestly admired the hell out of that. I got that nigga, but he damn sure got me back and took my cookie with him. Slick muthafucka. But I was still pissed with Tot. I trusted that nigga, but I did kill his brother, so we were even. However, I was sure he wouldn't see it that way. Hopefully, he could put his anger aside to help me out, because I'd hate for him to see his brother sooner than he wanted.

I know I'm talkin' reckless for a nigga who was one heartbeat away from meeting my Maker, and I knew my grandma told me to be better, but that shit took time. Right now, I had to fight to get the Feds off my back, and I needed to get some people on my team like fast. I'd work on my Christian love later. I was giving Terrence, Tot, and Trinity all passes, so damn it, that had to count for something. *Give a nigga a break here. That shit ain't instant.*

"Hey, Vernon. How are you holding up?" Stein asked, interrupting my thoughts as he sat down at the table.

I shrugged. "I'm holding."

"That's better than not."

He had a point about that shit.

"I just wanted to let you know where I was with the self-defense strategy—"

Self-defense. Back to that bullshit. On the real, I was beginning to question this muthafucka's credentials. I put my hand up, halting his words. "Stein, I'm a convicted drug lord and murderer who just murdered the cop who got my black ass locked up. Who the hell do you think you're going to sell that bullshit self-defense story to? There are some muthafuckas in the world who can't see shit right in front of them, but even Ray Charles can see that shit wasn't no self-defense."

"You hired me to be your attorney. If you don't have faith that I can win this thing, then why do you have me here? I'm doing the majority of this shit pro bono, because for some reason, I feel that deep down you're a good person."

"And I feel that deep down you're a good attorney, but let's count the facts here. You didn't get me off the first time, and this time you couldn't even get me bond. I'd say you need some help if I plan on seeing the light of day. I'm just putting it out there."

Stein was growing some hella balls hanging around me. He was gonna fuck around and be one gangsta-ass white man.

By now, Stein was beet red. "Well, do you have any suggestions?" he asked with a slight attitude.

"First, I suggest you take the attitude out of your voice. You came at me, and I came right back. That's just me. Get used to it. Secondly, you need to talk to Trinity."

Stein frowned. "Your ex?"

"Yes. She's my best bet since Detective Marsh kidnapped her and was the one who instigated this whole fucked-up plan. You have to tell her and Terrence that I didn't shoot at them and get them to help me. If they feel that I'm not a threat, maybe I can turn this thing into a hero story for me. I went along with Big Cal's plan in order to rescue Trinity, and I shot Big Cal to protect Trinity as well as myself. You think you can arrange a meeting with the three of us?"

Stein contemplated it. "You might be on to something here, Vernon. I'll work my magic and see what I can do."

Relief washed over me that he gave my plan full consideration, and I thanked him.

Stein looked at me in shock. "Wow."

I hunched my shoulders up. "What?"

"You thanked me. Did those bullets mess up your neurological system?" he joked.

Damn white boy had jokes. Hanging around me was lightening his shiny-suited ass up.

"Man, get the fuck outta here." We shared a brief chuckle, and then my mind drifted to Flava. "How are Adrienne and Flava doing?"

"Adrienne is still in love with Sonja. Sonja's case should be brought to trial in the next month or so. I think we have a really good chance of winning it."

"Has Flava asked about me?" It was odd that I hadn't heard anyone say anything about her.

"Only that she hopes you rot in this hellhole for running after Trinity instead of focusing on her. I was told to relay that message whenever you asked about her."

"Figures. Flava is always gonna be the same."

"Maybe you should try caring for her the same as she does for you. Just a thought. Underneath the rough exterior, she's just looking to be loved by you," Stein advised.

Since when did this dude become my personal advisor? "Who the hell are you now? Dr. Phil? Make up your mind which personality you want to be, because I need for you to be Stein in the courtroom."

"I'm just an attorney who's seen you through a lot of bullshit. You fucked over Trinity, and you see what happened. It's not often we find the real deal, and you've found it twice. Be grateful." He stood up. "You know, outside of you, I have a life too, Vernon. My wife divorced me while you were doing your stint, so I happen to know a thing or two about regret. It's not always about you. Sometimes you have to give a little to gain a lot."

On that note, Stein walked out of our meeting room. When the guard placed me back in my cell, I thought about what Stein and my grandma had said. Maybe I was a selfish bastard who deserved everything I'd gotten. If Flava got off and I got off, I was gonna make it my business to pursue a real relationship with her. She deserved that. I was gonna take care of Princess and let Trinity and Dreads live their life. And if I could, I might even drop a rose on Big Cal's grave. I hope my grandma was praying hard for me, because for me to do all of that, it was gonna take a hell of a lot.

Chapter 21

LaMeka

"I know you and your bitch-ass boyfriend had something to do with me getting fired," Tony yelled when we came to pick up the boys from his parents' house. "And for all I know, you had something to do with my financial aid, too."

"I didn't have nothing to do with that shit. And neither did Gavin. We only just heard about what happened from Misha, and your friend told her."

Tony's dad held him back. "Tony, don't lose your cool. Calm down, son," his dad attempted to coax him while his mom began to cry.

"You better listen to your daddy, because what you're not gonna do is think you gonna come at me and Meka. That's what's not about to happen. Ya feel me?" Gavin yelled while I desperately tried to block him from moving closer to Tony.

Never had I regretted a decision more in my life. Tony's mother begged me to see the boys. She even gave me a grand for Tony's support. She'd claimed that she missed them and wanted to squash the beef between us, so I agreed. I took the boys over there. Tony wasn't supposed to be home when I picked them up. When he got home, his mom was leaving to bring them to me to avoid conflict, but we pulled up at the same time she was leaving. Now here I was in this mess with Tony again.

"Fuck you! I ain't feeling shit you gotta say, white boy!" Tony pointed angrily at him.

"Fuck you, homeboy! You've been wrecking my life, and you want me to feel sorry for you because you got a dose of your own medicine. Bitch, kick rocks," Gavin hollered.

"You both need to calm down. Tony, you need to stop because you don't know who did it," Tony's dad yelled. He turned to Gavin. "And you need to stop disrespecting my house and my son."

"Mr. Light is right," I pleaded to Gavin. Honestly, I loved the fact that Gavin was sticking up for me, but this was Tony's parents' house, not a street corner.

Gavin fell back, pacing. "I apologize because this is their house, but I ain't sorry about disrespecting their son. Their son needs to learn some respect before he can get some. That's the reason his damn status is leaked all over the block now."

After a moment, Tony calmed down somewhat. "Okay, then. So just tell me. Did you all do it or not?"

I went to speak, but Gavin put his hand on my arm to stop me. "Since you want to play confessional today, you speak up first. Were you the one who sent that dude to vandalize my car? Were you the one who broke in my house and trashed it? Were you the one who called children and family services on us? See, you're doing a whole lot of fact-checking and asking questions, but you ain't being straight up your damn self."

"You called children and family services, Tony?" his parents asked in unison.

Tony swallowed hard. "I don't know what you're talking about."

Gavin and I looked at each other knowingly. That confirmed it all to me. "Exactly. We don't know what you're talking about either. Ol' lying-ass muthafucka," Gavin grumbled.

"Look, I don't want any problems. The boys are strapped in their car seats, and we need to go. All I want is for you to leave Gavin and me alone. That's it."

Tony's nose flared, but he knew there was nothing he could do about the situation. He gave up and huffed, "If I find out, I swear this ain't over."

Gavin stood toe-to-toe with him, looking him dead in his eyes. "And if you do start something, I'm telling you, ain't a corner of this earth where you can hide that I can't reach you. Believe that. If I wanted to, I could make you a non-issue right now. I choose not to for the sake of the boys. Your best bet is to fall all the way back and live your life. Real talk," Gavin shot at him in a tone I'd never heard.

"I think you better leave and take your boyfriend with you," Tony's dad said. "He's not gonna threaten my son in my face. I won't tolerate that."

"It's all good, Pop. I'm gone." Gavin walked to the car.

Eyeing Tony and his parents, I issued my final plea. "Just leave us alone, please."

On the ride home, I had to question Gavin about his threat to Tony. I'd never seen Gavin so ruthless before. Not even with the dude in the club. There was just something in his tone and the way he threatened Tony that got next to me. I just couldn't put my finger on it.

"What was all of that about? 'There ain't a corner on earth where you can hide' stuff."

"I was just shit talkin'." He continued to stare out the window.

"Stop cursing in front of the boys."

"My bad. I'm just pissed right now."

"And I'm not?"

He pointed at himself. "I didn't say you weren't. I was just explaining why I cursed. Come on, man. It's been enough already. Let's not get into it too."

"I'm just asking because I know when someone is just running off at the mouth and when someone is making a threat. That was a threat, baby."

He threw his hands up. "Of course it was. I'm your man. I'm supposed to protect you," he defended.

"I get that. That's not what I'm saying. It sounded to me like that threat was literal, not figurative."

"Literal or figurative, it doesn't matter. He'd just better leave us alone," he spewed. "Now that's what matters."

That was it. It'd surfaced. When someone claims they'll ruin you, the majority of people mean they will report them or plague them, and then there are those people who literally mean they will ruin you. That latter half, that was what Gavin sounded like, and that was what I was not used to feeling from him. I pointed at him. "See. That's the attitude I'm talking about. How can you make a literal threat like that? You said that shit like you were in the mafia or something."

"You cursed in front of the boys," he corrected me, being a smart-ass.

"Whatever! So are you going to answer me?" I asked, flipping right back on the subject.

He cleared his throat before speaking, his tone calm yet final. "Okay, yeah, it was a threat, Meka. But that's it. That's what a man does for his woman. And I don't want to talk about it anymore."

I eyed him. *Mm-hmm.* Gavin was an open book, so for him not to want to discuss this with me only meant one thing to me—he was still hiding something from me. I knew it. I could sense it. No one just makes literal threats that they can't back up. No one. I didn't know what the secret was, but this time I wasn't going to stop until I found out. I wanted to be with him, but I wasn't for lies and games. He'd just better hope his little secrets didn't come to light, or he was definitely gonna be single again. And I meant that in the most literal of terms.

Chapter 22

Trinity

I couldn't believe that Dreads was back at home with me. I'd gone through so much to prepare for this day. He was a little sore, and the stitches in his side caused him to ache, and he even moved a bit slower, but he was alive and well. He had all his neurological functions, and his health was damn near perfect. Aside from a few small scars from the bullet wound and surgery, you wouldn't even know anything was wrong with Terrence.

More importantly, a few of the detectives on the force and our attorney had gotten the DA's office to rule Terrence's shot on Pooch as self-defense. That was pretty easy to do given that Big Cal was Terrence's cousin and considering Pooch's history with all of us and the law. After I spilled my guts about Big Cal kidnapping me and explained how Pooch was jealous over my relationship with Terrence, it made my baby look like the hero he was. He got mad props from the force and the family for not killing Big Cal his damn self. It took some convincing, but given his community involvement, everybody rallied around him. Thank God Pooch made it. With Pooch surviving his gunshots, even if Dreads had gotten charged, it would've been an aggravated assault charge at best, which I was positive would've been thrown out of court or easily won. The law has so many loopholes in it that it was all about finding the right one. But the best ones are always the ones that have deep pockets and deep connections. Since Terrence had both, he didn't have to worry about a thing. Good, because I didn't get him back from the grave to have to live three to five years without him because of another damn bid.

Now that I had him back, I was going to do everything in my power to make his life easygoing and comfortable. Consuela and I made sure that the house was going to be Terrence friendly until he was completely recovered. With the downstairs guest bedroom being central to the kitchen, breakfast area, and dining room, it made for a relaxation oasis. Therefore, I turned it into a temporary master's suite complete with a Sleep Number bed for him, and I even got a reclining massage sofa chair for the room. I purchased a brand-new fifty-six-inch wall-mounted television complete with a Blu-ray player with all of Dread's favorite movies like *Scarface*, *Car Wash*, the *Good Times* collection, and every *Friday* movie that Ice Cube made, just to name a few. I'd brought his PS4 and all his games into the room along with a mini-fridge. I had the stair climber and some free weights set up in the back corner of the sitting area so he could exercise when he needed. I even moved half of Dread's wardrobe downstairs to the closet so he wouldn't have to want for anything. I'd rearranged my schedule to sit out one semester of my classes and only go into the gallery one day a week. I was devoting my time to making sure my Dreads was back at 100 percent in no time.

"I can grab the bags," Terrence said as we walked into the house.

"No. I have the bags. You just go inside."

"I'm not handicapped," Terrence grunted and held his side as he walked.

"I know, baby, but you have to take it easy." I brought the bags in and set them down in the living room, then shut the door. "I just got you back. Let me get you better." I walked up to him and cradled his face in my hands.

"That's right, Mr. K. Listen to your wife," Consuela concurred.

His eyes fell before he drew in a deep breath and released it. He was such a man. Allowing me to help him would be an adjustment. "Okay, li'l mama," he relented, then kissed me.

His kiss—so sweet. I didn't think I'd ever realized how soft and sweet his kisses were before. It was like I was discovering so many things that I'd once taken for granted. I just wanted to savor every moment as if it were my last with him. Holding him close for another moment, I allowed it to sink in. My Dreads was home.

He pulled away and looked up the stairs, then looked back at me. "As much as I hate to admit this, I may need a little help making it up there." He pointed.

"No help needed." I grabbed his hands. "Come this way. I have a surprise for you." I beamed as Consuela and I walked him to the guest bedroom.

As soon as we entered, we heard, "Daddy!" The next thing we saw were little people barreling toward us.

"Not too hard," I coached the kids as they each hugged him.

"Are you kidding me? They can hug me as hard as they want," he said, his emotions evident. "What's up, Terry? And my big girl, Brit! Look at my Princess!" he gushed as he hugged each one tightly.

"We missed you, Dad," Terry said.

"And we made you cards," Brittany added.

"You did?" Terrence's face lit up as each of them handed him a card, even our little Princess.

"Did you make this for me?" he asked Princess.

She nodded. "Yes, Da-da," she said, and that was all she wrote. Terrence's and my eyes misted, and we wiped tears to keep them from falling.

Excited, Terry shouted, "And look at your room."

Terrence looked around. "What? What is all of this?" he asked with amazement as he wiped a few tears from his eyes.

Consuela walked up and wrapped her arm around my shoulders. "It was Ms. Trinity's idea. She wanted you to be comfortable. So we arranged everything for you. You don't have to want for anything."

"That's right." I looked around at my handy work proudly before I introduced him to all the features of his own plush man cave.

He walked slowly to the bed and sat on it. "This is amazing, baby. You've outdone yourself. Thank you so much."

"And I know you are concerned about the money, but please don't be upset—"

He pulled me to him and planted the sweetest kiss on my lips to shut me up. "Woman, hush. I can't be mad at this. I'd never be mad at this."

"Gross," Terry and Brit said in unison.

"Oh, shut up, you two." Terrence laughed. "How do you think you got here?" he teased, and then he looked around. "Where's Tyson?"

"In the nursery. He's sleeping."

"I want to see him the moment he wakes up," Terrence said. "So let me check out these cards." He picked them up, and the kids hopped on the bed with him.

Just then, the phone rang. I went out to the living room and answered it, even though I didn't recognize the number.

"May I speak to Mrs. Kincaid, please?" a man asked.

"This is she. May I ask who this is?"

"Hi, Trinity. This is Attorney Jacob Stein," he said, and I plopped down on the recliner as if the wind were taken out of my sails. Because it was.

"Attorney Stein," I repeated slowly.

"Yes. Is this a bad time?"

"Yes. Wait, no. What is it that I can help you with?"

"I was wondering if I could meet with you. I need to speak with you about Vernon."

Nervous energy slowly crept up my spine, and I bit my lip. "Speak to me? About what?"

"I'd really rather speak with you—"

"I'm not meeting you, Mr. Stein, unless I know exactly what this is about. Forgive me for being rude, but when it comes to Pooch, I don't trust anyone who's affiliated with him. Not even you."

I could sense his hesitation and his frustration through the phone, but I didn't care. If he couldn't talk now, I couldn't talk later, period.

"Understandable. To make a long story short, I want to discuss using you as a possible character witness for Vernon's defense case."

The laugh escaped me before he could finish his sentence because I knew he was fucking lying. "Okay. Is this you, Ryan? Aldris? I know someone is joking on this line."

"I assure you this is no joke, Trinity. I really need to talk to you about this matter," Attorney Stein persisted.

"No, you don't, because the answer is no." Venom spewed out of my mouth like molten lava. "That bastard was a part of my kidnapping scheme. He assaulted me while I was restrained during the kidnapping and nearly caused me to lose my husband. Not to mention he killed my cousin-in-law. Have you lost your mind?"

"I can assure you that he had nothing to do with the actual kidnapping. Also, please give credit to Vernon for what he didn't do. He didn't shoot at you or Terrence.

You're blaming him as if your cousin-in-law, as you put it, didn't have a thing to do with it," Attorney Stein tried to reason with me.

"You have a lot of nerve. You can't assure me of a damn thing when it comes to Vernon, as you put it, and I don't give a good damn what he didn't do at the time. Pooch has done so much to me in the past that I can't even keep up with the number of cases he should've caught by now. If you need a witness, you better invent one because it will not be me, Mr. Stein. And that's a fact you and Pooch better damn sure remember," I snapped, abruptly ending that call.

I went to the kitchen and grabbed a bottle of water and took a swig. I couldn't believe he had the nerve to consider me for Pooch's defense, but knowing Pooch, it was probably his twisted-ass idea. *Let him get free so he can come after Terrence and me? Shiiiitt. Not me. Not in this lifetime.*

I walked back to Terrence's room and saw that he had two pills in his hand. "What are you taking?"

"Pain pills. I'm hurting." He chugged them both with a glass of water.

"You should've eaten something first."

"I'm cool. I just need to deaden that pain. Who was on the phone?"

"It's not important," I lied, waving off his question and choosing not to tell him right then. "Where did the kids go?"

"You know them. They aren't going to stay in one place too long. Brit took Princess to have a tea party, and Terry is upstairs playing his PS4. Brit said she was going to bring me some tea." He laughed, which evoked small giggles from me as I explained how much they truly had missed him.

He motioned for me to come to him, and I did. Clasping the sides of my waist with his big hands, he drew me close to him. "I've missed you all too." He kissed my stomach. "I need you." He leaned his forehead onto my stomach, his voice husky with emotion. "I need you so bad."

"You need to concentrate on your strength."

"I need to make love to my wife." He gripped me firmly about my waist. "Please."

His touch sent shivers up and down my spine. God, I loved this man. "Baby, I want to. Believe me, I do, but this is your first day home. Can you please just rest today? For me?"

He let out a reluctant sigh. "Just for you and just for today."

A look of understanding and satisfaction washed over my face as I turned to leave to allow him to rest.

"Wait. I have this room by myself?"

"I figured you'd need alone time to fully rest and—"

"I got more rest than I can tolerate in the hospital. Please don't isolate me at home. I like what you did, but I don't want to be here by myself. It would feel like I'm still in ICU. Consuela is cooking dinner. Come on. Lie with me."

Obligingly, I kicked off my shoes and sashayed over to the bed to lie down with my baby. Snuggling close to him, he held on to me firmly, stroking circles on my back as I lay my head on his chest. The sound of his heartbeat made my heart swoon. His heart. My heart. I swore they beat in sync. I loved this man with everything inside of me. From the feeling permeating between us, I knew he felt the same.

"This is what I need. Right here."

"You and me both," I agreed.

Soon we both drifted off to sleep in each other's arms.

Chapter 23

Charice

"Welcome to the Grand Cayman Islands," the staff greeted us as we walked into the luxury resort.

"We" meaning Ryan and me. Yeah, I couldn't get out of this one. However, I'd sexed the hell out of Lincoln just yesterday, and I promised him that I wouldn't be giving my cookie to Ryan on this trip. I had set my plan in motion. Last night, I tossed and turned, feigning menstrual cramps. Ryan looked like he was gonna blow a gasket when he heard those two words slide out of my mouth.

"How may I help you?" the receptionist asked us.

"Yes, I have a reservation for two. The name is Westmore," Ryan said.

"Oh, yes, Mr. Westmore. You have our five-star honeymoon cabana with the honeymoon package. Are you newlyweds?" she asked excitedly.

I laughed. "Hardly." It slipped out before I knew it.

Ryan looked back at me. "We've only been married ten months, Charice, so yes, we are still newlyweds," he said with a little irritation in his voice as he and the receptionist eyed me.

"I was only joking. Besides, we've been together so long it hardly feels new to me." I weaseled out of that comment.

The receptionist broke the tension with a cheerful grin. "Oh, you feel like old soul mates. I get it," she cooed.

Old roommates is more like it. I linked my arm through Ryan's. "Oh, yes. We've been hanging in there together for a long time." I faked loving emotion.

Ryan's demeanor changed back to the chipper mood he had been in when those words slipped from my lips, and he smiled at me. "And I wouldn't trade her for the world."

"Me either, baby." *But I would trade you for Lincoln.*

Ryan gave her his credit card to finalize the charges, and then she gave us our information packet. "Okay, Mr. and Mrs. Westmore, here are your keys to your cabana. You have day and night staff members here for your every need. Marco is your designated bellhop. Claudia is your daytime housekeeper, and Suzette is your nighttime housekeeper. You also have Juan and Rose as your butlers. They can provide anything you need. If there is any issue with your cabana, please do not hesitate to notify us. Here is your receipt and some information about the islands and different amenities and activities that we have available for you. Do you have any questions for me?" she asked.

"No. Thank you," Ryan and I said.

"Okay, then. My name is Nessa, and if you need anything, I am here. Our manager would like to welcome you, and then our hostess, Luanna, and Marco will drive you to your cabana," she explained before she turned to get the manager.

I peeped at the receipt. Fifteen grand for five days. *Damn.* Ryan was gonna be pissed that he couldn't get any cookie on this trip. Oh, well. People in hell wanted ice water, but they couldn't get what they wanted either, so why should I feel sorry for Ryan? Savage, I know, but he made me like this. Judge your mama, not me.

The manager came over, and I swear I could've copped a squat on the floor. People irked the hell out of me with how they just fawned over Ryan. You'd think celebrities were God Himself. People would fall over backward to praise and please them. Of course, I expected nothing less than top-rate service for spending fifteen grand in the establishment, but the praise was what got me. Let's be for real. Fifteen grand may be pocket money for us, but it was nothing to sneeze at. There were people in the world getting their cars repossessed who only had fifteen grand left in car payments, and we were fortunate enough to have that kind of money to blow on a trip for just two people. But sometimes people were just too much. They went overboard just because Ryan had money, and he was in the elite NFL. It's not like Ryan was the humblest person in the world, or at all, for that matter. He ate that shit up. He should've been an actor or singer because it was always lights, camera, and action wherever he went.

"Oh, Mr. Westmore, my name is Yuri Avant, and we just want to say thank you so much for choosing to stay with us. You and your beautiful wife are most welcome here, and if there is anything we can do for you please do not hesitate to ask. We want your stay to be one you remember for a lifetime," he said, shaking Ryan's hand the whole time.

"Thanks a lot, Yuri. We appreciate that," Ryan said.

See what I mean? *Why is he calling that damn man by his first name, Yuri, instead of Mr. Avant?* Who in the hell gave him the rights to call that man Yuri? He didn't know him. He should've addressed him formally just like Mr. Avant addressed him. Not *the* Ryan Westmore. And the sad part was the manager would still kiss his ass.

"It's no problem at all, Mr. Westmore. You're very welcome. Very welcome. I'm willing to bet your Super Bowl chances that you'll enjoy yourself." He laughed. And there it was. Kiss ass. Muah. Muah. Muah.

"Then I know I'm going to enjoy myself, Yuri." Ryan chuckled.

"Well, Ryan, let's get going. I'm sure Mr. Avant has plenty of patrons to address. We don't want to hold him up." I tugged on him, growing tired of this charade.

Mr. Avant then shook my hand. "I hope you enjoy your stay, Mrs. Westmore. Please let us know if there is anything we can do for you."

"Thank you, Mr. Avant."

The fact that he didn't correct me to ask me to call him Yuri let me know that he preferred being addressed by his surname. Point proven.

When we arrived at the cabana, I nearly choked. They didn't lie one bit about the ambiance of the cabana. Large bouquets of roses filled each room and there were rose petals on the bed. In the center of the bed was an arrangement of chocolates with a bottle of rosé and two champagne flutes. The huge whirlpool tub had white tealight candles lit all around, and the surround-sound system played soothing R&B music in the background. On the kitchen island were three trays: a cheese tray, a fruit tray, and a dessert tray. There was a flat-screen television everywhere, it seemed. Everything was absolutely beautiful.

"Is everything to your liking?" Luana asked us.

"Yes," we confirmed, still taking in the brilliance of the cabana.

"I've placed your luggage in the bedroom," Marco informed us.

With that, Ryan thanked them both by peeling off a $50 bill for each of them. They both thanked us graciously for the tip, wished us a wonderful stay, and went about their way.

"This place is so amazing," Ryan said in awe.

"It really is."

I continued to take in our beautiful surroundings as I entered the bedroom and unpacked my luggage. Suddenly, I felt two arms around my waist. "What are you doing?"

"Trying to find out how amazing it can be." He leaned me back into his chest and kissed my neck. "I just want to sit you in the middle of that dessert tray and skip dinner," he whispered.

"Let's unpack first."

"Damn the luggage. I need to unpack this cum built up in my nuts," he whined.

I turned to face him, unbothered by his tantrum. "We have plenty of time for that. I'm hungry, we need to unpack, and we still need to check on the kids."

"How about we unpack later, eat the food off the trays, and call the kids now so we can get to our business?" Ryan asked me. "We need to beat Mother Nature to the clock."

"If I don't get a real meal, you're going to be shit out of luck, Mother Nature or not."

He gave in, and I called Juan to set up a light lunch on the terrace. I'd arranged for us to have a couple's massage immediately following lunch and then to do a little shopping. Then for dinner, I made reservations at the hotel restaurant, and I made plans to watch a show immediately after that. Yes, you guessed it. I was making our time here as busy as possible. If he was too exhausted to have sex, then I definitely wouldn't have a care in the world.

I called the boys, and we both spoke with them to make sure they were doing all right. By that time, lunch had arrived, and Ryan went with Juan to set everything up, so I called Lincoln.

"Hey, you," I cooed, watching Ryan closely.

"Hey, baby. Enjoying your honeymoon?" he joked.

"Hardly." I sighed. "Wishing it were you and me. This place is spectacular."

"We'll have to go one day."

"You're so wicked." I giggled.

"So where is your husband?" he asked sarcastically.

"Eating up attention as usual. He's sickening."

"Careful. You almost sound like you don't love the man anymore. A wife should never sound that way," he playfully teased.

"That's because I don't. My heart only beats for one."

Caught off guard, he paused, exhaling deeply. "I love you so much, Charice."

"And I love you too, baby. Too much," I said just before Ryan entered the cabana. "So is Lexi giving you any problems?"

"Leave him, Charice. This is crazy," Lincoln pleaded.

"She's being a big girl for her daddy. That's good," I said, looking up at Ryan. "I'm just checking on the baby."

"Tell Lincoln to take care of our little bundle of joy," he said loud enough for Lincoln to hear.

"Tell Ryan I'm fucking his wife and I want to marry her," Lincoln said.

I laughed nervously. "Oh, okay. That's good. Just give us a call if you need anything."

"I need you," he pressured. "Leave him, baby. Please."

"Our lunch is ready, Ricey. Come on," Ryan rushed me before heading back out onto the terrace.

"I'll talk with you later, Lincoln. Kiss Lexi for me."

"I love you, baby. I really do." The sadness in his voice came through so clearly.

"Ditto," I whispered and disconnected the line.

Emotion overcame me when I powered the phone off. So much so that I rushed to the bathroom because tears had found their way to my eyes. I longed to be with Lincoln, but I was trapped in this marriage with Ryan.

Why couldn't things have been different? Why did I have to jump to marry Ryan? Why didn't Lincoln just confide in me from the beginning? Why did we have a perfect love now in such an imperfect situation?

My heart nearly ripped in half listening to Lincoln plead for me to be with him, but I just couldn't bring myself to put my feelings first. I did what I always did. I pulled my emotions inside, dried my tears, and put on my happy face. It was time to pretend to love Ryan. After all, I was his wife.

Chapter 24

Mike

Is this what karma felt like? Please let me know. My heart was heavy. I hadn't spoken with Lucinda all week. The first couple of days were by choice. I was tired of refereeing her and Aldris around each other and even more tired of having her second-guess my feelings for her over bullshit behind Aldris. My stance against talking to her was pretty easy because Lucinda didn't reach out to me either. After a couple of days, I began to feel bad and really miss my baby, so I tried to reach out to her only to find out that she still wasn't talking to me. No answered calls, no return phone calls, and no return texts. Nothing. I even went to her condo because surely she couldn't avoid a face-to-face conversation, but she wouldn't even answer the door. Now I would think that maybe even if her car were sitting plainly in front of her condo, she could've possibly left with a friend, but not when I could hear her inside the condo laughing at whatever was on television. Yep. She straight ignored me.

How did I know? Well, after the fifth ring of the doorbell, which I could clearly hear was working, through the blinds I saw her get up, turn the television off, and go to the back of the house. I wasn't being stalkerish. I simply missed my lady, that was all. Didn't she miss me, though? Didn't she even care? I couldn't help but laugh at myself. I was starting to sound like a complete bitch.

I knew what was really bothering me, though. All our issues had one common denominator—Aldris. How could my relationship grow if her ex was a constant concern? Even if that ex happened to be my former best friend. For that, dating Lu was fucked up on my part. I'd never denied that. All I was saying was that I couldn't help that I loved her. Was it really wrong to date Lu after she broke up with Aldris? I mean, I didn't cause the breakup, and I damn sure didn't approach her even when I wanted to. She was never his actual wife. There was no scandal, no affair. Aside from pissing off Aldris, how was I wrong? And why was karma fucking with me when I tried to do everything right? I didn't tell Lu to fall for me. I didn't force my feelings or hers. In the grand scheme of things, I believed we had these feelings for each other because it was honestly meant to be. Either karma was being a bitch right now, or Aldris was the problem. Maybe it was both. Whatever it was I didn't like it. Not one bit.

"Hi! You've reached Lucinda. I'm unavailable to take your call at the moment, but if you leave your information, I will call you back as soon as I get a chance. And if not, you have to try to catch me again. Have a good one, *mis amigos!* Beep," I said along with her voicemail. I'd heard it so much I could recite it verbatim at this point.

"Hey, Lu. It's me, baby, again." My discontent bubbled to the surface. "How long are you going to be mad with me? I'll admit it. In hindsight, I shouldn't have taken you to Nikolai's and steppin'. It was a player move I used to do, but you know how I feel about you, babe. I just wanted you to honestly be a part of my life. You know. Enjoy the things I liked to do. I promise you, outside of my babies' mother, Nikolai's and steppin' is the closest anyone has ever gotten to me. You know me. You have my heart. Please just answer the phone. Please," I pleaded. "Call me. I love you."

Being stuck at the house with nothing to do had driven me stir-crazy. I was off work for two days without parental duties because my kids were visiting their grandma, and I didn't have any plans and damn sure no visitors. Even though I thought I still had a woman, I still felt like a damn bachelor. This was the perfect opportunity to be snuggled up with Lu in the bed watching movies and making love. Before I got excited over that idea, I decided I had to get out of the house. I showered and headed over to the basketball courts to grab a pickup game with some of the fellas out there and relieve some stress.

When I got there, there was a game in motion on one court, so I headed to the empty court so I could clear my head. Halfway on my trek to the other court, I heard my name and turned around to find Rod and some of the guys we used to work out with at the gym, and Aldris.

"Yo, Mike," Rod yelled. "You too scared to come over here and join us?" he joked much to the fellas' amusement.

"What?" My heated gaze fell on him. "What the fuck you just say to me?" I walked over there with an attitude.

"Pipe down, dude. I was just fuckin' wit' you. You're the one acting all brand new. Going to the other court and thangs."

The disbelief was unreal. I pointed to myself. "Hell, you didn't call me for no pickup game. If you ask me, y'all acting brand new."

Rod shrugged. "Fair enough. But you're here now. You just gon' bypass us like that?"

"I didn't even see y'all. My mind was somewhere else."

"Somewhere like wondering why Lu ain't talking to you? I remember that feeling, you know, when she was my fiancée," Aldris recalled callously.

"You know what? Fuck you, Dri!"

"No, fuck you, Mike!"

Rod and one of the guys from the gym jumped between us to prevent us from fighting. "Y'all calm the fuck down," Rod demanded.

I shot an accusatory point toward Aldris. "He fucking started it."

"Me?" Aldris pointed at himself. "You're the grimy one here. I'm not going behind your back and fucking your girl."

"I never did that. I keep telling you nothing happened while you were together, damn!"

"Nothing ever shoulda happened," he hollered. "So what you saying? Y'all done fucked, Mike? Is that it? Have you fucked my ex-fiancée?"

Nope. Like this game, this conversation was a wrap. What I wasn't about to do was discuss with him and all these niggas on the court what happened in my bedroom. I waved off his questions.

"Man, I'm out, 'cause that right there ain't even none of your fucking business." I turned to walk off.

"You must not be hittin' right," Aldris sneered mockingly.

The sounds of chuckles set a blaze through my system, and I spun around ready for this verbal assassination. "Oh, no! I hit that Spanish Fly just right. Believe that muthafucka!"

By now, I was back in the middle of the group, intent on charging Aldris. He wanted a fucking fight, and I had it for him. The way I felt, I needed a reason to blow off steam. Rod and the dude held us back from charging at each other.

"And that's why she can stay away from you for so long, huh? Damn. If you was hittin' it just right, then she should be missing it enough to call you. Lame-ass, limp-dick muthafucka," he spewed as a few of the guys tried to stifle laughs.

"Bitch, who you think you coming at?" I asked, trying my best to bulldoze my way through Rod at this point. "For real, dawg. I'm sick of yo' shit!"

"Hey! Hey!" Rod brought my attention to him with light pats to the cheek and gripping my shoulders. Once my eyes landed on him, he addressed me. "Let it go, big baby. It's all good. You want to work that shit out? Do it on the courts. How about that?"

"I'm in," Aldris said tensely.

I looked at them and nodded. "Yeah. I'm in."

"All right! We have ourselves a real street ball game now," Rod said before turning to face the other guys in the group. "Dri, you and Lee are wit' me. Mike, pick your team."

I looked the guys over. Sal and Dion were the best two guys I remembered from the gym, so I picked them. But I made damn sure to make a mental note that Rod chose not to be on a team with me. The other three guys sat down on the bench to watch us play. At the tip-off, my boy Sal came down with the ball. He passed the ball to me, and I passed it to Dion. Dion couldn't get off a good shot, so he passed it to me, and I went inside. Aldris was right there and shot a bow straight to my face.

As I fell down and ate the concrete with a hard thud, Aldris grabbed the ball and then ran up the court, finishing with a dunk. "Foul! That was a fucking foul!"

"This is street ball. Ain't no fouls." Aldris winked with sinister eyes.

"Oh, so it's like that?" He nodded with a smug look on his face. "A'ight." I took off my T-shirt.

"Oh, shit, fellas. It's gettin' real now. Big Mike done took the shirt off. Got the six-pack showing. Flexin' the muscles and shit," Rod joked.

Hopping up from the ground, I spat, "Fuck you, Rod!"

"Hostile." Rod continued to poke fun at me.

"First team to twenty," I called out.

Aldris threw the ball to me roughly so that I could in-bound. "Two up."

After that, it was on. I got off two good bows to the side of Aldris for a hard lay-up. We went back and forth like that all game long. I caught several shoves, a bow to the mouth, and a bow to the eye, but it was all good. He wasn't gonna win this game. I had a bruise on my face and a little blood trickling out of my mouth, but I didn't give a fuck about that. Besides, I was tearing up his side and stomach with bows and shoves, and I did manage to catch his ass in the mouth once, too.

"Game point," I yelled out. We were up 18–17. One more two-pointer and it was a fucking wrap.

My male ego wouldn't allow me to let my teammates make this last shot. I had to make it against Dri. I just had to. I passed it to Dion who shot it back to me, and even though Sal was wide open for a three pointer, I took it inside to dunk on Aldris, and that muthafucka clotheslined me in the throat. I hit the ground with a loud thud and turned around in just enough time to watch his ass shoot a three-point shot to win the game. Nothing but muthafucking net.

"Game over," Aldris yelled as Rod and Lee all high-fived him and celebrated.

I wanted to just lie on the ground. I got fucked up and I lost. Slowly, I got up and hobbled over to the bench. Sitting down, I wiped the blood and sweat from my face. All the fellas walked over to the bench.

"Maybe next time, bro," Rod said with a soft pat to my shoulder while drinking his bottle of water. I nodded and wiped my face again.

"Nah. It ain't happening next time either. Grimy mutha-fuckas always end up falling flat on their ass." Aldris looked dead at me.

That was it. *Fuck that game and fuck him.* I jumped up. "You got something to say to me nigga, then say it."

"Gladly." Aldris walked up face-to-face with me, pushing Rod back.

"Nah, Rod, let him go. Let him say what he gotta say."

Rod threw his hands up, and all the fellas stood back.

"You ain't nothing but a grimy-ass muthafucka. Ol' fake-ass cat. The only way you could find or get a good woman is by scoping out my situation. You just mad because I've always been better than you. Ever since we were kids, I had the better behavior, better grades, better clothes, better girls, better cash flow, and better swag. You ain't nothing but a muthafuckin' hatin'-ass bastard who played Mr. Clean-up Man to get what you never would've had a chance in hell of getting. And your problem is you don't know your role, and you didn't play your position. That's why your raggedy ass is going to end up without Lucinda," Aldris spewed as I stood there and let him get it off his chest.

I ain't gonna lie. That shit cut me deep. I'd always admired Dri. I looked up to him, and yes, I was a little jealous sometimes when we were school-age because he'd get the first new pair of Jordans or some shit like that, but real talk, I always had mad love for him. Even today. I coulda balled harder and roughed him up more, but I didn't, because he was my boy even if I wasn't his. To hear him talking reckless like this on some shit from when we were boys caused a separation in my heart for him. He wanted to throw away our friendship over a woman who didn't want him anymore because of his actions, and this time it worked.

"Wow. So that's what it is, huh? You think I've always been your little sidekick? Well, Batman, Robin is flying solo from now on. And by the way, I'm taking your ex-fiancée with me. So you got it, chief. You won all the battles, but you lost the war. The sad part about that is you lost the war on your own. I'm just capitalizing on it. As for my position, it's up top with your ex-fiancée's legs spread wide on my shoulders. Now hate on that, you punk muthafucka." On that note, I grabbed my bag and walked away.

The next thing I felt was a hand on my shoulder, and I instantly turned and swung. Aldris ducked and caught my ass with a one-two combination in the face. I fell to the ground, and he kicked the shit outta me before Rod and Lee grabbed him. Then I felt a glob of spit hit the left side of my face.

"Hate on that, bitch-made nigga," Aldris yelled.

Adrenaline coursed through my veins as I jumped up and wiped his spit with my towel. I was prepared to go toe-to-toe with his ass this time, but Rod and Lee kept him bound, and Sal and Dion blocked me from them while ordering me to leave. As badly as I wanted to get at that nigga, I shrugged it off and did as they'd suggested. Instead of going home, I drove straight to Lucinda's condo.

"What do you want—" she answered the door brashly, then gasped when she saw my face. "Oh, my God! What happened to you?" she shrieked and pulled me inside.

"Your ex-fiancé is what happened. At least this time you answered the door."

Confused, she asked, "Why would he do that? Let me look at your face."

Was she serious right now? As if Aldris and I hadn't been at odds over her ass since before she and I officially became a couple. I shrugged her off. "Because of you, Lu. Why else?"

"He just attacked you like that?" she asked somewhat in disbelief.

Part of me wanted to lie and say yes, but I opted for the truth. "During a game of basketball on the courts. He was talking shit, I was talking shit, and shit just got outta hand. I'm fine." I plopped on her couch. "Where's Nadia? I don't want her to see me like this."

"At a birthday party," she answered before going to the kitchen. She came back with a hand towel full of ice. "Put this on your face." She sat beside me.

I put it to my face and turned to her. "We need to work some shit out. I need to know where we stand, because on the real, I'm not going to war for you if we ain't gonna be together. I just got my ass kicked by my best friend of twenty-three years who is no longer a friend of mine at all, over you, and I'd like to think that was for a reason."

She huffed and crossed her arms. "I don't know if it was for a reason, Mike."

I put the ice down and turned my body completely facing hers. "What are you saying, Lu?"

For a moment, she sat hardened in her stance. Then she released a sympathetic sigh and leaned back on the sofa. I knew then that she was ready to talk, and I was ready to hear it, because after the events of today, we had to be clear about what it was we were doing. Biting her lip, a nervous habit of hers, she admitted, "Mike, I like you, but every time we begin to get closer, something pushes us back. I feel like we are on two different emotional levels, and even though you say you love me, I can't believe that."

Ain't this about a bitch? I just got my ass kicked, and she says I don't love her? What the fuck? I was beginning to think I was stuck in the fucking Twilight Zone. "Lu, are you kidding me right now? I've lost my best friend, my best friend, over you. You have a relationship with my kids. Every chance I get, I try to show you how much I care. I messed up on our last date, but damn, everybody makes mistakes. I'm trying to be more active in your life, but I'm confused. You want me, then you act like you don't. You say it's important for me to be a part of your life, but when I try, you tell me that I'm moving too fast. If we're stuck in neutral, it's damn sure not because of me."

Lucinda sat forward, sliding her hands down her face. Clasping her hands together, she turned to me and nodded. "You're absolutely right. I can't argue with that."

Well, after that admission what the hell could I say? She threw me for such a loop that I couldn't say shit. I gazed at her for a long while before barely stammering out, "Okay. Um. Well. Okay."

"You're wondering where that leaves us?" she asked, eyeing me closely.

"Well, yeah."

"I don't know," she said and stood up, pacing back and forth. "I don't know if we have enough of anything to move forward. I feel horrible because I know that you've given up a lot for me, and I can't say that I'm ready to give up on us, but I just don't know if what I feel is enough to keep trying." She let out a pained groan, then she turned and faced me. "I fought so hard for Aldris, and I lost. I just don't know if I have any fight left."

Her words hollowed me. I loved Lu, and I couldn't lose her like this. If I did, Aldris would be right, Jennifer's plan would fail, and I'd lose her forever. It wasn't going down. Not on my watch. Too much had been put at stake for that.

Standing, I walked to her. "Are you kidding? No one I know has more fight than you, Ms. Lucinda Rojas. You encourage me. You inspire me. You have the ability to prove the entire world wrong." I grabbed her hands and held them in mine. "Look at me. I literally hated you for Aldris because I didn't know you, and now, here I am head over heels in love with you. Who does that? Where they do that at?"

Getting serious again, I continued. "Perhaps we were both wrong. Did you need more time to heal from your relationship with Aldris? Absolutely. Did I fall in love too fast? Positively. But here we are. Together. You're my friend and lover. I don't know how this will turn out, but I know I care enough about you to see how far we could go. Maybe we'll make it, and maybe we won't. But I plan on enjoying the ride for as long as you'll allow me to. Let's get mad at each other and make up. And go out and stay at home. And laugh and cry. Talk and yell. Let's do all of that because that is the only way we will know if this is worth it. I don't want you to fight for me, Lu. Just be with me, and I'll do the rest. That's all I ask," I pleaded with so much sincerity it shocked even me. I had never been so into a female before in my life. It had to mean something.

Her hand fell to her chest, and her caramel cheeks turned rosy red. "Damn. You might've just stolen my heart."

Lifting her chin with the curve of my forefinger, I pressed her gently. "Might've isn't good enough."

Caressing my face, she declared, "Let's start over."

My heart soared. *Music to my ears.* "Sure." Extending my hand to hers, I clasped it and lightly shook. "My name is Michael Johnson, but they call me Mike."

"It's a pleasure to meet you, Mike. My name is Lucinda Rojas, and they call me Lu."

"Nice to meet you, Lu. It's my pleasure." I snapped my fingers. "You kinda remind of this chick I met once named Spanish Fly."

"Oh, yeah? I heard that too. From what I know of her, she's a bad chick," she played along as we both laughed.

Moving my hands to caress her face in my hands, I made my request known. "Let's try for real this time, Lu. Please."

She sealed that request with a kiss. That was all the confirmation I needed. I pulled her to me and held her tight in my arms. Her scent was intoxicating as I ran my fingers through her hair and slid my hands down her bodacious booty. I wanted her so bad and not just in a sexual way. I wanted her to be mine forever. I kissed the nape of her neck, and she moaned.

"I want you," I whispered in her ear.

She pulled back and grabbed my hand. "Let me reintroduce you to my friend, Spanish, last name Fly," she said seductively. And that was all she needed to say.

Chapter 25

Ryan

Three days. Three whole days. I'd set up this romantic trip for Charice for our honeymoon, and we'd been having a lot of fun. We'd done everything imaginable on the islands for three glorious days except have sex. She'd managed to keep us so tied up during the daytime and nighttime that by the time we got back to the cabana, the only thing either of us wanted to do was sleep. I tried to be slick and set my phone's alarm for five o'clock in the morning so I could get some early morning nookie, and you wouldn't believe that she was already up and at the resort gym. I found a nice little note telling me to be ready by the time she got back because she had a big day planned for us. I wanted to tear some shit up.

Who the hell takes a honeymoon vacation and doesn't have sex? Who? Let me answer that one for you—no one. Even virgins gave it up by the second day to their husbands, so I couldn't understand what the fucking problem was. It damn sure ain't like either one of us were virgins. Shit, I'd conquered that pussy back in high school, and I had triplets to prove it. True enough, my plan was to get Charice pregnant, but shit, I had to be able to get some sex before I could concentrate on impregnating her. Hell, without one there sure as heck couldn't be the other. Besides, pregnancy could come later. I needed to be deep in a warm hole now because I was on the verge of losing my damn mind officially.

Although I hated to admit this, it was my truth—if I knew giving her the dance studio was going to deter her from the bedroom, I would've waited until after she'd gotten pregnant to give it to her. I would've had to come up with another plan to bounce back after Lincoln opened his mouth and squealed like a pig. That would've been the simplest thing to do because I was always a man with a plan. If I didn't have one, then I could damn sure think of one. You could bet your ass on that. She spent all her time at the studio or doing something for the studio. It was already the best ranked in the state and was in the top ten of the region. I get that she wanted to be number one in the country, but I needed her too.

Maybe karma really does exist. Why, you ask? Well, I could picture in my head Charice feeling the same way when I went into the NFL. Hell, she'd told me. But I just wanted to concentrate on my career, so I damned my family to hell. Now she was damning me to hell. *Wait a minute. Perhaps I could use that as a key point. You didn't like it when I did that to you. Well, maybe not.* It sounded good in theory, but I didn't think it would go over too well with this new Charice. She'd only get offended and tell me that it was in fact karma, and then I'd never get any pussy.

Honestly, I was getting downright pissed off about it. I was so pissed off, in fact, that I opted to stay at the cabana while she shopped on day four. Day four. I'd stayed in bed while she worked out, came back, showered, ate breakfast, and left. She kept asking me if I would join her, but I just grunted and rolled over. Yeah, I was being a bitch, but it'd been months since I was intimate with my wife, and it was beginning to take a toll on me. I'm not like her. Women are so resilient. They could go years without sex and be perfectly fine with that, but not a fertile, sex-craved, heterosexual male such as myself. We needed that shit like we needed oxygen. We couldn't survive without it. So here I was trying everything to keep my mind off of the fact that I was not getting any. I'd watched television shows, then a movie, then played one of those in-house hotel video games, ordered room service. Everything.

"Forget this shit," I said aloud as I reached in my carry-all bag and grabbed a bottle of lotion. "This is gonna have to do for now." I headed to the bathroom.

I sat on the lid of the toilet with my shorts around my ankles, a towel across my lap, and my lotion in my hand working its magic. Soon, I was lost in the moment of relieving myself. As I thought about Charice, the more intense I became, and just when I was about to reach the point of no return—

A loud gasp rocked me as my eyes flew open to the woman standing before me. "I'm so sorry, Mr. Westmore," Claudia, the housekeeper, apologized as she scurried back out of the bathroom.

"Oh, shit," I yelped, jumping up.

"I'm so sorry, Mr. Westmore. I knocked and no one answered, so I thought . . . I assumed . . . I'm so very sorry," she apologized profusely outside the door.

Washing my hands, I said, "It's okay. Uh, just give me a moment. I'm a little, uh, embarrassed."

"I'll wait outside."

"No, I'm coming out now." I emerged with my shorts and T-shirt on and eased past her.

"Mr. Westmore, I can come back if you need more time," she began and stopped. "Sorry, that didn't come out right. What I meant to say was—"

The irony of the situation couldn't be described as anything other than hilarious. The whole universe was in on a conspiracy to give me the blue balls. I couldn't help but laugh. As I began to laugh, she laughed, which caused me to laugh even harder.

"I bet this one will be on your top-ten list of adventures on the job. I'm sure you've seen it all."

"*Ay-ay-ay!*" she said, putting her face in her hands. "I'm just happy you're taking it so lightly. My coworkers have seen it all. I've only been on the job for a month, so this is my first. Well, there was the one guy who loved to eat breakfast in the nude, but we all witnessed that one."

"Great! So not only am I in the top ten, but I'm also number one by default."

She put her hands up. "Oh, but don't worry. I won't tell anyone. We are held to strict confidentiality, so we cannot reveal names. It could cost us our jobs, and I'm not trying to lose my job. Your secret is safe with me," Claudia explained.

"That's good to know," I sighed in relief. "You probably don't know who I am, but I have a reputation to uphold."

She nodded. "I know who you are. Did you assume because I'm a young female housekeeper that I don't?"

Embarrassed again, I confessed, "Actually, yes."

"Well, Mr. Westmore, my father is a huge sports fanatic, and he had six girls, so he treated us like boys. I probably know more about football and basketball than I do housekeeping," she joked. "So I do know you—star running back for the Giants."

"You get a TD for that. I'm impressed. Shocked, but impressed." She seemed fairly young, and I wondered why she wasn't in college versus working at some high-end hotel chain. "Let me ask you a question, how old are you?"

"You are as blunt as the tabloids said." She looked at me in amazement.

"I'm sorry. I was just wondering because you seem so young."

"I'm twenty-one."

"Are you in college?"

She patted the towels in her hands. "That's what the gig is for. I'm saving up enough for one term so that I can go. I have to pay term by term on this salary."

"What do you want to be?"

"A sports journalist. What else?" She laughed with a shrug.

"Duh. Well, good luck with that. It will all work out. I'm sure of it," I said as my cell phone rang. It was Charice. "Yo," I answered. "Hey, babe. Shopping for another hour? Ricey, come on. Okay. All right. Bye." I hung up and threw my phone down on the bed.

"I'll just come back," Claudia said, placing the towels in the bathroom and turning to leave.

"Wait. No. You can stay so you can finish up to get to your other cabanas."

"I only have three. They want me to learn to give top-notch service. You're actually my last cabana for the day."

"Do you mind staying? I could use the company. Please."

"Umm, your wife—"

"Is going to be shopping for another hour, and if it weren't for her selfish ass, you wouldn't have caught me in the bathroom in the first place. What the fuck does a man have to do to make love to his fucking wife?" The tirade flowed out before I realized I'd said it. She just stared at me. "Wow. I can't believe I just said that out loud. Damn. My bad." I was truly slipping. This fucking no-sex thing was driving me completely out of my character.

"Umm, maybe I should be going," she said nervously. "Just a little tip though. It's your honeymoon. Maybe she's waiting to surprise you, Mr. Westmore. Well, anyway, call me or Suzette if you need anything."

I plopped down on the bed and massaged my throbbing dick through my shorts. It'd been a long time since this side of me emerged, but here it was rearing its ugly head. Charice could thank herself for that.

"Wait," I called out to Claudia.

She turned around. "Yes, sir."

I observed her. Legal. Long, dark hair that she kept in a ponytail. Probably a native of the islands by her complexion. There was nothing spectacular about her looks body-wise, but that was cool. Legal. She had a pretty face, though. Round with full light brown eyes. Eyelashes for days. Pretty white teeth. Cute button nose. Soft and succulent-looking lips. Yeah. The lips are what got me. Did I mention that 21 was legal?

"Claudia, I'd like for us to be friends."

She eyed me suspiciously. "Friends?"

"Yes, friends. You know, have each other's back."

"Oh, I already told you, Mr. Westmore, I won't say a word. Not to your wife or anyone about what was said or done. I told you I need my job," she assured me.

"Good. But as your friend, I would like to help you out." I picked up my cell phone. "How much do you need for your classes for the rest of the year?"

"About forty-five hundred dollars, why?"

"I'd like to take care of that bill for you. All I need to do is call the bank and have a money order drawn up."

"But why would you do that for me? I don't need hush money. I told you I wouldn't say anything."

I stood up and walked over to her. "It's not what I don't want you to say. It's what I need you to do."

"Do what?" she asked cautiously.

"Please don't get offended. I wouldn't ask, but you know my situation, and I would like for a friend to help me out, and in return, I will help a friend out. Strictly confidential of course."

"Do what?" she asked again more firmly.

I looked down at my package, and her eyes followed. "Just a little mouth work is all I need. You know, a warm hole. That's it."

"You want me to—"

"Yes. If you say no, I understand. We're still friends, but I just couldn't do you the favor. If you say yes, we're still friends, I'm relieved, and you're forty-five hundred dollars wealthier. So what do you say?"

"I'm not a hooker," she said, offended. "Nor am I a madam for hire."

"I never called you that, nor did I call you a madam. I'm not even hiring you. I'm just doing a favor for a friend who would do a favor for me. Is there any harm in that?" I tried to coax her.

If she didn't make a decision soon, though, I'd have to kick her out before Charice came back. So what if I was wrong for what I was doing? Charice was wrong for withholding sex from me. That was my God-given right as her husband. Since she took it upon herself to dish it out when she felt, I was gonna get satisfied how I pleased. Besides, as long as I wasn't screwing anybody else, it wasn't technically cheating. This was simply a service just like getting your carpet cleaned. I needed my dick vacuumed.

She stood there in deep contemplation. "Are you serious about the money?"

I called the bank that I used here and had everything arranged in a matter of twenty minutes. All she had to do was come down with a valid identification and pick it up. Just like that.

"I'm that serious. Should I call my money people back and have them shred it, or will you be picking it up? Time is of the essence. I've already killed twenty minutes. We only have forty left." I looked at her with a "hurry up and make a decision" expression on my face. "It's just a one-time deal that stays between us friends."

Claudia knew she wanted and needed that money. Where else was she gonna get it? Her looks were merely average, and her body, while slender, had no "pop" to it. Charice beat her in appearance and presentation ten times over, so I was doing her a favor by allowing her a part of me anyway. No woman generally appealed to me unless they were as fine as or finer than my wife.

Trust me. It ain't as simple as it sounds, because Charice wasn't just a dime piece. She was a whole dollar bill. I was fucking hurting, so Claudia had better tap into this treasure she was given because if I fucked around and found someone else or actually got some from Charice, she could call it a wrap on this deal.

She nodded. "No one can know," she said, walking over to me. "And I don't swallow."

My dick damn near high-fived me, but I kept calm to ensure she knew I held the upper hand. "Of course no one can know, and you most certainly will not swallow. In fact, I insist that you use a guest toothbrush and the travel-size bottle of Listerine afterward."

She seemed impressed. "Wow. How thoughtful."

Thoughtful my ass. She wasn't going to save my soldiers in her mouth and spit them in a turkey baster and then in the next six weeks have my black ass on the news because she said I got her ass pregnant. Not on my watch. I knew exactly what I was doing. I'd been in the league long enough to know exactly how the game worked. Hell, even the bank account she was getting the money from was set up under a different name. Yes, that's how I rolled. Women have a nest egg. I was sure Charice did, so why the hell shouldn't I? I was always one step ahead of the game, always.

"Oh, shit." I moaned as her mouth slid up and down. "Damn, girl." I looked down at her. "You're pretty damn good just to be twenty-one."

She giggled. "Thanks. My boyfriend wants this done all the time, so I've become a natural—"

"Okay. A little less talking," I cut her off, leaning my head back and enjoying the feeling of being in a warm mouth.

Besides, I didn't want my moment fucked up by her beginning to feel bad because of her man, or thoughts of her with another man invading my moment. The less I knew about her, the better. That way, if anything did come up, I could deny like no other. If I didn't know shit about her and she didn't know shit about me, then she couldn't prove anything.

"Fuck, I'm about to explode." I gripped her head, moving her mouth up and down faster and faster. As I felt my cum moving to the tip, I grabbed the bunch of tissues I had, quickly held myself, and then released into it. "Oh, yeah." I oozed out.

We both stood, and I pulled my shorts up over my waist. I promptly walked her into the bathroom and told her to spit in the toilet and flushed it, just to be safe. Then I gave her a toothbrush, watched her brush, and gave her some mouthwash and watched her rinse—twice. Then I flushed my tissues down the toilet. Oh, and trust me, I grabbed that toothbrush, too. There's no such thing as being too careful.

She smiled at me as we stood in the bathroom. "You good?"

"Hell yeah. Thanks, and you can pick that up today."

"I take it this won't happen again," she said as she prepared to leave. "Unless you'd like to see me tomorrow."

I shook my head. "I'm good. Thanks," I answered. Number one rule in the game: don't make the same "mistake" twice.

"It was a pleasure to meet you, Mr. Westmore. Good luck on your upcoming season, and enjoy the rest of your stay," she said, showing me that she would stick to the agreement.

Just before she left, something dawned on me. "Claudia," I called out to her.

"Yes, sir."

"You said you have a boyfriend. It didn't seem like you felt bad for doing this. Why is that?"

She turned and looked at me, and then she admitted, "The whole truth of the matter is my sister is in her third year of college. Her tuition is paid for, and it's all because she used to work here. She told me there would be days like this. I didn't get it at first. Today, I understand. It's like you said, we are friends doing each other favors. What's there to feel bad about?" she explained, and with that she left. I couldn't help but admire her hustle. She was gonna go far in life. Real far.

Once she left, I immediately began tidying up, and I jumped in the shower. Even though I'd had an awesome release, I still had a build-up. I was so backed up it wasn't even funny. I refused to call Claudia back, and Suzette was a woman in her late fifties. I didn't do women old enough to be my mother or grandma. That was just nasty. I'd keep a hard-on if I had to do that. Everybody should have a limit, and that was mine. What I didn't have was patience for this lack of sex from my wife anymore. The moment she got in, I was getting some, period.

"Ryan," Charice called out. "Oh, Ryan, hey, babe. Where are you? I bought a bunch of cool things for the boys and cute outfits for Lexi. You should see them. Ryan?" she asked again.

I could plainly see her from where I was standing, and she looked delectable. She'd taken off her sun hat, shades, and flip-flops. Now all I needed to go were those thongs and that sundress, but I could do the rest. I flipped the lights off and eased up behind her.

"What the hell?" she asked, startled.

"Shhh, baby. It's me," I whispered in her ear as I held her close to me.

"What are you doing?" she asked as I ground my hard-on against her backside.

"You," I said, pushing the top half of her body forward.

The palms of her hands hit the bed with a thud as I gripped her about the waist. I pushed her dress up her back, revealing her nice, plump ass cheeks swallowing a black lace thong. I palmed one ass cheek in my right hand and caressed her kitty through the thong.

A grunt escaped from my lips. "Damn. I almost forgot how sexy you are. I'ma rip these damn thongs right off you and give it to you nice and hard."

"Ryan, what are you doing? Stop this. Stop this now," she demanded.

She went to stand up, and I pushed her back down, this time flat on her stomach. I straddled her and pressed her hands down with mine as I interlocked fingers with her.

"Come on. This is what you want, right? It's been so long I can't remember anymore. Please your husband, Ricey. Please me." My voice came out rough and forceful.

"You're hurting my wrists," she whimpered, panicked. "Let me go. Get off me."

"Stop screaming like I'm raping you," I bit out tensely as I tore her thong at one side.

"What do you call it? You're forcing yourself on me."

"No, I'm making love to my wife. It is my God-given right to make love to my wife. It's a duty for us to plea- sure each other, and since you won't voluntarily pleasure me, I figured you wanted it rough. I didn't bring you on this trip to be treated like one of your fucking girls. I'm your husband. Please me!"

She struggled beneath me, but I overpowered her by ten times her strength. I flipped her over and pressed my body mass on her as she tried to push me off her. "Please, Ryan. Don't do this like this," she begged as her lip quivered.

Now I was angry. "Why are you fighting me? I shouldn't have to beg for this. Why are you doing this to me, Charice, huh?"

She stared at me with such intensity as if she had a million things to say to me. Then she paused and swallowed hard. "I . . . I don't want to . . ." She took a deep breath. "To . . . get pregnant," she stammered and looked away.

Wait. Her reluctance to sex me was because she didn't want to get pregnant? So I was fucking my own self up from getting sex? She was afraid of getting pregnant because she knew that's what I wanted. This was why I wasn't getting any? Damn. I wanted a baby, but I had to make her feel like it wasn't all that important. At this point, it wasn't that important. The sex itself was. She was gonna get pregnant. I wasn't giving up on that, but for now, I just needed to be with my wife. That was it.

I caressed her face. "Baby, I understand. You may not have thought I listened when you told me that you didn't want any more kids, but I did. I heard you loud and clear. If you don't want more kids, you don't want more kids. I can respect that. But what I need is to have my wife back. What I need is to make love to you and have you make love to me."

She stared at me a moment, and then she nodded. "Okay," she said barely above a whisper. She closed her eyes as I lifted her legs and pulled her thongs off. When I eased her dress off and spread her legs, I saw tears trickle down her cheeks.

"It's okay, baby. You don't have to feel like you're disappointing me."

She wiped her eyes and shook her head. "I'm just . . . this is so emotional for me."

"Let me make it better," I whispered, kissing her favorite spot on her neck and making her moan instantly. That was the signal. Worked every time. I held her close as I lovingly eased inside of her love nest. *Yes. This is what I need right here.* "I love you, baby," I whispered lovingly to her over and over again.

As I stroked her, she cried with each thrust. With each thrust, I made love to her more passionately and more lovingly to show her that she could trust me as her husband. I thought it was sweet that she was actually in tears. It made me love her that much more. I savored the moment as I slipped in and out of her slippery seduction. Finally, I was home. Finally.

Chapter 26

LaMeka

Ever have that feeling that things are just too perfect? I swore I was not looking for trouble or being so used to things not going my way that I couldn't accept peace. That was not it. I mean the type of perfect that causes a person to sense the storm brewing in the midst, except they can't see it and they don't know when it is coming, and they can't even prepare for it, but they just know it is lurking and waiting.

Things had been just too normal. Too quiet. Too perfect. Neither Tony nor his family had bothered us. Nothing at all. I did receive my child support, but for Tony to blow up the way he'd done normally meant he would try to get back at me or do something foolish, which usually translated into withholding support as if he were hurting me. But I'd actually gotten it and on time. His parents weren't acting reckless at the mouth or being demanding. Gavin was being overly loving and nice. At work he wasn't being overbearing or harsh. He was helping me with my coursework—not that he wouldn't. It was just that his help seemed more voluntary than normal. I was happy about that, though, since I was only one semester away from my associate's degree in nursing. Next stop: bachelor's degree in nursing and becoming an RN and maybe even full steam ahead to a PA. The only things that seemed normal were Misha, my mom, and the boys.

But even that was changing. My mom was looking at buying a house and moving Misha with her so I could have my space, but I assured her it wasn't necessary. She told me nothing had changed, that she'd still take care of LaMichael during the day and keep Tony Jr. in the afternoon. She wanted to start a small in-home daycare, and Misha could help in the afternoon, even if she did nothing but watch Tony Jr., so she could tend to the other children. I could pay Misha to do that so she'd have a little money to do what she needed or wanted. The plan sounded good, but I didn't want them to feel like they were a burden to me.

Everything had seemed to be going so right. Since Gavin wasn't going to tell me what the hell he'd meant that day, I was going to find out. I'd been making a habit of going to his house more and more, but still I didn't see, hear, or find a thing. I wanted to give up and just take Gavin at his word, but in my gut, I knew better. If there was one thing I vowed to do for the rest of my life, it was to listen to those gut feelings and inner voices. They aren't just there for no reason. That was God's way of saying, "You'd better listen to me." I hadn't listened in the past, and I'd suffered gravely for it. I was listening now. As a matter of fact, I was listening and leading my own investigation.

"Meka?" Gavin asked as he opened his front door.

I nodded and walked in. "Yep. Me." I headed back to the bedroom.

"I called and didn't get an answer, so I hopped into bed. It's ten o'clock at night, baby. We have work tomorrow," he said, following me.

I put my overnight bag down beside his dresser and stripped down to my tank top and panties. "Yeah, I know. I was studying for my final on Friday, and then I showered." I folded my clothes and placed them on top of his dresser.

"Where are the boys?"

"With Misha," I explained, getting my toiletry bag out and heading to his bathroom.

He followed me. "Not that I don't like this, but you didn't tell me you were coming over tonight. I mean, I don't care at all, I'm just saying you caught me off guard. I would've made it special, ya know? Cooked something, got some chocolates, you know, get my romance on for you, baby."

I looked back at him and laughed. *Liar.* I caught him by surprise. That was the reason why this was bothering him. That was why it bothered me. "Really? We're officially a couple now. My house is your house, so yours should feel the same to me. There's no need for you to prepare for me to come over every time I come. This is my home." I turned on the sink faucet and started brushing my teeth.

"I know and it is. I just like doing romantic things for you. At least get you some roses or something. You know how your man does." He eased up behind me.

"I do. You don't bring flowers to my house. I don't need them at yours. It's cool." I rinsed my mouth with mouthwash and wiped my hands and mouth with a paper towel. "Have you eaten?"

"Yeah, I had some Church's tonight."

Nodding my approval, I turned and kissed him on the lips. Then I walked into his bedroom, lay across his bed, and flipped on the television. Soon I heard his footsteps in the bedroom.

"It's a welcome surprise, ya know. Having you here with me," he said, standing over me with his arms crossed.

I flipped on my back and motioned for him to lie on the bed with me. He crawled on the bed, and I wrapped my arms around his neck. "I'm glad you like my surprise. I love you, Gavin."

"I love you too, Meka."

Even though the next day was a workday, we had a couple of beers and snacked on some chips like it was the weekend. We even stayed up and watched a couple of television shows together and played a game of Spades in his bedroom. I had to admit I loved the time we spent together. Nobody knew me better than he did. Not even Tony. That was why it bothered me that he was keeping secrets from me.

I drank a swig of my beer. "I have to ask you something, so don't be offended, okay?" I blurted after the last show went off.

He set his beer on the nightstand. "Okay. What's up, babe?"

"How come you never talk about your brother or to your brother? I know he's your family and everybody deals with their family differently, but you are such a family-oriented person, it just seems you two would be closer."

He sighed. "Our mother raised us, but that doesn't make us close. My brother and I are like oil and water, and I just got tired of trying. I'd love to be closer because he's my brother, but that's up to him."

"What happened?" I pried.

"Ugh. It's a long story about things that happened a long time ago. I really don't want to get into the specifics tonight." His focus went to flipping the remote back and forth.

I put the palms of my hands up. "I'm sorry. That's your right."

"No, no, you're good."

"How long has it been since you last spoke with him? Surely, one of you can make the first move one day."

He chuckled and kissed me. "You are something else. You can't save the world, baby. But I thank you for trying."

He leaned back. "I haven't really talked to my brother in months, and honestly, I'm better off because I haven't. I hate to feel that way, but I do."

I realized the conversation was dampening his mood, so I decided to let it go for tonight. I looked over at him. "Umph. I thought you were better off because of me," I joked.

"No, baby. You make me better. You complete me," he said seriously. I smiled at him, stroking his cheek. God, I loved this man. "I'm about to take a shower. Care to join me?" he asked seductively.

I crawled toward him and kissed him. "No, baby. Enjoy your shower. I'll be waiting right here for you so we can get all hot and sweaty again."

"Why don't you come to the shower with me, and we can get hot and sweaty and clean all at the same time?"

"'Cause I'm clean now and I want you clean. Nothing beats great oral than clean hygiene. So go get ready for me," I coaxed.

That melted him. "All right. I'll be right back, baby." With that, he disappeared into the bathroom.

He ain't slick. I told him when I got here that I was already showered up, so he knew I didn't need to join him. If sex was on his mind, he would've been all over this booty the moment I stripped down. He was trying to keep me close where he could keep an eye on me. Men. Typical and predictable. Why, oh, why would he do that? Something was up. I ran into the bathroom acting as if I needed tissue to make sure he was in the shower.

Immediately after I left the bathroom, I grabbed his cell phone. *Damn it.* I needed his four-digit PIN code to unlock it. I tried his birthday and mine, but they didn't work. So I left it alone. Next, I went through his wallet. Credit cards, debit card, social security card, license, gun license, nursing license, bonus cards for grocery shopping, and $62 with a photo of me rounded out all the contents in his wallet.

Maybe I was going crazy. Maybe I was putting too much on a very small subject. Maybe I was so unhappy in my past that I couldn't allow myself to be happy with my present. Perhaps it was me. What I wasn't going to do was question my man to the point where I drove him away from me, so I put his wallet down and sat on the bed to watch television. I would make it up to him as soon as he eased under the covers. And from this point on, I wasn't going to doubt him again.

Just as I settled back, his house phone rang, and I picked it up. "Hello?"

"I'm sorry. I must've dialed the wrong number," a man said.

"Wait. I probably should tell you that this is Gavin Randall's house if that's who you're looking for."

"Oh! Then I do have the right number. May I speak with him?"

"He's actually in the shower. Can I take a message for him?" I asked, grabbing a pen and some paper.

"This is his brother, Gary, and who might I be speaking with?" he asked.

I gasped. "Oh, my God! Hi, Gary. I'm glad to know that you called him. I can't wait to tell him that you did. I know it's been a while since you spoke to him. Forgive me. I'm just rambling. I apologize. I am his girlfriend, LaMeka. It's a pleasure to talk to you."

"Okay, well, if you consider two days ago a long time, then I guess so. You must talk to your siblings every day." Gary chuckled.

"Two days ago?" I questioned. Didn't Gavin just recon-firm to me that he rarely talked to his brother, and it'd been months since he had? I knew my gut wasn't off.

"Yes. LaMeka, is it?" he asked.

"Yes, it is."

"I really have to run, but can you tell Gavin that since he won't be at work tomorrow, I will catch him this weekend when I come down."

"He'll actually be at work tomorrow."

"He will?"

"Yes, he definitely will. At nine a.m. sharp."

He huffed. "That lying little . . . never mind. I shouldn't have said that. LaMeka, it's been a pleasure. Do me a favor, and don't tell my brother I'm coming tomorrow. Please."

"Okay, I can do that."

"Thank you, and you have a good evening," Gary said.

"You do too, Gary."

I wanted to be upset, but I was more concerned as to why Gavin would lie to me about his family of all things. He knew just about everything about mine, and he knew before I decided to give our relationship a chance, so why in the hell couldn't he be honest with me about his? Why was it such a big deal that he kept his family and me separate? If he'd talked to Gary just two days ago, how come he didn't know about me? Something wasn't right. For all his fancy talk, if I found out that I was just a booty call, or worse yet, that this fool had some type of secret family in another state, I was going to see red—blood, that is. I was so anxious I wished it was the next day already.

"That shower was just what I needed, baby." Gavin came running into the bedroom and put on his T-shirt and boxers. He turned to face me. "What's wrong?"

I just stared at the television. "Nothing. I'm just into this," I lied.

"Oh, okay," he said, picking up his cell phone and then his house phone, pressing the caller ID buttons.

Good thing I had enough sense to delete his brother's call from the phone or I'd never find out the truth. *You ain't slick enough this time, Gavin Randall.* I knew it was too perfect. I knew it.

Chapter 27

Charice

I was an emotional wreck. I had no choice but to have sex with Ryan the last two days. He was on me like he was literally going to take it, and I believed he literally was. How could I explain that I didn't want to have sex with my own husband? Ryan wasn't stupid by a long shot, and truthfully, Ryan knew how my sexual appetite was, especially with no kids around. I couldn't see that one going over well at all, especially after he lied and said he could accept that I didn't want any more kids. Yeah, right. Ryan never just accepted anything. He was just more concerned with having sex with me. Try as he might, he didn't know I was on birth control, and he didn't know for a reason. No babies were coming out of this womb unless I absolutely wanted it, and if I did want it, it damn sure wouldn't be with him.

I could've avoided the sex with him if my menstrual cycle plan hadn't fallen through. He busted me on that one, because on our first night there, he actually came and jumped in the shower with me. The first thing he made note of was that my period obviously wasn't on. To save face, I explained that I thought it was menstrual cramps before, and I kicked myself in the ass for not locking the bathroom door. It took some true Houdini shit to keep his ass off me that night. He got out of the shower first to try to create an ambiance to put me in the mood, so I had to think fast. Thank the good Lord every room had a phone in it. I called the housekeeper, Suzette, to come down and clean up for us that night, then stalled until she arrived. When I came out, I told Ryan that I called her because I wanted everything to be fresh, and then got him to come with me to one of the clubs so we could party until the room was clean. Crisis averted. I kept his ass at the club until nearly four in the morning. Then we stopped by one of the all-night eateries to grab a bite to eat. By the time we made it back to the cabana at five in the morning, all we could do was fall onto the bed and sleep. I tried my best to keep the same type of routine going until he messed me up that afternoon. Then he made sure he beat me to the punch, waking me up at 4:45 in the morning to have sex yet again. I was going to get up fifteen minutes earlier than my normal routine just to avoid having sex with him again, but when I rolled over, he was already staring at me. *Shit*. He had his way with me until eight o'clock in the morning.

Now we were back home, and I was scared as hell to face Lincoln because I knew he was going to ask me if I kept my promise not to give Ryan any sex, and I couldn't lie to him. I knew this was important to him because he felt the one thing he had over Ryan was that the treasure between my legs belonged to him. And it did. I won't lie. Ryan was good at what he did, but in my heart, I didn't enjoy it. It was more a chore than anything else. It's weird to explain. I guess the best thing to say is that I allowed myself to relax so that I could be in the moment, but I couldn't bring myself to any type of completion or actual pleasure because I didn't want Ryan. I had to relax, because if I didn't, Ryan really would've had to question me. It was one thing to tell him I'd been withholding sex because I didn't want to get pregnant, but it was a completely different situation when your wife wasn't turned on by you. One had nothing to do with the other. Ryan would've seen straight through me if that were to ever happen.

I wanted Lincoln. I wanted to leave Ryan and be with him, and God knows after this vacation, I had to put myself first. I had to find a way to leave Ryan and be with Lincoln. I owed it to myself and to Lincoln. I couldn't keep hurting like this, and I couldn't hurt Lincoln anymore. I knew the boys would be mad with me, but I just prayed that eventually they would understand and forgive me. My heart couldn't take it. I had to be with the man I loved.

I was so nervous about meeting up with Lincoln that after we got back from our vacation, I'd actually had Ryan stop on our way to the house to pick up Lexi. This way, Lincoln couldn't question me, and I didn't have to feel the pressure of having to lie to him, and it worked. I had to get away from Ryan first before I admitted what happened to Lincoln. Prayerfully, by that time, I'd be lying in his bed at night, and it wouldn't make a difference.

Today, Lincoln was coming over to pick up Lexi, and I was really hoping that Ryan would leave the house as he normally would, but he was hanging around today. It really didn't matter. It was probably for the better. Ask me no questions, I'll tell you no lies. Besides, he was just picking her up anyway.

Ryan had answered the door for Lincoln when I came down and saw Lincoln sitting down on our living room sofa. "Lexi's things are ready. You can pick her up out of the bassinette and leave if you like. I know you don't want to be around him." I pointed in the direction that Ryan had just left.

"Actually, Ryan told me to stick around for a moment." Lincoln looked at me, confused.

I shrugged as Ryan came back into the living room. He had a T-shirt. "I just wanted to give you a little token of my appreciation for watching Lexi for us. I know she's your daughter and all, but I have to admit when I'm wrong. You have honestly been a man of your word and not interfered with my family, and I appreciate that. I was wrong about you. Perhaps we all can coexist together," he summarized, giving Lincoln the T-shirt.

"Oh, from your trip?" Lincoln asked, looking at it.

Ryan smiled, wrapping his arm around my shoulders. "Yeah, I picked it up myself. You could use it for practice or something. You ready for camp, bruh?"

"Yeah, as ready as I ever could be. We gotta watch these rookies. Show 'em how it's done," Lincoln said, amped up.

Ryan and he slapped hands. "Hell yeah! All things aside, on the field you're a beast, and I'm counting on that good blocking so I can make some great scores. I'm sure Andre is looking for the same."

"Yeah, you know I got it on lock, especially with Carter. All roads lead to the Super Dome in February," Lincoln said as they slapped hands again.

"Hell yeah," Ryan concurred. "But you know I'm always focused on getting a little aloha in my vocabulary, too. I'm sure you'll be back in for your fourth straight season."

"You too man. The Pro Bowl was amazing, wasn't it?" Lincoln laughed.

"Shit yeah. Gotta get more of those in my life," Ryan agreed.

Okay, what the hell was going on? I was standing here having an out-of-body experience. These two hated each other. Literally. Ryan bought Lincoln a gift, and Lincoln accepted? On top of that, they jumped straight into football as if they'd always wanted to be on the same team? Was I dreaming this shit up? Nope. I pinched myself to be sure. When in the hell does a man who's fucking another man's wife suddenly become cool with that man? When has a man who's hated another man for being with a woman he wanted ever suddenly been cool? I was shocked and appalled.

I patted Ryan's arm and tried to break up this New Edition reunion moment. "We're cutting into Lincoln's time with Lexi."

Ryan pulled me to him and kissed my cheek. "Look at my wife. That's generally code that she wants some alone time with me," he joked.

I shook my head no toward Lincoln. He laughed. "Well, I should be going anyway," he said, putting Lexi in her carrier and grabbing her diaper bag.

"So how did you two enjoy your trip? I never got a chance to ask." He smiled at us.

"It was great," I blurted out. "We saw a lot of things on the island and had a lot of fun. We partied to the wee hours of the morning. I'm still recuperating. In fact, as soon as you leave, I'm gonna sleep like a log," I said, quickly trying to hurry him out the door.

"Yeah, Ricey shopped a lot. Spent a lot of my money, but that's cool. That's what the trip was for," Ryan bragged as we walked Lincoln to the door.

"Well, that's great. Sounds like you two had a partying good time," Lincoln added as he opened the door.

Ryan shrugged. "Yeah, but you know how I roll. Couldn't leave without getting my romance on."

Instantly, the color drained from my face. Lincoln stopped dead in his tracks and turned around. "Oh, yeah? That's great," he said, looking directly at me. I put my head down.

Ryan laughed. "This is weird to say to you, but we carried on like we were making a baby that last day, didn't we, Ricey?" he said playfully as I glared at him. "I know we're agreeing not to have a baby right now—"

"Right now?" Lincoln asked with his eyebrows raised. "So you two are thinking of having a baby?"

"No," I intervened instantly. I gave Ryan a hard stare. "We already discussed this, Ryan. We aren't having a baby, Lincoln," I tried to reassure him.

"He said not right now, Charice," Lincoln repeated.

"Right now, we're not. Maybe down the road or something when things get a little less hectic. I don't know. It's an open discussion. Right now we're not, but, man, you couldn't tell it. I swear we went half on one," he joked.

"Half. Wow. That was an amazing time." He smiled. "Well, let me let you two lovebugs get back to your, umm, baby making. I've got Lexi." He walked to his SUV.

"Lincoln!" I called out.

"I've got Lexi, and no, I don't need anything. Do you, Charice. You all have fun together with your alone time. Please don't let me hold you up," Lincoln said, and with that he jumped in his car and left.

"Lincoln has really come a long way," Ryan said as we walked into the house.

"You know what? I need to go to the dance studio. I'll be back," I rattled off and ran upstairs to grab my shoes and purse.

"Okay, well, I'm going to the gym," Ryan called out to me.

Son of a bitch! I had to get to Lincoln. I had to let him know it wasn't like that. I couldn't believe Ryan would say some shit like that. Maybe he was trying to test the waters to see if Lincoln was truly over me. He couldn't have found out about the affair. Ryan could be slick with withholding information, but there was no way in hell he'd plot like this. He couldn't hold it in that long. He would've blown up on the spot. His ego and pride couldn't let him hold it in. I'd be damned if his ignorant ass was going to mess up my relationship with Lincoln again. If I had to leave him on the spot, I would!

I wished so badly that I would've followed my first mind back on the islands. When Ryan asked me why I was withholding sex from him, I came within two seconds of telling him that I was in love with Lincoln, but in one split second, I changed my answer to not wanting to get pregnant. I'd thought about my boys and the fact that I was scared of Ryan's reaction. With him damn near close to taking my body against my will, I didn't know what he was capable of if I'd admitted an affair at that moment. So I folded. Now I was wishing to God that I hadn't. I should've told him and let the chips fall where they may.

By the time I ran downstairs, Ryan was already gone. I pulled out of my driveway and drove down to Lincoln's house. I used my spare garage door opener and backed my car into his garage. I let it down and ran inside his house. He was standing in the kitchen, brewing.

I put my hands up. "Baby, listen to me. It wasn't like that. I swear to you it wasn't," I said, walking up to him.

He pushed me back. "Get away from me," he said tensely. "So you're telling me he's making it up."

"Yes!"

He stopped and eyed me. "So you didn't fuck him?"

I swallowed hard. "Listen to me. I . . . I did, but it wasn't like how he's making it sound."

"Wait. First you said it wasn't true. Now you're saying it is, but the way it happened is a lie. What the hell does that even mean? Fucking is fucking, Charice!"

Tears fell from my eyes. "It's not coming out right. It's so complicated," I cried as I wiped my eyes. "If you'd just let me explain—"

"Explain what? That you are playing the both of us? You want to have your cake and eat it, too? When you get off the phone telling me you love me, do you just go and make love to him as if what I said didn't matter? You're scandalous. I can't believe I trusted you. You say Ryan is the bad person, but you're nothing but a female version of him," he yelled, pacing back and forth.

"Baby, I'm not playing you. I swear to God I'm not. He was going to rape me if I didn't give him any. I had to. I didn't want to tell you because I knew you'd be upset. I just couldn't bring myself to tell you."

"You want me to think he was going to rape you, and you've still been living in the same house with this man for a week? You are not a fool, Charice, and neither am I. Not anymore." He crossed his arms with a sense of finality.

"Lincoln, wait! No, baby." I ran up to him and grabbed him. "I'm serious. I am getting my divorce ready. I'm leaving him for you. I swear it. Please, baby, don't leave me. Don't do this. I love you," I cried as I held him by his waist.

Lincoln glanced down at me with sad eyes. He pulled my arms away from his waist and held my hands. "Charice, I love you. I've waited so long to hear those exact words. It's too bad that words are all they are. I don't believe you any more than I believe he was going to rape you. Go home to your husband. We are done," he said tensely as he gently pushed me back.

His words pierced the depths of my soul. *Done. No way can we be done. Done? Like done, done?* No, I couldn't lose him. Not again. Not again. "Lincoln, please," My teary pleas spilled out as I fell to my knees in despair. "I can't take being without you again. You have to believe me. I put that on everything I love. Everything! You know my heart. You know I'm on birth control, so I'd never be able to get pregnant, because I don't want to. I'm asking you to trust what you already know."

"No, I don't. I don't trust shit. I don't have to believe shit. For the first time, I realized I'm the only one in this triangle who is living up to any type of commitment, and

I'm the one who's not married. I'm not doing it anymore. No more," Lincoln spewed. "Get out of my house. Leave the garage door opener and all the spare keys on the counter on your way out."

I stood up with a tear-drenched face. "It's repeating itself."

"What? What's repeating itself, Charice?" Lincoln asked angrily.

"Karma," I explained. "We did this before. We allowed Ryan to separate us before. This happened in Dallas, and it ended up horribly. We walked away from each other, and I ended up married to the wrong man. Don't you see, baby? Don't do it again. If we let go now, we'll never find our way back again. We are meant to be together. I need you to believe that this time. Just believe it."

Lincoln walked out of the kitchen and plopped down on his living room sofa. Lexi was sound asleep in her bassinette despite all the commotion around her. I followed Lincoln to his living room. He was in deep contemplation as I kneeled in front of him.

"You have me, baby. All you have to do is hold on. I'm not trying to trick you or anything. This is real." I pointed back and forth between us. "I'm divorcing Ryan to be your lady."

Despite himself, tears fell from Lincoln's eyes, and he let out a wail that sounded like it contained years of pain and anguish. He cradled my face. "I love you, but I don't believe you. And I've never felt like that about you until now."

"What can I do?" My pleas continued because there was no way in hell I was letting him go. "Do you want to go with me to file the divorce? What? What do I need to do?"

"Leave him now. Damn the waiting. Leave him, move in with me today, and then file. That's the only way I'll know it's real," he blurted out.

"What? You know I can't do that. I have to get things straight for my boys and—"

"Exactly." He stood up. "Exactly what I thought you'd say. Leave, Charice. This is not what you want."

"Lincoln, if I walk out this door, if I leave this time, I'm not ever coming back to you. So you think about this. Think about this before you let me go. If I walk out, it's final. I can't put myself through this again."

Lincoln looked away for a few moments, contemplating my words. "Fine, Charice. You win. I won't let you go," he said slowly. I ran up to hug him, but he stopped me. "But . . . that doesn't mean I trust you. It just means you have to prove it to me. I'm not your puppet anymore. So go home, figure your shit out, and when you get it together, you'd better pray to God I still want to be in this relationship."

"Oh, Lincoln." I tried to hug him again.

He put his hands up, signaling me to move back. "That is all the leeway I can give you. Please go before I change my mind or say something I regret." He turned and walked me to the kitchen entrance that led to the garage.

I turned to look at him. "Baby, I love you," I said sadly.

He huffed. "We'll see." And with that, he slammed the door shut.

Chapter 28

Aldris

I kept replaying that horrific night in the hotel room, the restaurant, and the basketball courts. All of it was just stuck in my head like a broken record, especially listening to Mike and Lu giggling, kissing, and snuggling. It was enough to make me throw up. My only saving grace was my iPhone with its AirPods. If I didn't have that little device, I would've had to sleep in the car or go to jail for murder. Why did I continue to torture myself? I knew Lu was with Mike, but I just couldn't let go of the idea that it was not meant to be. I couldn't let go of our relationship. In my heart and in my head, Lucinda was my wife. If only I could get her to see that as well.

How in the hell did she get over Mike's tirade in the hotel just like that? When we were together, if I pissed her off, I'd be in for a full week of ass kissing. I couldn't tell you the extreme pleasure it gave me to walk in on Lu and Mike arguing. I was like a kid in a candy store. And I'd even thought I had a little hope when she told Mike that she couldn't hate me. In my mind, that could only mean that she loved me, but sadly, I was mistaken. She didn't love me enough not to get romantic with Mike. Now I'm not saying they were nasty enough to screw while I was in the hotel room, but they might as well have done just that. I couldn't even think about it no more. *Ugh.*

The only joy I had in my life with regard to those two was that I knew I had severely put a monkey wrench in Mike's special night with Lucinda. Well, that and whipping his ass on that basketball court that day just gave me a warm and fuzzy feeling down on the inside. But seriously, what kind of man takes his woman on the same lame-ass date that he took his jump-offs on? Mike was lower than low for that, and Lu deserved so much better. Hell, she had better in me.

I prayed that she would see that Mike was nobody she needed to be involved with. What kind of life could he give her? He had three damn kids already. Count 'em: *uno, dos, tres.* Three! I ain't knocking anybody who had a bunch of kids from finding love. I was just talking about Lu and what she needed and what she didn't. Mike was no good for her and Nadia. I just hoped that Lucinda finally saw that this time around. Not just for the hopes that I could win her heart back, but for herself. She could say what she wanted, but Mike was nothing more than a rebound man for her broken heart, and the moment it healed, he'd be out of a lady. As he should. Waiting to see that happen was driving me crazy because it wasn't happening fast enough.

Since all of those events had taken place, I'd been throwing myself into my work. I had to focus on something besides Lucinda. Besides, National Cross was excited because they got 200 percent out of me every day as they expected with this new position and raise. I hadn't seen Jennifer or Jessica much since I got back from my trip to Illinois. I'd called to check on Jessica and her several times, but that's all the interaction we'd had. At least until today. It was a Saturday night, and I didn't have a thing to do, so when Jennifer called me and asked me to pick up Jessica to give her a break, I was happy to oblige and welcomed the opportunity. Besides, I needed her about as much as she needed me.

When I pulled up to Jennifer's house, there was a gray Infiniti parked in her yard, and I had no idea whose car it was. I figured it was probably a girlfriend of hers and they were about to go out.

"Hey, Al," Jennifer said plainly as she answered the door.

I looked at her in amazement. "Hey." I walked in. "Where are you going?" I asked, admiring her ensemble. She was looking hot.

"Daddy!" Jessica barreled into the living room and hugged me.

"Hey, baby!" I hugged her back. "Are you ready to go?" Instantly, my eyes floated to the man sitting on the sofa. "Who are you?"

He stood up with his hand outstretched. "How are you, my man? The name's Braylon, but they call me Bray."

I slowly shook his hand. He was a real cock-diesel-looking Negro. He was taller than me by a couple of inches and looked like he ate steroids for breakfast, lunch, and dinner. His brain was probably the size of a peanut. *Oh, I know damn well Jennifer isn't going on a date.*

"Bray, huh? Well, I'm Jessica's daddy. What are you doing here?" I asked while Jessica packed up her bags.

"He's here to take me on a date," Jennifer confirmed, then instructed Jessica to get her favorite pillow.

"Jennifer, can I talk to you for a minute?" I asked. We walked into her kitchen. "You didn't tell me you were going on a date."

She looked at me sideways. "I didn't realize I had to. You're not my man." She folded her arms.

"I get that, but you could've given me a little courtesy of knowing what the hell is going on. Besides, I don't know this cat, and he's at your house and in front of my daughter. Come on. Not to mention, he doesn't look like the sharpest knife in the drawer."

Jennifer threw her hands up. "Hold up! You ran your ass halfway around the world to chase your ex-fiancée, and you have an issue with me going on a date? I can't believe you."

"No, what I have an issue with is you bringing this clown to your house. How do you even know this cat?"

"He's one of the trainers at my gym."

Surprise, surprise. "Figures," I mumbled.

"What's that supposed to mean?" Jennifer laughed sinisterly.

I shook it off. "Nothing. Look, I just feel like you could've done this in a better fashion. That's all."

"Well, there are plenty of things you've been doing lately that you could've done better, but you didn't," she shot at me. "Don't be mad because I'm taking your advice and living my life."

"Oh, so you're still mad about the day I left?" I asked, having an epiphany. "Okay, yes, I was rude to leave you down there handling your business, but you don't have to go and do—"

The slap to my face was quick and fierce. I mean, she slapped the hell out of me.

"You are really full of yourself. How dare you assume that I'm doing this because of you? I'm dating because I want to go out with a man who can show me a good time because he genuinely likes me. Me, Aldris. If you want to chase Lucinda for the rest of your life, so be it. I don't give a fuck. But what you don't get to do is tell me you don't want me and then trip because I'm going out with someone who does." She walked off, ending the conversation.

As mad as I was because she slapped me, I deserved it. She was right. If she wanted to go out, I had no right to interfere, but that wasn't my complaint. My complaint was that I didn't want strange-ass men around my daughter. Right now, she was a little too heated for me to tell her that, and I was a little too heated to bring the subject back up. I walked back into the living room where Jessica, Jennifer, and Meathead were sitting.

"Are you ready, baby?" I asked Jessica.

"Yes, Daddy." She stood up and hugged Jennifer. "Good night, Mom. Have a good date."

"Good night, sweetie. I love you." She kissed her forehead.

"Good night, little mama," Bray whatever said to Jessica.

"Her name is Jessica," I corrected him.

"Good night, Aldris," Jennifer said, ushering us to the door.

"Good to meet you too, Jessica's daddy," Bray whatever shouted.

"Likewise, nobody," I called out over my shoulder.

"Leave now," Jennifer gasped as she opened the door, and she pushed me out before shutting the door.

Jessica and I got in the car. "You don't like him, do you, Daddy?" she asked after she was buckled in.

"I just don't know him."

She laughed. "That means you don't like him. Don't worry. I don't like him either."

I laughed. "Why not?"

"He's an airhead," she said.

I burst out laughing. Yep, she was definitely my child. With that, it was time to change the subject from the airhead. "Well, we'll have fun tonight."

Jessica bounced up and down excitedly in her seat before turning her focus back on me. "I have a favor to ask, but you have to promise to do me the favor first before I ask," she said.

Even though I cut my eyes over in curiosity of this favor, I needed to make things up to her in a major way, so instead of questioning her like I should have, I gave in. "Okay. I owe you. Shoot."

"Can I play with Nadia?"

Damn it. I knew I should've pressed her for information first. I gripped the steering wheel and swallowed hard. "Let me see if I can pull some strings for that."

"Tell Ms. Lucinda I really would love to see Nadia."

If only it were that easy. I sat there contemplating how in the hell I would make that happen. I was almost positive that Lucinda wouldn't answer my phone calls. She hadn't done that since we'd broken up. If by some fluke chance she actually made up with Mike, I could guarantee she wouldn't answer. I figured my best bet would be to head to her house and pray that she was there alone with Nadia.

When I pulled up to her condo, there was a space right beside her car. *Great.* She was home and alone. I instructed Jessica to stay in the car while I attempted to pull this off. If it worked, I could possibly be looking at some alone time with Lucinda, which I needed desperately. Maybe I could finally prove my love and prove that Mike was not the one for her.

She answered the door after the second time I rang the doorbell. "Aldris?" she asked with her arms folded.

"Hey, Lu," I said shyly.

"What are you doing here?" she asked with a slight attitude.

"Look, I know we're not together anymore, but I really need to ask you something."

Scoffing, she shook her head in disgust. "Ask me what? Ask me have I seen Mike's face since you pummeled it at the basketball courts?"

The fuck? After that blowup at Nikolai's she was back talking to him? Couldn't be. Not the Lucinda I knew. Hell, the question came out before I had time to reel it back in.

"So you're talking to him?" I refused to believe they were actually talking after all of that. Was she for real?

"I can't believe you. Did you really think beating him up was going to separate us? Or was it your evil attempt at spoiling our date at Nikolai's?" she sneered.

Okay, maybe I should've called first. This wasn't turning out how I'd planned. I never thought I'd walk into the middle of World War III. I put my hands up. "Look. I was just trying to tell you the truth. As for the fight, well, your boy had that coming to him. I'm not here for all of that. I really need to ask you something."

"Like what?" Her voice was thick with revulsion. "Ask me if I'm back with Mike? So what, you thought you could slide back in the front if you could keep us apart?"

"Huh? What? No. Lu, you've got it all wrong."

"Really? Let me get this straight—you're not trying to break us up?"

Okay, that wasn't an easy one to answer because the answer was yes, but at the time, that wasn't what I was there for. "Lu, cut me some slack. Please. I just wanted to ask if Nadia could play with Jessica. I'm sure Nadia misses Jessica, and I'm positive that Jessica misses her. I just wanted to know if I could come over with her and let the girls enjoy each other. I'm sure we could work that out."

She stood there for a moment and eyed me. It was then that I heard commotion in the background. I peered past her and saw Mike's three kids and Nadia playing in the living room. I guessed they were back together, but still, this was for my daughter, so even if I had to endure their relationship, I would to please her.

She put her hand up, shaking her head back and forth. "You are truly certifiable. Sure Jessica wants to see Nadia. How stupid do you think I am? Using your daughter as a ploy to get next to me? How low can you go? As you can see, that will not be happening. Nadia is playing with my man's children. We have a nice combined family over here, so you and your little tactics can kick fucking rocks."

Using my daughter to get next to her? That shit offended the hell out of me. "Whoa! Wait a minute, Lu. I think you need to back it up a little bit and watch your words. This is my daughter you're talking about. I don't give a shit what goes on between me, you, and Mike. I would never use her as a ploy."

Now I loved her, but she was seconds away from crossing a line with me. I may not have been the world's greatest dad, but I took my relationship and feelings for Jessica very seriously. I didn't give a damn who you were.

She rolled her neck and pursed her lips. "I think you're the one who needs to back it up a bit. Back it up off my doorstep with that foolishness. Please. Over here begging for some alone time and using our daughters as bait. Boy, stop. I'll tell you what. Tell 'Jessica' that that won't be happening," she sneered menacingly, using those dumb-ass air quotes.

Her words knocked me back a few. I'd never believe she'd stoop so low, and it pissed me off. Not only was I pissed, but I had an epiphany. For the first time, I looked at her from a brand-new lens, and she was the most ignorant woman on earth to me at that moment. I couldn't believe that was the same woman—correction: chick—I was going to marry. *Marry?* What the fuck was I thinking about? She had the nerve to mock my relationship with my daughter. What kind of human being does that? No matter if she believed me or not, there were just some things you didn't do, and messing with me about my kid was one of them. If she wanted it to be over, fine. I didn't need an immature ex-stripper slut who'd slept with my best friend like her in my life anyway.

"You know what. Never mind. You're right. It won't be happening, and not because you said so, but because I'd rather leave my daughter to play in the street than bring her over here with your immature ass." I turned to walk away.

Just then, Jessica got out of the car, and I stopped. "Ms. Lucinda! Hi! Is it cool? Can I see Nadia?" she asked excitedly.

"Jessica, get back in the car. We're leaving," I demanded.

Lucinda gasped. "*Ay Dios mío!*" she said as she stepped outside and shut the front door. She pulled me back toward her. "Wait, Aldris, I'm so sorry. I thought—"

I turned back toward her, snatching my arm away. "I already heard what you thought, and you disgust me. I get that we're not together. And you know what? Admittedly, deep down a part of me hoped that we could have the alone time to actually talk, but fuck that and fuck you. Of all people, I would've thought you'd know me better than to think I'd ever use my child as a pawn."

"Aldris, there's just been so much that you've done. I just thought . . . I am really very sorry. I should've known better. I apologize." She held her hand over her heart with tears in her eyes. "If Jessica wants to come and play, you all are welcome."

I looked back at Jessica, who was sitting in the car sulking. It hurt me to see her upset, but there was an issue at stake that was far greater than her hurt feelings. I wasn't about to give in. Call it pride or whatever, but the little bit of it that I did have left, I was going to take it with me, get into my car, and spend time with my own daughter. To hell with Lucinda Rojas.

I turned to face her. "No. You go ahead with your little 'combined' family with Mike. Jessica and I are going to be just fine," I said angrily, using the same dumb-ass air quotes she did, and I turned to walk away. But I had more to get off my chest, so I turned back around. "You know, I just have to say this. You and Mike, you two deserve each other. I don't have to stand here and deal with this shit. I don't know what I was thinking about chasing after you after the shit you pulled."

Lucinda covered her mouth as tears streamed down her face. "Aldris, I'm so sorry. Please just calm down, and let's talk about this. Not just this. Everything."

"Now you wanna talk? Fuck that. I know I made my mistake, but you two are as low as and arguably lower than me. My ex-best friend and my ex-fiancée. How nasty is that? You didn't see me cheating with Trinity, LaMeka, or Charice, or going after them when we broke up. No. I would never cross that line. Regardless of what I did, I still had enough respect and love for you and myself not to cross that line. But I should've known you were more his speed than mine anyway. You said so yourself in the beginning. You're a round-the-way kinda chick. Remember that? Humph. Well, I need class in my life. For you to lie your ass down with my best friend only proves that you belonged in Club Moet, and that's exactly where I shoulda left you. Scandalous ass." With that, I walked off and got in my car, not even giving her a slight chance to respond.

"I can't play with Nadia?" Jessica asked.

"No, but don't worry. We'll have a great time together. Anything you want to do, I'm game."

"Even tea parties and playing dress-up?" She giggled.

I gripped the steering wheel, making a mental note to shut my mouth and quit agreeing to terms before I knew them from this point forward. "Yes, even tea parties and dress-up."

She laughed. "This is gonna be fun."

"You bet your as . . . Yes, it will, honey. Yes, it will." I looked at my vibrating cell phone showing Lucinda's contact info. I hit IGNORE, and that time, I meant ignore for good.

Chapter 29

Terrence

It felt great to be back. Since my release from the hospital, Trinity had been absolutely amazing. She had devoted her time to me in a way that only she could. I was so blessed to have a woman by my side who took her vows to heart—in sickness and in health—and for that alone, when I got back to 100 percent, I would forever shower her with whatever she wanted and along with everything she needed. That was my greatest issue. My strength wasn't back completely, and even the simple things sometimes proved to be a feat. I hated feeling handicapped. I couldn't play ball with Terry or hold Tyson or Princess too long. I was a man, so it bothered me that my wife could pick up a box when I couldn't, or that I had to take sit-down breaks when we went out somewhere as simple as the grocery store. Trinity didn't care because her focus was on helping me get better. Hell, she'd have me on bed rest until all cylinders were working if she could. As a man, that bothered me.

It affected everything, and when I say everything, I mean everything. Plain and simple, it bothered me tremendously in the bedroom. I couldn't perform the way I normally could. Basically, anything that required me to put in the work was out of the question, so Trinity was stuck running the show there too. She didn't complain, and she claimed that I still satisfied her, but I didn't believe that for one second. I knew how I used to put it down, and these days I couldn't lay down a pickup stick, let alone some pipelines, no matter how hard I tried. While I was grateful that Trinity stuck beside me through it all, I wasn't convinced that it didn't bother her. How could it not? If it bothered me, I knew it had to bother her.

Another issue I had was with Thomas. I'd made my peace with Aaron shooting me and his death. I'd even gone to his gravesite and told him that I'd forgiven him. However, now that Thomas was over the sadness of losing his brother, he was pissed with Pooch. I was too, but it was time to leave well enough alone. I had had to say goodbye to two family members in two years' time, and after the deaths of little Charity and Aaron, I refused to go to any more funerals. Thomas was going to have to learn to let the anger go. I doubted Pooch would ever be released from prison again, so unless he planned on breaking inside the prison or setting up a hit, he had no choice but to let it go. At least, that was what I was sitting in my living room trying to convince him of.

"How can I just let this go, man?" Thomas asked, drinking some more of his beer. I glanced at him. His eyes were red, and his beard had grown out. I was really worried about him.

"Look, I know it's rough, but think about the stress your mom has been through. Do you really think she needs to see you go to prison or, worse, in a box beside Aaron?"

He eyed me. "You all right?"

His concern came from the grunts I had released simply trying to sit back against the sofa. The pain from my injuries was debilitating. "I'm cool. Just a little pain," I assured him as I reached in my pocket and popped a pain pill into my mouth.

Accepting my answer, he set his beer down and continued his pleas to go after Pooch. "But check it. Look at all he put you through. Setting you up on trumped-up charges, taking your girl, trying to shoot you, and not to mention what he did when he found you and Trinity hanging out in the park. Speaking of, let's not forget all the ill shit he did to her. Dogging her out, beating on her, dogging your kids—"

I put my hand up. "All right! All right! That's enough. Shit." He was making me want to go get his ass my damn self.

"Nah, man. That's the ish you need to hear. We have to think of a plan to put this bitch to sleep once and for all. For you, me, Trinity, and Aaron," Thomas said, hitting his fist on the coffee table.

I exhaled deeply and looked Thomas directly in the eyes. "You know how I got this big, nice house, my career, my loving wife, and my beautiful kids back? By being smart," I said matter-of-factly, pointing my index finger to my head. "Making smart moves. Not letting my emotions take over to the point where I do stupid shit. That shit you're talkin' is stupid, and it's reckless. I'm mad. You're mad. Hell, the whole family mad. But some shit you just have to let God and time handle. That's real talk."

Heated, Thomas stood up. "Let's talk about what this is really about, T. You're pissed because my brother shot you and slept with your wife. Rather than defend his honor, you wanna be a pussy and cop out."

What? That guy was on some wild shit now for real. My cousin—his brother—had lost his life behind that bullshit, and he was claiming I didn't care. Yes, it hurt to know that Aaron betrayed me, but I was man enough to realize that Aaron had issues. He'd also been trapped undercover for years under Pooch, and the mental damage was real. He didn't know how to press the off switch, and that drove him insane. On top of that, he was jealous, and he wanted what I had. Shit, who didn't? I was just as foolish over Trinity as Aaron and Pooch were. Did that mean I wanted to see him or anybody else die over that bullshit? No. Hell no. I knew better than anyone else that there was no coming back if God decided it was your time to check out of here. That was some shit I'd never in my life play with ever again.

At any rate, it was time for Thomas to leave, because there was some shit you just didn't say and lines that you didn't cross. He was at his limit. "I think you better leave, because not only is that not true, but you making me wanna kick your ass for it."

"Then use that anger. Use it toward Pooch. I've admired you my entire life. I get that you've always been smart, a smooth operator. But it's time for the inner goon to stand up. How you just gonna let that nigga take away our family and not do something about it?"

"'Cause I wanna live to grow old with my wife and see my grandkids and great-grandkids. My priorities are different, Thomas. Once you get a wife and a child, then you can talk to me about an inner goon. When you have a family, your own family, there's some stuff you just let go of, and you do it for them not for yourself. I'm good with seeing that nigga rot in prison if it means I can live my life and be happy and alive."

He laughed cynically. "It's always about you and your family. What about your extended family?"

Fine. He wanted to play that game, so I flipped the script on his ass. "Are you asking your mother to set up a hit on Pooch? No. You want her to be at peace. That's all I want too. For you, my entire family, and myself—peace."

"Fine. If you won't help me, I'll figure it out on my own."

Before I could try to stop him, we saw the door open. Just then, Trinity and the kids walked in the house. "Hey, baby!" she greeted me as the kids ran to the sofa where I was sitting. "What's good, Thomas?"

"Hey, babe. Hey, kiddos. Speak to your cousin Thomas," I instructed my kids after hugging them.

"Hey, Thomas," they said in unison.

He smiled and nodded at them. "Sup, kids. Sup, Trinity."

By then, Trinity had made her way to the sofa, so she bent down and kissed me. "Everything all right?" she asked, eyeballing Thomas.

Signaling for her to let it go, I shook my head as I kissed Tyson's forehead. He was sleeping like a log. "Kids, how about you all go play outside for a bit?" It didn't take them but a split second to hit the backyard.

"I'm going upstairs to lay Tyson in his crib. I'll be back," Trinity said and playfully blew kisses at me.

After the room was cleared from my wife and kids, Thomas and I stared at each other for a few minutes not really having much to say on the subject. I'd put my feelings on the line, and he put his out there. I was just hoping he'd see my point of view.

"I know you have a life now, but my brother was all I had," Thomas said sadly as he gulped down some beer, obviously trying to mask his pain.

"Not true, my man. You have me. Always."

He glanced over at me and swiped a tear from his eye.

"Listen, Thomas. Just don't do anything. Let it go."

We dropped the subject and got quiet again when we heard footsteps coming down the stairs. We both knew it was Trinity, and the last thing I wanted was for her to worry about me or Thomas when it concerned Pooch. Hell, I didn't want her worried about Pooch at all. She'd been through enough behind the men in her life, including me, and my only wish was for her to live happy and unbothered. I owed that to her.

"What's going on?" She crossed her arms.

Thomas picked up his beer. "Nothing, Trin. Just choppin' it up with my cousin. I'm 'bout to head out."

"Okay, well, you're welcome to stay for dinner," she invited him.

"Nah, I don't want to intrude on the family time," Thomas said snidely.

After that slick-ass comment, it was definitely time to see Thomas to the door. I didn't want to feel disrespected in my home, because then we'd have a new set of problems. I stood up and winced in pain.

"Honey, sit down. You're hurting," Trinity ordered, coming to help me up.

"I'm fine, Trinity." I shooed her hands away.

"No, you're not—"

"I said I was fine, damn." I didn't mean to be harsh, but I was tired of being petted, and I was tired of everyone telling me what to do.

She cleared her throat as she and Thomas looked back and forth between me and each other. Finally, she spoke again. "I'm going in the kitchen to start dinner. Thomas, it's always good to see you." She turned and walked away without giving Thomas or me time to respond.

I could tell she felt embarrassed, and that made me feel horrible. She was only trying to help. "Trinity," I called out, but she kept walking. "Damn," I mumbled. I knew I had fucked up.

Thomas laughed devilishly. "You might be right, cuz. You got enough issues to deal with at the house. I'm out."

With that, Thomas shook his head and left. I walked to the door to make sure it was shut and locked, then went back to the living room to sit down. I plopped down on the sofa and pulled out two more pain pills and swallowed them. I closed my eyes and tried to will the pain and Thomas's request away.

"How many pain pills have you taken?" I heard Trinity ask.

"Just this one," I lied.

"I'm not trying to be mean or anything, baby, but you may need to calm down with that. At least a little bit."

"If I'm hurting, I take them with caution. Why should I even explain this? I'm the one in pain here, not you." I opened my eyes to see her standing in front of me.

"Fine," she said, irritation displayed all over her as she threw her hands up and turned to walk away.

Fuck me. I'd done it again in less than five minutes. What was wrong with me? I stood up. "Trinity. Wait. I'm sorry. I didn't mean to snap at you. I'm just frustrated and tired."

She turned to look at me. She looked angry, as if she were about to plow into me, but then she just exhaled and shrugged her shoulders. "Okay. I love you, Terrence. I just want what's best for you. I hope you remember that."

"I know," I said as she went back to the kitchen.

I sat on the sofa, and soon sleep found its way into my eyes. Yes, this was what I needed. A relief from my pain and my troubles.

Chapter 30

Pooch

Day in and day out of this muthafucka was driving me crazy. For the first time in a long time, I felt alone. Most of my fam was locked up or dead. I hadn't talked to my mom in years. She'd wanted me to get out of the game ever since Pops died, but I didn't, so we kinda kept our distance. My sister was the only one who kept in contact with me, but that was limited. She had kids of her own, and she didn't need or want any heat around her because of my issues. Trinity hated me. Lisa damn sure hated me. And there was no question that Flava hated me. To top that off, I was broke as a joke for the first time that I could remember, and I hadn't seen my daughter in forever.

The only people on my team and by my side were Adrienne and Attorney Stein. I couldn't tell you how sick and tired I was of entertaining Adrienne's ass when all she wanted to do was discuss her kids and Flava. I didn't give a damn about her kids, and why would I want to hear her talking about how much she was in love with the woman I was gonna try to get with if I ever got out of this bitch? I was cool with a whole threesome every now and again, but that broad was acting like we were the new black Brady Bunch. I didn't give a damn about her. To me, she was damaged goods. A woman scorned.

Not to mention she was only one visit or phone call away from Wolf. After I set his ass up, ain't no way I wanted to cross paths with him again. Don't get me wrong, Pooch ain't scared of no muthafucka, but that don't mean I went knocking on the devil's door either. You stay alive longer in this game by staying low-key and only dishing out heat when it's brought to your doorstep. Bring that shit to another nigga if you want to. Nine times outta ten, that's your ass. Trust me. I'd seen it too many times to count.

At any rate, I was glad to have some contact with the outside world even if it was with Adrienne, although she was not on my list of important people. Then Stein gave me the bad news: Trinity refused to help. Ain't that a bitch? I had a chance to shoot her ass and Dreads's if I wanted to, but did I do it? No. All because of this fucked-up love I had for her. Why couldn't that love shit inside of me just die? This bitch had a true gangsta heart. She cheated on me, got pregnant with Terrence's baby, risked her life to save his, slapped my ass while I was shot, and had the nerve to arrogantly deny helping me. Using my catch phrase on me. Who the hell did she think she was? I'd killed niggas for lesser offenses. If it weren't for me, Memorial Gardens Cemetery would've been a family affair not only for Big Cal, but for her and Terrence, and she was treating me like this. See why I was pissed about my emotions?

That was what I was trying to tell my grandma: mutha-fuckas ain't just gon' let you do right. Here I was trying my best to turn over a new leaf and be a good person, and that bitch wanna act stupid. In the words of Forrest Gump, "Stupid is as stupid does." And she was 'bout to see who the stupidest nigga was in town. My motto: use what you got to get what you want.

"Sup, Adrienne." I gave her a hug.

"Hey, Pooch. How are you holding up?"

"It is what it is. You know. I'm Pooch. I'll survive," I told her as we sat down.

"Made any new friends?" she asked me, smiling and shit.

New friends? Where the hell did she think I was? In a clubhouse? This wasn't *Camp Rock* or *High School Musical* or another one of them crazy-ass Disney Channel shows I couldn't stand. This was the state penitentiary. You didn't make friends here. You made alliances. Right now, the only alliance I had was my roommate, and me and that nigga just spoke to each other. This was exactly why I didn't like to fuck with her. She had no clue.

Instead, I laughed that shit off. "Nah, man. Same ol' same. Talkin' wit' my roommate and biding my time. How's Flava?" I shifted the conversation before she started pissing me off with these ignorant-ass questions.

"Her trial is Monday. I think she's gonna win. You know I'm going to be there for her every step of the way."

"That's good. Tell her I said good luck and to keep her head up. Let her know I'm still thinkin' 'bout her and that I'm sorry for all this shit that went down."

"I'll tell her, but you know she's still pissed with you. I keep telling her that you love her and that you are sorry, but she ain't trying to hear that. She may come around once all this is over. She has to so we can be a family." She reached out and held my hand.

That's that dumb shit. Straight lu-lu. "Yeah. Keep talkin' to her."

"Stein is working hard on your defense. He's still gonna try to get Trinity to testify on your behalf, though. I brought what you asked me for," she said, dropping her voice low.

"A'ight. Slide it all to me under the table nice and slow," I instructed, and she followed. "I appreciate this. You did good." I winked at her.

"Anything for my man and my woman."

Her man? Flava had really driven this heifer "cuckoo for Cocoa Puffs." "Well, thanks. Tell Stein I said I'll see him next week." I stood up. It was time to dismiss her.

She stood up. "I can stay longer if you want."

"Nah. Get home to your babies. I got some business to handle anyway."

"You're so thoughtful." She rubbed the side of my face. "I wish Flava could see that you only did what you did because you wanted to see your daughter. I will have to talk to her some more. We can't let her break up the family."

She was just as gullible as she wanted to be. No wonder Wolf was able to reel her in with a few kind words back when her sister left him, and he went whining to her through letters. Hell, Flava too, for that matter. I'd told her that I was hurt by Trinity for lying about my son and taking my daughter away, and that was why I agreed to Big Cal's scheme to get rid of Trinity. At the time, I was so ready to get out of prison and so pissed off with Trinity about my son, I would've done anything Big Cal asked. At any rate, I knew Flava would believe that, and I needed somebody on my team. I figured it may as well be her because she was free and she was in contact with Flava. It really wasn't a lie. In some ways, that Christian thing was working out. It just wasn't the whole truth or even the primary reason for me agreeing to the scheme, but a reason was a reason was a reason.

And there went her crazy ass talking 'bout family again. She had me fucked up. That sounded like some ol' cult shit to me. *She ain't 'bout to get me outta prison, dress me in red robes, and have me drinking the Jesus juice. No haps.* The next thing I knew I'd be sitting in the middle of the expressway playing the guitar and singing "Kumbaya." *Shittin' me.* It was official. Adrienne had to go.

I grabbed her hand and winked at her. "Atta girl. You do that for me. Keep talkin' to Flava and having her back for me."

"Of course," she agreed and walked up to me.

Before I knew anything, she pulled me to her for a kiss. That bitch had some soft lips, and she was the best kisser I'd ever had. No lie. Yes, even better than Trinity. Of course, Trinity wasn't much for kissing, and it wasn't her kisses that had me insane anyway. As bad as I needed some pussy, her kiss was actually satisfying. No wonder Flava was just as in love with her. I bet she could eat the hell outta some pussy. I had to resist the urge to imagine her giving me a blow job, or I'd be as hard as a rock. Okay, so maybe I needed her to stick around for little bit if I got out of this joint.

"Damn, girl."

She winked at me. "Didn't know I had it in me, huh? Just a little pre-celebration kiss for your release and Flava's. That's all."

"I can't wait to get to the actual celebration."

"I can't either. It's going to be a three-way blast," she said seductively.

Down boy. No rising for the occasion. Down, I willed myself. Okay, so one good weekend with Adrienne, but that was it.

"I will talk with you later."

"Okay, Pooch. Hold it down, baby." She hugged me. This time I hugged her back.

"Hold it down for me too."

That was when the guard came to take me away. As we walked, the guard spoke up to me. "You got it?"

"Yeah." I handed him two $100 bills.

"Nice doing business with you, inmate." He opened the door to my cell. "Don't get caught, or it's me and you," he whispered.

"A'ight, CO Smith. I got you. Just make sure that room-mate of mine stays gone for a while."

"I've got Johnson under control." He unlocked my cuffs.

"Thirty minutes. That's it."

"Cool. One more question."

"What is it, Smalls? You know you're on your thirty minutes now, right?"

"Yeah." My attitude was evident. I hated these fuckin' pigs. "You think you can hook me up with some pussy?"

He laughed. "That's gonna cost you five more."

"Damn." I shook my head. "Ain't nobody free or cheaper?"

"Yeah, you can get that fine-ass dime piece who came to visit you for free, but you gotta pay me five for the room. Other than that, it's five for the woman."

Greedy bastard. "A'ight. I'm straight."

"Lotion will become your best friend. Well, either that or a booty hole," he joked, but I didn't see shit funny.

Did they get a kick off this gay shit that went down in the prison? Man, please. The day I became cool with that was the day I was gonna hang myself. Real talk. If that was all I had to be proud of, then I was gonna hold on to that forever.

Speaking of, I grabbed my lotion bottle and headed to the side of the bunks. You already know the deal. Five minutes later, I was pressure free, and that left twenty minutes to handle my real business. I pulled out the pre-paid cell phone that Adrienne snuck in for me. Thanks to CO Smith I didn't have to do a search, courtesy of my $200 that Adrienne brought as well. Stein was a great lawyer, but I had to take some shit into my own hands. Starting now.

"Hello." Trinity's voice came crashing through the phone.

"Good to hear your voice, Trin."

She gasped. "Pooch?" she whispered. "How the fuck did you get my home number? And how the hell did you manage to call me without it being a collect call? Are you out?" she rolled off in a barrage of questions.

"It's good to hear from you too. I got your little message, and I must say I'm pissed about it, but I guess I trained your coldhearted ass well."

"Are you out?" she asked again more demandingly.

"Doesn't matter. Here's what does. I need your help. You have to testify on my behalf."

"I don't have to do shit," she sneered.

Oh, the advantage she had with me being locked up. I took a deep breath to keep my composure. "No, you don't, but here are the facts: I could've shot you and your husband, but I didn't because I care about you. I love our daughter, and I want a chance to be free to do right by her. Real talk. So on the humble, I'm askin'."

I swear to God it took everything in me to remain calm and humble myself to her mercy. What I really wanted to say was that I would find her and choke her ass to death if she didn't do it.

"You don't care about Princess. She doesn't even know you. She has a daddy in her life, and as for Terrence and me, well, I guess you shoulda taken the shot, you rotten bastard," she said tensely. "How'd you get my number?"

My jaw locked tight. My inner goon was screaming to be free. I could hear his ass now: *Get that bitch, Pooch. Ooh, get her! See why nice guys finish last? Plan B.*

"Fine. You don't have to help me, but ask yourself this: do you want to spend the rest of your life lookin' over your shoulder? See, what I'm promising you in exchange for your testimony is peace. You and Terrence free to be happy and live your life. I won't interfere. That's my word. I just ask that when I'm released and I get my shit together, you give me the opportunity to be in Princess's life, but if you don't give your testimony, you'll always wonder."

"What is that supposed to mean?"

"Come on, Trin. You ain't stupid. Far from it. But I'll break it down for you. If you don't help me, you better be ready for war at anyplace or anytime. Now are you willin' to risk that? You could be in the park wit' the kids, shopping at the grocery store, or just sittin' at the traffic light and shit could go down. Do you want to take that chance? What if Brittany, Terry, Princess, and Tyson are wit' you? You just got your Dreads back. Do you wanna risk that again?"

"I know damn well you ain't threatening me. How the fuck you form your mouth to ask to spend time with Princess and the next thing you tell me is that you're going to get at me and my family if I don't give you what you want? You heartless bastard. I gave you two and a half years of my life and a child, plus I subjected my other two children to your foolishness, and this is how you do us? They're kids, Pooch. I can't believe you. No, as a matter of fact, I can."

"Well, what can I say? I told you I had to get myself together first before I could be the father Princess needs." I swear people don't listen. I was trying to be a Christian about it. She was forcing me to be a gangsta. So I gave her one last peace offering. "I put it to you this way. I can guarantee nothing will happen to any of the kids regardless of your decision. See, I do have a heart, but trust me, that's only because Princess is my child, and she will need her brothers and sister later in life. What I can't promise is the same for you and Terrence. Now it's your choice. You can wait it out and see how long you get to be parents, or you can live in peace for the remainder of your lives. That's all I can offer you."

She paused for a long while. Then she sighed. "If I do this for you, you have to promise me one more thing."

She was really trying my fucking patience and using up my time. "What, Trinity?"

"That you leave Princess alone. Let me and Terrence raise her and be parents to her. I won't turn her against you, but she won't be allowed to see you until she's eighteen, and then it will be her choice if she wants to get to know you. Giving me peace means absolute peace, and this is the only way I can ensure that," Trinity bargained.

"But I want to take care of her—"

"Then put your money into an interest-bearing account for her until she is eighteen. But don't send it to me. Leave her alone, and let us raise her. Those are my terms. Take them or leave them."

Give up my child for my freedom. Now that was a hell of a decision. A year ago, I probably would've jumped at that deal because being a father didn't mean shit to me. In the strangest way, though, being locked up made me want to be a father. I guessed it was part of the opportunity to try again, or maybe being a father gave me some kind of hope to keep me from going back to prison. I didn't know. I had to look at this logically. What kind of example could I possibly be for Princess? Not to mention, I had to get myself together, and all of that was based on if I even got released. Wouldn't it be better for her if she lived her life without me, at least until she was old enough to make her own decisions and live her own life?

"Will you promise to keep my sister informed about her? Send her pictures and things as she grows up?"

She swallowed hard. "I can do that."

I sighed heavily. "Then I'll agree to it. I'll leave you and Terrence completely alone and Princess until she's eighteen in exchange for your testimony."

"For real?"

"Yes. Now do we have a deal or what?"

"Yes. I'll call Attorney Stein on Monday. You'd just better not go back on your word."

"I promise I won't. I've got to go. And, Trinity, thank you."

"Wow. Gratitude has never been your forte."

"I told you I do have a heart."

"Bye, Pooch."

"Bye, babe."

Even after we hung up, I stared at the phone for a second. Deep down, I'd always love her ass just as much as I hated her. Thug passion, you gotta love it. I hid my phone, and then a little while later, Johnson came back to the cell.

"What's up, young cat?" he asked.

"Nothing, old man." I gave my respectful greeting to him as I climbed on the top bunk.

I thought about my new plan to get out of this hellhole. I couldn't wait until my trial. Freedom was just Trinity's testimony away.

Chapter 31

LaMeka

I was so thoroughly pissed with Gavin that I gave him the cold shoulder all night long. He kept asking if anything was wrong, and I kept dismissing him. Finally, Gavin decided to leave well enough alone, and eventually, we fell asleep back-to-back instead of in each other's arms the way that we normally would. Generally, when I was that pissed, I tossed and turned all night, but last night, I slept well. In fact, I slept too well. I kept having pleasant dreams about Gavin. I even had a dream about our wedding day. I'd never dreamt of that day before. Not that I didn't eventually want to get married, but I just never took the time to think about it. Hell, that dream seemed so far out of reach for me when I was with Tony that I guessed I just got used to being a man's old lady instead of his wife.

The whole thing had me thinking. I had a really good man in Gavin. Compared to what I had and what I'd seen, there was no comparison. A real man was hard to find, but a real good man was even harder to find, and I had both qualities in Gavin. A real man was someone who financially supported himself and his family. Who does the manly things, you know? Changed the oil on time, cut the grass, and fixed things around the house all without having to be asked. But a good man? Oh, he was going to be the one who encouraged you, helped with the kids, supported your dreams as well as your household, and proved that you were his one and only, not just his number one. Hell, I didn't have anything real or good in Tony, and in Gavin I had both.

Now that a cooler head prevailed, I felt bad for setting Gavin up. I wasn't satisfied with what I had or the lack thereof in Tony, and now, I wasn't satisfied with what I had in Gavin. What in the hell was wrong with me? His family had nothing to do with our relationship, and perhaps I was being intrusive by forcing the issue. It wasn't like I didn't know who Gary was. He was his brother, not some gay lover. Not only that, but I was also inviting drama to his job, which I did not condone. I realized that I might get caught in the middle of some true bullshit because I really didn't know what the true deal was with his family. Now I regretted my decision to go along with Gary's plan because I had no clue of the ramifications of being a party to this scheme.

Once at work, I made the decision to tell Gavin before it was too late. It was already a few minutes after nine, and I figured his brother might not even show up, but in the event that he did, I had to be truthful with him.

I went to the main nurse's station, where Gavin was standing and reviewing the charts. "Hey, you got a minute?"

He looked down at his watch. "I'm kinda busy now. Can we talk in, say, ten minutes?" he asked without looking up.

"It's kind of important."

He shrugged. "Now you want to talk," he quipped, still not looking up at me.

Now was not the time for his petty attitude. "Listen, I was an ass last night, but I really, really need to talk to you." I hoped my admission was enough to get him to sense the alarm in my voice.

"Don't worry. He doesn't have much time to speak to anyone these days," a man's voice floated from behind me, causing both Gavin and me to turn around.

Gavin sucked his teeth. "What are you doing here?"

"Is that any way to greet your only brother?" Gary asked.

Gary was almost the spitting image of Gavin, but one thing was notably different. Gary looked like he had plenty of money. There was money, and then there was *money*. I'm talking about *money*. He had on a tailored suit and a French-cuff shirt with diamond cuff links. Even his speech reeked of sophistication and class. He literally looked like he stepped off the pages of *Forbes* magazine. I was amazed. I expected, hell, I didn't know what I expected, but it damn sure wasn't that. What the hell was really going on?

"I told you I wouldn't be at work today," Gavin snarled.

"Well, imagine my surprise to find you here," Gary said curtly.

"Meet me at my house later. I get off at six tonight," Gavin said quickly.

"I don't have the time. I have an important dinner meeting scheduled with some developers, and I can't cancel it."

"Well, I'm in the middle of work too. I'm sure you understand."

He chuckled. "Our father is this hospital's number one contributor. I'm positive they won't mind you taking a break to speak with your beloved brother."

Hold up. Wait a minute. Number one contributor as in financial contributor? That man told me he grew up poor. He was raised by his mother, who raised two boys and struggled on her own. Was that even the same person who told me these things?

At that revelation, I couldn't help but intrude. "Excuse me. Did you just say, 'contributor'?"

From a distance, I heard someone say, "The shit hath hitteth the fan," and I turned to see Sara and Jeanine with one of my classmates standing in the cut. *Great. An audience.* Just what I needed.

"Yes, I did. You must be new here," he said.

I nodded. "Yes, I'm a student going through—"

"Let's just go in the breakroom," Gavin said to Gary, cutting me off.

Gary gave me the full once-over. "Let me see if I can take an educated stab at this one. LaMeka, right?"

I blushed and nodded. "Yes, and you must be Gary."

"The one and only."

Gavin's eyes flew up in surprise. He stepped forward between us with his hand up, tossing a stare back and forth between Gary and me. "Wait a minute. How do you know her name?" Gavin asked.

"So you haven't told your family about us?" I blurted out more in shock than anything else.

"There are a lot of things that Gavin doesn't tell me about," Gary butted in with an attitude.

Gavin looked at me, ignoring his brother. "No, I haven't, but there is a perfectly good reason for that." His expression looked suddenly panicked.

He was panicked, and I was livid. All this time he had been with me, he'd been laughing it up with my mom and sister, wining and dining me, hitting this good stuff between my legs, staying at my house, and playing Daddy to my kids, and his family didn't know about me when it was obvious that they most certainly communicated? Oh, hell yeah, I was blown the hell up.

I placed my hands on my hips. "So what was that good reason, Gavin?"

He looked at his brother, then back at me. "Let's not do this here."

"Then where?" My annoyance was at an all-time high. "I'm tired of being in the dark."

Gavin held his head. Aggravation showed on his face. He looked around at the crowd that was drawing together. "Everybody get back to work. Gary and LaMeka, come with me," he said sternly.

Gary and I followed him into one of the staff break-rooms. As I passed Jeanine and Sara, they just shook their heads at me as if to say they felt sorry for me. I didn't know what was going on, but today was the day I got my answers. Gavin shut the door as Gary and I looked back and forth at each other.

"You shouldn't have come here. I told you I'd deal with you when I had a chance," Gavin spewed at his brother.

"You shouldn't have lied to me. You said you weren't going to be at work, and imagine my shock when I found out you were going to be here," Gary shot back.

"And just how did you find that out, might I ask?" Gavin asked, folding his arms across his chest.

Gary laughed and nodded toward me. "Your friend told me."

Umm. Now would be the time that my anger shifted. *Damn white boy. Ain't nothing but a snitch.* As Gavin looked at me, I looked away.

"So, Meka, when did you talk to my brother?" he asked, walking up on me. "Hmm? You wanna fill me in? Because I don't ever remember me giving you the phone and saying, 'This is my brother, Gary. Talk to him.' I think I would've remembered something like that," he said angrily.

"Well, he called while you were in the shower last night. I didn't think there'd be any harm in you talking to your brother since you told me you hadn't spoken in months, which apparently was a bald-faced lie on your part."

"I didn't lie. I said we haven't really talked in months. Meaning we've spoken, but he doesn't listen to me, and I don't listen to him. We have a very complicated relationship. You had no right to stick your nose where it did not belong."

Pisstivity reactivated. Did he just say what I think he said? "Excuse me? Where it didn't belong? You betta hold the fuck up. I don't know who you think you're talkin' to, but I'm not one of these little girls you can raise up at and think I'm just gonna take it. I will bring it to you, so don't take it there with me, Gavin." My anger had moved me from classy to sassy in zero seconds flat.

"And there it is." Gary pointed as he sat down with his legs crossed. I hadn't even noticed that the snitch had poured himself a cup of coffee and was watching us. "This is why we bump heads, Gavin. Right here."

"Shut up, Gary," Gavin scowled.

"What is he talkin' about?"

"Nothing," Gavin said, then turned to his brother. "Shut your mouth, Gary, before I shut it for you."

"Ooh. I'm so scared," Gary said cynically. "Why don't you just tell her for Christ's sake?"

I pushed Gavin. "What is it, huh? You've got a baby's mama? No, I know what it is: a secret family up north somewhere. Maybe you're a down-low man."

Gavin gripped my shoulders. "Everything I've told you about me is real, but you're crossing the line. I don't have no secret family, outside kids, and you know good and fucking well I'm not gay. Stop it and finish your rounds. We'll deal later."

"We deal now or not at all," I demanded. "Now I'm not stupid. Either you're a liar or your brother is one. I want to believe it's him, but you have to tell me so."

Gavin looked at me as if the weight of the world were on his shoulders. Then Gary heaved a long sigh. "Oh, for Christ's sake! I can't take this melodrama anymore. LaMeka, Gavin is not going to tell you. He's so much like our mother it's pathetic."

"Muthafucka." He turned his full attention to Gary. "Shut up, and leave my mother's name out of your fucking mouth," Gavin snarled.

"You shut up." Gary stood up. "He probably told you that he and I grew up with our mother, who was poor. That's true, but she chose that lifestyle. She had the opportunity to be a woman of great power, but she chose to live like an animal all to keep us away from our father. Our father, Gerald Randall, is one of the wealthiest and most powerful men in Virginia. I moved in with him by choice when I became a teenager. I begged my brother to come to get away from the life Mama was providing for us, but no. Mama's boy had to stay. Had to protect his mama," Gary said harshly.

"Say one more thing about Mama and your ass is gonna be in one of these hospital beds in the ER," Gavin said angrily.

Gary cringed. "I perish the thought. County ER is a melting pot for the homeless, helpless, and the hood." He made a fist reminiscent of the Black Panthers and looked at me.

It was my turn to be offended and appalled. "Excuse me?"

He pointed at me. "This is what I'm talking about. Dad put you through college, Gavin. He set you up with a trust fund even though you had Mom's meager life insurance that she only left for you. He hand-picked a college just so you could become one of the greatest doctors in the world, despite the fact that he offered you a plush job within the firm. All you had to do was make a choice to be a reputable son of his. You gave it all up to be a damn nurse in the county ER and bed women of lesser stature," Gary proclaimed.

"Lesser stature," I repeated as if I didn't hear him correctly.

"Yes. I'm sure you don't know what that means—"

No, the fuck he didn't. I looked at him and rolled my eyes, interrupting him. "I know exactly what that means, and as long as you don't call yourself referring to me, then you can say it as much as you like."

Gary laughed. "You're a feisty one. But of course I wasn't referring to just you." He stood and faced me. "I was referring to you and all the other women he's dated just like you and your kind."

"My kind? What kind is that? Educated women?"

He chuckled. "You're cute. You know what I mean, gal. Black women."

"You son of a bitch!" I was two seconds from showing him exactly what the hell my kind could and would do, but Gavin jumped between us.

"Oh, don't go all 'ghetto' on me, please," Gary said, throwing his hands up in a condescending way. "I actually kinda like you, though. I can see why Gavin does. There's nothing like a little hood one in your life. You can do all the things with them that you can't with your wife. Dad and I both have one of you in our back pockets because your little freaky asses sure know how to make a man holler just to get a dollar," he joked.

The next thing I knew, Gavin hauled off and punched his brother square in the jaw. Gary went reeling back and fell straight on his ass. "Now you holla, muthafucka," Gavin said angrily. "Don't talk to her like that."

He sighed and got up, holding his face. "I figured this was going on. Why can't you do like Dad and I ask you and get what you need from these women and move on? Dad says it's time to find a wife and give him a grandbaby. For heaven's sake, keep Meka. Surely, she'll be willing to take your cash to take care of her baby's daddy and her little ghetto offspring. I'm sure she has some. They all do. Find a nice, wholesome, educated, Christian white girl. Marry her, and have a son or daughter, and get your freaky on the side." He moved his jaw. "Damn. This is gonna swell, and if you knocked out my crown, I'm gonna hurt your ass."

I couldn't believe what I heard. Had I gotten involved with the offspring of the Ku Klux Klan? *Oh, my God.* This was some shit I never bargained for. Of all the things I expected, I never expected this. Gavin was blacker than some black men, and his brother, and apparently father, were the biggest racists I'd ever met in my life. What had I gotten myself into?

"Fuck you, Gary, and fuck Dad too. I'm not living my life for y'all. I never have and I never will," Gavin spewed. "And what you will not do is disrespect my woman like that. Not now. Not ever."

"Fine. See how long you keep your job if Dad pulls his funding from this damn dump. Whether you like it or not, you're stuck with us. You can change women, but you can't change blood," Gary said sardonically.

Immediately, tears sprang to my eyes. What had I done? I'd fucked up so bad, and now the outcome was real. My relationship with Gavin was doomed, and it was my own fault. As much as I loved him, I couldn't be with him, because Gary was right. His family would not allow it. I couldn't believe that, in this day and age, I felt like it was 1964. My heart was broken. It was in that moment that I thought of the possibility of being Mrs. Gavin Randall and how that would never come true.

"Meka, baby, are you all right?" Gavin asked, holding me by my waist.

I shook my head. "I'm just gonna go."

"Don't leave like this. Don't pay any attention to him. You and I know what's real between us." Gavin wiped my tears.

"Gavin . . ."

"Baby," he begged. Everything in him was begging me not to let him go.

Gary's cold stare penetrated our moment, and I glanced over at him in disbelief. His look said it all. Pure disgust. I turned back to Gavin and hugged him. "I love you."

He held me tight, breathing a sigh of relief. "I love you too, baby—"

"But it will never work," I cut him off. "We aren't meant to be. Listen to your brother." I caressed his face.

"No!"

I nodded as more tears fell. "It's okay. Just promise me, promise me, you'll marry someone who loves you just as much as I do." I let him go and walked toward the door.

"Meka! Don't leave me," Gavin said, sounding hurt and defeated.

As I went to respond, Gary intervened. "Go, Meka. You made the right choice. I knew I liked you," Gary mocked.

Horror, embarrassment, and sadness overcame me as I swung the door open before Gavin could open his mouth. I headed straight for the time clock and punched out.

"He broke up with you, didn't he?" Sara asked as all the nurses looked at me.

"No, bitch. I broke up with him." I hauled ass out of the hospital, leaving them and Gavin behind. I could say one thing: I got my answers. Now that was all I had.

Chapter 32

Gavin

"Now perhaps we can get down to business," Gary said as if LaMeka didn't just storm out of the breakroom.

"Go to hell." I left him where his evil ass stood and ran out after the love of my life. As soon as I reached the floor, I saw Jeanine and Sara. "Have you seen—"

"She clocked out and left," Jeanine stated, cutting me off.

I ran toward the entrance where I knew LaMeka parked. I was furious with Gary, with her, and most of all with myself. I should've told her the truth from the beginning. I should've told her that my father was a high-powered technology mogul worth millions of dollars. I should've told her that my brother was his right-hand man and that he and I were both heirs to the throne of the Rand Technologies empire. Even though my dad was disappointed in my career paths and choices in women, he still wouldn't deprive me, because I was his son. How I wished to hell I wasn't.

I didn't tell Meka because I knew it would scare her off, and I didn't want that. Not because my family was a bunch of white-collar multimillionaires, but because, to their core, they were nothing but a bunch of redneck bigots. My dad's motto: do business with them, do lunch with them, and even "do" them, but do not settle with them. "Them" being any woman of a different culture, but especially black women. He was cool with having black friends and business associates and, hell, even screwing a black woman, but what he did not condone and would never condone was his pure white blood mixing with any other race. If my wife and kids were not 100 percent Caucasian Americans, then there would be hell to pay.

That was why my mom chose not to deal with him and tried her best to keep us from him. She said my dad was a hypocrite and a racist, and she refused to allow him to turn her boys into hateful creatures like him. She tried, but she lost Gary along the way. You see, our dad refused to help my mother unless she allowed him into our lives, and my mother refused to get help from our dad because she didn't want him in our lives. Gary wasn't truly racist, just materialistic—another one of my dad's traits—so once my dad was able to find us and latch on to Gary, it was a wrap. He wanted the best of everything that Mom couldn't afford to offer him, so when my father showed up willing to give us everything we wanted and more, Gary shoved his good home training down the tubes for the promise of a more comfortable life. I guessed after faking for so long, he'd actually begun to believe in that crap, but it wasn't my brand of bullshit.

In the past, I'd allowed my dad and brother to come between me and my lady at the time because I was too afraid to walk away from them. In a family as powerful as mine, you don't just walk away from them. It was like a forced marriage. I wasn't like Gary, and I never would've dealt with our dad, but I allowed my dad into my life at the request of my brother. I thought I was doing the right thing by giving Gerald a chance. At first, I was a little bitter that he had never been there when we were growing up, so anything he wanted to do for me, I took it just to be spiteful, but taking it came with a price. My dad had funded my education and a portion of my lifestyle, so I felt indebted to him. Hell, I was indebted to him, and I found out quickly that with Gerald everything was business, even family. "An eye for an eye" to him meant "I helped you, so you abide by my rules." Leave it to his prejudiced ass to loathe the thought of his sons being with another race, especially the only race I was attracted to: black women. Regretfully, I allowed the perks and my indebtedness to him to get the best of me a few times with a few women. I chucked it up because, at the end of the day, the women I was involved with didn't mean much to me—at least not enough for me to turn my back on my family.

Regardless of their cruel ways, Gerald was still my dad, and Gary was still my brother. So when they grew tired of me playing in the massa's house, as they called it, I'd always let my lady friend go about her way. But not this time. This time it was real to me. I loved LaMeka, and no matter what I had to do to keep her, I was going to do it. Even if it meant risking everything known and unknown by turning my back on Gary and my father.

"LaMeka, wait!" I caught up to her just before she got into her car.

"What, Gavin?" she asked as I caught her door and refused to let her open it.

"I should've told you."

"You think?" she asked with an attitude as she wiped her tears.

"Don't put all of the blame on me. You went digging for answers, and now you have them. You should've let me handle it. You should've trusted me to handle it."

"Trust you? You've been living at my house, all up in my personal affairs, and being around my family, and you didn't think that I should know that your family is a rich clan of racists?"

That was the wrong word choice. It was true, but currently, it wasn't the time to play the blame game. I was trying to salvage my relationship, not end it. I steepled my hands, trying to explain what I meant. "No, I'm saying you should've let me tell you in my own way and in my own time."

"And what time was that going to be? When they lit a cross in front of my house?"

"That's not fair—"

Her finger poked to my chest, thwarting my words. "No, what's not fair is that you bulldozed your way into my life knowing that we could never work. You knew your family wasn't ever going to approve of us, and you led me on this dead-end trail anyway."

My mind was turning aimlessly. I couldn't fathom losing my girl. Not over this bullshit. I had to pull her back into our space. When she was wrapped in the bubble of us, she felt safe and loved. I had to nestle her in that place. I pulled her to me about the waist. "How can my love for you be a dead end? I don't care what my dad or my brother thinks. I love you, and I won't let you go if you don't let me go."

My desired effect had no bearing on her now. She had hit fight-or-flight mode, and she'd bypassed fight straight into flight. She pushed me away and looked at me as if I'd lost my mind.

"Are you crazy? Never mind. I know the answer to that. Yes, you are. You only have yourself to think about. On the other hand, I have a mother, a sister, and—as your brother so eloquently put it—two little ghetto offspring to look out for. I'm not going to war with them. I have enough on my plate without pissing off two men who could crush me and my entire family."

"Are you saying I'm not worth the fight? That what we have isn't worth the fight?"

"No! I'm saying that you must pick and choose your battles, especially when you aren't prepared for the war. I just left eight years of hell. I didn't get out of that to sign up for a lifetime of it. I love you, Gavin, I really do. The mere fact that you couldn't tell your family about us until you had no choice shows me that you aren't ready to go to war either. If you aren't, then what the hell are we fighting for? How long are we going to be together before they influence you to drop me? How long should I wait around to find out when that will be? As much as I love you, Gavin, I refuse to put myself or my children through that. We deserve better than your maybes."

What she'd said ached inside my heart so deeply that I hadn't realized that she'd opened her car door and gotten inside. When it all boiled down to it, she had a helluva point. The sad part was that I'd never looked at it that way. I only wanted to protect her from my family, but no matter how I tried to swing this, it would still seem as though I was hiding our relationship. Feeling the sting of her words, my eyes watered, and I choked up.

Despite being choked up, despite being a part of this godforsaken family, and despite all the reasons she should leave me, I had to plea for her, for us. "Meka, baby, I'm sorry. I swear to you this is not just a maybe. This is real. My love for you and the boys is real. Just give me a chance to fix it."

Her hands gripped the steering wheel, and she seemed to be contemplating my request, but then she heaved a long sigh and shook her head. "No. You had a choice to do that from the start. You played Russian roulette with our relationship. Well, I'm sorry, the game's over, and I'm pulling the trigger. I'm done, Gavin."

The moment she pulled off, everything I'd struggled to hold in came out, and I bawled my eyes out right there in the parking lot. My heart felt as if someone had ripped it out of my chest, and I could barely breathe. I'd never in my life loved a woman so completely. Meka was more than my heart. She was my soul mate. It was in that moment that I knew she was supposed to be my wife. Yet this time I knew that our breakup was for real. This wasn't as simple as me not telling her how many women at the hospital I dated like before. Meka was gone, and there was nothing I could do about it. I had no one to blame for this mess but myself, because if I had just been straight up, then things could've worked out differently.

After a few minutes, I pulled myself together as best I could and walked back toward the hospital.

"I told her you'd break her heart, white boy," a dude said as I walked past him just before I made it to the entrance.

Of course, it was none other than Tony leaving from his counseling session. A rage swelled up inside of me, and without thinking, I turned around and punched his ass right in the stomach.

"You muthafucka," he gasped.

Just then a couple of nurses ran up to me and jumped between us. "Come on, Gavin. Let it go. What's wrong with you?" Jeanine asked.

"I'm sick of yo' ass." My pent-up anguish spewed out at Tony. "Leave me the fuck alone, and leave Meka alone."

During his coughing spell, he pointed at me. "I got you, my dude. Best believe I got you." He finally stood upright and added, "Oh, and from what I heard, you ain't got no choice but to leave Meka alone your damn self." He hobbled off while the nurses stood guard around me to ensure I didn't go after him again.

The next thing I felt was someone grab my arm. It was my brother, who pulled me away from the entrance of the hospital to the side of the building. "What the fuck is wrong with you? Has that blackberry pussy got you that whipped? Damn. Chasing her down and fighting. Oh, and let me guess, her ex or baby's daddy was the one in front of the hospital, the place you work and are supposed to remain professional at. Have you lost your damn mind?" Gary spouted off.

Yeah, I was the right one on the wrong day today. He could get it too. I punched him in his mouth. "Shut your fucking mouth about Meka."

He held his mouth. "You have lost your damn mind!"

"You're damn right. I've lost my mind so much that I'm insane, muthafucka."

And I was. Anybody could catch these hands because I was insane with hurt and rage. Only one person could settle me—Meka. With erratic breathing, I paced back and forth wishing this muthafucka or any muthafucka would.

"Say one more—and I do mean one more—muthafuckin' word and I'ma stole on your shiny-suited ass. With the mood I'm in, I'm good to issue ass whoopins all day long."

Ignoring my warning, he chuckled and continued to taunt me. "It is that good. Well, damn." He sighed. "You're sounding just like one of them now. Acting all ghetto. This place and these people are beneath you, and you aren't doing anything but letting them bring you down. The saddest part is that I actually admire LaMeka, and if she were white, I would tell you to marry that girl."

Snatching him by his collar, I forced him into the side of the building, making his back hit with a thud. "The best thing for you to do is to leave me alone, and don't come around me or call me again." Then I released him and let his body crumple to the ground.

Standing and dusting himself off, he said, "That's impossible. Since you are one part owner of Rand Technologies, I have to communicate with you."

"I want to sell my portion."

"That's not an option."

"There's always an option."

"Not on this and you know it," Gary said sternly. "You know, Dad may not be perfect, but damn it, Gavin, his rules aren't hard to follow. You just need to stop looking for love in all the wrong places. She's a woman just like any other. You'll get over it."

I withheld my rage long enough to deliver my final demand. "You and Dad can go to hell. Tell him that I want to sell my portion of the company so he can buy me out. I love LaMeka, and whatever I have to do to get her back I will do, even if that means cutting the both of you loose."

With that demand left lingering in the air, I left him where he stood and found my supervisor to let her know I was leaving for the day, and I called in for the next day as well. I was going to go to my house and have a few beers to kill this pain inside of me. All I wanted was to be left alone. And thanks to my family, I probably always would be just that—alone.

Chapter 33

Lincoln

As I sat in my theatre room studying film tape of past games against the Baltimore Ravens with Rico and DaQuan, I felt like I had the weight of the world on my shoulders. Thoughts of Charice and Ryan filled my head like black clouds overcasting my life. The peril of being in love with someone who was unavailable to me was damn near more than I could bear. I was shocked that I had lasted this long without nutting the hell up.

When I thought about it, the whole blowup with Charice couldn't have come at a better time. The week after that massive fight, we had to report to summer training camp to prep for the season. It gave me time to clear my head and deal with my emotions and gave her time to handle her business. Hell, I'd performed better this year at camp than I had my rookie season when I was trying to impress the GM and coaching staff in Dallas. Part of it was because I was forcing myself to keep my mind off of Charice, and the other part was to keep from deflating Ryan and telling him the real deal.

He was sickening. He walked around like his shit didn't stink, giving everybody the impression that his life was a bed of roses. I'd bet he'd keep it low-key if the team and staff knew that his baby girl was really my daughter, and that his oh-so-loving wife was my secret lover. *Yeah, bitch, brag on that.*

Anyway, I'd been back from training camp for five
days, and it was apparent things hadn't changed. Charice
brought Lexi to see me, but she didn't bring any type of
paperwork that proved she was actually leaving Ryan. I
didn't bring it up to her because that was my time for
my daughter, and I wasn't going to taint it with another
blowup with her mother. Furthermore, I refused to
ask despite how badly I wanted to know. I was tired of
chasing behind her and begging her like a damn fool. It
was time for her to prove some shit to me. If she wanted
me, she would.

"Man, I've studied more film than I have my entire career. Let's call it a wrap and go out," Rico said, breaking
my train of thought.

DaQuan gave him a pound. "I'm down wit' that, yo."

I drank a swig of my beer and eased down in my recliner. "A'ight then. I'll holla at you guys." I gave both
men a pound.

As they stood, Rico turned to me. "Man, Linc, come out
with us. You stay cooped up in this house like you're an
old-ass man. What the hell has got you so in the dumps?"

I waved off his question. "It's nothing."

DaQuan laughed. "Man, please. The way you put on a
clinic at training camp, you were stressed about something. Hell, I was ready to put more funds on your
contract, nawimean?" he joked.

We all howled in laughter at that one. "I'm just showing these young ones what I got."

Rico hit my leg. "Okay, well, let's unwind. Your daughter is staying with your parents for the weekend. So
what's the deal? My bad, unless you have a woman
coming through."

DaQuan laughed and hit Rico. "If he had a woman, he
damn sure couldn't have put on a clinic at camp. That ass
would've been too tired from working that back out."

"I'm straight. You two have fun for me."

"Suit yourself," they said in unison. Then I got up and walked them to the door.

"So what are you guys going to get into?" Curiosity got the better of me as I opened the front door.

"We'll probably hit up a restaurant. You know, get our grub on and then hit a couple of clubs or a titty bar. You know how we do," Rico joked.

"My vote is on the titty bar," DaQuan joked. "I'ma call up a couple more fellas and see if they are down. Be easy, Linc." He hugged me with one arm before he walked to his SUV.

Rico looked at me once DaQuan drove off. "Stop pining away for her. Forcing yourself to stop living your life isn't making her leave any quicker, if she leaves at all."

Rico was one of my best friends since high school and the only person outside of Charice and me who knew of the affair. He was like a true brother to me, and I knew he'd never tell, especially with all the shit I had on him. I knew enough dirt on Rico to get him kicked off the team, out of the league, and be put in prison. No lie. So the respect and the vow of silence were mutual. I really didn't want to confide in him, but I had to tell somebody. The shit was eating away at me.

I gave him some pound. "I hear you."

He shook his head. "Still as stubborn as ever. I'll let you deal with it how you want to deal with it. I'm just saying the shit ain't healthy. You have to look out for Lincoln." He pointed to my chest.

"Be easy. Deuces."

He turned to leave and threw up his two fingers. "Be easy."

I knew what he was saying was the truth, but I didn't feel like being bothered with much of anything or anyone. I knew I was in a funk, but he'd never been in love, so he didn't know how it felt to have your dream right at your fingertips but just beyond your grasp. I felt like a dog chasing his own tail. You know it's there, but you can never get it. I just wanted Charice to make a decision so I could either live my life with her or move the hell on, because this limbo shit was not going to cut it.

I plopped back down on my recliner and pressed play to keep studying the film when my cell phone buzzed. There was a message from "Yours Only," otherwise known as Charice.

Yours Only: Hey u. I know we haven't talked this week, but I just wanted u 2 know I was thinkin' 'bout u. I miss u.

Tiger: Thinkin' 'bout me? Miss me? What's the deal, C? U know what, never mind.

Yours Only: I wanted 2 talk 2 u in person. Just didn't want u 2 think it was excuses. Tryin' 2 get some things straight about my dance studio first. Just don't want him tryin' 2 take what I've worked so hard 2 build up. U understand?

Tiger: Yeah. I understand. Loud and clear.

I pressed the call log on my phone. "Yo, Rico."

"What it do, son?" Rico answered. "What's good?"

"What time are you guys going out?"

"We're heading out in a couple of hours or so around nine thirty so we can eat first. Then we're gonna club hop. Don is going with us, and you know his wife would kill him for going to titty bars." He laughed. "Why? What's up?"

"Swing by and pick me up."

"Word?"

"Word."

"Say no more. Be ready to roll at nine."

"Will do."

As soon as I hung up, my phone buzzed. It was another message from Charice.

Yours Only: Tell me u ain't mad, please. I love u.

Tiger: I ain't mad. Do u, babe. Deuces.

Yours Only: Deuces??? Do me??? What r u sayin' 2 me???

Tiger: Nothing.

I got up and headed to the shower to get ready to chill out with my boys. As I was walking, I got another message from Charice. Now she wanted to do all this fucking talking. Oh, well. I read the message.

Yours Only: We need to talk. Name the place and time.

I powered my phone off and went to my closet to pick out what I was going to wear. It was time to get my boogie on and start living a Charice-free life. Nobody had time for those games, and I was done playing house. I was beginning to see that it would always be excuses from her because she had no intention of leaving her lavish lifestyle with Ryan. She could have the lifestyle, but she wasn't going to have me. She made her choice. *I hope she chose wisely.*

By nine, I was fresh dressed like the million-plus bucks I was worth, looking dapper in a V-neck all-black T-shirt with a white Balmain distressed denim jacket, black Balmain denim jeans with all-black Balmain B-Glove high-top sneakers, and an all-black Yankees fitted cap. To add to the style, I rocked my brand-new Rolex and Super Bowl ring. Topping off with my favorite cologne, Kenneth Cole Black, I was ready for tonight.

"Linnnnnc! What it do, baby?" Rico yelled as I opened my front door. "Look at that boy. Fresh! Those kicks are bananas."

We gave each other a one-arm hug. "Man, I can't compete with you. Word, you ready to turn up?"

"No, my dude, I'm ready. Are you ready?"

"Ready as hell!"

We were rolling six deep with the crew: two of us to each car. My boys decided to do old-school rides: DaQuan's '85 Chevy Caprice, Don's 1969 Shelby GT 350, and Rico's 1973 Chevy Chevelle SS. All of them were fully restored and had premium-color paint jobs with rims. Having an old-school car was sort of our thing on the football team. My car of choice was a candy-coated pearl black convertible 1971 Oldsmobile Cutlass complete with a V8 engine, 350 horsepower. It reminded me of myself: class and sophistication both in the name and on the outside, but 100 percent bad boy on the inside. Tonight, I felt like my Cutlass. It was time to let my inner bad boy out for a ride.

"All right! All right! I wanna give a major shout out to my boys from the Giants football team visiting us tonight. This song goes out to you guys," the DJ shouted playing Drake's song "Back to Back" as we lounged in the VIP section of the 40/40 club.

It was one in the morning, and I was having a damn blast. I'd received about six more texts from Charice and deleted them all. I didn't have time for that shit. I loved her, but I was finally starting to see that my love—or rather, my patience—had limits. I'd always love her, but I wasn't going to be anybody's fool, not even hers.

Anyway, we'd been all over the city eating, drinking, and partying. We finally ended up in the VIP section at one of the most elite clubs in the NY, and I was feeling right. Four beers, two Crown Royals, one Hennessy and Coke, and one bourbon shot later, I was tipsy as hell and dancing my ass off up in the VIP with about ten different females' numbers in my pocket.

"How does it feel to be out?" Rico joked when I finally sat my half-drunk ass down.

I laughed as we tapped glasses. "Damn good, bruh. Fuck C," I slurred.

"Well, my dude, I'm 'bout to get out on the floor—" he was saying when security tapped me on the shoulder.

"Sup, big Brice?" He gave me a pound.

"Ain't nothing, Linc. Yo, there are two females over there trying to get in VIP who want to get your autograph," Brice said, pointing to the ropes.

They were fine as hell, especially the one with the caramel complexion. She had one dimple, light brown eyes, and beautiful light brown hair. Her mocha-complected friend was a catch too, but caramel did something that only Charice had done for the past two years—made my dick jump.

I hit Brice. "Hell yeah. Let them in. I got caramel."

"You can have caramel. You know I love blackberries." Rico laughed as we slapped each other five.

We stood up as they approached us. "Ladies," we said in unison. I motioned for them to have a seat, and they both smiled and greeted us with a hello before they sat, and we followed suit.

After we were seated, Caramel outstretched her hand to me. "I'm Mona Sims."

I shook her hand. "Pleased to meet you Mona, and I'm—"

"Lincoln Harper," she finished. "I know. I'm a huge fan of football and of yours." She smiled at me. "And this is my friend Diamond Banks."

"Hello, Diamond." I nodded toward her. She smiled, and my boy immediately introduced himself. "And I'm his teammate and best friend, Rico Cortez." He shook Diamond's hand first and then Mona's. "Pleased to meet you ladies."

"We won't trouble you for long. I just saw you and wanted to get your autograph. Other than catching a few away games, I've never been close enough to you to ask," Mona said to me.

"What makes me your favorite?" I grabbed a napkin as she reached in her purse and gave me a pen.

"My little brother adores you. He plays football for his middle school and even plays your position. He calls himself Little Big Truck. You became my favorite because you're his."

"Damn, ma. Either that shit is real sweet or you run some good-ass game," Rico chuckled, drinking some more of his Henny.

"My girl doesn't need to run game. We are the game," Diamond said seductively to Rico as he threw his hands up.

Mona pulled out her cell phone. "See?" She showed me a picture of her and a little boy who looked similar to her. He was in his football uniform, with my number, and the caption underneath said: Me and my baby bro, Ashton aka Little Big Truck. "That was taken last year at their first playoff game."

I liked that. "Well, tell your brother that the Big Truck said good job and keep up the hard work. Did they win?"

"That game, but they lost the next one by one point due to a field goal in overtime," she said, sounding disappointed.

"You love your brother, don't you?"

"More than my own life," she answered with conviction.

I signed two napkins, one for her and one for Ashton, and then I handed them to her. "Here you go."

She read hers silently and then she read his aloud. "Aww, it says, 'To Little Big Truck aka Ashton. Make me proud on the field! Best wishes, Big Truck aka Linc Harper.' He's going to love this. Thank you." She shook my hand and stood up.

I stood up. "Wait. Are you leaving?"

Diamond waved her hand, and that was when I noticed she was snuggled up under Rico. He already had her hooked before I could sign an autograph. "She's leaving. I'm going to hang out with Rico, girl."

She huffed. "Diamond!"

Diamond cut her eyes at her. "I'll be fine. You have to work. I don't."

"Work? On a Sunday?" I asked, bringing my attention back to her.

"Not really. I just have some case files that I have to read over."

"Case files?"

Diamond giggled, her tipsiness showing. "I'm a dental hygienist, and she's an attorney. We're sorority sisters and best friends, but my girl doesn't know how to hang out anymore. Who studies case files on Sundays?"

"The same type of person who studies film tape on Saturday nights," Rico said, hitting my arm. "Ain't that right, chief?"

Mona and I looked at each other and laughed. "I'm sorry. I really have to go. Just look out for my friend since she insists on staying?" Mona asked.

I grabbed her hand. "Hey. Well. Wait. What time do you have to be at work tomorrow?"

"Anytime I choose. It's voluntary, but there's something I need to do."

"Hang out with me for a little bit. I promise I won't keep you long. I mean, unless you have other reasons like you're married or in a relationship." She eyed me skeptically. "Don't make me beg." I hit her with the puppy-dog eyes.

Hiding behind a soft blush, she sat down. "Only for another hour." She crossed her legs gracefully as she settled back into the plush couch. "And I am very single."

It was my turn to blush, my deep dimples on full display. "Good." I fanned for the waitress to come over. "What are you drinking?"

"Nothing. I'm driving."

"One drink won't hurt."

"So says the man who's never tried a drunk-driver case. Besides, I think you're toasty enough for the both of us."

"Funny. A glass of rosé?"

She shrugged and held up her index finger. "One glass."

I turned to the waitress. "Can you bring me back two glasses of rosé?" As the waitress left to get our drinks, I noticed that Rico and Diamond were in their own world as Mona and I sat there bopping our heads to the music. "So what law school did you attend?"

"NYU."

"Good school. How old are you?" I asked more so for my purpose than hers.

"Old enough." She chuckled. "Don't you know it's impolite to ask a woman her age?"

"My bad. It's a habit of my profession to ask."

She pointed at me. "Gotcha. In that case, twenty-seven."

"You and your brother are far apart in age."

She giggled as the waitress handed us our drinks. "Yes, Mama's little mistake in the Easy-Bake was what I called him," she said, bringing me to chuckles. "My parents went off to celebrate their fifteenth wedding anniversary and came back with more than they left with," she joked. "But he is my heart and joy. The main man in my life besides my daddy. It's just hard to get back home to see him."

"Hmm. Where are you from?" I asked.

"Connecticut."

"Wow, a suburb lady." It wasn't every day you ran across high-society girls in the VIP.

"Surprised that I'm not some rough-around-the-edges chick out of the Bronx?"

"To be honest, yeah, kinda."

"Diamond is the New Yorker. She's from New Rochelle. We actually met in undergrad at FAMU, and we both applied to and were accepted into NYU programs after we graduated."

"Didn't want to stay in Connecticut?"

"Connecticut is nice. It's calm and plain. I wanted to go to a Southern black school and then move to New York. That's always been my dream."

"Why?"

"You ask a lot of questions."

"You answer them so well."

My answer must have caught her off guard because she blushed before taking a sip of her rosé. "Honestly, I felt like Southerners are more in tune with our culture. I've never felt that living in Connecticut. And well, being in New York was my revolt against my good-girl image."

"So this is your bad girl image that I met?"

"No, this is my 'I've grown the hell up, and I have a career to build, but I still love New York and hanging out' image," she corrected me. "Enough about me. I've dominated the conversation, please tell me about you."

Leaning in close to her, I bit my lip. "I've enjoyed it. You're refreshing."

She laughed as some wine drizzled on her chin. "That's one I haven't heard." She dabbed her mouth with a napkin. "Ball players don't use words like 'refreshing.'"

"And attorneys from Connecticut don't hang out in clubs in New York," I shot back at her. "There's always more beneath the cover of a person, good girls and athletes included."

She nodded. "I like that, and my apologies. Athletes," she said, catching my subtle hint. I'd never liked the phrase "ball players." My career was my career just like anybody else's, but I was way too twisted and intrigued by Mona to be offended.

"But I'm still a bad boy from Queens, so I guess I'm just coming home."

"Home is where the heart is," she said as we touched glasses.

"Can we dance?"

She paused for a moment, then shrugged slightly, flashing a dazzling smile. Her eyes sparkled when the light hit them. I was mesmerized. "Sure," she answered.

We set our glasses down, and when she got up, the most beautiful donk was on showcase for me. She was absolutely gorgeous. As we headed to the dance floor, I couldn't help but notice how her body oozed sexiness in those black leather pants, an emerald green sleeveless top, and what looked like five-inch stilettos. How that trunk carried those shoes so gracefully I would never know. She had a tattoo of a butterfly with her name inside on her right shoulder, and when she flipped her hair back, she smelled like passion fruit. What really got me was her purity. Besides her fineness, her innocence turned me on. However, that ass told me she was a stone freak in the bedroom, and if she wasn't, she was one in training, and I was dying to be the teacher. Appropriately, the song "She Got a Donk" filled the airwaves as we ground on the floor to that one and the next three.

As the song slowed, she wrapped her arms around my neck, and I rested mine around her waist. "Mona, I've had a ball with you, but I have to tell you something."

She rolled her eyes. "I knew it. You're married, right?" she said, quickly removing her arms from around my neck.

I laughed. "No, I'm a bachelor, and no, I'm not gay, before you ask. What I was going to tell you is that you're fifteen minutes over your limit. It's been an hour and fifteen minutes."

She laughed and hit her forehead. "I'm sorry. It's just hard to trust—"

"I get it," I interrupted knowingly.

"I better get the hell out of here."

"Can we exchange phone numbers?"

She swallowed hard. "I don't know."

"No drama in my life. Seriously. I just want to be able to talk, and perhaps take you out one day." *No drama anymore now that I'm officially out of this damn love triangle.*

She bit her bottom lip. "All right, Mr. Harper." She handed me her business card, and I gave her my cell phone number. "Don't have my number on Craig's List, please."

She had jokes! "I should tell you the same thing."

"You can trust me."

"You can trust me too. You'll see." I winked at her.

Blushing, she quipped, "We shall." She turned to walk away.

I pulled her back and cupped her face. "So you're gonna leave me hanging, ma?"

She wrapped her arms around my neck and hugged me tight. Then she pulled back and kissed my cheek. "Thanks for a good time. If you call and we actually get that real date, then you'll get a real kiss. These lips aren't for cheap thrills. If you want them, you gotta work. Good night, Lincoln."

Shit, she was hitting a nigga on all cylinders. *Mutha-fuckin' Mona.* "Good night, Mona."

I watched her sexy ass sashay out of VIP and all the way through the club. Mona was the truth. She had major game, and no lie, she pulled me in hook, line, and sinker.

When I walked back over to the couch, Rico was already tongue-deep in Diamond's mouth. "Dude, you ready?" I asked.

He heaved a sigh. "My man. Can you grab a ride with Don? I'ma take Diamond home," he said, staring at her seductively as she bit her bottom lip.

"A'ight. You two be safe."

"Always," they said in unison, never looking up at me.

"Hey, wait a minute," Rico said, putting his hand up to stop me. "You aren't leaving with Mona?" Rico asked.

Diamond laughed. "Mona is a good girl. That's not happening. I'd be surprised if you got her number."

"Well, Diamond, be surprised." I showed them her card.

Diamond's eyes bugged out. "Well, shocked I am. For more reasons than one." She giggled, tipsy as hell.

"I've got this under control. Believe that. I'll holla at you." I gave Rico some pound before leaving to find Don.

It was three a.m. by the time I slid on my basketball shorts and wifebeater. After a nice, hot shower, I felt good despite still being tipsy. If I couldn't fall in between a nice pair of sexy legs, I opted for falling into my nice, big, and empty bed to go to sleep. As I fell backward into my bed and turned on my fifty-two-inch flat screen, I had to admit it felt good to go out and have fun instead of sitting in the house hoping and wishing for Charice to come back to me. I looked over at my nightstand and saw the picture of her and turned it down. It was clear to me that it was time to move on with my life and let Charice have hers with Ryan.

I picked up Mona's card off of my nightstand. I chuckled to myself at our conversation at the club. She was intelligent, sexy, confident, caring, and I could not stop thinking about her.

"I apologize for calling so late. I know it's rude, but I just couldn't stop thinking about you," I said to Mona after she'd groggily answered the phone.

"I must say that even though I hate being awakened out of my sleep, this is a pleasant surprise. I'm shocked."

"Well, I'm glad that you're pleasantly surprised even if I inconvenienced you. I just wanted to know that you made it home safely, and I wanted to hear your voice.

It was a pleasure to meet you, and I really enjoyed your company tonight."

"Same here. It says a lot to me that you thought enough to call. I'm starting to understand that there is a lot more behind the cover of Lincoln Harper."

"Well, I hope that it's enough to make you want to get to know what's behind the cover of Lincoln Harper."

"It is."

"So it's a date between us, right?"

"Yes, of course. Whenever and wherever you'd like."

"Don't say that to me. I'm intoxicated and horny. I might take it the wrong way. I'm trying to be a good guy."

She laughed and, man, that was intoxicating. "Why fight it? You're a bad boy, and I haven't lived in New York without getting a little bad girl in me."

Now I knew I was drunk, but I could've sworn I heard a little seduction in her tone. "Are you flirting with me?"

"Just like you're flirting with me, and we both like it," she said sexily.

I bit my lip and moaned. "Damn."

"Lincoln, I don't know what it is about you, but you have me feeling a kind of way, and I know it's not the rosé talking."

"I feel the exact same way." I stroked on myself. "I really wish you were here with me."

"Then I'd never get to work tomorrow, because we both know if I were there with you, some things that we are both thinking about would go down."

"I love your realness."

"I need to go."

"Before you get in trouble or so you can go to work?"

"You already know the answer to that one."

I laughed. "Yeah, I do. So I guess this is good night again, Mona."

"Good night again, Lincoln, and by the way, I should be finished up tomorrow about three o'clock."

"Three o'clock, huh?" I asked, picking up on her not-so-subtle hint.

"Yep, three o'clock."

"Sweet dreams and rest up."

"Ditto," she said, and we hung up. I couldn't wait for three o'clock. Just as I set my phone down, it buzzed. I picked it back up. It was another message from Charice.

Yours Only: Linc, baby, please talk to me. I love you so much, and I'm sorry if you feel like I keep hurting you. Please believe me.

Tiger: It is what it is. There's nothing left to say that hasn't already been said. And I'm cool with that. I understand. Good night, Charice.

Yours Only: Where do we stand, Linc?

Tiger: The same place we've always stood. Nowhere.

I turned off my phone, and then I grabbed all the other telephone numbers that I'd collected that night and threw them into the trash. For now, it was all about sweet dreams of Mona and our three o'clock date.

Chapter 34

Lucinda

"Hey, Aldris. It's me again, Lucinda. I was calling to tell you that I'm sorry, and I wish that you'd pick up the phone so I could tell you this in person, or at least call me back. I overreacted. That's so unlike me and I'm, I don't know, so frustrated by everything that has been going on. Well, anyway, I'm sorry again," I said into his voicemail for the tenth time in over two weeks.

Yes, I'd been attempting to apologize to Aldris for that long. It really got to me that I reacted so harshly to him and, in essence, to Jessica. It was rude, disrespectful, and highly uncalled for. It was just that I was sick of him interfering with my relationship with Mike, but I never wanted things to end up like this between Aldris and me. I wanted us to be able to be cordial with each other. Now it was a mess.

The crazy part was that, despite the cruel things he said to me, I couldn't even be mad at him for them. I deserved it. When I looked back over what he said, he was right. Forget cordial or anything remotely close to it. If I had found out that he was dating one of my girls, I wouldn't ever have words for him again. In fact, I might've been caught up on murder charges. Fucking Jennifer was bad enough, but Trinity, LaMeka, or Charice would've been grounds to knock his block off. Real talk. He reacted a lot better than I would have in that situation because there's no coming back from that. Despite that, he wanted to be with me. It was funny how shit was different once you turned a mirror on yourself. At the time, it didn't seem so bad. Aldris and I were over, and Mike and I were together. Simple as that. Now it didn't seem so simple anymore.

The entire situation had been bothering me since it happened. Mike told me that I made a mistake and to let it go, but I couldn't. Something on the inside of me felt low and horrible, and I wanted desperately to correct this wrong that I had done. It was a good thing that I was spending the day to myself. I could free my mind of everything that bothered me, including disrespecting Aldris. Nadia was heading to my mother's house for a while so that I could get a break. I needed one just to be one with Lu.

I put my cell phone down and walked into Mike's bathroom, where I found him in the shower. I smiled to myself as I opened the shower door. "Can I join you?"

"Shit!" Mike jumped, running the water over his head. "You scared the hell out of me, Lu. You know how I am about my showers. It's my private time. Maybe we can bathe together later on tonight," he said, closing his eyes and letting the water stream across his face.

Aldris would've never turned me down. *Showering together was the sexiest and most romantic thing we shared,* I thought as I plopped on the bed and waited for the laptop to boot up. I shook my head. I couldn't believe I'd just done that again. That had been happening a lot lately. My mental comparisons. It was like I couldn't stop it. Everything Mike did lately, I critiqued it with Aldris. I had to stop that. They were two different people, and this was a very different relationship, but sometimes I wished he would do some of the things that Aldris used to do without me having to ask or feel like I was begging for him to do them.

Suddenly, I felt a kiss on the side of my cheek, disrupting my thoughts. "Sorry, Lu, I need to get ready for work. How's my baby feeling?"

"Ready for this much-needed rest." I sighed as I surfed the internet. "I'm about to make sure Nadia is dressed so I can drop her off at my mom's."

He scratched his head. "Did you forget my kids were coming over this weekend?" he asked me as he put on his dress slacks.

I stood up and stretched. "No, I figured you were picking them up once you got off this afternoon."

"Actually, their mother is bringing them by here. She should be here in the next fifteen minutes."

"Who's going to watch them?"

"Well, you, baby. Who else?"

Excuse me? Me? Maybe I woke up in an alternate universe, because I do not remember this shit whatsoever. "Umm, how did you figure I was going to watch them when you never discussed this with me?"

Mike turned to look at me. "Lu, I thought by you and Nadia spending the night last night that you were doing that for me. You know their drop-off time on my weekends is at nine in the morning."

"Then why are you working on your weekend?" I asked him with my arms crossed. "I stayed here last night because you said I shouldn't leave after midnight taking Nadia with me. I agreed, so we stayed. You never said anything to me about keeping your kids. I'm not even going to have my own child."

Mike crossed his arms and put his index finger to his lips. I hated when he did that. He always thought he was about to say something profound and intelligent when he did that. "Well, Lu, the same way you come as a package deal, so do I. I don't have any problems watching Nadia for you. I thought we both understood that."

This fool had really lost his mind. "It's not about me not accepting you as a package deal. It's about common fucking courtesy. I would never just toss Nadia off on you without making sure you had nothing else planned."

"Even if I did, if you needed me, I'd be there for you," he said, irritated.

"And I am there for you, but that doesn't mean it gives you the right to not consider my feelings or my time."

"You can't sacrifice a little alone time just to help me out? Is that what you're saying to me?" he asked, visibly upset.

"No." I threw my hands on my hips. "I'm saying that you are inconsiderate and that the next time you plan something for me to do, you'd better ask first."

"I'm sorry. I thought we were in a little thing called a relationship where certain things were a given. My bad. I guess I'll just ask my girlfriend to have my back the next time even though I didn't know those were the type of things I should be asking for." He stormed into his bathroom to finish dressing.

I threw a pillow at the closed door. "*Puto!*" I went to Michaela's room to check on Nadia.

"Are you ready, baby?"

"Yes! Can I take my Moxie doll over to *Abuela*'s house?"

"Umm, yeah. We might not go, but if we do, I'm not dropping you off."

"Why, *Mami?*"

"I have to keep Mr. Mike's kids for him until he gets off of work."

"Oh, yeah! I get to play with Michaela." She jumped up and down. "So we get to stay here and all play together?"

"Maybe. If I watch them, you all can watch the kid's stations. I'm not fussing with Michaela over that today.

So don't be asking me about BET or MTV on her behalf, and I mean it."

Don't get me wrong, I loved Mike's kids, but we had different ways of raising our children when it came down to certain things. They were sweet kids, but I felt they were a little misguided. Mike let them eat way too much candy, go to bed on the weekends way too late, watch way too many adult-oriented shows, and the thing that really burnt me up was that they called me Lucinda, not Ms. Lucinda. I always made Nadia respect him by calling him Mr. Mike, and I would've hoped that Mike would do the same, but no. When I tried to talk to him about things like that, he always had an excuse. If I brought up the candy, he didn't see how it hurt since they regularly went to the dentist and had perfect teeth. When I brought up the weekend bedtime, he said they already went to bed early during the week for school, so why couldn't they have leeway on the weekends? When I mentioned the adult-oriented shows, he thought they would get exposed to it somewhere, but at least at home, he could monitor it. I didn't even bother to bring up the whole Ms. Lucinda thing because I might've slapped him if I heard his thoughts on that one.

Soon I heard them barreling down the hallway. "Hey, Lucinda," they all shouted.

"Ms. Lucinda."

"Ms. Lucinda," they all said with an attitude. See what I meant? I could've popped the 'tude right down their throats.

"Hello, kiddos." I hugged each one of them.

Mike trotted down the hallway. "Look, kids, I have to go to work, so you'll be with Lucinda today until about five this afternoon. Don't give her any problems. Do you all understand?"

"Yes, Dad," they all said in unison.

"Good. Give me a hug so I can go." They each hugged him tightly.

Then he walked over and hugged Nadia and grabbed my hand. "Thank you," he said, giving me those damn puppy-dog eyes that no longer worked for me.

"Whatever." I fanned him off. "I've got them."

He smiled and winked at me. "That's my girl." He kissed me on the lips as the kids made gagging noises. "See you guys later," he said throwing up his deuces and heading to work.

"Can I watch the *Beyoncé Live* concert?" Michaela asked.

"We're hungry," the boys said in unison.

I rubbed my forehead. *Here we go.* "No, Michaela. You can't. Watch some Saturday morning cartoons. Now what do you all want for breakfast?" I was flooded with requests. Pancakes, waffles, eggs, grits, and other breakfast items were shouted out by the boys in the midst of Michaela whining about not getting to see Beyoncé.

An hour later, everyone had eaten and the kids were running around like chickens with their heads cut off as if they didn't just chow down on a home-cooked meal. After another couple of hours of monitoring the television, stopping the boys from fighting each other, and listening to nonstop chatter about Big Time Rush and Justin Bieber, I was ready for a break. I loaded the kids up and went to my mom's house. Thankfully, when we got there, my brothers and sisters were playing softball in the backyard, so Mike's kids and Nadia fell right in line.

I grabbed a bottle of water and plopped down at the table in the kitchen, rubbing my forehead.

"I thought you were resting today," my mom said as she sat across from me.

"That makes two of us," I mumbled. "Mike had to work."

"So their mama couldn't drop them off later?"

"She must've had something to do. The order says he gets his kids at nine, so they stick to it," I huffed.

My mom shook her head. "So he just sprang it on you, huh?"

"Yep." I flipped through the new issue of *Essence*.

My mom flipped through her magazine and finally she heaved a heavy sigh. "Lucinda, I don't want to pry, but I just have to say that I don't think you're ready for this." I sat up to speak, but she put her hand up to stop me. "Let me finish. I know you like Mike. He's a good guy, but this whole thing went entirely too fast for you. You weren't even over Aldris before you were in Mike's arms."

"I am over Aldris." I sounded more definitive than I felt.

"Maybe now, but then? Really? You were engaged to the man for a year and a half, and then you break up, and within three months you were with Mike."

"I'll admit it wasn't the best decision in the world, but I do like him."

"Like him enough to play house? He's got three children. I'm not knocking it, but that takes a lot more responsibility than what you're used to handling, and from what you've told me, you two differ in how you raise your kids. Going back to this Aldris situation, how do you even know you're over him if you never gave yourself time to get over him?"

Smacking my pursed lips, I shook my head. "I may not have had time to heal from what Aldris did to me, but I was over him the moment I found out he cheated with Jennifer. And as for Mike and me, we're making it work."

My mom chuckled and pointed at me. "You know who you sound like?"

"Who?"

"Just like your father," she said seriously. "He left me to prove that he really didn't love or need me. Maria had filled his head with nonsense because she was younger and wanted what I had. He was running from tough times and real love. He spent those years with her 'trying to make it work' because he was afraid to admit he was wrong. She used him up, faked a child on him, and in the end, he wound up right back where he started—with me. But that's what happens when you're with someone trying to make things work versus being with the one working things out."

Speechless. I was completely speechless. Those were the most profound words I'd heard in a long time. I didn't know how I felt about what she said, but it spoke to me deep down in my soul. In fact, those words were still on my mind as I stood at Aldris's door.

"I'm surprised you answered," I said to Aldris as I stood at his front doorstep.

He shrugged. "So why are you here?"

After my mom finished talking to me, I decided to leave the kids with her and take a drive to clear my head. I drove around aimlessly until I decided that I needed to speak with Aldris. It still bothered me that we were now on bad terms, so I wanted to clear the air. Whether I made things work with Mike or not, I just couldn't take ending things with Aldris on the note that it ended on. And so here I was standing in front of Aldris, who had no shirt on and basketball shorts, trying to correct my wrong and not look like an imbecile.

"Did you get my messages? I've called you."

His nostrils flared. "I got all ten messages," he said tensely. "And I received every call. Why are you at my house? Don't you have a combined family to tend to?"

"Look, Aldris. Things between us took a turn for the worse. I've gone over and over in my mind how they got so bad. I don't know where we went wrong, but I do know I don't want us to hate each other. I was wrong on so many levels for so many things. Regardless of who did what to whom, I just want you to know that I forgive you, and I was hoping that you'd forgive me too. Not just because of the incident with Jessica, but with Mike, too."

Aldris put his head down. "Is that all?"

"Yes."

He looked up, his expression like stone. "I appreciate the comments." He prepared to shut the door.

"Wait! So you're not going to say anything?"

He shook his head. "No, I'm not. I've already said my apologies and done my begging. It wasn't enough for you, so while I appreciate the comments, I don't forgive you. I know I'm not perfect, and I don't pretend that anybody else is either, but there are some things that just aren't fixable. I've learned that lesson from you. I accepted it and moved on. I think it's time you did the same thing too." With that, he shut the door in my face and to any type of friendship or relationship we ever had.

Wow. I slowly walked away from his house. Our house. The flower I planted in the garden was still growing and blooming. I walked over to it and admired it. As I looked at it, tears began to fall from my face. Unlike this plant, our relationship had not stood the test of time, and it was both of our faults. I cried because the plant symbolized something I'd probably never have—a never-ending love.

As I got into my car, the car Aldris bought for me, I continued to cry. Everything around me was a reminder of my life with Aldris, from the way I wanted Mike to act even down to the new-car fragrance in my car. With all the ill shit that had happened between us, why could I now only remember the happy times with Aldris?

"Hello?" I answered my cell phone, trying to straighten my voice.

"Hey. Is everything okay?" Mike asked.

I cleared my throat. "Yeah. Everything is cool."

"I was just checking on you and the kids."

"We're fine."

"Nobody is giving you any problems, right?"

"No. We're fine."

"Are you sure you're all right?"

"Yep."

"Still mad at me?"

"No."

He sighed. "Okay. Well, I guess I better get back to work. I was just checking in. I love you, baby."

I exhaled as I rubbed my forehead. "Okay. I'll talk with you later. I love you too, Aldris," I said and hung up the phone.

Oh, shit! Did I really just say that? I thought as I finally cranked up my car to leave our house—I mean, Aldris's house. The immediate ring of my phone from Mike told me that I absolutely did. I hit the RINGER OFF button.

Shit. Shit. Shit.

Chapter 35

Lincoln

"Close your eyes. I have a surprise for you," Mona purred.

"What kind of surprise?" I asked, closing my eyes.

"The kind that you won't get to see if your eyes aren't closed," she teased as I heard her walking into the room.

"My eyes are shut. I promise."

"Okay. Open up," Mona ordered.

I opened my eyes and gasped. "Shiiit. Lawd have mercy." I rubbed my hands together.

The sight before me left me horny and speechless. She wore a halter bra and matching thong that were in my team's colors with my number on each cup of the bra and the front of the thong. Red stilettos adorned her feet. Damn, she was gorgeous.

She tossed her hair. "What do you think?" she asked as she modeled the ensemble for me.

I stood up and walked to her. "I love the sentiment, and I think you are sexy as hell. I can't wait to get this off of you." I bent down and kissed her neck.

She giggled and wrapped her arms around my neck. "Your kisses are amazing. I love our time together."

"You do?"

She nodded. "Uh-huh."

"I do too," I confirmed as I sat in the chair, and she straddled me.

Her soft hands caressed my face. "Sometimes I have to pinch myself because I still can't believe this is real. My boyfriend is Lincoln Harper."

"Well, believe it, baby," I murmured as we shared a passionate kiss.

Yes, Mona was officially my lady. It'd been three weeks since we first met, and we'd been nonstop ever since. For our three o'clock date, I'd planned a nice, private picnic for the two of us. We ate and talked, and talked, and talked. It felt like I was reconnecting with an old friend versus getting to know someone I'd just met. We had the strangest connection to each other. We could pick up on each other's thoughts, finish each other's sentences, and the attraction both mentally and physically was through the roof.

Surprisingly, we still stuck to our core values. I wasn't comfortable bringing her to my house because of my daughters, and she refused to let me know where she lived. A plus. I liked that she didn't just go against all her values because I was the great Lincoln Harper. I appreciated the instances of reservation that she had with me. It was refreshing because it showed me that my status wasn't what she was after nor was it what she cared about. So we ended up staying at a hotel. The sex was safe and great. I brought my own condoms, and she insisted that I use them. No, she wasn't better than Charice in the bedroom, but that was only because Charice knew me well enough to know exactly what I liked and how I liked it. Mona would get there, and I was happy enough with her to patiently wait for her.

We'd seen each other nearly every day despite our schedules, even if it was only for fifteen minutes. She was the first person I spoke to every morning and the last person I spoke with at night. She'd flown out to meet me for our first preseason away game, and we were in her hotel room spending some quality time together when she showed me her custom-made lingerie.

I know what you're wondering. Charice, Charice, Charice. Outside of visiting my daughter once, I hadn't spoken to her. That wasn't because she hadn't tried, but because I was done with that situation. She'd called me once to tell me that I was overreacting and that she really was working to get things resolved. Yada yada yada. Same shit. Different day. You'd think she would've picked up on the hint that I was done with her, or better yet, figured out that I had someone new in my life, but that would require her to care enough about me to find out what was really going on in my life. As you can see, three weeks and one girlfriend later, she still had no clue. But she loved me, right? Exactly.

The only thing that bothered me about having to deal with Charice was the fact that I couldn't talk about Lexi to Mona without revealing who her mother was. She asked, and I just kept telling her it was a long story and that I needed to know where this relationship would go before I revealed all the details behind my baby daughter. She understood and never pressed. She just wanted to confirm that I was not with her mother, which I could wholeheartedly assure her of. Once she heard that, she was straight. We were straight.

As we kissed, Mona's work cell went off. She pulled back from our kiss. "I'm sorry, baby. I have to get this," she said getting up.

"No problem."

"Brent, this better be an emergency," she said to her assistant. "What do you mean he's recanting his statement? Shit! His mama got to him again. Look, have Leslie go through the other evidence. Make sure that it still sticks.

Get the reports back on the car immediately, and contact Judge Patterson to subpoena him. I'll be back tomorrow to tie up any loose ends. I'm having a blast, or I was. I will. You too. Bye." She hung up the phone and turned to me. "Sorry," she threw out, looking and sounding aggravated.

"Problems with a case, I take it." I walked over to the bed and began massaging her shoulders.

"Yes. It's taken me three months to build this case. I need that testimony." She huffed. "God, this feels so good. Brent told me not to worry, to have fun, and to tell you he said hello." She leaned against my chest as I continued to massage her.

"Tell him I said hello too, and he's right, you know? You don't need to worry, because it will all work out. You'll make it work."

"You make even the worst problems seem so small." She sighed away her anguish.

Sensually, I kissed her neck. "I'm your man. That's my job."

She released the most tantalizing moan, and that did it for me. Our passion ignited, and we began to sex each other as if it were going out of style. The way she softly called my name and moaned deeply as I penetrated her made me feel like a damn king. The way she gave herself to me during lovemaking was so pure, virginal almost. She was like an angel. I could see myself falling for Mona.

"Lincoln, baby, don't stop. No one has made me feel so good," she moaned, breaking into my thoughts as we hit our climax.

As we lay there basking in the afterglow of our love-making, I had to address what she'd confessed moments ago. "I'm happy that I'm the only one who's made you feel this way. It makes me feel as though I'm all you need."

She turned to face me, snuggling close and running her hand across my face. "Lincoln, thank you for being patient with me," she whispered.

"What do you mean?"

"I know that you're probably used to all kinds of spectacular sexual antics."

"I'd rather have what I have with you and know it's real than be with a ho who can make my head spin around. Trust me. I'm satisfied. Don't worry."

She rubbed my chest. "What makes you so different? You can have your pick of any woman, beautiful and experienced, yet you're so down-to-earth and willing to be committed. Don't you want to 'sow your royal oats'?"

"That is one James Earl Jones line I wish would die." We both howled in laughter. "No, I don't. I sowed more than enough oats when I first got into the league. Believe me. This is the good side of my bad boy. Now I want something real. A real relationship with real love."

"How'd I get so lucky?" she asked aloud, sounding as if it was aimed more toward her than for me.

"I've been asking myself that same question every day for the past three weeks." I kissed her on the top of the forehead. Tilting her chin to look at me, I made a confession. "I went out that night just to have fun and get a bunch of numbers for females who didn't mean anything, and instead, I met you. I threw away every number I got that night, Mona. I don't know where this is going, but I want to stay on the ride with you for wherever it will take us. As long as it's just me and you, I'm all in."

Tears welled in the corners of her eyes, and I softly wiped them with my thumb. Clearing her throat, she looked away and began to shake her head. "I have a confession to make," she blurted out.

The moment it flew from her lips, my body tensed up. *Oh, dear God. Tell me this woman was not married or in a relationship. Lord knows I can't take anything worse, like any sexually transmitted diseases. I know we used protection, but still, only abstinence is 100 percent.*

Maybe there's a child she doesn't want me to know about. Damn. Damn. Damn, I thought in a fast flurry.

I sat up and so did she. I swallowed hard as I looked her in the eyes. "What is it?"

She interlocked her fingers with mine. "There is a reason I was hesitant to hang with you that night at the club or give you my number."

She's married. Fuck me. "What is that reason?"

"Umm. I'm nervous telling you this because I don't know how you're going to take it."

I pulled my hands free. "Baby, you're making me a little bit nervous."

"Listening to you talk about the things you want, you know, a chance at a real relationship—a committed one—is something that I don't know if I can give you. Well, I mean I could give that to you, but I don't know."

I shook my head. "Mona, you're not making sense to me, baby. Break it down. You just said that you don't know if you can be in a committed relationship with me, but then you could, so I'm lost. Do you or don't you want to be with me?"

She sighed and rubbed her forehead. "I'm sorry I'm jumbling this all up. What I'm saying is that right now I am feeling like that is what I want, but the commitment part is what troubles me."

"I'm not asking you to marry me, Mona." She nodded as if she agreed and understood what I said. "I'm still confused. Do you want to see other people? Is that your bad girl thing? I mean, if you don't want to be monogamous, then let me know."

"No, baby, it's not that—"

"So what is it?" I cut her off because now I was irritated.

"I haven't had a boyfriend in four years," she blurted.

I was a little shocked by that, but, I mean, she had just passed the bar and was trying to get her career off the ground, so it was understandable. Maybe she just had cut buddies because at the time she didn't have the time to pursue a real relationship. That had to be it. She was scared to tell me that the last four years had been nothing but sex for her. Most women hated to admit that because of the double standard. However, I wasn't going to be judgmental of that. I'd done the same because of my career.

"We've all gone through that phase. You had cut buddies. I get it. Your career came first, and rather than be committed, you just got what you needed. Baby, I'm in the NFL. That's damn near a lifestyle for a lot of athletes." I chuckled, looking at her.

She looked at me seriously. "Well, unless a lot of athletes' cut buddies are gay men, then you can't compare them to me."

"Huh?" I scratched my head. "You dated gay men?"

"No. When I turned twenty-three, I had a thing with my friend, Kita." I looked at her, still confused, and she exhaled and continued. "What I'm saying is I became a lesbian after my experience with Kita, and up until I met you, I had not been with a man."

I was completely taken off guard. "So you mean to tell me you weren't interested in me that night at the VIP?"

"Yes, I was. That's why I stayed. I was shocked because you were the first man to interest me in four years. When you called me that night, it was my first time being turned on by a man in four years."

My thoughts floated back to that night. No wonder she was strictly about getting the autograph, and then there was Diamond's comment about her being shocked for more reasons than one that Mona had given me her number. It made perfect sense now. She liked women.

"How come you didn't tell me this before?" No lie, I was a little upset.

She shrugged. "Did it really matter? I was single when I met you. Cynthia and I had broken up four months before." She fanned off the thought. "She was worse than a man. Wanted every skirt that smelled sweet to her, and I got tired of that," she explained, immediately going into the story of Cynthia and her as if I knew all along she had been a lesbian.

She had to back the hell up. The last relationship I knew of was with a man named Matthew. Where in the hell did he fit into all of this? "But what about Matthew? Your ex-boyfriend?"

She held my hands as she settled down to give me her full explanation. "He is my ex-boyfriend. The one who broke my heart by getting Brittany, one of my so-called friends, pregnant. That happened when I was twenty-two. I thought he'd be my husband, but he got her pregnant, and to add insult to injury, he gave her the life that I spent two years building. During that time, Kita was my backbone. I knew she was gay, and it'd never bothered me before. I never knew I was actually her type until I had a moment of weakness and she inducted me into my first lesbian experience.

"At first I was pissed and ashamed. I have very strong Christian values, even though I break a few rules, but being with a woman was never on my menu. It's kinda like the first time you ever tasted a chocolate bar. Once you've had a good experience with that first taste, you crave it again. So I started a two-month secret affair with Kita. She wanted me to come out. I didn't. We split on good terms, but she wanted someone who could embrace being a lesbian just as she had. Then I found out Matthew married Brittany. That did it for me. I turned my back on men and lived my life as a proud lesbian woman. I sowed my 'royal oats' with a few women until I met Cynthia. She was my longest relationship. She was a young attorney like me, and we just clicked. One year and three affairs later, I was done with her and her promises to stop being unfaithful. I remained single to get back in tune with myself, and then I met you in the VIP."

I didn't know what to say to that. Part of me was intrigued. What man didn't fantasize about a threesome with his lady and another woman? Shit, that was like the ultimate sexual fantasy for every heterosexual male in America. Yet the other part of me, the part that wanted to settle down with a normal life, was pissed.

"Wow." I stood up and walked into the bathroom.

She followed me. "You're pissed," she commented more as a question as she crossed her arms.

I peeled off my used condom and flushed it down the toilet. "Yes and no. I mean, how could you not tell me something like that?"

She threw her hands up. "I'm positive there's some shit I don't know about you, Lincoln."

"Well, I can guarantee you it won't be hearing me tell you, after sex no less, that I used to booty bump another man."

"That is so hateful and judgmental, which is exactly why I was cautious with telling you," she said defensively.

"I'm not hating on anybody. If that's what you're into, by all means, live your life. You have to take account for it, not me. What I'm pissed about is the fact that you didn't tell me. Come on, Mona. Don't you think that is some pretty pertinent information? While you were telling me about NYU and FAMU, you could've said, 'Hey, by the way, I'm gay.'"

"Bisexual," she corrected me.

"Whatever."

"So I guess that's changed your whole outlook on me, huh?"

I sighed and leaned against the sink. "Only about the lying."

"I didn't lie. I just didn't know how to tell you, Lincoln. I didn't think we'd get this far, so I told you when I felt comfortable."

"So why did you choose to tell me now?"

"Because I don't know if I have enough inside of me to stop lusting for a woman. If we continue this, I have to really examine what it is I want, because you satisfy me, but in six months when the honeymoon phase is over, I don't want to be wishing for some kitty."

I stood there for a moment taking in all that she had said. Talk about blown away. I never would've guessed in a million years that she switched teams. Never. Then suddenly I laughed. I laughed so hard she began laughing. "Well, if you do, you know, lust for some kitty, just promise me I can be a part of it. I am a man after all."

She threw a towel at me. "Typical. You ass." She giggled. "Then we'll have a problem, because I can't share you."

"And I can share you?"

She approached me. "If you keep putting it on me like you've been doing, then you don't have a thing to worry about."

"Not even Cynthia or Kita?"

She smiled at me. "Cynthia or Kita who?"

I pulled her to me by the waist. "That's what I want to hear. I can work with you on this, but you gotta promise not to keep things from me. Can you do that?"

She raised her right hand. "I promise," she said, and I planted a kiss on her. "And I'm sorry for not telling you sooner."

"Apology accepted. No other shocking surprises, right?"

"No, other than that, I'm an open book, which is probably pretty plain and simple."

Since the air was clear, we continued enjoying our time together, which included a shower together. In the shower, we were able to joke a bit about her confession, and she explained in more detail about her lesbian bedroom experiences. Hell, I was hard as a brick just listening to her talk. This whole bisexual thing might be good for at least a try or two.

After we showered, I left to get ready so we could go out to dinner. Diamond was supposed to be in town, so Rico, DaQuan, and I were all going to meet up at a restaurant with our lady friends and chill out. Once I got back to Mona's hotel room, I was mesmerized. She opened the door, gazing at me, in a fitted dress that barely reached midway down her thighs and hung off one shoulder. A simple long teardrop necklace adorned her neck, and she wore one bangle bracelet and a beautiful diamond butterfly ring on her finger. Of course, she sported some more killer stilettos, and her makeup and hair were beautiful and flawless.

"You take my breath away." I couldn't contain myself from another compliment as we headed to the lobby, where the limo with the others waited.

"And you're handsome yourself."

In the lobby, a couple of photographers snagged our picture, which I didn't mind. We were single. It wasn't like sneaking with Charice, who had a calculated plan for every meeting we had as if she were 007. Regardless of Mona's sexuality, I didn't have to hide her, and that mattered most to me.

In the limo, we all enjoyed each other's company. When we arrived, there was no waiting period at all at the restaurant. The food was great, and we were given three bottles of their very best champagne. Good, good times.

"I envy you all. We married men don't have the plea-sure of having our female companions here, so we have to dine together," I heard from behind me. It was none other than Ryan.

I turned to see him, Don, and Randy together. "Hello, fellas," we all said as we gave each of them a pound.

Diamond gasped. "You're Ryan Westmore. The one on all the billboards."

Playboy didn't miss an opportunity to flash her his million-dollar pearly whites. "That would be me. And you are?" he asked, taking her hand.

"Diamond Banks," she bumbled, gushing over Ryan.

Ryan brought her hand up to his lips and kissed the top. "It's a pleasure to meet you, Ms. Banks."

Rico pulled her hand back. "How's your wife, Ryan?" he asked, shooting daggers at Diamond, who put her head down.

He cut his eyes, peeping Rico's game. "Busy as ever. The studio and the kids keep her plate full," he said, and then turned to me. "Good to see you, Lincoln, and out on a date. I thought you were going for a title for the NFL's most single eligible bachelor for a minute," he joked, and only Randy, his team do-boy, laughed.

"Funny. You should be a regular on Comedy Central." I wanted to knock his block off.

Don smiled at Mona. "Good to see you again, Ms. Mona. Glad you two hooked that up."

Ryan turned to Don. "Oh, so you've met her before?"

Don looked at him and nodded. "Yes. I actually hang out with the single eligible bachelors, as you put it, from time to time, unlike some married men."

Mona turned to face Ryan. "Well, I'm proud to have ended that single streak." She extended her hand to his and shook it. "I'm Mona Sims, Lincoln's girlfriend. It's a pleasure to meet you."

Ryan gasped. "Wow. Girlfriend. I didn't know. It's a pleasure to meet you as well." He looked skeptical.

With a smirk, I said, "There are a lot of things I don't tell, unlike some people who waste no opportunity to brag on themselves."

"With a woman as beautiful as Mona, you should waste no opportunity to brag either," Ryan quipped.

"Your wife must love your compliments," Mona shot at him.

"I'm sure she does." His pure arrogance was on full display.

"Then save some for her. She'd probably appreciate them more. I'm a one-man-compliment kind of woman." Mona gripped my hand on the table, then turned to drink some champagne as Rico and I chuckled. "Here, baby," she said, feeding me another strawberry.

"Tell Ricey we said hello," I said to Ryan, who I could feel staring at me and Mona as we continued to playfully entertain one another.

"Yeah. Will do," he said slowly. "You fellas enjoy your dinner. Ladies," he acknowledged before walking off with Randy behind him as Don trailed, giving me the thumbs-up.

"He is as arrogant as he is portrayed," Mona said to me.

"And then some. But enough about Ryan Westmore."

After that show Mona put on, there was no place else I'd rather be than with her. As I tried to push the surprise meeting with Ryan out of my mind, it kept creeping to the forefront because I knew it was coming: the quiet before the storm. Now that Ryan knew about Mona, it was only a matter of days, possibly even minutes, before Charice knew. And once she knew, I didn't even want to think about the shit storm that would arise. However, I'd deal with that when the time arrived. For now, it was all about quality time with my one and only—Mona.

Chapter 36

Aldris

"You're it," Jessica yelled as she tagged me, and I chased her all around the backyard.

"I'm gonna get you!" I caught up with her and tickled her senseless.

As I put her down and watched her run off to her playhouse and play, I couldn't help but smile. Actually, I had Lucinda to thank for my moments like this. By her disrespecting me to the point where I was able to back away from her, it allowed me to focus on what was really important in my life with Jessica. It also allowed me to refocus and rebuild other things in my life such as my career and my faith. I'd finally begun going back to church and even rebuilding my relationship with my mother. I'd even stopped drinking. Well, not completely, but I'd reduced it to social occasions only. I had learned how to live my life without Lucinda. I'd learned to move on.

Honestly, Lucinda's apology sealed the deal. Although I wasn't able to fully forgive her for her little tirade, it was closure. She'd admitted that she was just as wrong as I was and apologized for everything, so that was enough for me. I didn't need to prolong any conversation or pretend that we could ever be friends. What was done was done, and my conscience was finally free. I could live my life without regrets.

"Jessica! Dinner is ready," Jennifer yelled out of the back door.

Jessica whined. "Daddy, I want to stay out here with you."

I walked toward her and crouched down so that we were eye to eye. "We can play tomorrow after church. You have to eat your dinner."

I held up my pinky. She wrapped her little pinky around mine to seal our pinky promise. We walked inside together, and I directed Jessica to go wash up as I went to the kitchen, where Jennifer was making Jessica's plate.

"Smells good."

She turned to face me, cutting her eyes up and down at me. "Don't act surprised. You know how I do."

"And still as cocky as ever."

"Always."

Grabbing my keys, I leaned on the doorframe, preparing to head out. "I guess I'd better go. I promised Jessica I'd play with her after church tomorrow. Is that cool?"

"You know I don't have a problem with that," she said, straining to reach the saltshaker in the cabinet.

I put my keys down, walked over, and grabbed the salt and pepper for her. "Here, shorty. Why would you put it up this high knowing you can't reach it?"

"I normally have a step ladder in here, but your daughter is forever moving that thing. Anyway, thank you."

"You're welcome." I turned to walk away.

"So what are you eating for dinner?"

"Umm, it's probably going to be a Papa John's and Bud Light night, tonight."

She turned to face me. "You're welcome to stay for dinner if you'd like."

I looked skeptical. "I don't want to intrude. Besides, I figured that Meathead was probably coming over."

"His name is Bray, and we broke up."

I faked sadness. "Oh, really? I'm so sorry to hear that."

She laughed. "No, you're not."

"You're right. I'm not. Why did you break up with Bray aka Meathead?"

"You are crazy." She shook her head in disbelief. "Well, I broke up with him because he wasn't my cup of tea. All muscles and no brains, literally. No book sense or common sense."

"Hell, I could've told you that. I think Jessica could've too." She threw a dish towel at me.

"Just for that I should un-invite you!"

I ran and grabbed a plate. "Too late. I've already touched the plate, and don't make me stick my finger in the food."

"Whatever. Make your plate."

"Daddy, you're staying for dinner?" Jessica asked as she sat at the table.

"Yes, I am." I smiled, watching her elation as I washed my hands.

After we all made our plates and sat down, I blessed the food. We talked, joked, and laughed all during dinner, and afterward, we decided to play some family games. I stomped Jessica and Jennifer in *Scrabble,* and they stomped me in *Twister.* After the *Twister* game, Jessica took her shower, and I tucked her in bed.

When I was done, I walked into the kitchen and grabbed my keys. "She fell asleep before I even left the room. She's tired."

"She's really enjoying spending time with you. I hope it remains consistent like this," she said as she stood there washing the dishes. "I'm sorry. I wasn't trying to be mean."

I walked over to her and grabbed a dish to dry it. "I understand. I haven't always done right by her. When things go bad in my life, I tend to shut everybody out, but I'm trying to learn not to do that, especially not to Jessica. No matter what is wrong with me, I can't push her away. She doesn't deserve that from me."

Jennifer smiled at me. "I'm glad to hear that. You sound like you're really pulling yourself together. I'm proud of you." She dried her hands off and turned to face me.

"Thanks. That means a lot."

I had to step in front of her to put the dish up, and once I did, she kissed me on my cheek. "Thanks for the help."

I stood there for a moment staring down at her. That was when it hit me. No matter what I went through with Lucinda, she was right there. She had my back. I'd left her in the middle of sex to run behind a woman who didn't appreciate me while I had one who did all this time. I'd been debating whether I should pursue Jennifer for the past couple of weeks. I'd made up a million and one excuses as to why she'd never take me back, but I wanted her. I felt like it was our fate. We'd separated, been married, and been engaged to different people, and we'd still ended up back in each other's lives. To me, that meant one thing: Jennifer was meant for me.

Standing there in her khaki shorts and V-neck T-shirt, she looked sexy as hell. Her hair and makeup were always flawless, and her body was always banging. Those thick thighs were making me salivate to spread them. Maybe cheating on Lu with her was inevitable, because I desperately wanted Jennifer in the worst kind of way.

She swooped her hair behind her ear and timidly asked, "What?"

That was all she wrote. Wrapping my hand around her neck, I bent down and kissed her, tenderly nibbling at her lips until she responded vigorously. Our lips locked, and our tongues danced and tasted each other with wild abandon.

"I want you so bad, Jennifer," I grunted out between our moans.

It was as if those words snatched her into reality. "I refuse to be your rebound from Lucinda. Please leave before this gets out of hand."

"What? No. I promise that's not what this is."

"Then what is it?" she asked, folding her arms defiantly.

Pressing my body closer to hers, I caressed her face. "It's me realizing that you've always had my back even when I acted stupid or chased other women. It's me realizing that you are a good woman and the mother of my child. It's me saying to you that I want you, only you. I want to see where things could go between us. I want to be your man again." With that, I kissed her.

This time she didn't stop me. Our lips met teasingly at first. Then as we gave into the heat that grew between us, we delved in with passion. I lifted her up and gripped her bottom, and she wrapped her legs around my waist as we continued our sensual reunion. I carried her into her bedroom. After gently placing her on the bed, I stood back to admire her for a moment. Jennifer's lust-filled eyes called out to me as she gently bit her lip and beckoned me with her index finger. I captured her lips as my hands roamed from her behind, around her stomach, to her breasts. I gripped the bottom of her shirt and began undressing her, gently teasing her with feathery kisses on her neck.

"Please tell me that this is real," Jennifer whispered as we continued to kiss and caress each other.

"This is real, baby, and I'm not going anywhere anymore."

"In that case, I want you to be my man again."

"Then it's official. Aldris and Jenn again." I winked at her.

I stood to kick my shoes off, and Jennifer lay back, watching as I undressed myself, and pointed to her nightstand. I reached in to retrieve the prize and covered myself with protection. As I hovered over Jennifer, we gazed at each other lovingly for the first time since we dated in college. She stroked her fingers down my face and nodded. I captured her lips in a kiss and made our reunion official. With a gentle stroke, I lovingly slid into her. The moment I sank between her thighs I felt at home again. I wanted to pleasure her slowly and completely so that she would have no doubt where my heart and my loyalty lay. In and out I glided as I reclaimed Jennifer as my woman, and more importantly, she reclaimed me as her man. This time I'd do it right. No cheating. No Lucinda. Nothing but . . . marriage, yes, marriage to my baby's mother. The only woman for me.

"Al! I'm about to come, baby," she moaned.

I held her close as we released together. "Ooh, Jennifer."

"I love you," Jennifer cried out.

Moments seemed like hours as we lay relishing our newfound union. After our raging climactic urges and our breathing returned to normal, I pushed her hair out of her face. "Do you really? Love me, I mean."

She swallowed hard. "I always have."

Leaning my head against hers, I admitted my feelings. "I love you too." There. I'd said it. The proclamation had been issued. Jennifer had my heart. She hugged me tightly, realizing that I was once again hers completely. Pausing for a moment, I took a deep breath. "Marry me, Jennifer."

"Huh?" she asked in disbelief.

"Marry me. Please."

"I . . . I don't know," she stammered.

"Why not?"

"It's so sudden—"

I put my index finger to her lips and explained my reasoning. "If I hadn't messed up seven years ago, you'd already be my wife. I'm just picking up where we left off. Please. Marry me."

She exhaled, running her hand over her forehead in thought. "As much as I want to say yes, let's just wait, and if in a month that's still what you want, then we'll do it. We'll elope."

"I understand. Fine. One month. But you'll see. You're just delaying having a husband by thirty days." I sealed our commitment with a kiss. "I love you, Mrs. Sharper."

Chapter 37

Terrence

"Push, nigga!" Thomas yelled.

"Don't fuckin' yell at me." I strained to lift my legs with the weights on them. This shit was hard enough without Thomas breathing down my fucking neck.

It had to be "fuck with Terrence" day today. For the life of me, I couldn't understand why everything was going wrong. It was as if the planets aligned together specifically to piss me off. It all started early that morning when I was awakened out of a perfectly good sleep by the pain in my leg. I knew I shouldn't complain since I cheated death, but being alive and in pain hardly seemed like a consolation prize to be grateful for. After I woke up, I realized Trinity wasn't in the bed with me or in the room. At four a.m.? Where in the hell could she be at that time of morning besides in the bed with me? I used the intercom system to check our bedroom. She answered sleepily, and the next thing I knew, she ran through the bedroom door. That was when she informed me that most nights after I was sound asleep, she'd sneak out and go to bed upstairs because I shook the bed from my pain and groaned all night. Of course, I never thought anything of waking up to an empty bed at seven or eight in the morning because I always figured she got up early for the kids. I never figured she was leaving my ass on stuck.

Then one of my property deals fell through. I was anticipating sealing this deal because I wanted to get on the big playing field with the heavy hitters. However, this bum leg kept me away from being able to mix and mingle the way I needed to in order to accommodate the needs of my potential clients. They felt I was incapable of handling their demands, so the deal fell through and with it my hopes of getting in the majors with the heavy hitters.

Now I had to deal with Thomas's ass coming over and pissing me off. As a way to mend our relationship, after I refused to plot to kill Pooch with him, I'd asked him to come help me work out during my rehab sessions several times. He'd turned me down every single time, but today, he decided to change his mind and mend things with his big cousin. Today of all days. That was cool until he came in my rehab session trying to take over. My therapist had great patience, but I could tell that Thomas had managed to start wearing on even his nerves. *Yeah, well, join the club.* He was wearing on my nerves too. And with the day I was having, it didn't take much. I was ready to be done with this session so I could be with myself in peace and officially put an end to "fuck with Terrence" day.

"I appreciate the fact that you came over here, but I don't want to get him upset and frustrated," Eric, my physical therapist, said to Thomas. "We thought it was a good idea to invite a family member over for encouragement. I don't want to confuse that with brow beating."

Thomas, who had been working out with me, stood up and wiped the sweat off of his face with a hand towel. "And you're the reason why my cousin is still limpin' around this muthafucka today," he said harshly to Eric. "This nigga is a one hundred percent thoroughbred hood nigga. And you're treatin' him like a simp," he hollered, and then pointed back and forth between him and me. "We don't respond to encouragement. We respond to threats and haters. You're a white boy, so you wouldn't understand."

Eric's mouth dropped and then his nose flared, signaling that Thomas had angered him. "Let's take a ten-minute break."

"Yes, let's," Thomas sneered as Eric walked out of my home gym.

I looked over at Thomas. "What the fuck is your prob- lem, man?" I pushed myself up slowly to go grab a bottle of water. "I invited you over to help me, not run my physical therapist away," I scolded him, then limped over to the cooler where he was standing.

Thomas sucked his teeth. "That's what I'm doing. Helping! It's your pussy-ass emotions coach who's not helping you. I mean, for real, dawg. Where did you get this dude from? I get it. This is the type of person black folks with real money hire. All you needed was a couple of big niggas from the block to push you around, and I bet that leg would be healed by now," he fussed.

"I'm looking to be healed, not beat up. He's a doctor. Wait a minute. Why am I even explaining anything to you? You're not a doctor."

"Look, you're the one who needs to get better. Not me. You're the one who's limping around here like you got a kickstand in your leg. Not me. You're the one who is self-conscious 'cause you can't put it down in the bedroom on your wife anymore. Not me. So if you want to get better so you can dick your girl down the right way, you better start with accepting some tough love."

A rage built up inside of me, and I pushed Thomas straight into the wall. "Be clear, muthafucka. Don't you ever bring up anything about my and Trinity's sex life ever again in your life. Do you hear me?" I watched him catch his balance and stare at me. "Talking to me like you done lost your fuckin' mind. Gon' make me catch a case in this bitch." I was irritated with him, this training, and this day.

Thomas laughed, and I looked at him as if he were foolish. "And you say you don't need me pissing you off. Felt good to get that anger out, didn't it? You felt like a man again made whole. It's the most effort I've seen you put into your rehab yet." He drank his water. "It's okay. Soon you'll thank me."

"Fuck you," I mumbled as I drank some water.

Within a few minutes, Eric came back into the gym. I guessed he'd calmed down enough to deal with Thomas.

Hell, I hadn't. Maybe I should've taken that ten-minute break with Eric, 'cause I knew if I asked Thomas to leave, it would give him more ammunition, and I wasn't in the mood for that shit.

A part of me got so mad with Thomas because I really was self-conscious of and embarrassed by everything he mentioned, especially the fact that I felt I wasn't able to please Trinity like before. It does something to a man's pride when your money or your equipment ain't right. It's different when you're single, but when you have a lady, especially one you wanna keep, ooh, does it fuck with you. If Trinity were a bald-headed scallywag, then I might not feel so self-conscious about it, but being that I'd nearly gotten killed by two other men because of her, it was safe to say my wife was one bad lady inside and out. Hell, damn a dime. She was a whole $100 bill, and her pussy had to be worth a million bucks.

I got back to my workout, hoping to release more of my anger and irritation.

"You need to focus and push," Eric said firmly.

"Come on, boy. Do it for the sex," Thomas taunted me.

"Shut the fuck up, Thomas!"

Eric looked at Thomas. "You know, the race is not given to the swift but to those who endure to the end." He was big on the Bible. "Now push," he said firmly again.

Thomas fanned him off. "Well, he needs to work harder at giving a hundred, because this ninety-nine and a half he's puttin' out just won't do," Thomas sneered, paraphrasing one of our grandma's favorite church songs as ammo against Eric. "Now push harder, cuz!"

"Kiss my ass, Thomas!"

Eric pointed to himself, obviously upset. "I am the professional at this, and I believe I know what's best for him. I've helped successfully rehabilitate many people in my day," he said tensely. "Now push, damn it!"

"And I bet if you had put a loaded gun to their feet and shot at your patients, they would've gotten cured a lot faster, too," Thomas shot back. "Quit actin' like a punk."

"This shit hurts!"

"Shut up and push," Eric and Thomas yelled in unison, letting the emotions of their argument get the best of them.

I looked at the both of them. "Who the fuck are either one of you talkin' to? Both of y'all standing up here sounding like two bitches instead of grown-ass men." I pointed at Eric. "It's your job to get me better, not get into petty arguments with my cousin." I pointed to Thomas. "And if it weren't for your jealous-ass brother, I wouldn't even be in this situation. Now this shit hurts. Somebody get me my pills!"

I looked up and noticed Eric looking at the enraged expression on Thomas's face. "I'm sorry. You're right, Terrence. I'm just gonna go see if I can find your pills," he apologized, getting up fast to look around the gym.

Thomas blinked away the tears that unexpectedly formed in his eyes. I knew I'd cut him deep. "So the truth comes out, huh? That's really how you feel, dawg?"

I sat there with my chest heaving up and down from the rigorous workout and the pain. "No. Quit fucking being sensitive. I'm just hurting, and I need my damn pills."

"Pain or no pain, that's fucked up. We supposed to be family," Thomas said, gathering his things.

"Come on, dawg. You know I didn't mean that. I'm just in pain. Getting mad at me because it's—" I stopped in midsentence.

"Because it's the truth?" Thomas asked, raising his hands as if to ask if he finished my sentence, which he did. He laughed sinisterly. "Well, it may be true, but that doesn't make you any less fucked up for saying it. I'm out."

"Come on, Tot. I just need my pills."

He bent down by the bench and picked up a bottle, and then threw it at me. "You mean this empty bottle of pills?" he asked nonchalantly.

I shook the bottle and even yanked the top off. Nothing. Not even one. "This can't be right. I know I had a couple left. I have another prescription. I have to get upstairs and ask Trinity where it is," I panicked as Thomas shook his head and left.

"Maybe you should lay off the pills," Eric said to me.

"You know what? You can leave for today. I'm done."

When was this day going to end? Instead of rehab, I felt like going to the boxing club and knocking a nigga's head off, and if I weren't in so much damn pain, I'd probably go. This led me on my quest to find some more pain pills as soon as Eric got his ass out of my house.

Just as he left, my cell phone rang. I didn't have time for no arguments with Thomas. But it wasn't Thomas. In fact, I didn't immediately recognize the number. "Hello?"

"May I speak to Terrence?" a man's voice asked, sounding unsure that he'd reached the right number.

"This is he. Who is this?"

"This is District Attorney William Casey. Is now a bad time?" he asked, obviously put off by my rudeness.

"No, I'm going through rehab, and I'm in pain. What's going on, William? Why are you calling me?"

"I hope you start to feel better. I'm sorry to call, but this is important." He sounded equally irritated with me. "I'm calling you because you've become a really good friend of mine, and I wanted to talk to you about something before it becomes official."

"Talk to me about what?"

"I wanted to ask what the hell is wrong with your wife. If she is being coerced, we can handle that, but I need to know what's going on," he rattled off angrily.

"What the fuck are you talking about?"

"Oh, dear God. You don't know," he mumbled as if he had some type of damn epiphany.

"I don't have time for this. I have to find my pills."

"You'll make time if you know what's best. According to some paperwork from Attorney Jacob Stein, there is a new witness willing to testify on Vernon's behalf that he was actually providing protection for you all and his shot on Officer Marsh was nothing more than self-defense."

"What? Wait, but who could testify to that?"

"Your wife," he seethed. "She's listed as the key witness."

"That's a mistake—"

"Mistake my ass. If your wife's name is no longer Trinity Kincaid, then you're right, it is one. Since we both know that's not true, you need to find out what's going on. I don't mean to come off on you like this, but your freedom is at stake, and I don't like being embarrassed."

I was confused. "What? How? What?"

"I thought the same questions when I heard. Believe me. I don't know what the hell is going on, but if your wife testifies on Vernon's behalf, that's the same as recanting her original story. Since no formal charges were ever brought on you, if she recants her story, then the State will take over, and we will have no choice but to formally charge you with aggravated assault and possibly even attempted murder since Vernon's injuries were life-threatening. If she testifies on Vernon's behalf, I can pretty much guarantee your conviction. At the minimum, you're looking at five years on aggravated assault. I won't even go into the sentencing for attempted murder. Five years is long enough for you to get my point."

I pinched myself. Yes, I was awake. I looked at my cell phone. Yes, it was William's personal cell and not a prank caller. This could not be real. There was no way Trinity would ever betray me like that. Not over Pooch. No way. Somebody was lying. Somebody had to be lying. *Somebody better be lying.*

I rubbed my forehead, which was now throbbing along with my aching leg. "Look, you have to be wrong. I know my wife. She'd never do this to me. Not in a million and one years. Not ever. Not in infinity. Not even in death. This is bullshit. Somebody is lying."

"Well, if it is bullshit, then why is there an order for Stein granting Trinity immunity against perjury charges in exchange for her testimony? She will be free and clear, and you will be known as inmate 123456 again. So you can live in your dream world, or you can find out what the fuck is really going on before your wife frees your sworn enemy and gives you a one-way ticket back to federal lockup," he said with assurance. "I need to know what's going on so I can protect you and Trinity if needed. Let me know." Without another word, he hung up.

I stared at the phone in disbelief for a few minutes, and then out of nowhere, the lump in my throat moved down through my chest to the pit of my stomach. Then anger took root and began spreading like wildfire. I limped as fast as I could out of the gym through the house. I hopped up the stairs using only my good leg, taking them two at a time. I was so fucking blown. When I got to our bedroom, I swung the door open with such force that it hit the wall and the walls in the entire room shook.

Trinity jumped as she folded clothes. "Baby? What the hell is wrong? You scared the life out of me. Thank God my mother has the children," she said, nervously holding her chest.

"What's wrong with me? What's wrong with me? What the fuck is wrong with you? And where the fuck are my pain pills?"

She quickly slid my nightstand open and threw the new prescription on the bed. "I put them in your drawer." She was so nervous that her hands were shaking. "Baby, what's wrong? You're scaring me."

I took a deep breath. "I'm going to ask you this, and you'd better be honest. You'd better be clear, and you'd better be muthafuckin' honest. More importantly, it'd better be wrong." She stood there looking at me as if she were going to run for the hills at any moment. "Are you a character witness for Pooch's trial?"

She bit her bottom lip. Then she closed her eyes. "Who told you that?"

I gripped the handle of the door and shoved it against the wall so hard part of the doorframe broke off. "It doesn't fuckin' matter who told me what. It matters if it's true. And that's what I need to know is if it's true." Fear, panic, and heartache gripped me in a chokehold, and I broke down in tears. "I need to know if you agreed to vouch for your ex over me without even talking to me about it."

She put her hands up as tears streamed down her face. "Baby, let me explain. I didn't want to tell you because I didn't want you or Thomas to flip out on me. I wasn't doing it to spite you. I was doing it to help us. If I testify for him, he's going to leave us alone and let us raise Princess without interfering with our lives. He just wants to be free, and since he didn't actually shoot you, I figured it would finally mean peace for us."

I shook my head in disbelief. "Are you fucking crazy? Have you gone insane? You honestly believed that shit? This is the same man who worked until he got out of prison just to come back and help murder your ass and mine. The only reason he didn't is because he figured Aaron was gonna double-cross him. You don't think that once that fucker is out he's gonna finish what Aaron started?"

"You don't know him like I do. Something about him seemed different, like he was being sincere. I know he's shady, but Pooch's alternative is staying in prison the rest of his life, and I believe he'd agree to anything to escape that sentence. Besides, if I don't do it, he threatened to do something to us. What if he actually gets released by some fluke? Do you really want to live a life in fear not knowing when that fool will strike?"

I hit my head. "Yes! Because I know it's never gonna happen in a million years. Trinity, he would agree to anything to escape that sentence. Even if it meant lying to you and making you believe that he'd actually leave us alone if he was out. Pooch may be many things, but a saint is not one of them. I would've taken my chances on knowing this fool is gonna get locked up. Do you really think a convicted murderer and drug dealer who got released by the same cop he killed is gonna beat a murder wrap a second time? Think, Trinity, think. Gawd damn it."

"Baby, I know that you're upset about me agreeing to do this, but as long as I've known Pooch, I know one thing, and that is if he is desperate enough to make a deal with you, then you'd better take it. He never breaks his deals, and he always keeps his promises. I'd rather testify and be prepared than to not testify and not know."

"Well, then you can kiss me goodbye." She shook her head in confusion. "Your little deal means you'd be recanting your statement, Trin. You made it seem as if Pooch had to be the mastermind behind Aaron's plot when you gave your statement to get me off. If you go back on it, it means you lied about his intentions."

"But Stein is going to grant me immunity for my statement. I worked that out with him to protect myself."

"Good looking out for yourself, Trin, because you damn sure wasn't looking out for me." I knocked the books off the bookshelf.

She jumped. "Terrence, you're scaring me. What does this have to do with you?"

"Your little deal. Your little recanting of your story," I said snidely, showing my sheer and utter anger. "It means that the State can and will bring charges on me for shooting Pooch. If you change your story, you get off, he gets off, and I get a free ticket back to the slammer for aggravated assault or, at the worst, attempted murder. I will probably end up doing five years at the least."

She gasped. "No. No. No. They can't do that to you!"

"They can and they will if you testify."

She paced the floor. "Well, what if I get Pooch to agree to testify on your behalf? He owes me."

My eyes bucked. "Are you listening to yourself right now? You're actually considering me going ahead and having to stand trial for this shit. And even if I did, what leverage do you have over him?"

She snapped her fingers. "Princess."

I laughed with annoyance. "The same child he promised to let us raise in peace if you testified for him? So he still gets everything he wants. Us with no peace, a spot in Princess's life, and freedom. Congratulations, Trinity. You've put us right back at square one, only this time, I'll be right back in prison again. Oh, yeah, and he can have full access to you and our family anytime he wants unless you get back together with him. Win-win for Pooch. Lose-lose for us." I clapped my hands. "You are fucking amazing." I hopped over to the bed and grabbed my pain pills, wincing in pain.

She ran around to where I was. "Baby, I don't know what to do." She reached out for me as I struggled to pop the top off my pills. "And you don't need pain pills. You just had some two hours ago."

I swatted her hand away and shrugged her off me, nearly catching her in the face with my elbow. "Back the fuck away from me. What the fuck do you care about this for since you're sending me back to prison?"

"Dreads," she pleaded, her voice thick with emotion as she tried to reach out to embrace me.

"No!" I moved away from her. "I don't need you to fucking coddle me like I'm some gawd damned baby. I'm not Tyson. What you're going to do is call Stein and tell him that you aren't going to give that testimony. That's the first thing. The second thing you're going to do is stay the fuck away from me and stay out of my path."

I swallowed two pills without water and hobbled back toward the door. Trinity ran up to me to try to stop me. I stopped her and gently pushed her back.

"I'm not playing." I pointed my finger in her face. "Leave me alone, because I'm this close, real close, to losing my muthafuckin' mind on you."

I limped out of the door and slammed it so hard it bounced back open and fell partially off the hinges. After all I'd done for her, loved her, rescued her, fought for her, got shot for her, nearly died for her, she goes and pledges her loyalty to Pooch? *Wow*. They always said nice guys finish last, and now I saw why. It was shit like this that turned a perfectly good man bad. This had to be the climax to "fuck with Terrence" day. I had to call William back and tell him the deal. The way I felt, we'd definitely need police protection, but not from Pooch. Trinity would need it from me. Tears sprang to my eyes as I thought of the betrayal of my own wife. In Pooch's words, I was definitely gonna remember that shit.

Stay tuned for the conclusion, *Never Again, No More 6*.